Novels by
ANN BEATTIE

Chilly Scenes of Winter
Distortions
Falling In Place
Secrets and Surprises

Published by
WARNER BOOKS

Ann Beattie
CHILLY SCENES OF WINTER

WARNER BOOKS

A Warner Communications Company

WARNER BOOKS EDITION

Copyright © 1976 by Ann Beattie
All rights reserved.

This Warner Books Edition is published
by arrangement with
Doubleday & Company, Inc.,
245 Park Avenue,
New York, N.Y. 10167

Warner Books, Inc.,
666 Fifth Avenue,
New York, N.Y. 10103

 A Warner Communications Company

Printed in the United States of America

First Warner Books Printing: May, 1983

10 9 8 7 6 5 4 3

To my *mother* and *father*

Chapter 1

"*Permettez-moi de vous présenter Sam McGuire,*"
Charles says.

Sam is standing in the doorway holding a carton of
beer. Since Sam's dog died, he has been drinking a lot of
beer. It is raining, and Sam's hair streams down his face.

"Hi," Susan says without looking up.

"Hi," Sam says. He takes off his wet coat and spreads
it out on the rug. He goes through the living room to the
kitchen and puts two six-packs in the refrigerator. Charles
follows him into the kitchen.

"The one who doesn't speak is a friend of Susan's from
college," Charles whispers.

Sam rolls his eyes to Charles and holds his hands
cupped in front of his chest, moving them up and down.

"Hi," Sam says to Elise, walking back into the living
room.

"Hi," Elise says. She does not move over on the sofa.

"Move over," Sam says, sitting down next to her.
"How's school?" he says to Susan.

"I'm sick of it."

"Beats walking the streets," Sam says.

Elise giggles. "Are you a streetwalker?" she says.

"Me? What are you talking about?"

"Weren't you just talking about streetwalking?"

"In a manner of speaking," Sam says.

"I wonder how our failing economy has affected that?"
Elise says.

"You wouldn't know, huh?" Sam says, punching her shoulder lightly.

Elise looks bored. "Didn't you bring beer with you?" she says.

"Yeah, but I don't like you. You wouldn't move over for me, so I won't give you any beer."

Elise giggles. No matter what Sam does, he always has great success with women.

"What if I get it myself?" Elise says.

"Ah!" Sam says. "An aggressive woman. Are you an aggressive woman?"

"When Susan and I take to the streets we're very aggressive," Elise says.

"I wouldn't doubt it," Sam says. "College kids are nuts now. You probably do hit the streets."

"Are you drunk?" Susan says.

"No. Just trying to be cheerful. My dog died."

"We're eating in five minutes," Charles calls.

Elise goes out to the kitchen for a beer.

"What happened to your dog?" Susan says.

"Had a heart attack. Eight years old. Everybody's dog lives longer than that."

"Is your heart bad?" Elise says, coming back into the room. She puts the beer can on the floor, sits down, puts her head against Sam's chest.

"How much do you charge for doing a little something more?" Sam asks.

"I bet you think that because I'm a nursing student I don't charge anything at all," Elise says.

"Keep it clean," Charles calls from the kitchen.

"Sam's drunk," Susan says.

"Come and eat," Charles says. He has made chili, and puts the pan on the table.

"What would Amy Vanderbilt say?" Sam says.

"Not much of anything now," Charles says, dishing up the chili.

"What are you two talking about?" Susan asks.

"Amy Vanderbilt," Sam says.

"Who's that?" Elise says.

"Are you kidding?" Sam says.

"No. Who is she?"

"A dead woman," Charles says.

"She jumped out a window," Sam says. "Excuse me—fell."

"You've heard of her, haven't you?" Charles says to his sister.

"No," Susan says.

"Shit," Sam says. "These two."

But everyone is in a good mood during dinner. They are in a good mood until the phone rings, just as they finish. Charles is putting on water to boil for coffee.

"Hello?" he says, phone wedged between chin and shoulder, trying to undo the coffee lid.

"I'm so glad you're there."

"What's the matter, Mom?"

"If you weren't there I was going to kill myself. I've been in the bathtub, trying to get the pain to go away. The pain won't go away."

"What are you talking about? Where's Pete?"

"Is the appendix on the left or the right side, Charles? I think that must be what it is."

"Susan," Charles says. He gives her the phone, walks away, still trying to undo the lid.

"Of course I believe you," Susan says.

Charles doubles up, clenching the coffee jar, his face twisted in mock agony. Susan makes a motion with her free hand as if she's swatting him away.

"You didn't take any medicine, did you?" Susan says. "Where's Pete?"

"He's probably under a rock," Charles says.

"Don't take anything. We'll be right there," Susan says, putting the phone down. "Come on," she says to Charles.

"Where the hell is Pete?" Charles says.

"He's not there. Aren't you coming?"

"Shit," Charles says. He hands the unopened coffee jar to Sam.

"Charles, she's in pain. Please come on."

"She's not in pain. He's out with some barfly and she's acting up."

Charles stalks through the kitchen to the closet, gets his jacket. Susan puts hers on without buttoning it and walks out the front door.

"Shit," Charles says to Sam. "Even your dog had the good sense just to lie down and die." He opens the door that Susan slammed behind her and goes out into the rain. He knows the Chevy won't start. It never starts when it's wet. He fishes around for his car keys, finds them—can't lose any time there—and reaches around Susan to unlock her door.

"Susan, you've got to stop letting her upset you. She's either drunk or in a bad mood because he's out with some woman. She's done this a hundred times."

"Are you going to lecture me or drive over there?" Susan asks.

"Shit," Charles says. He slams her door and walks around to his side. The car starts the first time he turns the key.

"What are you worried about?" he says. "You know she's faking. Isn't she always faking?"

He is driving fast. The "cold" light is still on. The car skids around a corner. Susan is biting her nails.

"You *know* it's all in her mind," he says.

No answer. He puts on the radio, slows down a little. Maybe if the situation lacks drama she'll be calmer. He hates it when his sister gets nervous. He hates it when his mother makes crazy phone calls. On the radio, George Harrison is singing "My Sweet Lord." Charles rummages in the ashtray for a cigarette, finds one, rummages in his coat pocket for a match. There is no match. He throws the cigarette back in the ashtray.

"Don't be nervous," Susan says.

In five minutes they pull into the driveway. All the lights are out in the house. Deliberately, to make it hard for them to find her.

"Upstairs!" their mother calls. They run up the stairs and find her naked on the bed, her robe bunched in front of her. There is a heating pad, not turned on, dangling from the bed. A small light is on, for some reason on the floor instead of the night table. There are things all over the floor: *The Reader's Digest,* Pete's socks, cigarette packs, matches. Charles picks up a book of matches and two cigarette packs. Both empty. He drops the matches back on the floor.

"Where's Pete?" Charles says.

"The pain's over here," Clara says, running her hand across her side. "I didn't take a laxative. I knew I shouldn't take a laxative."

"Where's Pete?" Charles says.

"Chicago."

"What's he doing in Chicago?"

"Leave her alone," Susan says. "I think we should get the doctor."

Their mother has stringy dyed-red hair. Charles puts the light on and sees red smeared all over her pillow. Lipstick. She wears purply-red lipstick, even to bed. She had silicone implants before her marriage to Pete. She is sixty-one now, and has better breasts than Susan. Charles stares at her breasts. She is always naked. The television is turned on—a picture, but no sound.

"You're going to be all right," he says automatically.

"You hate me!" she says. "You don't want me to be all right."

"I despair of your ever acting normal again, but I do want you to be all right."

"My side," she says.

"You're going to be all right," he says, walking out of the bedroom to the hall phone.

"The bathtub," Clara says to Susan.

"What about the bathtub?" Susan says.

"It's full of water, I tried to soak the pain away."

"Let it be full of water. It's all right."

"Empty it," she says.

"What does it matter if the tub has water in it, Mom?"

She looks like she might start crying. Susan lets go of her hand to go empty the tub. Charles is on the phone. He is arranging for an ambulance.

In the bathroom there is another heating pad, plugged in and turned to "high." Susan pulls the plug out. There are movie magazines all over. Susan walks through them to pull the stopper. A cigarette is floating in the water. Susan reaches down carefully, not wanting the wet cigarette to touch her arm. There is a magazine at the bottom of the tub. Susan jerks her hand out.

"They're coming," Charles sighs.

"Help me!" Clara screams.

Charles puts the light on in the hallway, goes into her bedroom and holds her cold hand. She grabs his hand tightly, her false fingernails digging into him. He pulls her robe over her.

"I was going to kill myself," she says.

"I know," Charles says.

"Of course you weren't," Susan says.

"What are they going to do to me?" Clara says.

"Examine you at the hospital. I would have taken you in my car, but I know you like the ambulance better."

"Which side is the appendix on?" she says.

"The right, I think," Charles says.

"I think the left," Susan says. "Maybe the dictionary. . . ."

"Don't go!" she says.

"All right," Susan says.

They sit on either side of her, Charles holding her hand, Susan resting her hand on her mother's hair.

"What day is it?" she says.

"Thursday," Susan says.

"What day?"

"Thursday," Susan repeats.

"He said he was coming home Thursday," Clara says.

"Believe me, I wish he could be here," Charles says.

"I know it's my appendix," Clara says. She moves in the bed. The robe falls off her.

Susan rides in the ambulance. Charles follows in the car, deliberately driving much too fast in order to keep up with the ambulance, even though he knows the way to the hospital. Once he nearly turns the car over. When he gets to the hospital he is shaking—at least it looks like appropriate emotion. He sits with Susan, waiting. She bites her nails. He puts money in the cigarette machine. Nothing happens. He pushes the coin release. Nothing happens. After a while the doctor comes out and tells them that there is nothing physically wrong with their mother. She has been given a sedative. Her doctor is on the way.

Charles and Susan leave the hospital, go out to the car, begin the drive home. Soon the doctor will call and hint strongly that their mother should go back to the mental hospital.

The rain has stopped. Charles turns on the radio. Elvis Presley is singing "Loving You." Elvis Presley is forty. Charles turns off the radio. Susan wipes tears out of her eyes.

When they get back to Charles's house, all the lights are turned off. Charles goes out to the kitchen, still in his coat, and opens the refrigerator for a beer. Susan comes into the dining room and sits down across from him.

"I wish I had some cigarettes," Charles says. "You don't smoke, do you?"

"No."

"Or drink?"

"Wine, sometimes."

"You don't even like beer?"

"No," she says.

He finishes the can, says good night, and goes into his

bedroom. He puts on the overhead light and sees Elisé and Sam naked in his bed. He turns the light off, closes the door quietly, and stands in the hallway staring at Susan, still at the table.

"I should have known," Charles says, going into the living room. He puts two pillows side by side at one end of the sofa and lies down, still in his coat.

"You should have," she says.

"If you don't smoke or drink, do you do that?" Charles says.

"Yes," she says.

"Figures," he says.

"I'm turning off the lights in here," he says, getting up and turning them off.

"Okay," she says. She is still sitting at the table when he falls asleep.

Chapter 2

Riding to the hospital in the morning, Charles remembers going to the hospital with his father to get his mother and the new baby sister. There were two baby sisters, but one of them was born dead. His father told him that, but he told him not to let his mother know that he knew.

"How did they get there?" Charles asked.

"You don't know that? I thought you already knew that."

Charles had asked his father that question before, when he was sitting on a stool in his father's workroom. His father said: "I guess you've heard of screwing?" Charles had not. He nodded that he had. Charles's father gave him a nut and a bolt. "Imagine that this is you," he said, pointing to the bolt. His father gave it a twirl. Charles took it back from him and tried to twirl it, but he dropped the bolt. His father thought that was very funny.

Charles's gift to his new sister was a package of four number two Unger's Westover pencils (yellow). He put them on the mattress under her feet. Later he took them back and used them.

Charles liked his father. He died suddenly, at thirty-nine, on the bus coming home from work. He has foggy recollections of Pete at the funeral. Pete worked with his father. When his father died, Pete came over one evening with a bag of oranges. He came other evenings, too, at his mother's invitation, bringing with him apples, grapefruit, pears, and finally boxes of Whitman's chocolates, flowers,

15

and a briefcase with his pajamas and toothbrush. One night not long after his mother married Pete, the fuses blew. Pete climbed downstairs and called up a lot of questions. He couldn't fix it. Charles went down to help, carefully trying one fuse, then another, just as Pete had. "Could your Dad fix the fuses?" Pete asked. "Yes," Charles said. Pete had cursed and beat his hands on the cinder block wall above the fuse box until they were bloody. Another time when Susan took some of Pete's wood to make arms for a snowman, Pete pulled the wood out, spanked her with it, made her look out the window at the snowman as she got her spanking.

"If he's at the hospital, he's sure to want us to hang around to go to dinner with him. We're not going to do it," Charles says.

"I feel sort of sorry for him," Susan says.

"You can go to dinner with him if you want."

"No. I'm not going to go to dinner with him."

"You just feel sorry for him."

"I do. She's crazy almost all the time now. And something you don't know. This will really make you feel sorry for him. He thought she'd be less depressed if they got out more, so he signed them up for six months of dancing lessons. She wouldn't go, and he couldn't get his money back, so he went alone the first night. He said they were all old people, and he didn't go back either."

"He's a jackass," Charles says.

They are only a few blocks from the hospital. It has started to snow.

"I'll just take what I can get," Charles says. "We can walk." He pulls into a parking place.

"I don't want to get out," Susan says.

"She's okay. She can probably come home."

"This is a lousy vacation," Susan says.

"We'll have a turkey on New Year's Day. We'll have Sam over."

"I don't even like turkey."

"We'll have a ham."

"You're always thinking about food."

"Susan. Get out of the car."

"Do you love me?" Susan says.

"What the hell are you talking about? Will you please get out of the car?"

"You curse all the time. Can't you answer me?"

"Of course I love you. You're my sister."

"You don't act like you love me. It seemed when I came back like I'd never left because nobody missed me."

"Susan. I work five days a week at a lousy job and miss my lover at night. On the weekends I go out and get drunk with Sam, and then I get sick. Your mother gets sick all the time and calls me in the middle of the night and at work. I'm just not in a very good mood."

"Well, it shouldn't be like that. You should do things you enjoy."

"I don't have any money. It's all I can do to pay the bills and buy Sam drinks, because he doesn't have any money either."

"But you could get that girl back."

"I can't get her back. She's not coming back. Christ."

"You curse all the time."

Charles opens his door, gets out, and closes it. Susan's door does not open. He goes around to her side of the car, bends over, puts his mouth against the window. "Get out or I'll kill you," he says. She opens the door.

"You're in a strange mood," he says. "When I was growing up this would have been called 'an identity crisis.'"

"You always try to make yourself seem older than you are. Why do you do that?"

"I guess on second thought you're a little sure of yourself to be having any sort of crisis."

"Were you nice to that girl? If you criticized her all the time, that's probably why she left you."

"Stop talking about her. It's depressing me."

"What did she look like? Then I'll stop talking about her."

"She was pretty tall. Maybe five-nine. She had long brown hair. Blond. Brownish-blond. She was the librarian in the building I work in."

They go up the steps to the hospital, across the circular drive, and through the revolving door. There are brown plastic sofas everywhere. Charles puts his hand on Susan's shoulder and guides her to the left, where several women in white uniforms sit behind a desk. He asks his mother's room number, thanks the woman, and guides Susan toward the elevators. To the right, down a short corridor, is a chapel. There is no one in it.

"You meant it, huh? You really aren't going to ask anything else."

They get in the elevator. He stands to one side, pushing floor numbers for the people who enter. It's a slow day— only one man in a gray overcoat, one man in a brown jacket, a teen-age girl with a yellow ski-jacket and hiking boots, and a fat oriental nurse.

Their mother's room is the first to the left when they get off the elevator. She shares it with another woman, who is white-haired and fat, a little older than their mother. Both women are asleep. Charles and Susan look at each other, then back out the door.

"I'll talk to a nurse," Charles whispers. Susan follows him. At the nurses' station, Charles asks how his mother is. The nurse says that a doctor will talk to him about what she calls "her condition." He asks to see the doctor. The doctor isn't in yet. When will he be in? The nurse thinks two o'clock. She calls it "P.M." She has square, shiny fingernails and a perfectly round, auburn bun. She looks down at sheets of paper. All Charles can see is her neck. She has a long neck, fairly thin, skin quite pale. He asks if the doctor will call him. He will. He leaves his number. They do not go back to the room.

"If we stick around, Pete will show up. She looked

okay. As long as she's not hooked up to anything she's okay."

Susan walks beside him silently. They push the "down" button for the elevator and wait a long time. A woman in a wheelchair rides past. She has on a flowered bathrobe and pink slippers with embroidered flowers on them. A flowered scarf holds her hair back.

"Let's do something today," Charles says.

"What do you want to do? What about Elise?"

"Elise. Hell. I forgot Elise."

"Couldn't she come?"

"Sure. Sure she could come. I just forgot about her."

"You don't like her, do you?"

"Not much. Do you?"

"She lives on my floor. She came here because her mother's an alcoholic."

"*Your* mother's an alcoholic."

He opens the car door for Susan. He unlocks his own door, sits down, and laughs.

"I can't think of anything nice to do today," he says.

Susan rubs the moisture off the side window with her hand, looks out at the slush.

"In answer to your question," she says, "I don't like her very much. One of the guys I used to go with lived with her when they were freshmen."

"So what's she doing here?"

"She asked if she could come."

"Maybe we'll like Elise better if we can think of something to do with her."

"Do you think Mom would ever really kill herself?" Susan asks.

"I don't think so. She always says that."

"She looked like Esther Williams when she was younger," Susan says. "She's been old for so long."

"She'll get a lot older. She won't kill herself."

"We should have awakened her."

"We can go back tonight."

"Maybe we should have called Pete in Chicago."

"What should we have done? Called every hotel in Chicago? I should say every whorehouse."

"I don't think he does that."

"I don't care if he does it or not. I don't know why I said it."

Charles turns on the radio. Janis Joplin is singing the "la-de-dah, la-de-dah-dah" section of "Bobby McGee." Janis Joplin is dead. Susan is nothing like Janis Joplin. Susan speaks in precise, clipped rhythms, combs her hair into two carefully brushed sections (part down the middle), does what is expected—or what is unexpected behind people's backs. Susan does not drink Southern Comfort.

"Did you like Janis Joplin?" Charles asks.

"She was okay."

"She was great," Charles says. "All that flapping fringe and that wild hair and those big lips . . ."

"I guess men find her more attractive than women do," Susan says.

"That was so great—how she left all that money for a party in her honor when she died."

"I hope she doesn't kill herself," Susan says. "We should have awakened her."

Charles makes a left turn, pulls up in front of a car that is coming out of a parking place.

"I'm taking you to a Mexican restaurant," Charles says. "It's a great place."

"I'm not very hungry."

"Come on," he says. The song is over. Janis Joplin is dead. Jim Morrison's *widow* is dead.

The restaurant has round wooden tables and place mats with the sun on them. There is a blue glass vase with dried grasses in it. A hippie in a white T-shirt and jeans gives them menus.

"The *chiles rellenos* are great," Charles says. "And black beans."

"Fine," she says.

"Try to act enthusiastic. She's not going to kill herself. This is your vacation."

"This is *your* vacation," she says.

He is instantly depressed. He orders the first of four Bass Ales with his *chiles rellenos*. After lunch they decide to go to the art gallery, but on the way there they pass a porn movie and park and go there instead. Charles is a little uncomfortable being there with his sister, but he's also pretty drunk. He spends the first five minutes of the film looking around the audience. It's maddeningly light in the theater. His attention wavers between two light-haired boys two rows in front of them and the woman on the screen, caressing the neck of a Great Dane. He thinks that it is all predictable—the movie, the audience, the rest of his vacation. He wishes his father were alive; at least, then, somebody could get a few laughs out of him. If he tells Sam that he took his sister to a porn movie Sam will laugh at him. Sam. Elise. Janis. The Great Dane.

"What did you mean before when you said she was an alcoholic?" Susan says, walking up the aisle.

"Can't anything get your mind off her?" Charles asks.

Susan looks down, watching her feet leaving the theater.

"She's a heavy drinker," Charles says. "I was just exaggerating."

"What do you think happened to her all of a sudden?" Susan asks. "You know—she dyed her hair and started wearing those jersey things. . . ."

"If you want to know what I really think, I think that one day she just decided to go nuts because that was easier. This way she can say whatever she wants to say, and she can drink and lie around naked and just not do anything."

"Maybe when my sister died it did something to her."

"And it took nineteen years to register?"

"How long has she been crazy?"

"She was crazy when you graduated from elementary school, and that was . . . seven years ago."

"Maybe when he died . . ."

"Oh, who the hell knows? I notice you're not so concerned that you stick around here to go to school. She calls me almost every night. Or every day at work. How can I sleep? How can I work? I don't know what to do."

"Doesn't she talk to Pete?"

"She talks to Pete and then she gets on the horn to me. Sometimes they fight when she calls. She just dials the number and lays the phone on the table, and I pick it up and hear them screaming."

"We ought to go home. The doctor must be trying to reach us."

"Let's go to a bar," Charles says. "Then we can go back to the hospital."

"But the doctor won't be there again. We have to wait for his call."

Charles acknowledges defeat, but his shoulders feel very heavy when he shrugs them. He stops at a liquor store for a six-pack of beer to drink as he waits. He drives home slowly. He sulks. He realizes, with surprise, that he has forgotten to smoke all day. He decides to give up smoking.

There is laughter as he puts the key in the front door. Sam is laughing. There is a pile of clothes in the living room. Charles looks out the front door for Sam's car. Sam is laughing. Susan looks embarrassed.

"Goddamn it," Charles says. He squats and takes a can out of the six-pack, opens it, and has a drink. He offers up the can. Susan stiffens.

"I thought she was leaving today," Charles says.

"Come on," Susan says. "I'm not going to stay and listen to this."

"Well, what are we going to do? Go back to the hospital without having talked to the doctor?"

"I just don't want to be here."

"We could go over to Laura's, and you could tell her what a swell guy I am, and I could get her back."

"Come on," Susan says.

"Come where?"

"We can go to a bar. That'll please you."

"It would please me to stay here. But your friend is at it with Sam."

"Sam's your friend. You always do that."

Charles rubs his hand across the back of his neck. He is getting tired. He *is* tired. He picks up the rest of the beer and follows Susan out of the house.

"You drive," he says. "I'm tired."

"Where shall I go?"

"To the bar. And you're to blame if it doesn't make me happy, because you said it would."

Donovan is singing "Sunshine Superman" on the car radio. Mellow Yellow. Charles's car is yellow. It is an old yellow car with the trunk bashed in. He has nightmares in which he is thrown forward, into nothing. His car was hit from behind while he was stopped at a red light. A diplomat named Waldemere something-or-other did it. The diplomat was enraged. He showed Charles his license: "American driving license," he said. "Worthless." He wrote his name, embassy, and number in huge black letters on a napkin he got out of his car. On the other side of the napkin was a leaping fish. In the nightmare, Charles always screams. When he was hit, he just said, "Ugh." He and Laura were going to get married. They were going to have a dog from the pound. By now, that dog is dead. She said that she always had cats; now she wanted dogs. He agreed. She said that it was corny, but she wanted to go to Bermuda. He said that he knew how to snorkel and would teach her. They both drank Jack Daniel's on ice. He kept a bottle in his refrigerator, and when she was at his house they drank it straight. She had brownish-blond hair. Most women get upset if you can't tell if their hair is brown or blond. She didn't. He settled on brownish-blond in his own good time. She told him that Lauren Hutton had a wedge she put between her front teeth sometimes when she was photographed, and pointed it out on a Vogue cover photo. For that matter, she told him who Lauren Hutton was. Before Laura he loved three other girls: one of them he stopped loving, one he continues to sort of love, but she was no good for him, and the other one he never thinks about. Laura was the best of them. Laura made a dessert out of cognac and fresh oranges. A soufflé. Her cookbooks are still all over the house. He often craves that dessert, and the recipe is probably in one of those books, but he can't bring himself to look. He wants to think of it as magic. For the same reason, he never read a book about Houdini that Sam gave him for his birthday. He lies to Sam, says that he has read it. "What an amazing man Houdini was," he says to Sam. If she had married him and they had gone to Bermuda, he would still have a little tan left now. His arms are winter white. She gave him clogs. They are too loud; he is too conscious of them—he won't wear them. But he wears the undershirts. He can't tell them from his old ones. In a fit of depression, he once thought of unraveling the labels in the back because hers had some little gold rooster on the label. He could just throw all those out. And the cookbooks. He will never throw either out. Even the clogs. His house is full of her things. There are toenail scissors in the bathroom, photo-booth pictures of them on the kitchen cabinet. Sam says that he should call her again, too. Houdini miraculously breaks chain! Charles calls Laura! He lacks nerve.

"That bar," Charles points.

"That looks awful."

"It's okay. I've been there."

Susan turns down a side street and coasts along, looking for a parking place. It is almost rush hour. Traffic is heavy. She finds a place at the end of the street.

"Lucky," she says. She parks the car and gets out.

Charles sits there, imitating Susan earlier in the day. She comes to his window. "Out or I kill you," she says.

"That wouldn't be so bad," he says.

They get the last two seats at the bar. It is a long bar with red plastic bar stools and bowls of peanuts.

"What are you majoring in?" he says to Susan, and feels like a fool because a man next to him overheard. He considers following it up by asking Susan to see his etchings. Of course he can't take her home. Sam is screwing a woman in his bedroom. He had planned on a nap, but now he is balanced on a bar stool, making silly conversation.

"I don't have one," Susan says, and the man chuckles.

"It's my sister," Charles says, and the man turns away, pretending not to notice.

Charles orders a rum and Coke, figuring that that's probably what they drink in Bermuda. The rum and Coke tastes just awful. He wishes he had Susan's plain Coke.

"I'll tell you who's going to win the Super Bowl," a tall man in a black jacket says to a shorter man who is leaning away from him. "I am." He hits the short man on the back.

"Aw, Christ," the short man says. His face is sweating.

"You don't think I'm going to win the Super Bowl? I *am* winning the Super Bowl. Be tuned on Sunday, buddy, because that's when you'll see it."

"Drop dead," the short man says.

"I won't drop until I run that last quarter-inch to lead my team to victory," the tall man says. "Wait until Sunday and then you won't think I'm just some drunk in a bar. You don't think I can get in shape before Sunday? Eat steak and drink tomato juice, be in bed by ten. *That'll* get you in shape."

"Goddamn," the short man says. He pushes his empty glass forward.

"I'd better make one more try to reach the doctor," Charles says. "Do you mind sitting here?"

"No," she says. "Go ahead."

Charles walks through the archway to a wall phone. "Carla Delight is outta sight!" is lettered above the phone. There is a phone number, with the last number blacked out. Someone else has written: "Either 1,2,3,4,5,6,7,8,9,-0." Charles dials information, then the hospital. He finds out that his mother has a private phone, decides to talk to her. The phone rings once and is picked up.

"Hello," Pete says.

"Hello," Charles says. "This is Charles."

"I know my boy," Pete says. Pete sounds drunk. "How's my boy?"

"How's my mother?"

"I'd put her on, but she's a wee bit groggy now. She's doing just great, though. There was a little accident in here with the other lady, and she naturally got a little bit excited, but now she's calmed down just fine."

"What kind of an accident?"

"The woman fell when she was hooked up to the intravenous," Pete whispers.

"Oh God," Charles says.

"Cut up," Pete whispers.

Charles rubs sweat off his forehead. "We were by earlier, but she was asleep. Tell her that. What you can tell me, if you can now, is what they're going to do about her."

"Our girl's going to go home tomorrow," Pete booms. "They can't keep our girl down."

"That's good," Charles says. "She seems okay?"

"She's a wee bit groggy, but on the road to recovery."

"Tell her we'll be down later."

"Will do. Where are you now? How about dinner?"

"We're in a restaurant. We just finished eating."

"Oh," Pete says. "Well, you kids enjoy yourself. Mommy was just saying how she misses Susan and how she wants her home."

"Yeah," Charles says.

"I don't have to tell you that that invitation goes double," Pete says.

"Sure," Charles says.

"Well?" Pete whispers.

"Sure," Charles says again.

"Well?" Pete whispers.

"Sure," Charles says again. He is sweating. The tall drunk passes him, on the way to the bathroom.

"Heave ho, and away we go," the drunk says, clapping his hands.

"See you tonight," Charles says, and hangs up.

He goes back to the bar and sits next to Susan.

"Pete's there. I told him we'd already eaten."

"He's pathetic," Susan says. "I think he tries now. He just doesn't know what to do."

Susan has finished her drink and is sipping his.

"You'd better get one of your own before we hit it," he says.

She doesn't object. He takes an ice cube out of the glass and runs it across his forehead.

"Hot in here," he says.

"No it's not. Are you all right?"

"Yeah. I think it's because I gave up smoking."

She looks worried.

"The Super Bowl must be this Sunday," he says stupidly.

Laura's husband used to play football in college. His nickname was "Ox." "Imagine being proud of that," Laura used to say. "Don't drink so much," she used to say.

Chapter 3

He calls Laura from the hospital. He calls her from a phone in a sun room (it is labeled "Sun Room" on a plaque to one side of the door) on his mother's floor at the hospital. He holds a *Ladies' Home Journal* curled into a tight tube, but doesn't realize until halfway through the conversation that he is holding anything.

"Laura?" he says, "Can you talk?"

There is a short pause. She will say something ridiculous like, "Oh, we subscribe to too many now," and hang up.

"Hi," she says. "Jim isn't here. He's at a meeting."

"Maybe he's cheating on you. Maybe you should just assume that and cheat on him. With me."

"What?" she says.

"I thought I might as well get to the point."

"You did," she laughs. "How have you been? You didn't write back."

"I thought he might get the mail."

"He doesn't open my mail."

Her husband was nicknamed "Ox." How can she defend him in any way?

"He might ask questions, though," Charles says.

"I don't suppose you called to talk about him," Laura says. "Is everything okay with you?"

"I miss you. I'm miserable."

There is another long silence.

"My mother's in the hospital," he says. "That's where I am."

"She didn't try to kill herself?"

"She hit the scotch and plugged in a lot of heating pads—I don't know where she gets all of them—and thought she was struck with appendicitis, and now she's here."

"You're at the hospital now?"

"Yeah," he says.

"I'd come over, but Jim's supposed to be home at ten."

"Come tomorrow."

"I have to go to Rebecca's school tomorrow. It's a parents' day."

Rebecca is Jim's child from his first marriage. When he was Laura's lover he used to go to Rebecca's school every day, sit outside in his car until Laura picked up the child at noon. They usually got there at eleven. He always said he was going to lunch early. They kidded him about it at work. "Almost lunch time," they'd say as soon as he got there in the morning. But he only took an hour for lunch, so nobody said he couldn't go. He would sit in Laura's car, holding her hand. The car would fill with cigarette smoke.

"What time are you getting out? I could meet you there."

"I haven't planned it. . . ."

"I just want to see you for five minutes."

"Why don't you come at . . . two. You'll see my car there. I'll leave it open."

"All right," he says.

"I hope your mother's all right. Is she going to have to go back to that place?"

"No," Charles says. "I don't think so."

"It would be kinder to tie her to the bed," Laura says.

Jim's first wife is in a mental hospital. Laura has told him about visiting her—how they save all her letters, which are mostly about food, and how they stop on the way and get McDonald's Filet o' Fish, Kentucky Fried Chicken, macaroni salad, Heath Bars and Cott ginger ale, and how she does nothing but eat when they are there, everything together, a sip of ginger ale, some of the candy bar, the macaroni. It makes Laura sick. She gets dizzy, can't eat for a week.

"My sister's home from college," Charles says. "I've got the week off."

"That's nice. You two can do some things."

"We can't think of anything to do. Yesterday we went to a skin flick."

"That's horrible," Laura says.

"I thought of you."

"I'll see you tomorrow," Laura says. "I've got to go."

"Where are you going?"

"What's the use in telling you? You never believe me. I have bread in the oven."

"How domestic," he says.

"If you feel so bitter, maybe it would be better not to come tomorrow."

"I love you," Charles says. "I'll see you tomorrow."

He hangs up. A woman in a corner chair looks back at her knitting. A young man on an orange plastic sofa is asleep with his head on his overcoat, which is rolled up on the arm of the sofa. The young man has on a blue suit and shiny black shoes. The toes are too pointed. His tie, dangling from the sofa arm, is too thin. He makes gurgling noises in his sleep. Charles is always afraid of falling asleep in public places. He thinks that he will scream. He doesn't even close his eyes on buses any more. In fact he has started driving to work instead of taking the bus so he won't be tempted to fall asleep. Charles looks at himself in the mirror. It is an oblong mirror with a picture of the hospital painted at the top. Charles sees that he has circles under his eyes. His skin is pasty. In five days he will be twenty-seven. His eyes meet the woman's in the mirror. She looks down at her knitting again. He walks away from the mirror, puts the magazine on a table, tries to rub the creases out, gives up, thinks about going to his mother's room to join Susan and Pete, cannot, sits down.

"Is your wife having a baby?" the woman says.

"No," Charles says.

"My daughter is," the woman says.

"That's nice," Charles says. He and Laura were always worried that she would get pregnant. He frowns. The woman smiles.

"What are you hoping for?" Charles says.

"Health," the woman says. "Good health. That's what's important."

Predictable. Everything is predictable.

"She has three boys, so she's hoping for a girl," the woman says.

"That's nice," Charles says. He gets up and leaves the sun room. He walks slowly down the corridor to his mother's room. He sees the back of Pete's coat and turns around. He goes back to the telephone and dials his number. He is going to tell Sam to go to his place with Elise—it's depressing him. The phone rings twice. Sam answers it.

"Sam. It's been a rotten day and I'm tired, so I want you and Elise out of my bed when I get back there. I hope you don't take offense, but I don't want to sleep on the sofa again tonight."

"She's gone," Sam says. "She had me drive her to the train."

"Gone? Where did she go?"

"Home. She said that by now her mother wouldn't be drunk. Her mother always sobers up about this time so she won't have to make it a New Year's resolution."

"Oh," Charles says. "What are you doing there?"

"I just got back from the train. I was eating the leftover chili."

"I forgot to ask you for New Year's Day dinner," Charles says.

"Oh, yeah. I figured I was invited."

"Maybe I'll see you later, if I'm lucky enough to get out of here soon."

"Pete there?"

"Yeah. I'll have to think of some reason not to go out for a drink with him."

"How's your mother?"

"I haven't seen her yet. Tomorrow I'm seeing Laura."

"That's great. Did you call her?"

"No. Mental telepathy."

"Oh. You've just got a feeling, huh?"

"I was kidding. I called her. She was baking bread in her A-frame."

"I wish I had something to go with this chili," Sam says. "Don't you ever buy groceries? Maybe I could call Laura and she'd run some over."

"Hell," Charles says. "With your luck she probably would. With my luck she'd fall in love with you and be rolling around in my bed when I got back."

"I'll see you," Sam says.

"Yeah. Good night, Sam."

Charles walks down to his mother's room. His mother is sitting up in bed. The curtain is pulled around the other woman's bed. His sister is sitting in a chair beside the bed. Pete is dancing across the floor. He stops, embarrassed.

"I was demonstrating how to turn," Pete says.

"Go ahead," Charles says.

"I did. I already did it," Pete says, slapping Charles's back.

"He wants me to go dancing," Clara says.

Charles nods.

"Show some enthusiasm, my boy," Pete says, slapping his back harder. "Wouldn't a few twirls fix anybody up?"

Charles moves over to Susan's chair. He wants to sit down. He wants to sit down on her lap. He would like to be smaller, and her child instead of her brother, and then he could curl up and shut his eyes, and everyone would think he was being good, instead of being bad. It is wrong not to encourage Pete, who is trying hard to be helpful. He is just a jackass.

"Do you dance?" Charles's mother says. It is the first time she has acknowledged his presence.

"Yes," Charles lies, smiling at Pete that he is going along.

"What do you dance?" Clara asks.

Charles cannot think of the names of any dances. "The hula," he says.

Susan laughs. Pete frowns.

"Aw, he's just kidding. All young kids dance."

"The tango," Charles says. He has just remembered the name of that movie: *Last Tango in Paris*. Marlon Brando running around, cornering that Parisian, his dead wife, that young girl, the streets of Paris, all those people doing the tango, that girl running off, the streets of Paris, Laura. . . .

"The tango!" Pete laughs. Pete is getting mad. Susan looks down, trying not to show her smile.

"You don't tango," Pete says.

"I don't know the name of the dance I do," Charles says. "I just sort of move around."

"Well, you'd know what you were doing if you'd take a few lessons," Pete says. "That's what I've been trying to tell Mommy. Then at the convention she could take a twirl or two like the other wives. She doesn't want to go, because she just sits in the hotel room. We don't have to have that, do we, Charles?"

"No," Charles says. "She should go."

Pete smiles approval.

"Did you hear your boy say you should take a few twirls?" Pete says. Pete does not know how to get off a subject. Susan looks down, disguising a yawn. Clara reaches for the water glass and deliberately drops it.

"I'm so clumsy," she says, as Susan picks up the glass. Susan's stockings are wet. "How could I be a dancer?"

"We're going to take a museum tour when you're on your feet," Pete says. "We live in a city with a fine museum, and we're going to tour it."

"I don't know anything about art," she says.

"What do you have to know? You can look at a picture and enjoy it, right? What did you know about children until you had them?"

"I read Doctor Spock."

"There! Mommy's going to read a book about art and then hit those pictures!" Pete says, smiling broadly.

"If I ever get well," she says.

"You *are* well, honey. You're going to be looking over those pictures before you know it."

She closes her eyes. "I never saw a Picasso I liked," she says.

"He was a great painter," Pete says. Charles doubts that Pete knows who Picasso is.

"I guess I could look at some of them again," she says. Her eyes are still closed.

"That's the idea," Pete says. "Isn't it?"

No one answers. Pete moves over to Charles. "That's the idea, right?" he says.

"Right," Charles says.

"Maybe we should let her get some rest," Susan says.

"Rest those feet," Pete says, patting them under the covers. "Those feet are going to twirl you around the floor at the convention."

"I've never been to a convention," she says.

"Three weeks!" Pete says. "There are probably art galleries in Chicago. We can hit the pictures there, too."

"I don't know. I try to read books, but I never get through them."

"Just read the section on that artist you like," Pete says.

"What artist do I like?"

"You were talking about some artist. . . ."

"I said I never saw a painting of his that I liked, Pete."

"Well, you will in Chicago," Pete says. He grabs her foot and shakes it.

"See you tomorrow, honey," he says.

"I guess so," she says. "Where's my Susan's hand?"

Susan goes back to the bed and holds her mother's hand.

"Good-bye," Clara says.

"Rest," Susan says, patting her hand.

"I might not go to the convention," Clara says. "I might stay home and rest."

Pete's mouth opens, but he doesn't say anything. He smiles a big smile.

"See you tomorrow," he says.

"Where's my Charles?" she says.

"Oh, shit," Charles says, loud enough for Pete to hear. He walks to his mother's bed and gives her his hand.

"You were my first baby," she says. "I guess that doesn't matter to you, but it matters to me."

"What do you mean?" Charles says, but her eyes are closed and she doesn't answer. Deliberately. She wants them to leave thinking that she is still ill.

Charles tells Pete as they wait for the elevator that he and Susan are very tired—otherwise they'd enjoy that drink with him.

"You don't like me," Pete says. "I didn't kill your father. He just died."

The woman knitting in the sun room waves. Charles waves back. He looks at the phone. Two o'clock tomorrow.

"We're just not very much alike," Charles says.

Pete looks surprised; he expected some other answer. He pushes the "down" button again, straightens his coat collar.

"You're not coming to dinner either, are you?" Pete says.

"Yes we are," Susan says.

Pete smiles. "Ah!" he says. "That's good. We'll have a turkey." He turns to Charles. Charles can't bear to refuse.

"Sure," Charles says.

"What could I get that *you* would like?" Pete says.

Charles feels sorry for him. He remembers him dancing in the room, remembers Pete refusing to sign his report card when he got a "B" in conduct, how he had to stay after school every day for a week, until the teacher gave up, because of the unsigned report card.

"Olives," Charles says.

"Olives!" Pete says. "Any special kind?"

"Just regular olives," Charles says.

"They come in jars with big ones or the small kind," Pete says.

Charles does not like olives. Olives were one of the things Jim's first wife always asked to have brought to her. She would eat olives with Tootsie Rolls, and then drink grape soda. The foods Laura named made a great impression on Charles; he has trouble forgetting them.

"The big ones," Charles says.

"Big ones. I hope they can be found," Pete says, pushing the "down" button again. Pete talks about things tirelessly. The woman waves to Charles again. He pretends not to see.

"We should have olives and celery and all the trimmings," Pete says. "You know, Mommy wasn't up to cooking at Christmas, but she's up to it now. She'll be dancing around that kitchen."

"I'll come cook it," Susan says.

"That's very nice of you," Pete says.

Laura is baking bread. She is probably not still baking. It is probably out of the oven. The Ox is probably eating it. Charles is hungry; he would like some of that bread. More than that, he would like that dessert. More than that, he would like Laura.

"Kids dance nowadays, don't they?" Pete says, riding down in the elevator.

"Not much," Susan says. "Nobody does much of anything any more. I don't even think there are many drugs on campus."

"I should hope not," Pete says.

"Well," Charles says. "We'll see you in a couple of days."

"Right," Pete says. "Where are you parked?"

"To the left," Charles says.

"Me too," Pete says.

As they walk down the street, Pete says, "How's the car holding out?"

"It runs okay. Uses a lot of gas."

"If you ever want a good car wax, let me recommend Turtle Wax," Pete says. "That's really the stuff."

"I'll remember that," Charles says.

"No, you won't," Pete says.

"Turtle Wax," Charles repeats, not wanting to have to hear again that he doesn't like Pete.

"You don't like me a damn," Pete says. "But it'll be good to have you to dinner all the same."

There is an awkward moment when they reach Charles's car.

"Headed home?" Pete says.

"Yeah. We'll see you."

"I guess I'm headed there," Pete says, shrugging his shoulder toward a bar.

"Well, we'll see you," Susan says.

Pete nods his head. "See you," he says.

"Poor Pete," Susan says in the car.

"Nobody told him to marry her."

"She did. She told me that once. She told him that if he was going to come over all the time, he should marry her."

"Well, that should have told him," Charles says.

"I feel sorry for him," she says.

"Your friend left," he says. "I forgot to tell you."

"She didn't have a good time, I guess."

"What do you care? She's just some girl on your floor."

"Yeah," Susan says. "She might have had a good time with Sam."

"I don't care if she had a good time or not," Charles says.

"Sam's really something," Susan says. "Is he still selling clothes?"

"Yeah."

"Maybe we could ask him to dinner at Pete's place," Susan says.

"He wouldn't come."

"How do you know?"

"He doesn't like Pete."

"Does he know him?"

"We ran into him once in a hardware store. We were there to get a hammer for Sam. Pete got onto a thing about 'security systems'—how Sam owed it to himself to install 'a high-power security system.' He ran around pointing out locks and bolts. You know—Sam hasn't got anything anybody would bother to steal. He thought Pete was a jackass."

"You're the one who always says that. Sam probably didn't say anything like that."

"He said, 'What a goon.'"

"Maybe he'd go to dinner anyway. You'd like him there."

"Sure I would. I'd like to put him through that."

"He came before."

"That was when she was a lot better. The last time he came, her dress kept slipping off her at the table, and he was humiliated. You remember. You were there, weren't you?"

"I don't think so."

"Sure. It was just before you started college. Pete was

in Chicago. She kept saying, 'One of my men might be gone, but I have two others.' Sam was humiliated."

Susan combs her hair. She leaves her black mittens on, and Charles thinks that she looks like some weird animal with big paws. She's a nice sister. He wishes he could think of something to do with her.

"If you stop at a store, I'll buy something to fix for dinner," she says.

"You feel like fixing dinner?"

She shrugs. Laura likes to cook. Laura and the Ox are probably eating a late dinner together in their cold A-frame. Tomorrow he will see Laura. Laura's hair is longer than Susan's. Laura wears perfume. She wears Vol de Nuit. She gives Vol de Nuit to Jim's first wife for a present. They sit in the visiting room of the loony bin, smelling the same. Charles feels that he knows the woman, that he has been to the bin, but only Laura and Jim have been there. He hates Jim for getting to spend so much time with Laura, envies him the moments with her in the bin, visiting his first wife, thinks that he would be able to stand watching the woman eat, if only he could go there with Laura. Anywhere with Laura.

"I'm seeing Laura tomorrow," he says. "I called her from the hospital."

"That's good," Susan says. "I hope she's nice to you."

"She's always nice. She just won't leave her husband."

"Aren't there other attractive women where you work?"

"No. They all look and act the same, but the fat ones are a little louder, and the thin ones either bite their nails or twist their hair."

"They can't all be bad."

"I can't make myself look. When I do look, they all look bad."

He pulls up in front of a Safeway. "How about some money?" he says.

"I've got plenty of money." She gets out of the car and

he sits there double parked, waiting for her. He hopes she will buy oranges and cream and chocolate and make the dessert for him. When she comes back, she has bought a roasting chicken and stuffing and green peas.

"What's the guy you go with like?" Charles says.

"He's in pre-med. What do you want to know about him?"

"Are you going to marry him?"

"I don't know. He wants to go to Mexico."

"What for?"

"Just for a vacation. To buy a statue. He's very smart, but he's sort of nuts. I haven't wanted to call him since I got here. He's on a Mexico thing. He wears brown huaraches and a poncho. He saw the statue he wants to buy in the travel section of *The Times*."

"What do you two do?"

"He studies a lot. I fix dinner. Sometimes we go to other people's places. We don't do much."

"Has he got long hair?"

"Yes," she says. "How did you know?"

"Figures," he says.

"What's wrong with that?"

"Nothing. I wish I had become a surgeon. It's boring working for the government. At least I make enough money to pay the mortgage. Sam hardly makes enough to pay his rent."

"Why doesn't he live at your place?"

"My place? I don't know. That would look strange."

"What do you care what it looks like?"

"I don't know. I wouldn't want him there all the time. He'd get on my nerves."

"Sam doesn't get on your nerves. He's there all the time anyway."

"He'd bring all his damn women over."

"So what. Maybe they'd have friends."

"I'm twenty-seven years old. I ought to be able to find a woman if I want one."

"Do you look?"

"Not much."

"Aren't you lonesome?"

"Of course I'm lonesome. Why do you keep reminding me?"

"I don't like to think you're lonesome."

"I'm not that lonesome. I'm exhausted when I work, and Sam's around on weekends."

"But you're still lonesome."

"For Christ's sake, Susan."

"Maybe if you face it you'll find somebody."

"I'm seeing Laura tomorrow."

"That's not what I meant."

"Everybody's married. And if they're not, they're either fat or thin."

"You're deliberately not facing the situation."

"You're nineteen," Charles says. "Leave me alone."

"My age doesn't have anything to do with it."

"Susan, Clara's finally too bonkers to argue with me. Do you have to carry on for her?"

Susan looks out the car window. They are going around a traffic circle. A man is in the middle of the circle with a shopping bag and a cane. Cars swerve to avoid him. The old man lifts his cane and shakes it. Charles pulls around him, into the far lane where a Christmas tree lies. The car smashes through the tree.

"I'm surprised Janis Joplin appeals to you," Susan says. "She doesn't seem like your type at all."

"She was great," Charles says. "I saw her in a concert. I almost went to Woodstock. I wish I had gone to Woodstock."

"You would have been walking around in the mud, looking for a place to pee."

Charles laughs. "I thought you'd think Woodstock was glamorous."

"I saw the movie," Susan says.

"Do you go to movies with this hippie surgeon?"

"Sometimes. Not much."

"When he goes, I'll bet he likes Bergman," Charles says.

"Fellini," she says.

"If I weren't your brother, I'd save you," he says. "In a few years he'll be smoking Disque Bleu's."

Chapter 4

Charles gets up much earlier than necessary to meet Laura at two o'clock. There is a note in the kitchen from Susan, saying that she's gone shopping. There is also a note from Sam, that he didn't see the night before, saying "Just get your hand on her thigh and move it up slowly. That drives them wild." There is no signature. A plate with the remains of a chili dinner is next to the note. Charles puts it in the sink. He does not feel like washing dishes. He decides, instead, to go to the laundromat. He doesn't feel like going to the laundromat and stops at the front door with the dirty laundry basket to think whether there's some excuse to get out of it. There is not. He goes out to the car, notices that it has rained during the night. He inhales before he turns on the ignition. The car starts immediately. It delights him that his car is unpredictable. Turtle Wax, he thinks. Laura, he thinks.

He is the only man at the laundromat. His sheets are the only ones without flowers. A little boy sitting on top of the next washing machine drops his toy into the water and Charles has to fish it out for him. The little boy cries when he hands it back. The child's mother rushes over, picks him up, and disappears to the back of the laundry. The woman is pregnant. Her sheets have pink roses all over them. He looks at his pocket watch and discovers that the dryer is cheating him out of two minutes time. There is no one to complain to. If Laura were there, he could complain to her. Maybe Susan was right. Maybe he criticized her or complained too much. His vacation is almost over. He puts the clean clothes in the back seat of his car and drives to the school three hours early. Of course she is not there. He goes to a restaurant and orders breakfast. He is told that it's too late for breakfast. He gets mad and, for the first time in days, craves a cigarette. Instead, he orders a ham sandwich. He has finished lunch in twenty minutes. That leaves two hours to kill. He goes out to his car and sits there, shivering. Laura is still in her A-frame. He turns on the car radio to hear the news, but it's over. He has the opportunity to order a two-record set called "Black Beauty" if he acts now. He turns the dial. Merle Haggard sings about trading all of his tomorrows. He turns the radio off and starts the car. He drives around for almost an hour, then goes to the school and parks, waiting for her. He closes his eyes, remembers taking the Metroliner with Laura to New York, how he gave her a cup of water to hold for him while he got out an Excedrin. He always got headaches on trains. When the pill was on his tongue he reached for the cup and she smiled. She had drained it. The Excedrin was very bitter melting on his tongue as he got up to get another cup of water. The whole trip to New York was rotten. She hadn't wanted to go, but he had tickets to a play. He didn't know she didn't like Ibsen. That was early . . . when he first knew her. She was separated from Jim then, and living in a crummy apartment she wouldn't buy any furniture for. She smoked grass with him for the first time. She smoked all the grass, and Sam still hasn't gotten around to getting him more. Another time in New York he bought two grapefruit at a fruit stand, and the next time he looked at her the grapefruit were under her sweater. It looked very nice. She was very nice. He opens his eyes, convinced that he will fall asleep and scream, that she will walk up to his car and he will be screaming inside. The city is full of diplomats. He has been hit twice by them. Both diplomats were crazy. He gets depressed, sometimes, thinking that everybody is crazy. Except Sam. And then he gets worried that he feels that way about Sam.

He checks his watch. It is a gold watch that belonged to his grandfather. On the day his grandfather killed himself, he also shot two grouse. He went out in the morning for the birds, and in the afternoon for himself. They heard the story over and over when they were growing up about how their grandmother cleaned and cooked the grouse anyway. He studies the face of the watch, wondering whether his grandfather looked at it before he killed himself. She will be here in twenty-four minutes, he says out loud. He doesn't see her car, but she must already be inside the school. She is a devoted stepmother. She is devoted to everybody but him. He envies Rebecca. He has one of Rebecca's pictures that Laura left in his car by mistake. It is a crayoned picture of a flying red bird that looks like a flying pig. He takes it out and looks at it. He closes the glove compartment. Glove compartment. When people wore gloves. Years ago. His grandfather. There is a picture of his grandfather on a table in his mother's house. He was a plain-looking man, with white hair and puckered cheeks and a cravat. He built his own house. Charles got his house from his grandmother, when she died. It was not the same house his grandfather built. With the insurance money she had bought a newer one. His grandmother thought he was the only worthwhile member of the family. In elementary school, Charles had sung in the choir. His grandmother loved music. She left him her house.

Laura should be here. What is he going to say to her? He wants, somehow, to convey to her that her husband is a dull man. Since he is also dull, he wants to point out that she wouldn't be getting into anything unexpected; she would just be swapping a dull person who doesn't care much about her for one who does. That sounds awful. He will have to think harder. He puts his watch away. It is heavy in his pocket. He pushes it far into the pocket, not wanting to lose it. What would his old puckered-cheeked grandfather think of his rendezvousing with a woman at an elementary school?

She doesn't come. She's five minutes late, then ten. He turns on the radio, hoping to find out that his watch is inaccurate. There is a special report about a child's oven that blows up. Judy Collins. A financial report. He looks up and sees Laura's car, a black Volvo. Laura pulls up alongside his car, on the other side of the street. "I'm sick," she hollers. "I just came to tell you. I called, but you had left."

"What's the matter with you?" he says. Wind blows in his face.

"The flu," she says. "I'm really sick. I've got to go back to bed."

He looks at her stupidly. She looks very sick. Her hair is dirty. No question that it is more brown than blond. He stares into her eyes. They are bright. She has a fever. A car honks in back of her and she drives on. He thinks she is gone and can't bring himself to start the ignition. Her car pulls up alongside his.

"Hi," he says.

"I'm sorry I'm sick," she says, leaning across the seat. "I'll see you another time."

"Isn't there anything I can do for you?"

"No. I just want to go back to bed." She shakes her head. She looks awful.

"You shouldn't have come out."

"I thought of you sitting here. I knew you wouldn't believe I was sick."

"I would have believed you," he says, as indignant as she was when she said her husband didn't open her mail. But he probably wouldn't have. Even the bread-baking is in question.

"Will you call me?" he says. She nods, rolling the window up. Her car is moving slowly forward.

"I'm going to follow you," he says. "You're too sick to drive."

"I only have a fever," she says through the crack in the window, but he puts the key in the ignition, and she waits. The car won't start. It grinds, but nothing happens. When he is about to scream, pound the windshield, holler and curse, it starts. He follows her car. He follows it all the way to her house, which he can barely see from the road. It is a twenty-minute ride from the school, along streets he has never driven. He starts to pull into the drive, but sees another car and backs up, drives on. At the end of the dead-end street he makes a U-turn and coasts slowly past her driveway. What if she is dying? He sees her get out of her car and walk toward the house. He watches her until she disappears, then coasts to the end of the street. There is a lot of traffic, once he leaves her block. He keeps thinking about turning around, going to the house and saying something to her, no matter who's there. He lacks nerve. He's not sure what else he lacks, because her husband's no prize either. He is wondering about that when his car conks out at a stop sign. He tries to re-start it, but nothing happens. Finally, he sits there with the car flooded, cars pulling around him, head on the steering wheel. What the hell—it wouldn't hurt to grow his hair some.

Eventually the car starts, and he drives back to his house. Sam's car is out front. Charles pulls into the driveway and gets out, not bothering to put the car in the garage. The piece of junk doesn't deserve to be covered. He goes up the walk. Sam opens the front door.

"What are you doing here?" Sam says.

"What are you?" Charles says.

"I felt funny. I took off a couple of hours early. The flu's going around. I hope it's not that."

"If you think you've got the flu, what are you doing here?"

The wrong thing to say. Sam looks hurt.

"We can take care of you if you get sick," Charles says. He nods agreement with himself at Sam, whose expression changes.

"What happened to Laura?" Sam says.

"She's got it. She was awfully sick. I didn't get to talk to her. I followed her home. That's all."

Sam shakes his head. He is drinking wine. A bottle is on the floor by the chair.

"Wine?" Sam says.

"What are you drinking that for if you're getting sick?"

"I don't know," Sam says. "Where's Susan?"

"Shopping."

"I could go out and get food for dinner if there isn't any," Sam says.

"What would you go out for if you're getting sick?"

Sam shrugs. "What are we going to eat?" he says.

Charles gets a glass and pours some wine. It is French wine, instead of the Gallo that Sam used to drink. Sam sympathizes with the boycott. Charles feels sorry that he is getting sick.

"I guess I should call the hospital," Charles says. He gets up and calls. Pete answers on the first ring.

"Mommy did something that was a little silly," he says. "She had some laxatives in her purse, and she took them. She hasn't been feeling well today."

"Laxatives? What for?"

"She's going to be just fine, and fit as a fiddle for the Windy City," Pete says.

"Can I talk to her, Pete?"

"Sure you can. She's right here, and feeling better by the minute."

There is a lot of rustling and whispering.

"Hello?" his mother says faintly.

"I'm sorry you had a setback," Charles says. "You okay now?"

"Charles, I was in awful pain. It was like the night you

had to come for me. I was going to kill myself this morning and I went into the bathroom and took the laxatives."

"Made you weak, huh?" Charles says.

"Charles, the woman in the bed next to me died."

There is a loud rustling, and Pete's voice. "Charles? Pay no attention. Mommy's got her facts confused. The woman was discharged. Mommy's weak as a kitten from all those laxatives."

"Don't they watch her? Don't they know she's bats?"

There is a long silence. "We're looking forward to seeing you soon, too," Pete says. "I most certainly will tell her." Pete hangs up.

"Oh *Christ*," Charles says, slamming the receiver down.

"What's the matter?"

"She took herself a bunch of laxatives and she's talking about death again. He's there, no doubt telling her to try to foxtrot." Charles stops. He is surprised to realize that he remembers the name of another dance.

Sam shakes his head, swirls the wine in his glass.

"Nothing goes right," Sam says.

Charles picks up his coat from the back of the chair. "Come on," he says to Sam. "We're going to the store to get some good stuff. Bring those cookbooks with you."

"All of them?"

"There's only four or five."

Sam puts on his coat, picks them up.

"Under desserts," Charles says, closing the door behind him. "Look up soufflés. See if there's one that sounds like it's made out of oranges and cognac."

Sam cannot find it. Charles looks too, in the parking lot of the Safeway, but nothing even vaguely similar is listed. He ends up buying a Dutch Apple pie.

"I hate that kind," Sam says.

"I do too. Maybe I'll save it as a hostess present for Clara's dinner."

But on New Year's Day their mother is in the mental hospital. She is too sedated to have visitors. Pete is there, and Pete's brother, who flew in from Hawaii. Early in the morning Pete called to say that things were pretty good. The doctor did not think there would be much of a problem, and she'd be back home soon. She was taken to the hospital after she sat propped up in bed crying for an entire night. At noon, when Charles was fixing a bowl of soup to take to Sam on a tray, Pete called again. "You son of a bitch," Pete said loudly. "I know you don't like me and you never liked me, and from now on it's between you and your mother. I'm not calling you again. I'm not feeling guilty any more. You make me feel guilty she's here, when nobody could have taken better care of her. Talk to the doctors here about that, you son of a bitch." Charles called the hospital back, but there was no way Pete could be paged, and his mother had no telephone. The soup boiled over on the stove, and Charles tried to dab it up with a sponge, careful not to burn himself on the still-hot burner. The noodles looked disgusting clinging to the sponge. He put a napkin on a tray, the way his mother used to do for him when he was sick in bed, and then the bowl of soup. He could hear Sam coughing in the bedroom. The TV was in there, on a table Charles had moved to the foot of the bed. Even above the noise of the football game, Sam's coughing could be heard.

"You ought to have me call a doctor," Charles says, standing in the doorway with the tray. He feels his own nostrils unclogging as the steam from the soup rises.

"Everybody's got the flu. I don't need one."

"That cough sounds awful."

"Are you bringing me my lunch or not?"

Charles walks into the room. The announcer screams. The Dolphins have the ball. Sam sneezes.

"Don't get so close to me," Sam says.

"You've got a fever," Charles says. "I could feel the heat when I leaned over."

"Too bad the nursie isn't still here," Sam says.

"I'll bet she'd tell you to go to a doctor."

"I'll bet she'd jump into bed. Nurses are all amazing. I think nursing students are more remarkable than real nurses."

"Eat your soup."

"The last time I went to the doctor I had had a cough for two weeks—I'd shoot up in bed in the middle of the night, choking with it. He could hear me coughing. I coughed the whole time I was there. I told him that nothing worked but streptomycin. Naturally he wouldn't give me any. He said, 'Oh! You like that stuff, huh?' When the cough didn't get any better, I went back and asked for it again. He gave me some blue pills. That pissed me off, so I said, 'Isn't heroin good for coughing? Could you prescribe some of that?' Doctors. The hell with doctors."

Sam blows on a spoonful of soup, sips it. "Who was on the phone?"

"Pete. I guess he's loaded somewhere."

"Are you still going to have to go over there for dinner?"

"It doesn't look that way," Charles says.

"It's sort of pathetic," Sam says. "He tries to be nice to you and Susan now, doesn't he?"

"Yeah," Charles says. "He tries to be nice."

Charles is sitting at the foot of the bed. Sam leans around him to watch the huddle.

"You want me to move?"

"No. Stay where you are."

Charles gets up, wanders out into the hallway. Susan's clothes are thrown over a chair. She is taking a shower. When she gets out, he'll have to tell her that the shower had symbolic importance. Right after her boyfriend called she went in there. He picks up her sweater. Purple. Janis Joplin wouldn't have been caught dead in it. Laura wouldn't either. If Susan were Laura, he could throw off all his clothes, jump into the shower, say, "I love you, I love you, I love you." He sits down on the clothes-covered chair, thinking that he might be going out of his mind. If she doesn't call, he probably will. He goes into the living room and opens a drawer where there is a picture of Laura. It has a cheap silver frame around it—the kind that comes with photo-booth pictures. There is a white streak just under her chin. But her face is perfect. She has a heart-shaped face. She has large, white teeth that don't show in the picture. Her mouth is closed. She isn't smiling. "Why didn't you smile?" he said when she gave it to him. "I don't know. Everything's so complicated. It's all such a mess." Susan is right; he should have said how delighted he was to get the picture instead of criticizing her expression. She gave it to him when they were sitting at a drugstore counter, having a cup of coffee. She pulled it out of her wallet without comment. He thought that she was reaching for money, said "No, no." They never really understood each other. Most people can read signals; they never could. She'd be feeling good, and he'd think she was worried and not talk so she could think it out, when actually she was in a good mood until he stopped talking, and she thought there was something wrong with *him*. He tries to convince himself that the relationship was always doomed. They didn't understand each other, they didn't have a lot in common, she never said she was going to divorce her husband and never changed her mind, even after she said she loved him too. . . . It isn't working; he keeps picturing her on the carousel, sitting on a blue and gold horse, her hands tight around the brass pole, smiling at him. Well, he tells himself, that's a pretty rotten thing, if that's the best you can remember. It's not very significant. But it's as significant as anything else that's ever happened to him. He puts the picture back in the drawer. There's something wrong with putting her picture with unpaid bills. He takes it out and puts it on top of another table, against a vase.

"Finished," Sam calls. Charles goes into the bedroom.

"Sorry to yell," Sam says. "I didn't know where to put this."

"I'll take it. Is there anything else you want."

"I feel like puking now. No offense."

"No," Charles says. He carries the tray out to the kitchen. The phone rings.

"Hello?" he says. It is Laura. It has to be Laura.

"Hello," Pete says.

"Leave me alone, goddamn it," Charles says. "I didn't put her there either."

"That's not why I called," Pete says. "I called to say that when I called before I was a little upset. I wanted to ask you something."

"What?" Charles says.

"Do you think she'll ever get right again?" Pete asks.

"I don't know. What do the doctors say?"

"I can't understand them. There's something wrong with me, but I can't make any sense out of the things they say. Some young doctor—the one who lifted her wrist and said, 'What have we got here?' to her—talked to me all the time we were together about placem, placento, placenta research."

"You've got to be nuts to want to help nuts," Charles says.

"I think she senses that we all feel that way, so she has no incentive to recover," Pete says.

"Pete, before you even knew her she'd dance in the kitchen naked with the broom at night."

"She danced?" Pete says. "Yeah?"

"She seemed to be dancing. I don't know. I was so spooked that I got out of there fast."

"She senses that. She senses that we avoid her, and has no incentive to get well."

"Pete, you ought to try to forget all this for a while if you can and go back to the house and get some sleep."

"I'm in the house. It's a mess. I've got to clean it up, but I don't know where to start. She threw stuff all over."

"Go to sleep and forget it."

"I'm too loaded to go to sleep. Listen, I want you to

know that I didn't mean what I said before. I'm sorry to have said it."

"That's okay," Charles says.

"I wish I had a boy of my own. I think we'd be more alike than you and me. What you were saying."

"Yeah," Charles says.

"But it's too late now," Pete says.

"Yeah," Charles says. "Well, I'll be seeing you."

He hangs up and feels very guilty that he didn't offer to go over and help him clean up the mess. In the living room, he looks at Laura's picture. He is afraid the sun will fade it, so he puts it back in the drawer. He has looked at the picture for so long that when he sees Laura he's always surprised. Laura, for him, is always wearing a checked shirt, her hair always looks a particular way, she always has a deadpan expression. Not that he sees her much any more to be surprised. He looks down at an open magazine on the rug. "How Seriously Do You Take Yourself?" is printed in big black letters. Susan has taken the quiz, checking off the answers with small, neat checks. Susan doesn't have fits of depression; she doesn't buy expensive camera equipment only to discover she prefers skiing. He looks away. At the vase, where the picture was.

"That was Mark on the phone earlier," Susan says. "He's probably going to drive down and get me."

"Mark," Charles says. "Mark the doctor."

Her hair is wrapped in a turban. She is wearing slacks and a white shirt. She looks very clean and fresh. She will finish college, marry Mark, have children. Maybe even have an A-frame to vacation in. In Vermont. Or upstate New York. There might even be a maid to cook lamb chops.

"Go, go, go you bastard!" Sam hollers in the bedroom.

"Doesn't he know if he's coming or not?" Charles asks.

"He's coming if he thinks the car will hold out."

"What's wrong with his car?"

"He doesn't know."

"Then how is he going to decide if it'll hold out?"

She shrugs. "It's an old Cadillac," she says. "It eats gas, but it usually holds out. Except that there's one hose that always breaks."

"Wooooooo!" Sam shouts.

"I guess he's not dying," Charles says.

Susan unwraps the towel from her head, throws her hair forward and begins brushing it.

"Should we call the hospital later? To see how she is when the tranquilizers wear off?"

"She'll be nuts. That's how she'll be."

"If Mark makes it, he'll be here tomorrow. We can all go then."

"No," Charles says. "Anyway—I've got to go back to work."

"Oh, yeah. I forgot about work."

"It was sure a swell vacation," Charles says. "I can't complain."

"Do you get another vacation in the summer?"

"I just have two days left. Except for sick leave."

"Isn't it awful to have your life measured out like that?"

"I need the money."

"Couldn't you paint? You used to be so good at it."

"Paint? There's no money in painting. Maybe I could paint houses. I've thought about doing something like that. Sam and I kicked around the idea last summer. He's really going nuts at the store."

"I don't know what I'll do when I get out of college."

"It would help to have a major. But if you're marrying Doctor Mark, I don't guess you even need to finish."

"I want to go to school. I mean, I want to finish. I didn't go there to get a husband."

"Now that you've got one, why don't you just quit?"

"He's not even my husband. He's just my boyfriend."

"Propose to him," Charles says. "I wish I could propose to somebody and have them take care of me."

"I'm not going to propose to Mark!"

"Why not? Don't women propose to men now?"

"That's not why I'm not doing it. I just don't want to do it."

"Face it. You want him to marry you."

"Then he can propose," Susan says.

"How quaint."

"You deliberately get me on these subjects so you can goad me," Susan says.

"I know. I can be so unpleasant. Maybe if somebody took care of me I'd be in a better mood."

"Get that woman to leave her husband."

"It's more than a husband. It's a daughter and an A-frame."

"That's nothing. Women walk out every day."

"Not for me they don't."

"You should keep after her."

"She's sick."

"When she's well."

"Yeah," Charles says.

"Don't sound so defeated. You'll never be persuasive if you sound like that."

"What should I do? Read a Dale Carnegie book?"

"Who's that?" Susan says.

"What a generation. Never heard of Amy Vanderbilt. Never heard of Dale Carnegie. And you think Woodstock was a drag."

"I know it was a drag. It was nothing but mud."

"And nobody is into drugs any more, huh?"

"Not many people. I don't know . . . maybe I just don't know them."

"Have you got a lot of friends at school?"

"A couple that Mark knows are pretty nice."

"I don't have any friends. I just have Sam."

"Why don't you meet people?"

"Next you'll be telling me to dance."

Charles goes into the kitchen, looks through the cabinets to see what there is for dinner. Susan is right; he thinks about food too much. He picks up a package of dried peas, drops them back on the shelf. There is a large bottle of vanilla, a package of dried beans, a box of Tuna Helper, no tuna, a can of baby clams, two cans of alphabet soup, a canister with four Hydrox cookies (what happened to them? They used to be so good. Sugar. No doubt they're leaving out sugar), a package of Cheese Nabs, and a can of grapefruit juice. There is also a package of manicotti shells. They will have to go out for dinner. It is too cold; it was thirty degrees when he went out early in the afternoon to buy Sam some magazines.

"You don't have a hair dryer, do you?"

"Of course not. What would I be doing with that?"

"A lot of men blow-dry their hair now."

"I don't want all that junk around me. What would I have a hair dryer for?"

He is cantankerous. That's probably the real reason Susan's leaving. If Doctor Mark's Cadillac will start.

"Does Mark use a hair dryer?" he calls.

No answer. The rumble of the television. He looks at the thermometer on the window outside. It is twenty-eight degrees. The thermometer was a Christmas gift from an uncle in Wisconsin. An ornamental squirrel is huddled on top of it. It is made out of some plastic-looking black material. The squirrel looks like it won't make it. There is a black plastic nut in its paws. Charles goes back to the cabinet, looking for the jar of bird seed. He finds it, shoved to the back of the highest shelf. There is also another box of Tuna Helper there, and a jar of Heinz Kosher Dills. They will definitely be going out for dinner. Charles gets his jacket from the closet in the living room, zips it. Twenty-seven, and he still has trouble zipping his jacket. "You approach it with too much hostility," Laura told him. "You have to glide it up. You do it all wrong;

you jerk it. A zipper will never work if it's jerked." Laura used to zip his jacket for him. When she went back to her husband he couldn't stand to see the jacket. He went out and bought a raincoat, but that wasn't warm enough, and he had a sentimental attachment to the jacket, so eventually he started wearing it again. One of the girls he had once loved (the one he still sort of loves, but she's no good for him) gave it to him five years ago as a Christmas present. She got tired of sewing buttons on his blue pea jacket, and on Christmas morning he opened the box with the brown jacket in it. There was a chocolate heart wrapped in red foil inside. Where did she ever find a Valentine's Day heart in December?

He opens the front door and walks out into the snow with a pie tin full of birdseed. Fearing that the tin will blow away, he goes into the garage and looks for something to weight it down with. The only thing he can find is a shovel, so he takes that out and rests the handle over part of the pie tin. It looks silly—like some socialist emblem. At least now they'll eat. Walking back to the house, he glances over his shoulder. What is he doing in this neighborhood? Who are his neighbors? When he first moved in, a woman a few houses down—he can't remember any more whether it was the red brick house or the gray one—asked him to a party. He asked whether she'd mind if he brought a friend—the party was on a Friday night, and he always saw Sam on Friday night. He thought that afterwards he and Sam would go out for a few beers. He and Sam went to the woman's party (her name was Audrey. He's been trying to remember that for months), and met a couple who lived a few houses across from him (they told him which one—it was either the red brick or the blue with white shutters). They told him to stop by for a drink, but he forgot which house it was and was embarrassed to go knocking on doors. He kept thinking he'd run into them, but he never did, and he never got there for the drink. The party at Audrey's was pretty nice. At least he enjoyed it, until he began to sense strange looks, until he figured out that Audrey thought he and Sam were queer. Why would she think that? They even sat on opposite sides of the room. Audrey's husband was very nice. He was in a wheelchair, and had been for five years, after a car accident. He sold books. He also sold life insurance. On Saturday he sold flowers, helped the cashier who was his nephew. "I don't want to have time to think," he said. "I'd only come to depressing conclusions." "He's the most un-depressed man I've ever known," Audrey said. "He's a pleasure to be with." "And it keeps me out of the house," her husband said. Audrey looked terribly hurt. Later, Charles called (twice) to ask them to dinner, but both times she said they were busy. Once he saw her husband in his wheelchair on the avenue, trying to navigate down a particularly icy stretch of sidewalk that hadn't been sanded. He wanted to go over and help him, but he was embarrassed. He just went back to his car and drove home.

Charles is in the kitchen, looking out the window. Some children run across the lawn. One child is bundled up like the Pillsbury Doughboy. Charles remembers a picture from *Life* magazine . . . *Life* magazine . . . captioned "John-John, the President's son, spies his Dad and away he runs." John Kennedy, Jr. rushes toward the steps leading from the plane. If nobody is into drugs any more, John Kennedy, Jr., won't be a doper. With that smart father, he no doubt would have, otherwise. The kid will probably be a lawyer or a senator. Like the rest of them, he'll have car accidents. Charles is still a sucker for tabloids with headlines reading: "Onassis Keeps Skorpios as Haven for Vegetable JFK" and in smaller type: "Jackie Says She Can Never Leave Him."

He feels his head. He has been having strange visions, remembering strange things. He goes to the bedroom to check on Sam. Sam is asleep. His feet stick out of the covers. He has on thick red and white striped snowmobile socks that he was given at the office Christmas party. Actually, he didn't go to the office party. When he went back to work there was a note over his punch-in card, fastened with a paper clip. "Stop by for your Xmas Present. I couldn't buttonhole you at the party. Ed, in Sportswear." Sam was embarrassed to go ask for his present, but somehow Ed found out who he was and came over and gave him the present in the employees' cafeteria. "It's something anybody could use," Ed said. On Sam's present was written: "Number 80." Sam went looking for Ed a week later, to ask him if he'd like to join them for a few beers Friday night, and found out that Ed had been fired.

Charles thinks about turning off the television, but the sudden silence might disturb Sam. Sam's face is very white. He hopes Sam does not get pneumonia. Once Charles had pneumonia. That's how he got the sentimental attachment to the jacket. He was in the hospital for three days, and on the second night he got out of bed and got the jacket out of the metal closet and put it over the front of him, over the top of the white sheets. It was nice to have something familiar there. The room was pale green and white. It made him think he wasn't going to die. The girl kept coming and holding his hand, looking worried. She didn't want him to die, either. Why exactly had he left her? Why had he left any of them? Surprisingly, he left as many of them as had left him. He even left the first one, fifteen-year-old Pat O'Hara, when she told a mutual friend that he kissed sloppily. Maybe she never said that—maybe the friend made it up. The friend was a notorious liar. He remembers the friend: Bruce Laframboise, later captain of the football team, first one in high school to get a sports car, a short, muscular boy who, in high school, had blackened his front teeth with ink. His mother took him to the dentist. Mrs. Laframboise used to tell his mother that Bruce was a model child, except for that peculiar thing he had done. Bruce ended up working in a free clinic in Haight-Ashbury—at least according to Bruce, who was a compulsive liar. Either that or his sister was a compulsive liar, because she always swore that Bruce was, and everybody believed her. His next girlfriend was a stringbean named Pamela Byall, who became a veterinarian. He met her on the street the year after he graduated from college, and she said, "I've become a veterinarian, no thanks to you." Then there were the recent ones, the ones of the last four or five years. One of them lasted a year and a half. Pamela again. Pamela Smith, giver of the jacket. She started thinking that she was really a lesbian. He got tired of hearing about it. He'd go to bed with her, and she'd say, "It would be so nice to go to bed with a woman. What does it feel like to go to bed with a woman?" He told her he didn't think his perspective would help her. She bought a stack of books about lesbianism. Gay women's newspapers were thrown all over the house. She found all Sam's girlfriends terribly attractive, and said so to the girls. One night at a pizza house, he said, "I'm not going to have anything more to do with you" and left, leaving Pamela to pay for a green-pepper pizza. Good, he thought. That will be something to turn her against men. But she kept calling him, asking if she could come over and talk. "How can you turn your back on me when I'm so undecided?" she said. He always gave in, let her come over, and sat through a boring discussion of the beauty of women before they went to bed. She called him once and asked him to come pick her up at a gay bar because her car wouldn't start. He refused. She called again after that to get the number of one of Sam's girlfriends, and he hung up on her. He even got a Christmas card from her, with the female symbol on it, drawn with a red circle and green cross. "Merry Christmas, forgive and forget," she wrote on the envelope. Then she called him, but he said he wasn't feeling well. After Pamela there was a girl named Marsha Steinberg that he still has erotic dreams about.

Sam introduced them. He forgets how Sam met her. Probably a castoff, although he never wanted to ask on the chance he'd find out he was right. Sam always parts with women on good terms—so good that they call him to refer them to other men. Marsha Steinberg was very mixed-up when he knew her. She took a lot of amphetamine, although later she gave it up entirely and went to law school. She once did a pencil sketch of him that was surprisingly good—or at least it made him look surprisingly good. She had a brown cashmere sweater that she wore with slacks. The sweater shed all over the slacks. She had a dog that shed more. She was always covered with dog hair. Her own hair was very short. Short black hair, black eyes. He definitely loved her. She's now practicing law in Colorado. One day they went to the park and she fell asleep on his shoulder. It was a hot, noisy day in the park, and he couldn't believe that she'd fallen asleep. Policemen kept walking by, and he was terrified that she was dead, and that eventually he would have to call out to one of the passing policemen that the woman next to him was dead. But she woke up. He always loved her for that. Once he went to a hair-cutting shop with her and watched an inch get cut off her hair. "If you were sentimental, you'd scoop it up," she laughed. He should have done it, but it looked so ugly—those little clumps of black hair on the white floor. He couldn't touch it. He thinks about calling her sister to get her address in Colorado, but what the hell. What good can it do him if she's in Colorado? The girl he dated after Marsha was just somebody to pass the time with. She wasn't very pretty or very smart. He never thinks about her.

He looks out the window at the thermometer. Twenty-five degrees. He knocks on Susan's door.

"Do you want to go out for something to eat?"

"Sure," she says. She comes out. She has on the purple sweater. There is a small bump just above her lip.

"I'm glad you're not just hanging around waiting for her to call," Susan says.

He hadn't thought to do that. It's a good idea. He should wait. Eventually Laura will call. Maybe when Jim leaves the house for a minute . . . and who knows when that minute will be?

"I'm going to write Sam a note, in case he wonders what happened," Charles says. "Poor Sam. I hope he doesn't have pneumonia."

"He's got a good appetite, at least," Susan says.

"Yeah. We'll bring something back."

"I'm glad we're not setting out for dinner with Pete," Susan says.

Charles leaves the note on the dresser next to Sam, figures that he'll never see it, scotch-tapes it to the television screen, over Lauren Bacall's face. He puts on his jacket again, holds the door open for Susan. It is cold enough to wear his face mask, but his face mask frightens him. It has frightened him ever since he saw a television news program about bank robbers. The bank robbers had on face masks, imprinted with reindeer and diamond shapes. Charles always thinks he's a bank robber who will be caught when he wears his face mask. He also takes his hands out of his pockets when he passes a policeman. Otherwise—and he knows this is silly—he thinks that the policeman might think that he's hiding something. Still, his feet move all wrong when he passes a policeman. He weaves and stands too straight, and he's sure they'll stop him for questioning. When he drives, if he sees a policeman parked off the road somewhere in back of him, he keeps looking in his rear-view mirror. Sometimes he even checks the mirror if he passes a steep hill or a curve in the road off which they might be hiding. Once when he was eighteen years old he was pulled over by a policeman for speeding. He stopped so suddenly when he saw the blue light that the police car almost rammed him. The policeman was very jittery when he got out. "Pull over slowly when you see that light," the policeman said. Charles tried to say "Yes, sir," but he couldn't speak. He gave the policeman his license and registration. His hand was shaking wildly. The policeman looked at his hand for a second before he took the two pieces of paper. Then he shined his flashlight in the back seat of the car, and on the passenger's side. Charles watched the beam, transfixed. The policeman stood there, flashlight shining. Then he said, "Wait here," and disappeared. He came back with a ticket. Another policeman came with him and shined a light across the back seat again. They both walked away. Charles stuffed the ticket in his pocket without looking at it, turned the key and got ready to pull out. He pulled out right in front of the police car, cutting them off. The blue light went on again, but when Charles pulled over, they only pulled up alongside him. "What the hell's the matter with you?" the policeman hollered. He didn't wait for an answer. He tore off, blue light still on. Charles sat there, his leg jerking too wildly to drive. "Satisfaction" came on the radio. It was the first time he'd heard the song. It didn't help to calm him. Nothing did. When the song was over, his leg was still shaking, and he felt too light-headed to drive. He thought about dragging himself from the car somehow and crawling to the pay phone that was right in front of him to call Sam for help. Then he started talking out loud to himself, and that helped: "Okay, okay, it's just a ticket. They're not coming back. Take it easy." In a few more minutes he was able to drive. He had been on his way to an anniversary party for his parents at their best friends' house. When he got there he went to the bathroom, and without realizing what he was doing ran the water and took a shower. He didn't realize how strange that was until the host asked, "Were you showering, Charles?" when he came out of the bathroom with his hair soaking wet.

Charles pulls up in front of a Chinese restaurant, The Blue Pagoda. There is hardly anybody inside. Two booths

and two tables have been taken. The ashtrays on all the
tables are blue. There is a small paper umbrella stuck in
the top of the salt shaker. The waiter quickly removes it
when he puts down the menus. When he returns he has
blue napkins and chopsticks. They order: pork-fried rice,
moo-shu pork, spareribs. "No egg drop?" the waiter says.
"Egg drop," Charles says. "No egg drop?" the waiter
says. "Wonton?" "That will be fine," Charles says.
Faintly, Charles can hear Donovan singing "Mad John."
It's so faint that it might be Muzak, not Donovan at all.
And Charles might be imagining that the words are being
sung. A couple with a child comes in and sits at the booth
in back of them. "This *is* a German restaurant," the father says to the little girl. "It's Chinese!" the little girl
says. "If they don't have sauerbrauten, you'll just have to
suffer," the father says. "Sit up straight," the mother says.

"Wonton?" the waiter says, putting the bowls in front
of them.

"That's right," Charles says.

"Just made fresh?" the waiter says.

"Fine," Charles says. The waiter only knows how to
speak in the interrogative.

"You eat Chinese food with Doctor Mark?" Charles
asks.

"I don't think we've ever gone to a Chinese restaurant."

"I thought that was what people who were in love did."

"What?" Susan says.

"Listen to music, go to Chinese restaurants . . . that
kind of stuff."

"You always pretend not to know about things. You're
in love with that woman. Do the two of you go to Chinese
restaurants?"

"She eats with her husband."

"When she wasn't with him. You always pretend that
that time didn't exist."

"I don't want to talk about her tonight," Charles says. "I know she's not going to call."

Susan slowly sips soup. "I feel sort of bad about leaving you," she says.

"Why?"

"Oh, I don't know. That woman's sort of rotten to you, and I'll be leaving you with Sam sick. And her in the hospital."

"Your staying wouldn't make Laura leave her husband or Sam get well, and it certainly wouldn't spring her from the bin." Charles doesn't want her to leave.

"I guess you're right. Are you going to be polite to him when he comes?"

"What do you think I'd do? Act like some outraged lover?"

"I'm afraid you'll make wisecracks. I know you don't want him to like you."

"I don't think there's much chance of that."

"You always put yourself down. You always act dejected."

"I'm a mess."

She laughs, sucking spinach into her mouth.

"Hot?" the waiter says, putting the plates in front of them. He puts the dishes on the table, puts his hands on his hips, and says, "Okay?"

"Fine," Charles says. "Thank you."

"Thank you?" the waiter says, leaving. He stops at the next table. "You're not German!" the little girl says.

Once he and Laura went to a Spanish restaurant where the waiters poured a thin stream of white wine into their mouths from a leather wineskin. They ordered saffron rice and mussels and ate large, dark rolls. Laura told him that food started tasting entirely different to her after she stopped wearing lipstick. He wishes he could do something that would make him enjoy his food more. He eats all the time, but most of the time he hardly tastes it. His grandmother used to serve chicken bouillon before the

Sunday dinner to "make the tongue buds blossom." She always invoked strange metaphors: "Think if the earth were a big shoe and all that snow coming down was shoe polish." To this day, he feels that snow is a call to action.

"I was thinking about Grandma," Charles says.

"I don't remember her very well."

"I remember her smelling things. She always had her nose in the steam from a soup pot, she always thought their cat smelled bad, even when Grandfather had caught it and washed it, she always wore heavy perfume. What do you remember about her?"

"That her drawers were full of magazines she tied together in bundles and that she never untied the bundles. She always had things tied together. She'd tie two packages of paper napkins together with twine and put it on the kitchen shelf."

"She was nice," Charles says.

"Yeah. She was very nice. I remember that blue and lavender dress she made me. When it was washed the colors ran and made the lace blue, and she cut it all off and sewed white lace on."

Their grandmother died in her seat at a movie theater. There was a special movie about Greece. Men were there to show the movie and talk the audience into going to Greece. Everyone in the audience knew that she had died, and afterwards, their mother heard, more people than the men expected signed up on the spot for the trip to Greece. She was sixty-eight when she died. Their grandfather died two years and one day later. He was crossing the street with a bottle in a brown bag and a loaf of bread in another brown bag when a truck hit him. The truck was full of wheelbarrows that it was on the way to deliver to a hardware store.

"Almond cookie?" the waiter says, putting down a plate with four cookies on it.

"Tomorrow we've got to go see her, don't we?"

"Yeah. I'm not looking forward to running into Pete. He called today and told me I was a son of a bitch."

"He did not."

"He did. He said that I made him feel guilty. He called back and apologized."

"Was he drunk or something?"

"I guess so. I don't blame him."

"These are good," Susan says. "Almonds are supposed to keep away cancer."

"I thought that was apricot pits."

"Maybe you're right," Susan says, crunching into the second cookie.

"I saw a picture in a magazine of some Mexican doctor who injects people with apricot-pit extract. People go there and live in trailers and get injections. I hope if I get sick I don't get crazy like that."

"If I had it, I'd do anything. I'd go to Lourdes. I'd do anything."

"How the hell did we get started talking about this?"

"I probably started it. I'm so used to talking about diseases all the time with Mark."

"What conclusions has he come to?"

"You're not going to be nice to him, are you?"

"I told you I was. He's just a jackass."

"One of the doctors he knows has a theory that the cells react to music. He's trying to get a grant to play music to diseased cells."

"I'm sure he'll get it. There are a lot of jackasses out there waiting to give other jackasses money."

"You're so smart," Susan says.

"I'm not so smart. I'm just not a jackass."

"Are you sure it's okay for me to leave?"

"Sure," he says. "What color is the Cadillac?"

"Maroon."

"Maroon. Jesus Christ."

They pay the bill and leave The Blue Pagoda. It is bitter cold, and nobody is on the street. Charles drives down to the newsstand across from the train station and gets the late paper. A baby is on the cover: "First of 1975." He looks at the weather forecast, holding the paper near the floor so that the car light shines on it. Snow. He does not want to go back to work. He wants the car to hurry up and get warm. When they get home Sam is still asleep. On the note on the television is written: "Pete called."

"I forgot to get him food," Charles says to Susan.

"He's out for the night," Susan says.

"Should we try to wake him up to see if he's alive?"

"No," she says. "He's okay."

He is glad Susan is there. She doesn't tell him what to do much, but sometimes she does, and that makes it easier.

Chapter 5

At lunchtime (if only it were eleven again, instead of twelve-thirty) Charles goes alone to a restaurant at the end of the block. He orders a well-done cheeseburger, a salad without dressing, and a Coke. He thinks if he eats salad without dressing that when he eats it with dressing again it will taste good. All of the food is terrible. He oversalts it and is thirsty all day.

"Gimme a nickel," a black kid says to him as he walks back to the office, "and I'll do a somersault in the air for you."

Charles gives the kid a quarter. "You don't have to do a somersault," he says. The kid flips in the air.

"That's amazing," Charles says.

"My brother's working on a double flip," the kid says, and walks away to accost another man.

Back at his desk early, Charles puts on his earphones and turns on his cassette player: "Folk Fiddling from Sweden." After he has listened for a few minutes he dials his number.

"Hello?" Sam says groggily.

"I woke you up," Charles says.

"Glad you did. I was having nightmares. I dreamed you and I were hunting wolves, and there were so many of them we didn't know where to start, and if we didn't start soon . . ."

"God, I hope I don't catch this," Charles says.

Sam is panting.

"Is there anything you want me to bring you back tonight?"

"Can you get me some Mr. Goodbars?"

"Mr. Goodbars? They're no good for you when you're sick."

"Maybe they'll finish me off and I won't ever have to go back to work."

"I know what you mean," Charles says.

"Susan's doc didn't show. She's still here."

"Is she disappointed?"

"Doesn't act it. I'm not exactly too sensitive to the state of others right now, I guess."

"Take aspirin. She'll bring it to you."

"She does."

"Well, I'll see you tonight."

Charles hangs up. If Laura isn't still sick—she can't still be sick—she'll be leaving her house in an hour to pick up Rebecca. Lucky Rebecca. If Rebecca grows up to be like Laura she will be a heartbreaker. Maybe he will become like Humbert Humbert and get Rebecca. Because it certainly doesn't look like he's going to get Laura.

A woman from typing comes in to pick up two reports to do for him. The woman has on a blue dress that is unfashionably short and heavy black boots pulled tightly over her heavy legs. But her face is pretty. She was Laura's friend. He wants to think that she knows all about the two of them, but Laura said that she never told anybody. He wishes she had; then he wouldn't doubt, as he sometimes does, that it happened at all. He and the woman could exchange secret, knowing glances. Laura, they would both be thinking. She walks out with the piece of paper, and he looks at the big black boots walking across the blue carpet. Laura always dressed beautifully. She had suede boots and several pretty dresses, just a few but very pretty, and she always looked very delicate. Her husband is nicknamed "Ox." Charles has not gotten back to work, and he has been at his desk for fifteen minutes.

He has just cheated the government of five minutes. He cheats it of another two, turning his chair to look out the window, playing a little game and imagining that when he turns around Laura will be there, even though he knows that he would see her reflection in the glass if she were there. Even though she cannot be there, because she is getting ready to go for Rebecca. He wishes he were Rebecca's father. If he were her father and Laura were her mother they could be a family. They are already a family: Laura, Rebecca, and Ox. He imagines with horror that when he turns around they will *all* be there, that he will actually have to face the fact. He turns around immediately and looks at the piece of paper on his desk.

The woman from typing comes back. "There should be another piece attached to this," she says. He sits up a little higher so that he can look down at the boots. They are menacing. He wonders why she wears them. She couldn't think they're pretty. He reaches in the bottom of the basket on the corner of his desk. "Sorry," he says.

"First day back," he says.

"What do you hear from Laura?" he asks.

"Oh. I had dinner there last night. She went back to her husband," the woman says knowingly.

The A-frame. Ox. Maybe more freshly baked bread. So she's well.

"What did you have?" He can't contain his curiosity.

"Lobster Newburg. It was wonderful. I've been trying to lose weight, but with the holidays and that dinner, I'm never going to make it."

"You're going to think this is terrible, but I don't think I ever knew your name," he says.

"Betty," she says.

"That's right," he says. "I did know it."

He'd had no idea what her name was.

She stands there, smiling. He wants very much to know if she had the orange thing for dessert.

"I get into work and I become a robot," he says. "It's awful."

"I hate it here," Betty says. "But I'm lucky to have a job. My sister just graduated from Katy Gibbs, and she's been looking since before Thanksgiving."

"It's rotten," he says. "It's nice if you can have perspective on it and be glad you've got a job."

"I just am glad today," she says. "Most days I come in and hate it."

"Is your sister looking for work around here?"

"In New York. But if she doesn't find something soon she's going to have to come live with me. My parents kicked her out. They don't think she's trying, because they sent her to college and then to Katy Gibbs and all."

"Don't they read the papers?"

She shrugs. "I guess I'd better start this," she says, and turns to leave.

She's very nice, Charles thinks. Why couldn't you like her? He looks down at the piece of paper again and makes a notation on the pad. He has the eerie feeling that when he looks up Laura and Jim and Rebecca will be there. He throws his pen down. He gets up and picks up the pen, goes back to the desk and sits down. Lobster Newburg. That must have been delicious. That cheeseburger was awful.

He leaves at five-fifteen instead of five-thirty, stopping at the stand on the ground level for two Mr. Goodbars. The man who runs the concession is blind. "What have you got?" he asks.

"Not Laura" seems like the logical answer. He has got to stop thinking about her. It's true that he wasn't that wild for her when he had her. If he ever had her. When he *was with* her. Once when he was with her they sat at a drugstore having coffee and she gave him a picture of herself. *Remember something better* he says under his breath. "Two Goodbars" he says out loud.

"Thirty-two," the man says. The man reaches into an

open metal box and feels around for the change. The blind man is never wrong. Charles looks at the three pennies. Laura, he thinks. He drops the change in his coat pocket and zips the coat. Tries to zip it. He pulls more slowly. Sure enough, it works. He goes through the revolving door and into the cold. His car is a long walk away. He turns on the cassette player he is holding in his other hand and "Folk Fiddling from Sweden" blares out. It is still playing when he gets to his car. The lock is frozen. He kicks it with his foot. Much to his surprise, the lock turns. He drives to a store and buys a big package of pork chops and a bag of potatoes and a bunch of broccoli and a six-pack of Coke. He remembers cigarettes for Sam when he is checking out, in case he's well enough to smoke. He buys a National Enquirer that features a story about Jackie Onassis's face-lift. James Dean is supposed to be alive and in hiding somewhere, too. Another vegetable. Not dead at all. *East of Eden* is one of his favorite films. He saw it, strangely enough, on television shortly after he and Laura went to a carnival and rode on a Ferris wheel. He felt so sorry for James Dean. Back then he didn't feel sorry for himself at all. No reason to. Now he feels sorry for himself. Feeling sorry for himself, he gets back in the car and drives home. He thinks about Rebecca's bird trapped in his glove compartment. At a stop sign he closes his eyes and inhales, hoping to smell Vol de Nuit. Cold air sears through his nostrils. Turning onto his block he sees the man from Audrey's party getting out of his car. Charles stops, rolls down his window. "Hey," he says. "Hi. Hello."

"Hello," the man says. "Cold as a witch's tit, isn't it?" The man is wearing a black coat and scarf. He looks menacing.

"Yeah," Charles says. "Farmer's Almanac says we're in for a big storm the eighteenth."

"You were going to come for a drink," the man says. "Come for a drink."

"Okay," Charles says. "I'll get over."

"Any time," the man says.

"Good. Thanks," Charles says.

He feels good about that until he realizes that the man's car was parked far away from either the red brick or the white house with blue shutters and that he still doesn't know where he lives.

He runs with the grocery bag from the driveway to the front door. Susan opens it.

"It's awful out," she says. "How did it go?"

"I got through the day," he says, then realizes that that was melodramatic. He expects her to inform him that his attitude is wrong, but she doesn't.

"How are you?" he says. "Doctor desert you?"

"No. He'll be in later tonight. His car broke down."

Charles feels sorry for him because his car broke down. He does not want to feel sorry for the man.

"What kind of jackass wouldn't get rid of a Cadillac anyway?" he says.

He takes the groceries into the kitchen, then goes to the bedroom to see Sam. Sam is asleep, his feet again out of the covers. This time his fly is hanging open and his pajama top is all bunched up around him. Charles is sure that he is getting pneumonia. He backs out of the room, goes to the kitchen and gets a glass of grapefruit juice.

"What makes you so sure he doesn't have pneumonia?" Charles asks.

"He doesn't have pneumonia. He was awake for several hours today."

Charles is glad she's still there. He wishes the Cadillac would break apart in the middle.

"Would you like me to cook these?" Susan asks, taking the pork chops out of the bag.

He will never have that dessert again. "Sure," he says.

"After dinner we've got to go see her," Susan says.

He had forgotten. "I know," he says. "Pete call back?"

"No."

"I guess I'll get it in person then."

Charles checks the thermometer: thirty-two degrees.

"It's freezing," he says. He goes into the living room and lies down on the sofa. It reminds him of lying in the hospital bed, no energy to move, his mother sitting at his side, on top of her coat on a chair. The man who shared his room was named somebody-or-other Brownwell. Brownwell, it turned out, had an inoperable melanoma. Charles had no idea what that was, and Brownwell didn't either, and as hard as he tried not to, hands over his ears, Charles still heard the doctor say "cancer" through the thin screen that was pulled around Brownwell's bed. It was so depressing there. He'd wake up in the morning and see Brownwell's head against the pillow; the rest of his body already seemed to have shrunken up, given up, disappeared. Sometimes Charles would raise himself in bed the little he could to make sure that Brownwell was still there below the shoulders. Brownwell sat and stared. Charles's mother always asked Brownwell if he wanted a glass of water when she came and when she left. Once he did. Charles turns on the couch, trying to get the hospital out of his mind. The sheets were so stiff. Once he woke up a little to see Brownwell, who paced for four days until they discharged him, pacing by his bed. Brownwell stopped to pull Charles's blanket up. Charles pretended to be asleep and lay very still, but it was all he could do to restrain himself because he wanted to reach out and kiss Brownwell's hand. He almost did kiss his hand. Not because he straightened the sheets, but just because he felt so damn sorry for Brownwell. Every day when the doctor came to see him, Charles waited to hear the word "melanoma." He hung on the doctor's every word. "You're very alert today, that's a good sign," the doctor said. Another time, the doctor asked him if his mother was "emotionally disturbed." He never found out what his mother had done that made the doctor ask. Pete came every night—damn, he should like that man—and brought

Playboy and, for some reason, an inflatable plastic pillow he could blow up and put under the one on the bed. Actually, it came in handy. He was too weak to sit up well without calling the nurses to haul him up by his armpits, but with the pillow he was a little higher and could see a little more. Brownwell's son blew it up for him. The son was a cub scout. Brownwell looked like he could die every night during visiting hours. He looked better when his wife and son left. Charles gets up. He's going to remember as long as he lies there. He goes out to the kitchen and watches Susan pour Sam's leftover white wine over the cooking pork chops.

"I hope she's not so sedated she doesn't know us," Susan says.

"She fakes that. She almost always knows us."

He sits in a chair. The pork chops smell good. He is glad she is there, because he is too tired to cook. He shouldn't be so tired. He should have a checkup. He doesn't want to. They will find out he has an inoperable melanoma.

They eat dinner at the table, even though Charles and Susan told Sam that they should bring a tray to him in bed and bring chairs in for them to sit on to keep him company. Charles was secretly glad to see Sam get up, because that would keep pneumonia away. Nothing would keep inoperable melanoma away, but walking would keep pneumonia away. He shakes his head, trying to clear his mind so he can enjoy dinner.

"Did you get the candy bars?" Sam asks. Sam is very hoarse.

"Oh, yeah. They're in my coat pocket."

"Probably won't be able to eat that much, though," Sam says.

"Sure you will."

"I've got to get back to work tomorrow," Sam says.

"You're nuts. You can hardly stand up."

"Then let them send me to the doctor and send me home. That way I won't lose my job."

"Call them and tell them you're sick."

"Won't work."

"Bastards," Charles says.

"I'm lucky to have the damned job," Sam says.

"A Phi Beta Kappa is lucky to be selling men's jackets. Yeah."

"The money, I mean."

"Speaking of which, you've still got a twenty of mine for grass."

Susan looks up, surprised.

"Coming in end of the week," Sam says. He gets it from a woman whose son gives it to her. She puts it in her lunch pail. The woman works in the "Bath Accessories" shop. She's a nice woman—a dumb, nice woman. Charles met her once when he came to pick up Sam, and Sam was walking out with her. "I like being dangerous," she said, swinging the pail. "Only I don't got the nerve to use it. You boys have a good time. I'm dependable. My boy can get you more."

"One time Sam got a memo from the boss saying that he should wear a tape measure around his neck to make himself look more official," Charles says to Susan.

"He didn't."

"I did," Sam says. "God, did I drink a lot that weekend."

"You don't wear the thing, do you?" she asks.

Sam rolls his eyes.

"Oh, Sam, that's awful."

"I sort of think it's funny now. Another time, when I first started working there, he sent his brother around. His brother was a big fellow. He took forty-two extra long. And the guy told me he wanted a thirty-eight regular. He could hardly squeeze into it. What did I care. I rang it up. Next day the boss came around to congratulate me. 'That's right,' he said. 'The customer is always right.' "

Susan shakes her head and laughs.

"Laugh while you can. Wait until you get out," Sam says.

"She's going to marry the doctor," Charles says. "She's got no worries."

"It's nuts to get married," Sam says. "What would you get married for?"

"I never said I was getting married. He did."

"I should know," Charles says. "According to you, I'm so smart."

Susan looks at her watch. "I don't know when visiting hours are, do you?"

"We're family. I don't think it matters. It would be good to avoid the regular hours because we'd probably miss Pete that way."

"We ought to at least say hello to him. He's awfully upset, you said."

"We cheer him up a lot. We're such good-natured kids."

"We could try to act nice tonight. It could be a sort of rehearsal for you, Charles. For when Mark gets here."

"I already like him immensely," Charles says.

"I do too," Sam says.

"Will you let him in?" Susan says to Sam.

"When he makes his house call, you mean?"

Susan sighs.

"Iffen I don't shoot at the varmint from behind the moonshine machine," Sam says. Sam puts down his napkin. "Good dinner," he says. He walks slowly back to the bedroom.

"Let's get ready," Susan says.

"Let's do the dishes."

"Come on," she says. "We don't want to find her asleep when we get there."

Charles goes to the closet for his jacket. He takes out the candy bars and takes them in to Sam. Sam is propped up in bed, watching the news.

"Thank you," Sam says.

"Welcome," Charles says. "I got you cigarettes, too. Do you want them?"

"Not right now. Thanks, though."

Charles meets Susan at the front door, and they go outside to the car. He notices that the birds have eaten all the seed, and that he will have to put out more. Predictable: put out birdseed, it disappears, you put out more, it disappears, and so on. Susan is nervous. She wants to drive, and he lets her. He puts on the radio. John Lennon is singing "Mind Games." John Lennon thinks that "love is the answer." But John—what if she won't get out of her A-frame to be loved? The snow that was not predicted until the eighteenth has started to fall lightly.

"Road's getting slick. Watch it on the turns," Charles says.

"I drive Mark's car all the time," she says. She is in a bad mood. It always upsets her to see Clara in the bin.

"Stop at that drugstore," he says. "I'm going to get a pack of cigarettes. They all want cigarettes."

She stops in front of the drugstore, and he gets out and buys a pack of Camels. A woman in front of him is buying a magazine with Cher on the cover. "Bonos Bust" the headlines read. Cher, in a low-cut silver gown, is pictured holding their daughter, Chastity, and Sonny has his arm against his brow, as if shielding himself from the sun. The three people have all been cut out of separate photos and jumbled into this one. Charles stares at Sonny, who is wearing boots and fringed pants and a pink shirt. If you don't shield yourself from the sun you can get an inoperable melanoma, Charles thinks. He would not really care if Sonny Bono died at all, if he didn't have to be in the bed next to him. The outfits the Bonos are wearing look like something mental patients would put together. Except that then Cher would have on bedroom slippers with her silver dress. The bin. He pays for the cigarettes and walks back to the car. The announcer is talking about the at-

tempt to deport John Lennon. "Does anybody out there
want John out of the country? Call in and let us have
your views. You know, some people say the government
has harassed John. Some of our best citizens have written
letters or appeared in John's behalf. Should they continue? Should John Lennon stay in the U.S.A.? Call us
at. . . ." The announcer's message is followed by "The
Ballad of John and Yoko": "Christ, you know it ain't
easy, you know how hard it can be, the way things are
goin'. . . ." John sings about eating chocolate cake from
a bag. Now there's something nice to remember, one of
those crazy in-love things, like special songs and Chinese
restaurants. He didn't do enough of that. Even then he
was tired. Right now he is very tired. He rests his head
against the foggy side window. He closes his eyes and
imagines scenes that never took place: he and Laura went
to the beach, and she got sunburned and he rubbed Solar-
caine on her back; Laura cooked a ten-course Chinese
dinner for him, gave him a surprise birthday party; she
asked him for advice, and he gave her good advice that
made her happy; they ate Fudgsicles in a park in Paris.
Do they have Fudgsicles in Paris? They must. They have
a McDonald's. Revision of that fantasy: he and Laura
had a Big Mac in the Paris McDonald's, later went to the
top of the Eiffel Tower. Her eyes were wide at the Lido,
the horses racing to the edge of the stage. They climbed a
mountain in Switzerland, drank hot mulled cider. They
held hands and walked down a street in the spring. She
tripped, he fixed the heel of her shoe. She dropped a
scented handkerchief, he picked it up, smelled Vol de
Nuit. They were together at Christmas, and the house
smelled of turkey. She gave him a pineapple. He parted
her hair, smoothing his hand down in between brush
strokes. In a supermarket, she kissed his ear. They went
ice-skating, she in a long skirt, he in a long scarf just like
the Currier and Ives print that used to be in his sixth-
grade history book. In the rain in Mexico she bought a

big white bowl with a rooster in it that he carried. They had a villa and a maid, and where they were the water was so blue it seemed to burn. In actuality, they once had cheeseburgers at McDonald's on Saturday and were happy eating them there, in spite of the noise the children made and how downtrodden the people looked. Once he got in the tub with her, and she didn't kick him out. She taught him to play chess, and they drank a delicious, expensive French wine. She gave him a sweater, and he had it for a long time before he lost it. He gave her Vol de Nuit, and she smiled. Once he got in the shower with her and she laughed at him, but didn't kick him out. She did an imitation of the way he slouched when he walked; he imitated her distracted gaze. Nobody got mad. The roller coaster, and the Ferris wheel. They made cookies together. She took her picture in a photo booth to give to him. They ate at a famous seafood restaurant and had brandy. They got stoned and listened to Schubert. She sent him a valentine signed "Anonymous" and always swore that she didn't do it, even though it was her handwriting. He gave her a chair for her apartment, brought it to her in the rain. She sat in it. It was all wet.

He looks out the window at the snow. They are already at the hospital. There are three lights in a row, and a few cars. Susan pulls into a place at the end of the row, and they get out and walk toward the side door. A security officer points them to their mother's wing. Room 14-B. Walking to room 14-B he gives away four cigarettes and lights four cigarettes. He gives out a fifth on the threshold of his mother's room, turns to light it. "Don't shake," the woman says, holding his hands. She frowns at them, no doubt realizing she'll have little success. She exhales in his face.

"We're here, Mom," Susan says to their mother.

She is sitting in bed with a bright yellow ribbon tied around her hair.

"I'm going home tomorrow," she says. "They knew, they knew it was a mistake to put me here."

Susan looks at Charles.

"That's great," he says. "How are you?"

"Charles, they won't believe me, but a young doctor here does believe me that I nearly died in that hospital, and I had to get the card of laxatives from my purse and into the bathroom I went, only to get rid of the pain."

"What does the doctor say about the pain? What caused it?" ·

She stares at him. "The laxatives. So many laxatives. No one believes me that I almost died with the pain. I had to go into the bathroom and take them, those that I had with me from home, in my purse."

"Pete at dinner?" Charles says.

"Yes, he is. I want you to meet a very fine friend, Mrs. DeLillo."

"The lord have mercy on your soul," she says. "Do you smoke?"

"A cigarette. Yes," Charles says, extending the pack. She folds the pack into her hand, puts it down the front of her nightgown.

"Matches?" she says.

"Can you have matches?" he asks.

"What good are cigarettes without matches?" she asks. He gives her a book of matches.

"Charles, I'm so glad not to be dead. My first baby."

"We're having quite a snow," Susan says.

"Imagine the snow in Madison, Wisconsin," their mother says. "My girl goes to school far away," she says to Mrs. DeLillo.

"I don't have to imagine snow," Mrs. DeLillo says. "I can see it right out this window."

"My friend Mark is coming down tonight. He's going to drive me back."

"Who's that?" Clara says.

"I told you, Mom. Mark. The pre-med student."

"When did you tell me?"

"In a letter."

"I save all your letters. My second baby." She looks past Mrs. DeLillo, out the window. The lights in the parking lot are visible through the window. They light up the slowly falling snow.

"How long ago did Pete leave?" Charles asks.

Clara opens a night-table drawer. There is a piece of paper inside. She hands it to Charles. "Gone to dinner, 7:15, return approximately 7:45," it says. He should like Pete. He nods and hands it back.

"Charles, they don't believe me, except for the young doctor who knows I'm telling the truth, about the woman in the bed next to me dying."

"I'm not dead, I'm here," Mrs. DeLillo says. She lights a cigarette.

"She was discharged, I heard," Susan says.

"With a blanket over her head, honey?"

"I don't know. . . . I wasn't there," Susan says.

Their mother takes the yellow ribbon out of her hair. "When they put this on me, I said, 'Oh, the yellow ribbon of the old oak tree.' Everything you say to them here they think you're crazy."

"It's a song," Charles says stupidly. He looks at his watch. It is 7:40.

"Here's my family," Pete says, coming up in back of Charles and Susan.

"I'm Mrs. DeLillo," Mrs. DeLillo says.

"I should have called to save you the trip. Mommy's coming home tomorrow. The doctor says it was a mistake to have Mommy brought here, but since Mommy's so weak, she might as well rest up one place as another."

"And I've met my fine friend Mrs. DeLillo," she says.

"Thank you," Mrs. DeLillo says. Mrs. DeLillo has a green ribbon in her hair. Her hair is too short to hide the ribbon. You can see it going around both sides of her head.

"My Pete," Clara says. Pete is sweating. He looks like he's been drinking.

"Mighty cold and snowy out," Pete says. "I saw it start, sitting down in the cafeteria."

"Do you have snow tires?" Susan asks. She is better at making conversation with Pete than he is.

"*Studded* snow tires," Pete says.

"All my family take care of themselves," Clara says.

"Today was my first day back at work," Charles says.

Pete slaps him on the back. "Thatta boy," he says.

"You don't drive in the rush hour, do you?" Clara says.

"I have to drive in the rush hour. I have to be there at nine o'clock."

"Oh, Mommy knows the way things are," Pete says, slapping Charles again. "Nobody's going to put one over on Mommy."

"She's a sensible woman," Mrs. DeLillo says.

"Charles, when I came here the nurse reported something I said to the doctor, the young doctor . . ."

"What a fine fellow," Pete interrupts.

"And he came to me and he said, 'You know that song about the yellow ribbon on the old oak tree, don't you?' Charles, I was very sick in the hospital, but now that I'm not so weak I see that I'm not so sick. I told the young doctor that I was much improved, and if it hadn't been for the pain, you have my word of honor, Charles, I would not have medicated myself with the laxatives."

"They *give* you laxatives here," Mrs. DeLillo says.

"Talk to the doctor," Clara says.

"The doctor?" Susan says.

"He will tell you—the young one—that my word is good, and it was an accident that I made the mistake of taking the laxatives in the bathroom."

"Well," Pete says. "Let's not dwell on past mistakes."

"Did you get to see the football game Sunday?" Susan asks Pete.

"No," he says. "I didn't."

Susan seems to have run out of things to talk to Pete about.

"But I wish I had," Pete says.

Charles looks at Pete's shoes. They are shiny brown cordovans.

"What did the doctor say about a few twirls?" Pete says.

"Take them," Clara answers.

"Ya-hoo!" Pete says. He says it very quietly; it sounds absurd not being shouted.

"What has happened to Wilbur Mills?" she asks.

"He showed up in Boston where Fanne Foxe was stripping and got on stage drunk," Pete says, brightening.

"I knew that. I mean, how is he now?"

"A wife cheater," Mrs. DiLillo says. "You know the saying: 'Wife cheater, child beater.' "

"He's still there, as far as I know," Susan says. "In Walter Reed."

"I read that that place was a firetrap," Charles says.

"You be very careful when you drive to work tomorrow, Charles."

"I will," he says.

"Bring my fitch coat when you come tomorrow," Clara says to Pete.

"Yes, sir," he says. "Mommy's going home in style."

"In the meantime, in between time, ain't we got fun?" Clara says.

"What's that?" he says.

"Another song!" she says, delightedly.

"I remember that one," Mrs. DeLillo says. "Not so long ago, huh?"

"Do you remember that one?" their mother says to Charles.

"Sure," Charles says.

"No," Susan says.

"Mommy knows her music," Pete says. He looks at his watch. "Mommy," he says, "if we don't leave on time they come around, you know. Shall we say goodnight?"

"My Pete," she says. "And my Charles and Susan."

"Good-bye, Mom," Susan says, kissing her. "I'll be home in a while. I have to leave tomorrow."

"Be careful in rush-hour traffic," she says, pressing Susan's hand.

"I'll see you soon," Charles says.

"I know you will," she says, pressing his hand. "And my Pete."

"Tomorrow," Pete says. "Good night, honey."

"My family," she says.

In the corridor, Pete says, "What do you think?"

"Is she weak, is that why she's acting so strange?"

"What do you think?" Pete says. "She took herself a dozen laxative tablets. She's still not on solid food. Only soup and milk."

They walk past the guard's desk. "All clean," Pete says, flashing the inside of his overcoat. The guard does not smile. Charles glances at the book on the guard's desk: *Seventeenth Century Poetry*. Probably the only job the guard could get.

"I guess my asking you for a drink is getting to be a joke," Pete says. "I guess you wouldn't have a drink with me after I called and said that you were a son of a bitch."

"Sure I would," Charles says. "Maybe I should get Susan home, in case Mark is there, and meet you somewhere."

"Couldn't you come for a short drink?" Pete says to Susan.

"Sure I could."

"You mean you're both coming?"

"Sure," Charles says. Pete looks surprised. He smiles—the same smile he gave when he came to the hospital to visit Charles and saw his plastic pillow in use.

"Well, where do you get a drink around here?" Pete asks.

"I think there's a place a couple of streets over."

"Walk?" Pete says. "Do you mind walking?"

"No," they both say.

"That's good. My skin's still crawling."

"The place seemed pretty sedate tonight," Susan says.

"That woman in the room with Mommy is a dog killer. Cat killer. She had a house full of cats and dogs and killed all of them. I don't know the details. I said to Mommy, 'You never know. Keep on the good side of her.'"

They are walking together in stride, Susan breaking step occasionally to keep up.

"Oh man, when is this winter ever going to end?" Pete says. "This morning, driving down to the hospital I was tempted to take my credit card—did you kids know I have a BankAmericard?—over to the airport and fly to Florida. Three years I've been wanting to fly to Florida, get the hell in the sun. I thought to myself, you're freezing; you're sixty-three years old and you've never done anything exciting in your life."

"There's not much exciting to do," Charles says. The Paris McDonald's.

"Florida, hell, you might not call that exciting, but you know what I mean: to be where it's warm. It's colder than I ever remember it here this winter."

"I can't keep up with you," Susan says.

"Sorry, honey," Pete says. They slow down a little.

"Another thing I thought about was getting a Honda Civic. Your mother thinks the things are too small to ride around in. She says we'll be killed. I said, 'What the hell. We don't have kids. We don't have any big dog. We can get us a little car.' You know your mother." Pete blows his nose, drops the tissue on the sidewalk. "This morning I thought, I've got time to go arrange for a Honda Civic on the way to the hospital. I was damned early. Couldn't sleep. Got up to get breakfast, and it didn't take me any time to wolf it down. So I thought: do it, Pete. Get a Honda Civic. Hell, I never do anything."

"Get the car if it's important to you," Charles says.

"I don't know. . . . How do I know if it's important to

me? This morning I really thought I wanted to go to Florida. If I had, I guess I would have."

"I think you could use another car, Pete," Susan says. "Yours is pretty old now. Maybe you could hang onto it and let her drive it."

"You think I ought to get a Hondo Civic, huh?" Pete says. He pulls another tissue out of his pocket and blows his nose. "I should," he says.

The bar they walk into is called The Sinking Ship. Charles remembers that it's usually crowded with college kids, but most of them are away on vacation, so there's a strange mixture of businessmen and hippies.

"This is swell," Pete says. "You want to sit at a table, don't you?"

They move to a table against the wall. There is a framed newspaper picture above the table of Nixon, Bebe Rebozo, and Robert Abplanalp. Charles stands long enough to read the caption. The three are on a boat, it seems. They all look like Mafia characters. A waiter comes to the table.

"What do you want?" Pete says.

"Could we split a pizza?" Susan says.

"Sure we could," Pete says. "What would you like to drink?"

"Scotch on the rocks," Charles says.

"A glass of red wine," Susan says.

"A pitcher of beer for me," Pete says.

"Okay. And is that a plain pizza? Mozzarella?"

"Right," Pete says. The waiter goes away. His jeans have a small buckle across the back. He has on cowboy boots. The heels are scuffed.

Pete leans across the table. "Tell me something," he says to Charles. "What was the worst thing I ever did to you?"

Charles looks into Pete's face. Pete has a little broken vein on the side of his nose. Pete has a sharply pointed nose. There is a plaid blue-and-red scarf hanging unevenly around his neck. Pete combs his hair straight back. It is white at the temples, light brown back to his bald spot. Charles's father was very handsome. He had curly brown hair and a broad chest. When Charles was little, he used to have him stand next to his leg so he could tell how tall he was getting. He died on the bus coming home from work. He would have died in his car, but he left the car with Clara. Tuesday was grocery day. Charles hopes that there wasn't an embarrassing time for his father before he died—that he didn't scream in pain, or have to look into any of the other passengers' eyes. He wanted to ask the policeman who came to the house, but his throat always choked up when he was in the presence of a policeman.

"We don't dislike you," Susan says, patting Pete's shoulder. It is the first time Charles has ever seen her voluntarily touch him.

"Neither of you like me *much*," Pete says. "What did I ever do that was so awful?"

"One time when Susan was only about seven years old she made a snowman with some of your wood and . . ."

"Okay," Pete interrupts. "I remember."

Pete unfolds a napkin and puts it on his lap. He looks at it.

"But don't kids forget about things like that? Forgive and forget and all that?" Pete says.

The envelope from Pamela Smith, Charles thinks.

"I forgive you," Susan says.

"He doesn't," Pete says.

The waiter puts down the pitcher of beer. He puts a tray on the table and takes Susan's and Charles's drinks off it.

"I guess I'm not making you have a very pleasant time here," Pete says. "After all this time you went out with me for a drink, and I sit here talking about the past."

Maria Muldaur is singing "Midnight at the Oasis." She offers to be a belly dancer; the person she is singing to can be her sheik. "Maria!" a middle-aged man hollers, raising his beer glass. "Boogie," he says, bouncing in his chair.

"Aw c'mon," Maria Muldaur sings.

"Boogie," the man sings, rising again. The man sitting across from him reaches across the table and pushes him down. There is an argument. Charles expects one of the men to come flying at him, but the fight subsides. Once in a bar a man was thrown into his back. He was standing at the bar. He dropped his glass of beer. It went "clunk." Charles didn't know what had happened. Now he fears that people will fly into him at bars. He doesn't stand at the bar any more because that way he has his back to all of them. Once he had a nightmarish vision of a policeman coming at him—crashing into him, actually—telling him he had an inoperable melanoma. He was so scared he froze. When the policeman said his father was dead he froze. Charles adjusts himself in his seat, to reassure himself that he can move all right.

"How's college?" Pete says to Susan. "Have some pizza, Charles?"

"Thanks," Charles says. The pizza is very good. He thinks about asking Pete to order another. This is very nice of Pete. He wishes he could say something nice to Pete that he felt sincerely. He frowns in concentration.

"Pizza's hot, huh?" Pete says.

"Yeah," Charles says.

"I don't know, Pete," Susan says. "I can't figure out what to major in."

"Not interested in anything, huh?" Pete says.

"I sort of like psychology and French, but I don't know if I want to major in either of them."

"No point in it, huh?" Pete says.

Charles is surprised; Pete sounds like him.

"A French major wouldn't do me any good," Susan says. "Because it's the only language I know. To be an interpreter you have to know at least three."

"Parlez-vous français?" Pete says. "Hell. I used to know French."

Pete picks up the last piece of pizza. "I'll order another one of these," he says. "They're little."

"I forget everything," Pete says, pouring beer into his glass. "I know that on the way in you kids were telling me to do something."

"Buy the car," Charles says.

"That's right. Buy a Honda Civic."

Connie Francis is singing "Where the Boys Are." He saw that movie. Yvette Mimieux got raped. He would like to rape Laura. That's not even true. He would just like to have a cheeseburger at McDonald's with Laura. For almost half an hour he had not thought of Laura. He tries to switch his thoughts to . . . what was her name . . . Betty, to have an erotic vision of Betty. He sees a slightly plump woman in a dress and heavy black boots. He tries to imagine her without the black boots. It is impossible. The black boots will not come off her.

"I'm here, Connie," the man who was hollering to Maria Muldaur calls to the ceiling speakers. "Boogie, boogie," he calls.

The waiter comes to the table. "Another pizza," Pete says. "More to drink?"

"I'll have another one," Charles says.

"A Coke for me," Susan says.

"I'm set," Pete says. When the waiter walks away, Pete says, "She wouldn't come here with us even if she was out of the hospital."

"She won't go to bars?" Charles asks.

Pete shakes his head. "Anywhere. I tried to get her to take a boat ride this summer. They had a jazz band that played on the boat. You know, just a two-hour boat ride. Drinks and stuff. She locked herself in the bathroom. Said the boat would sink."

"Did you tell the doctor about that?" Charles asks.

"I forgot about it. I've told so many stories to so many

doctors. I'm always rambling about heating pads all over the house and how my bed pillow's been missing for six months, and about the look she gets that I can't describe. I'm always looking into doctors' faces, trying to do imitations. The last doctor wanted her to go for group therapy. She wouldn't go. Probably thought the chair would collapse."

Susan laughs. Charles smiles. God, I'm glad I don't live with her, Charles thinks.

"We ought to work on that," Charles says. "Group therapy."

"She wouldn't go," Pete says.

The second pizza is put on the table. Pete cuts a piece off with a little plastic fork. The tines are bent under. The pizza is very hot.

"I did an awful thing. When the pillow had been gone for a week, I cornered her. I cornered her in the kitchen. 'You tell me where that pillow is,' I said. She started to shake, looking right into my eyes, shoulders going back and forth. I was ashamed of myself."

"Ever find the pillow?" Susan asks.

"No," Pete says, draining his glass.

Mick Jagger begins "Wild Horses": "Tiiiiiired of living . . ."

It occurs to Charles that songs are always appropriate. No matter what record is played it is always applicable. Once, on a date in high school, when he was going to tell his date he loved her, Elvis Presley came on the radio singing "Loving You." It always happens: politicians are always crooks, records are always applicable to the situation. Charles shrugs off his sweater. Martha and the Vandellas start to sing "Heat Wave." Charles laughs.

"I know," Pete says. "It is funny. A grown man with a messed-up wife, and what does he do but sit around his office stewing all day, then come home and corner her about a pillow."

Susan laughs again. She pours some of Pete's beer into her glass.

Mick Taylor has left The Rolling Stones. Mick Taylor replaced Brian Jones. Brian Jones is dead. Women all over the world claim to have babies that are his. All the babies look like Brian Jones. Mick Jagger got dumped by Marianne Faithfull ("It is the evening of the day. . . ."), who took drugs with him, and married Bianca, who walks around with a feather hat and cane. She has expensive jewelry. They have a child. A daughter? Should John Lennon stay in the U.S.A.? John Lennon went to the Troubadour with a Kotex on his head. In reply to the announcer's query, a girl called to say, "I think John should stay here because he's such a groovy musician." "And what do you think about people being denied citizenship because of drug offenses?" The girl hung up.

Pete is having a very good time. He is smiling and wolfing pizza and looking all around.

"I hope they don't change their minds tomorrow," Pete says. "They always do that at that place."

"She was only there once before," Susan says.

"One night I took her there. She was home the next night, though," Pete says. "Then some doctor called. 'Who discharged your wife?' he said. He hung up on me."

Bob Dylan: "Time will tell just who has fell and who's been left behind. . . ."

Pete reaches in his pocket for his wallet. "Look at this," he says, handing his BankAmericard to Susan. She turns it over, looks at the front of it again, hands it back. Pete takes a twenty out of his wallet and puts it on top of the tray with the bill. The waiter picks it up.

"Back into the cold," Pete says. As they leave, Charles looks back and sees the man who screamed to Maria Muldaur with his hands over his head. His head is resting on the table. Lou Reed is singing: "Good night ladies, ladies good night. . . ."

The snow is falling fast now—big wet flakes that probably won't last.

"Thanks for having a drink with me," Pete says. There is a mustache of sauce above his top lip.

"Thanks for taking us," Charles says.

"Yes," Susan says.

"I wish I had kids," Pete says. "You kids are nice. But if I had my own kid it would probably be nuts about me, don't you think?"

"Well," Charles says. "Kids are so alienated from their parents now . . ."

"It's too late anyway," Pete says.

They break into a trot, Pete taking Susan's hand to guide her around slick patches. They are all out of breath and shivering when they reach the hospital parking lot. The three lights have been turned off.

"Well, I'll be seeing you," Pete says. "Thanks for having a drink with me."

"Good-bye," Charles says.

"Thanks again," Susan says.

"Hell, if you didn't have a drink with me, I don't know what kids would," Pete says. "I got none of my own."

Charles and Susan get in the car and drive away. He should have said something nice to Pete. He finds it impossible to bring himself to say something really nice. What is there really nice to say that wouldn't just sound foolish? Even the fruit that Pete brought to the house after their father died was always wrong. The time he brought the oranges they had just been sent a crate of oranges from neighbors visiting Florida. Their mother made them take all the oranges out of the refrigerator—there were a lot of oranges—and put them in the crate and hide the crate so Pete's feelings wouldn't be hurt. Charles had to sleep with the crate of oranges under his bed. He felt like there was a bomb there. He couldn't sleep. He tried to tell his mother that the Florida oranges were better; they should just mix Pete's in with them. The crate stayed under the bed. Every morning they had fresh-squeezed orange juice, and at school, in their lunch box, there was always one and maybe two oranges. Susan got diarrhea. Charles didn't; he always gave both of his oranges away. He gave them to a Japanese boy. None of the other kids wanted the oranges. They all had cookies. When he pressed them on the Japanese boy he took them without saying anything and put them in his desk. The second day he gave them to the Japanese boy Charles noticed that when the boy opened his desk the two oranges were still there. When there were six oranges the Japanese boy took them all home in a bag. The Japanese boy had no friends. He wouldn't talk to anybody, even when they talked to him. He'd say hello to Charles, though. He called him "Mister Oranges." Charles could never get beyond that with him. He asked him to come over to his house and play, and the boy just shook hands. When the oranges stopped coming, no questions were asked. The Japanese boy didn't come back for the sixth grade. Somebody in the class found out that he had gone to Japan.

Charles had the same teacher for fifth and sixth grades. Her name was Mrs. Witwell. Of course she was called Witchwell, or just Mrs. Witch. This name was given to her when Mrs. Witwell dressed up as a witch at Halloween to pay a call on a friend's first-grade class. She showed the fifth grade her getup: a long black skirt and blouse, pointed black hat and broom. She had powdered her face white. "The first grade will think I'm a real witch!" Mrs. Witwell said. Her fifth grade believed she was a real witch. The Japanese boy looked terrified.

Mrs. Witwell came to the funeral parlor. He was embarrassed to have her see him there. She came with an old lady, her mother. The book was signed "Eleanor and Dora Witwell." It was the same handwriting with which Mrs. Witwell criticized his penmanship. He got up and ran to look at the book when she left. He no longer has any idea what he expected to see.

He turns into his driveway, surprised that Doctor Mark's car still isn't there. He has trouble getting up the driveway; it's very slippery. After spinning awhile at the bottom, the car finally makes it halfway up, and he settles for that, putting on the emergency brake.

"That really wasn't bad with Pete," Susan says.

"He does try," Charles says. "I just don't feel comfortable with him. I was around him for so many years that I should, but I just don't."

"I hope he goes ahead and buys the Honda Civic," Susan says. "I think he's sad. Not to ever get to do anything."

"He's a grown man. There's no reason he can't bring himself to do anything. Living with her depresses him."

"He ought to get out," Charles says.

"Don't wish that on her," Susan says. "What would she do?"

"Plug in the heating pads, drink, read movie magazines. What she does now. I can't believe she loves him."

"It's hard to tell how she feels," Susan says.

"He should corner her and ask her that."

"That's cruel," Susan says.

"I know. I don't know. I feel sorry for them. I feel sorry for everybody."

"If you just categorically feel sorry for everyone, it must be something bothering you."

"That's profound," he says, taking off his coat. She hands him hers and sits down on the sofa, pulls the afghan over her.

"Can I say something you won't want to hear?" Susan says.

"I have to hear things I don't want to hear all the time. Go ahead."

"I think you're an egomaniac."

Charles laughs. He had been expecting something terrible.

"Yeah. So what?"

"So you dismiss *everything,* even helpful criticism. You refuse to think."

"Susan, I think all the time. I shake my head to try to stop the thoughts from coming."

"What do you think about?"

"Isn't that a little broad?"

"I know what you think about. You think about that girl. You deliberately make yourself suffer all the time because then you can be aware of *yourself.*"

"What's all this?" he says. "Some dollar twenty-five Bantam paperback philosophy? One of those books with multicolored arrows going off in all directions or something?"

"Don't you think I could have any thoughts of my own?"

"Everybody's thoughts are acquired. Where did you acquire yours?"

"I don't know, Charles. I just realized that what I'm saying now is true. You're infantile."

"Thanks for coming here to stay with me so you could put me down."

"It's not to put you down. I can tell it's not working. You're probably thinking of her right this minute."

"*You* keep bringing her up. Don't you notice that, Susan?"

"Just tell me whether I was wrong when I said that. Were you thinking about her?"

"I wasn't," he says. He was.

"You're even a liar. I know you were thinking about her."

"I was. So what?"

"It proves my point. That you dwell on it; you try to make yourself miserable. You've got to snap out of it."

"What'll happen to me if I don't?" he says. He really is curious, but she thinks he's making fun of her.

"You want me to preach so you can accuse me of

preaching. You always have to be in control, like a two-year-old."

Sam comes into the living room. He has on the same pajamas, the same ski socks.

"She's giving me hell," Charles says.

"I heard," Sam says.

"Hi," Susan says.

"Hi," Sam says. "Some woman *not* Laura called," he says to Charles.

"How do you know?"

"I know her voice. I'm very good with people's voices on the phone."

"A woman . . . who was it?"

"I should have asked. I was asleep. Wasn't thinking."

"Then it might have been Laura."

"No. I'd know her voice."

"Did she say she'd call back?"

"Yeah."

Charles shrugs. Sam sits down on the floor and takes the ashtray off the sofa arm, lights a cigarette and throws the match in the ashtray.

"This thing wiped the shit out of me," Sam says.

"Mark didn't call again?" Susan says.

"Nope," Sam says.

Sam sits with his elbows resting on his knees. He seems to have lost weight. His hair is dirty and stringy. He is still just as hoarse when he talks. Charles no longer thinks that he is dying of pneumonia. He is glad. He has known Sam since fourth grade, when Sam's family moved to the area. He remembers Sam's mother holding her son's hand, leading him into the fourth-grade classroom. Sam whirled and slapped her hand as they came through the door. Sam was a troublemaker. Charles was not. He worshiped Sam. Sam would pretend to have coughing fits so that he'd be excused to get a drink of water, and then he'd go into the bathroom and get the door off the stall before he came back. Sam was quick, and he always had the right tools with him. Once he got the handle off the drinking fountain, and when everybody came in from the blacktop and raced for the fountain, the handle was gone. He was too smart to have it on him when the teacher checked. He had put it in a girl's desk. After school the teacher watched Sam, so he couldn't get it. The next morning when the girl opened her desk she found it and gave it to the teacher. Sam waited until the end of fifth grade, but he finally thought of the perfect thing to do: throw a mud ball at her. The girl threw a mud ball back and hit him in the forehead. There was a rock or something in her mud ball, and he still has the scar above his left eyebrow.

Charles picks up a pile of mail and opens first a small blue envelope addressed to him in unfamiliar handwriting. It is a small blue booklet: "Why you didn't get a Christmas card from us." He begins reading: "Did you wonder, in all the holiday hassle, why you didn't get a Christmas card from Carolyn and Bud? The answer can be quickly given: Carolyn and Bud were having problems. But there's more to the story than that. After all, each could have sent a card. But each was too preoccupied during the season of brotherly love to do so. To wit: Bud told Carolyn a week before Christmas that he was going to divorce her for a blonde cutie. Carolyn cried, agreed. Bud ran off that night with the cutie, and Carolyn ran around in her sweat suit in the cold streets all night, crazy with jealousy. The next morning she found Bud back, but she threw him out. The cutie called: Please, Carolyn, take him back. I know he never loved me. Not on your life (jog, jog). Bud then got irate. Mad at both of them. Would Bud have thought of sending *you* a Christmas card? *Non, mesdames. Non, messieurs.* Would Carolyn? *Non.* But here's a late wish from her, and a 'Here's hoping your New Year is Merry.' " On the back page is written: "Sequel: Bud and C. are back together. How *tasteless* of C. to send this. Wait till Bud finds out. Will *you* be the one to tell? Love, C."

"Whew," Charles says. "Take a look at this, or did you already get one?"

Carolyn works at the store with Sam. Once he and Charles had dinner at their apartment. That was at least a year ago. How did they get his address?

"What do you make of that?" Charles says.

"I'm reading," Sam says.

"What is it?" Susan says.

"A crazy letter sort of thing from Sam's friends."

"Good God," Sam says, reading. "We went over there for dinner one time. Remember?"

"Good God," Sam says, tossing it back to Charles. "Isn't anybody happy? Or even sane?"

"Everybody's not crazy," Susan says. "You two are depressed all the time."

"You'd be depressed too if you felt like I do," Sam says.

"That's not what I mean. I mean all the time."

"You're not here all the time. How do you know?"

Susan sighs, goes into the kitchen.

"I'm too depressed to apply my usual trenchant wit," Sam says.

"I wasn't depressed until she started in," Charles says.

The phone rings. It is Pete, sounding very drunk.

"You don't want to hear any more from me tonight, do you?" Pete says. He does not say "Hello."

"Hello," Charles says, stalling for time.

" 'Hello?' " Pete says. "I *said* hello. Now I've got to know the answer to my question."

"Pete, you profess to love her. You're not going to do her any good going out and getting juiced the night before she comes home."

"Don't criticize me," Pete says. "Just answer my question."

"You asked if I was glad to hear from you, didn't you? I was, Pete, until it turned out that you were drunk."

"In my day a youngster would never *never* speak to an old man that way."

"Pete, you're not an old man. Try to cheer up. She's coming home tomorrow and it might work out this time."

"I've got one thing to tell you," Pete says. "I found the pillow. Do you know where I found it? In the attic. Some birds had gotten into it. It will never, never work out."

"Pete, maybe some friend of yours not so close to the problem could advise you better than I can. I don't really know what to say."

"What did you say was the worst thing I ever did to you again? I've forgotten."

"Pete, you're drunk. Where are you?"

"I'm at home. Where do you think my attic is?"

"I'm glad to hear that, because the driving is very dangerous. You're just drinking at home?"

"If *I* went nuts," Pete says, "I wouldn't have anybody to take care of me. My brother came from Hawaii. Now where is he? Running around an orchid patch. Eating macadamia nuts. I don't know. I don't have anybody but myself to depend on."

"Would you like me to come over?" Charles says.

"That's very decent of you. But I don't want you to come."

"Okay. I hope things go okay tomorrow. Take it easy, Pete."

"Are there any old people you like a lot?" Pete asks.

Charles does not know any old people. "No," he says.

"So what you're saying is that it's nothing personal," Pete says. "I'm glad to hear that. You're a very honest young fellow. Now tell me honestly, Charles, what was it you said was the worst thing I ever did to you?"

"In the bar I told you about the time Susan made the snowman with your wood. You never really did one particularly rotten thing to me, Pete. I don't hate you, and I

His first building wasn't bad. It was a ten-story brown brick building, and he walked up to his office on the fifth floor every day to keep in shape. Now he works in a mud-colored glass building and only walks to his office on the twenty-first floor once a week, on Friday. One Friday, walking up, his cassette player going, he saw an employee flatten himself against the wall, wide-eyed, frightened, obviously, of what might have been coming for him. The employee had acted very strangely. It was about the sixteenth or seventeenth floor and Charles was very winded, so he just lifted his hand in greeting. The employee ran under his arm, like an animal running out a gate. There were a lot of nervous people in the building, and it always seemed to him that quite a number of women coming out of the rest room looked as if they had been crying. Laura said that wasn't so; she had never seen a woman crying in the rest room. He was always surprised that so many people in the employees' cafeteria kept their plates on the wet brown tray. He always took the dishes off and put the tray in the rack, but most of the people ate right from the tray.

The knock on the door is Doctor Mark. He rushes in when Susan opens the door as if he's really glad to be there. He is as she described him. Passing him on the street, Charles might have thought he was a musician. His hands, circling Susan's back, are very large and graceful. In a bar, Charles might have mistaken him for a homosexual.

"How do you do?" Mark says, extending one of the big hands. Susan is still pressed against him with the other.

Charles shakes his hand. "Hello," he says.

"Mighty cold and snowy," Mark says. The big hand goes back around Susan.

"Can I get you some coffee?" Charles says.

"I take no artificial stimulants," Mark says. "But. Thank you."

"Milk?" Charles says. Is there any milk?

"I'm loaded with calcium for the day, thank you," Mark says.

Charles revises his opinion of him. He would never work up to Disque Bleu's. The most he can hope for is Gauloises.

"Sue, Sue, let me look at you," he says.

Definitely homosexual.

"It's very nice, you letting me barge in on you tonight," Mark says.

Charles frowns. Susan hugs Mark's neck, lets go of him to sit in a chair.

"May I stay the night? I'm afraid I'm. Much too late to start back now."

"Sure," Charles says.

"May I ask. How is your mother?"

"She's going home tomorrow, Mark," Susan says.

"That's *very lucky*," Mark says, emphasizing the words to convey that it is not.

"Just before you came Pete called, though, and he's drunk again."

"That actually *kills* brain cells," Mark says.

"I don't think he cares. He's so miserable living the way he does now," Charles says.

"That's it!" Mark says. "In the final analysis it's up to the individual. No amount of coaxing can make a person care who does not want to care." Mark's voice goes up loudly on the last five words.

Charles looks at Mark's feet. Soaking wet tennis shoes.

"Take your shoes off. I can get you some socks. . . ."

"No, no," Mark says, as if Charles had asked to see his penis. "I'm fine. Feet are fine."

"They're wet," Charles says.

Mark frowns. "Rose hips?" he says.

"What?" Charles says, leaning forward.

"Rose hips," Mark replies.

"He doesn't have any," Susan says.

"Ah," Mark says, as if delighted.

"How was your trip?" Susan asks.

"My trip. Well, I can tell you that it was long and cold, made less so by Brahms. A wonderful station that played much Brahms the last stretch."

"Are you a musician?" Charles says.

"I play piano. Unprofessionally."

Charles wants very much to ask if he's gay.

"How was the car?" Susan asks.

"Well. I can tell you it started off with problems. And a stopover at a service station was necessary because of overheating. Clouds of smoke came out of the car. A small puncture. In. The hose."

Charles breaks into a smile. That's it . . . the guy talks like a J. P. Donleavy character.

"Do you read Donleavy?" Charles asks.

"Donelly?" Mark says. He turns his head to the side. Charles wishes he had a kidskin glove to slap his cheek with.

"No, no, Donleavy! Yes. *The Ginger Man.*"

Mark looks at Charles, expecting the conversation to go on.

"Of course I don't read the number of novels I would like to," Mark says.

"What would you like to read?" Charles asks.

"You're being obnoxious," Susan says.

Charles is genuinely curious. He wishes Susan knew that. She misunderstands him, thinks he's obnoxious every time he's curious.

"Jane Austen," Mark says with gravity.

Figures. And probably Thomas Pynchon, too.

"I've got a copy of *Gravity's Rainbow* I'm done with. Would you like it?" Charles says.

The head turns to the side again. "By . . . ?" Mark says.

"Pynchon."

"Ah! Pynchon. *V.*"

Susan is filing a fingernail.

"Thank you, but I have little time to read novels."

"I guess med school is really rough," Charles says. "Susan says you plan to specialize in surgery."

"Neurosurgery, yes," Mark says.

"I read a thing in some newspaper about a doctor in some South American country who pulled a woman's eyes out of the socket and cleaned them and picked off tumors and put the eyes back. To cure her of migraines and double vision."

"God!" Marks says. "That's revolting. That's not possible, I'm sure."

"Oh God," Susan groans.

"No wonder people are afraid of doctors when they read things like that," Mark says.

"That's sickening," Susan says. "Did you make that up?"

"No. It's in the same paper that has a denial from representatives of Frank Zappa that Frank Zappa had a bowel movement on stage."

"Oh *God*," Susan says.

"I follow those rags for kicks," Charles says. "You know, they're still full of JFK gossip. JFK jumping out of women's windows when he was President, JFK a vegetable on Onassis's island. . . ."

Susan puts down the fingernail file. "I'm going to have something to drink," she says. "Is anyone else?"

"Oh. No." Mark says.

"Maybe I'll go to bed," Charles says. "It's been another long, though glorious, day."

Mark stands. "Thank you very. Much for your kindness," he says.

"You're welcome," Charles says.

"Good night," Susan says, going into the kitchen.

"Good night," Charles says.

In his dream that night Charles is sitting behind a desk—in his office, presumably—and Mark is standing in front of him. "Take a letter. Any letter," Charles says, and wakes up laughing. The house is silent. He hopes they didn't hear him. He lies there with his eyes open for some time, listening to the silence.

What if JFK *is* a vegetable somewhere? He closes his eyes and pictures Kennedy, round-faced and thick-haired, then sees him as a dancing green pepper, his smiling round face a little knob on top. He opens his eyes. Blackness. Kennedy's favorite fiction writer was Ian Fleming. Ian Fleming was turned into a neurotic by his crazy mother. He closes his eyes and pictures Sean Connery driving a broad-nosed sports car that metamorphoses into a corncob. He opens his eyes again. He is hungry. He imagines dancing apples. There is nothing good in the house to eat. Tomorrow he will go to the Grand Union and buy all his favorite foods. Grand. Holden Caulfield hated that word. He thought it was phony. That cover illustration of *Catcher in the Rye:* Holden in a big gray overcoat, hat turned around, pointing down his back. Saw a movie once starring William Holden that was scary. Can't remember the title or the plot, just the name William Holden. The dancing apples. "Aw, c'mon now, Mama. . . ." "Geooooooooorge Stevens!" George Washington. Famous portrait of Washington left unfinished because artist took on more than he could handle. Very ambitious artist. Washington who chased his slaves or Jefferson? Laura. Chasing Laura. "I'm gonna get you, Laura." Cornered in the library. "Are you crazy, Charles?" Government employees. If I were a carpenter, if Laura were a lady. First of 1975. Guy Lombardo waving his stick around, head moving more energetically than the stick, old Guy up there, shaking his stick. Guy Fawkes Day. Firecrackers. Fanne Foxe, The Argentine Firecracker. "Ya-hoo, I'm just a country girl from Argentina." The girl from the north country. She once was a true love of mine. Laura. Laura against the bookshelf: "What are you doing? Are you crazy?" "Aw, now, Sapphire, I can explain . . ."

Chapter 6

"You don't look like you had a very good night," Betty says to him.

"I didn't. There was a lot of stuff going on." In my head, he thinks. I'm going crazy. My mother *is* crazy, but they're letting her out of the bin today. This very day. Maybe she's already out. Maybe at lunchtime I'll get a phone call.

"This all?" Betty asks, taking two pieces of paper out of his basket.

"So far. More to come." Looney Tunes: "T-t-t-t-thu-that's all, folks!"

Betty walks out. She is not wearing the black boots; she has on a pair of brown high-heeled shoes. He is disappointed; he had come to think of the boots as part of an outfit. The boots made her look very . . . substantial. Damn.

He stops working on the report he has already stopped working on ten times, and fills out a requisition form for Steel City paper clips. In the third grade a boy hit another boy in the nose with a paper clip launched from a rubber band. The paper clip went flying across the room and went up the kid's nostril. The school doctor got it out. The school doctor was a heavy middle-aged man who told the kids to call him "Doctor Dan." Nobody called him anything. Once a year he weighed them and looked them over. "Doctor Dan finds nothing wrong with you," he said. He always called himself Doctor Dan.

He goes back to his report, finishes it, and leans back in his chair before starting another. There are only four more to do. If they're as easy to do as the last one, he can probably get half of them done before lunch. Of course, if he were going to lunch at eleven o'clock that wouldn't be true. Damn.

He looks at the next report. He fills out the first line, then drifts away, thinking about what a mistake it will be for his sister to marry Doctor Mark. Why should jerks like that get to tell decent people that they have inoperable melanomas? If neurosurgeons ever get to say that. They must get to say it. Sure. "An inoperable melanoma near the occipital lobe." He can just hear him saying that. Then he'll go home and screw Susan. No, he's probably just marrying her for respectability. He'll tell some poor jerk he has an inoperable melanoma near the occipital lobe and then run off to a gay bar. Then he'll run home to Susan. By then she'll have a lot of kids and not care if he's there or not. She'll have a Maytag and probably be so dumb that she'll let them take a picture of her with it—a green Maytag and several white-faced children. Her hair style will be out of date, her legs a bit too fat. One of the kids will not be looking into the camera. One will be in her arms. Doctor Mark will be to the far left, towering over his family: wife, children, Maytag. He will have a late model Cadillac: the Cadillac Eldorado. Where the hell is Eldorado? Probably some place full of humidity and peasants. Doctor Mark will probably be in one of those Dewar's profiles:

HOME: Rye, N.Y.
AGE: 35
PROFESSION: Neurosurgeon
HOBBIES: Squash; attending concerts
MOST MEMORABLE BOOK: *V.*
LAST ACCOMPLISHMENT: Told some poor jerk he had an inoperable melanoma.

QUOTE: "I think everybody should go to med school and get a high-paying job and get the little woman a Maytag."

PROFILE: Keen, aggressive. Plays squash and cuts brains with precision.

SCOTCH: Dewar's "White Label"

He looks at the report again. He has been doodling on it. Christ. He gets a fresh form and starts again. Susan is right. He would like it if he were an artist. Then he'd know fascinating people instead of women who cry in bathrooms. Even Sam's dog was more interesting than anybody that works in this place. Sam's dog was so smart she could lip-read. "Go in the other room" Sam would mouth to her, and she'd look dejected and walk into the kitchen. "Dinner," he'd mouth, and she'd run for one of her toys, prance with it in eagerness. One of them was a yellow squeaking bottle with a red dog face on the front called "Pupsie Cola." Even the names of her dog toys are more interesting than the names of the employees: Stan Greenwall, Bob Charters, Betty . . . Betty what? Maybe just Betty—Betty of the erotic dreams, the ones it will be difficult to have, since her dresses stick to her. When he sees her later, he will find out her last name. Then he can call her for a date, and maybe when he knows her better he can have erotic dreams about her. Maybe that will even make Laura jealous. She said once that Betty hardly ever had a date. Who would she date? Recently divorced Bob Charters, who flicked the back of his hand against Charles's shoulder when they were standing side by side at the urinal and told him now that he was divorced, he was looking to go yodeling in the gully? His own boss, who wears a button with the female symbol on it inside his trench coat and shows it to people with a laugh the way men turn over their neckties to reveal a naked woman painted in lurid colors? Or Bob White—he must have taken a lot of kidding about that name—who never says anything except in the elevators, when he says he's sorry to be there or glad he's leaving? What happens to girls like Betty if they don't get married, and how do they ever get a husband? How do they ever get to move to Ohio and have a fantastically reliable Maytag? He proposed to a woman once. She said she was already married. She said it pressed up against a row of books in the library, whispered to him to get away, people would see and think he was crazy. He was always cornering her—in restaurants, when the coat-check girl turned to get their coats, on the Tilt-A-Whirl, pressing her to one side before the machine even started and tilted them there. Well, maybe it wouldn't have worked out. Look where his mother and Pete's marriage ended up: in a corner of the attic, pecked to pieces by birds. But maybe his marrying Laura would have worked out.

He begins to write figures on the piece of paper. He is not making much progress. He will never get a promotion if he doesn't apply himself. When he was thirteen his mother made him take dancing lessons. They were given in a church basement that was always cold. The girls all had bad breath or big breasts he was afraid to touch. He was an awkward dancer, and he didn't improve. The dancing instructor hated him. She'd clap her hands together slowly as he and the girl he was dancing with whirled by, meaning for them to get closer. She always showed her bottom teeth when she clapped her hands. The woman refused to give him his diploma. She sent a diploma in the mail about a week after the course was over, but in the space where his name should have been was printed: NOT YOU. "That awful woman," his mother had said, and he had been flooded with relief that she sympathized with his inability to dance. "Dance with me," Clara had said. "Let me see whether you can dance." He told her that he couldn't, but she still made him. She towered over him—no chance of running into her breasts, thank God. And after a few twirls his mother dropped the subject, except for telling his father that his money had gone down the drain.

Another report finished, he takes off for lunch. He has fried shrimp and a beer and mashed potatoes that can be lifted all in one mound with his fork. He eats part of the potatoes and plays with the rest, pays the bill, and walks back to the office. Passing the typing pool, he sees that Betty is eating at her desk. He goes in and pulls an orange plastic chair up to her desk. Two women at desks in back of her who were talking normally begin to whisper. There is a brown vase on Betty's desk with four paper flowers in it. There are no pictures. There is a paperweight with a picture of a cat inside. Doctors tell old people, people whose mates have died, to get a pet—something to love. Betty must already have given up.

"Is that your cat?" he says.

"Yes. That was a Christmas present from my nephews."

"My best friend had a dog that died not long ago," he says. Why did he say that?

"Did it have heartworms?"

"What's that?"

"Heartworms. They can cure a dog once, usually, if they get it in time."

"I don't know what it died of. It just died."

Betty shakes her head. "Heartworms, I bet."

Betty is eating cottage cheese. She is trying. She is trying to lose weight so she will get a husband and not have to rely on her Siamese cat. Poor Betty. If only she were Laura he would love her madly, blindly, forever.

"You'll only have to type two more from me today," he says.

"Have you gone to lunch?" she says.

"I'm on my way back."

"Oh," she says. "Okay. I'll be down for them later."

He leaves, convinced that there's no possibility of romance. She should have said something witty. She is so dogged. But what could she have said witty? What's the witty comeback about a dead dog? If she were Hemingway, at least she would have said something strange—that a dead dog lying in the sun was beautiful. But she is Betty. She says Sam's dog died of heartworms, which can be cured once, usually. Unlike inoperable melanomas. He gets a drink of water at the water fountain, hoping to wash down the glutinous mashed potatoes. They are still right there, even after a long drink.

Why didn't you even try to be a painter? he asks himself as he sits down to begin another report. Why don't you paint at night? You could paint primitives—then it wouldn't matter if they were sort of sloppy.

The sun is in the middle of the window. In the morning it is on the left, at noon in the middle, and to the far right before it gets dark and he goes home. He amuses himself by thinking that the sun rises and sets in his window, that it is confined to this rectangle, that the window is like one of those games they have in bars, with the little squares that beep from left to right. If he doesn't find out Betty's last name or her phone number, he will be spending another Friday night in a bar with Sam. He would ask Sam to come along, but the women always fall in love with Sam. Except Laura. She just thought Sam was nice. Sam didn't fall in love with Laura either. Oh, hell—it was perfect. His best friend didn't love his girlfriend. The three of them could have knocked around forever.

At the end of the day (4:25 today) he leaves the building. Bob White is in the elevator. He wants to say "Bob White! Bob White!" to him, chirp it at him, and he bites his tongue. Susan is right; he is infantile. "Glad to be going," Bob White says. "Yeah," Charles agrees. "Going to juvenile court with my kid tonight," Bob White says. Charles looks at him for the explanation. "Threw a bottle through a window," Bob White says. Bob White gets out first, quickly walks through the lobby to the revolving door and disappears. Charles stops at the blind man's stand and picks up an Almond Joy. "What have you got?" the blind man asks. Sometimes, Charles is convinced, he just stops at the stand because the blind man's question has such a nice ironic ring. Going out of the building, he wonders if Marsha Steinberg would defend him if he killed Laura's husband. He has forgotten to ask Betty her last name. Well, all these things we forget are deliberately forgotten. Thanks, Freud. You probably would have forgotten too. The more exotic appealed to you. The more exotic appeal to me. He crunches into his Almond Joy.

At home, he sorts through the day's mail: a letter from the Humane Society saying that kittens are being thrown in the trash, a note left in the mailbox from Susan, thanking him for "a good time," a Burpee's seed catalog. The bed that Sam slept in is a mess in one bedroom. He did not make the bed he slept in the night before. He goes into the bathroom, which is relatively uncluttered, and soaks a washrag in warm water, rubs it over his face. It is quiet in the house. He turns on the television and lies in bed to watch it. Sam's snowmobile socks are hanging off each side of the bed rail. Like the coquette who forgets her handkerchief, Sam will be back for the snowmobile socks.

The evening news features a plane crash, the parents of a child who was roughed up in a Boston school, and a word about former President Nixon going golfing. There is a picture of the former President. He looks like a lean old mafioso.

HOME: San Clemente, California

AGE: 62

PROFESSION: Retired

HOBBIES: Going out to Bob Abplanalp's island, playing golf with ambassadors, shooting the breeze with Eddie Cox.

MOST MEMORABLE BOOK: *Six Crises.*
LAST ACCOMPLISHMENT: Surviving surgery.
QUOTE: "Y'know, I love my country."
PROFILE: Aging, embarrassed, a crook. This man will not live long.
SCOTCH: Yes, and pills, too, but don't tell anyone.

He turns off the television and goes out to the kitchen to fix dinner. The phone rings.

"May I speak to Elise Reynolds?"

"Elise. Elise left a few days ago."

"She did? To whom am I speaking?"

"Charles."

"And is Susan there?"

"Susan left, too."

"Where did they go? This is *Mrs.* Reynolds."

"Oh, hello, Mrs. Reynolds. Elise left before Susan did. I thought she said she was going home."

"This is the home, and I'm in the home, but Elise isn't in the home. Just where do you think she is?"

"I can't say, Mrs. Reynolds. Maybe she's back at school."

"Maybe you *murdered* her."

Charles almost drops the phone. He sits down, eyes wide. Let's see; she left the day before yesterday. . . .

"Mrs. Reynolds, get hold of yourself. I'm sure she's back at school."

"Did she tell you I was an alcoholic?"

Susan told him she was an alcoholic. "No," he says honestly.

"I *am* an alcoholic, but it's a popular misconception that alcoholics never sober up. They *do* sober up, and when they sober up they *search their nest.*"

"Is your husband at home, Mrs. Reynolds?"

"Didn't she tell you he was dead?"

Oh, Christ, he thinks. She's flipped out and there's nobody there.

"Well, he isn't," Mrs. Reynolds says. "She exaggerates everything. She's had him in the grave for five years. He's considerably older than I am."

"Okay, okay. I just wondered if somebody was there with you . . . if you're worried."

"I haven't had anything all day but a Peppermint Schnapps, and I *am* worried."

"Elise seemed to have had a fine time here. You know kids. They're unpredictable. I'm sure she'll return to your house or to school."

"Excuse me. I didn't realize I was speaking to an adult. I think we do understand each other. We know that when I looked in the nest, she had flown."

"Try not to worry, Mrs. Reynolds. It will work out okay."

"Where is Susan?" Mrs. Reynolds asks.

"She left this morning with her boyfriend for college."

He is going to call Susan and yell at her about this. Why did she bring that screwed-up girl to his house? What if Mrs. Reynolds tries to do something—call the police or something?

"You get back in touch if you get worried, Mrs. Reynolds."

Please don't get back in touch. Please leave me alone. I didn't like your daughter. I'm glad she's gone. You sound like another crazy woman, and I don't like you either. I will keep the phone off the hook. Laura. I can't keep the phone off the hook.

"You can tell that I'm concerned, can't you, Charles? I *am* concerned. Do I sound drunk to you, or concerned?"

"Naturally you're concerned."

"That's not what I asked! I asked if I sounded drunk."

"No. You certainly don't. You only sound concerned."

"I *am* concerned. It's a popular misconception that alcoholics aren't concerned. If I weren't concerned, I wouldn't be an alcoholic, Charles."

He has no idea what to say to terminate the conversation.

"Some people are unwilling to carry on a conversation once they find out that someone is an alcoholic, but you've been most gracious. Naturally, when we tend an egg, we look beyond the crack in the shell. We look to see the infant bird, to care for it, to care that it is all right. And since I haven't heard from Elise for so long, naturally I am wondering."

"Certainly you are. And I'm sure she'll get in touch."

You bet she will, that bitch, and Susan will see to it. Somehow.

"You can't know how reassuring it is to discuss this with an *adult*," Mrs. Reynolds says.

"Well, I'm sorry I can't be of more help to you, Mrs. Reynolds, but I'm certain that she's back at school now. She's okay, I'm sure of that."

She will be dead somewhere. Twisted and dead. And the police will find his fingerprints on her coat—he lifted her coat from the sofa when she was here—and they will come to work and arrest him.

There will be a scuffle—he will try to keep his balance when he stands to greet the policemen. He will have a bemused, curious look on his face. And one of them—the big one—will misunderstand and think he is preparing to fight his way out. Why else would he lean to one side, why else that rigid spine, prepared for a fight? The big one will pick him up and throw him through the glass, and he will fall twenty-one stories. Braced briefly and miraculously between two snow-cushioned tree limbs, he will scramble for safety, but lose his grip and fall from the tree to the ground, while the policemen look through the hole in the glass and slap each other on the back. A sex pervert; he deserved that fall, O'Hara.

He calls Sam to see if he knows anything about where Elise might be. Sam reports that his temperature is ninety-nine and that he doesn't know where Elise is. He

did give her fifteen dollars though. "All she was worth—
at the most."

"You *paid* her for it, you *paid* for it?" Charles says.

Things are really taking a new turn if Sam paid for it.

"It wasn't that overt. She told me she needed money. I
think she said she needed twenty dollars. I gave her fifteen, which is definitely all she was worth."

Sam sort of paid for it. Things are sort of taking a new
turn.

"But she didn't say anything about where she was
thinking of going?"

"The only thing even remotely related to travel that she
talked about was how she envied the Kennedys, except
for the amputee who has a bit of trouble with it, for being
able to go skiing."

"You don't think she took off for some ski lodge?"

"Not on fifteen bucks."

"She might have had more."

"Not in her wallet. Well, she had about ten or fifteen
more in there, I guess."

"You went through her wallet."

"She was showing me some pictures. I saw a little bit
of money in the back."

"It could have been hundred dollar bills."

"I don't think so. She was really grateful when I gave
her the fifteen. She should have been. Even with inflation,
that was a five-dollar lay."

"Okay," Charles says. "You don't know anything."

"Maybe you know whether my snowmobile socks are
at your place," Sam says.

"Yeah, they are."

"I looked all over the place for them before I left.
Ended up going to work in a pair of yours."

"Bring them back."

"I will. Why would I want a pair of your socks?"

"They'd better not be the ones Laura gave me."

"How should I know? They're a pair of navy blue socks."

"No. She gave me gray ones."

"Christ, you're nuts. My dinner's getting ready to burn."

"What are you having?"

"Stouffer's lasagna."

"It's good you're eating. Keep your strength up."

"You sound like somebody's grandmother."

"You're as testy as I am. Guess you've got a right if you've still got a fever."

"I've got a right if I have to stand here gassing to you while my lasagna burns up."

"Okay. Good-bye."

"Bye," Sam says.

Charles puts the phone back on the hook, taking his hand away slowly, debating whether it might not be wiser to let it dangle. Might as well let her call again, get it out of her system so she doesn't start that "You murdered her" stuff again. Murder. Jesus. Elise couldn't drive anybody to murder. Who would bother? Except all those murderers out there . . . the ones who'll wear rubber gloves and not have their fingerprints on her coat. In comes Detective O'Hara, out the window goes Charlie. *Then* she'll be sorry. Then, too late, she'll realize that she didn't want her husband and Rebecca. She'll go back to work in the same library, just to be in the building where he once cornered her against the bookshelf. Twice. Three times at least.

He puts a box of taco hors d'oeuvres in the oven and finds a beer in the bottom of the refrigerator that he decides to save to go with the tacos. Laura and her husband and daughter are probably having a nourishing dinner. They are having baked ham, sweet potatoes, asparagus, freshly baked bread, milk, and that dessert. Laura used to come home with him sometimes and cook dinner. She'd take off her stockings and go get a pair of the soft gray socks she had given him and stand in the kitchen in the socks, cooking dinner. In her dress and socks she looked like some bobbysoxer. If he had known her in the fifties they would have jitterbugged. She would have worn a ribbon in her hair, and a long pleated skirt, blazer, and white socks and saddle shoes. The socks would have a funny weave that looked like rivulets when they got twisted around a little. Gonna rock, gonna rock around the clock tonight.

The kitchen clock says five-thirty. That gives him enough time for a shower. But does he want a shower? No. He wants that beer. But doesn't he want it with the tacos? Yes. People's problems should end when they get home from work. They don't. No wonder men go home and knock their kids around. There's only one beer, which will be great with the tacos, but they want it immediately to cool their throat, so when the kid says that a wheel came off his bicycle the father looks at the wheel, picks it up, and pushes it over the kid's head, the kid goes around yowling, the wheel like a clown's ruffle, his wife says he's a beast, separates from him, divorces him. If only Laura would push a wheel over Rebecca's head. Not very likely. She goes to parent's day, is "room mother" for the kindergarten, bakes special gingerbread cookies for the kids, who all love her. "She was such a nice woman, you'd never think she'd push a wheel over her child's head." And, in fact, she won't. She'll just cook a nice nourishing dinner and then tuck Rebecca in, and what she does after that is too painful to think about. Maybe she will call him, though. She won't.

The phone rings as he is finishing dinner.

"This is a voice from the past," the caller says.

He swallows the last quarter inch of beer. It tastes foul.

"I have pretty eyes and long hair, and I call you every time I'm in trouble. Who am I?"

"Pamela Smith," he says, his voice gloomy.

"That's right!" Pamela Smith says.

"What kind of trouble are you in, Pamela?"

"Spiritual trouble."

He repeats this.

"I was in California. I got back just a couple of days ago. I called you last night."

"You were in spiritual trouble last night too."

Twenty-four hours of spiritual trouble. More or less.

"Was I ever. I've been out in Mendocino, working in a canning factory."

"That sounds like a drag."

"The whole California thing—I thought it would be wild, but there's no way to get money in California. I got a ride out with a dyke who ditched me in a bar in San Francisco. She crawled out a toilet window. Women are no better than men. Women are worse. You should have seen the beasts I worked with in the canning factory."

"Yeah. That sounds awful."

"I mean, there were some nice things about California. When you order a sandwich out there they bring you fresh fruit with it instead of potato chips. You order a roast beef sandwich, you're likely to get half a peach and a strawberry. In some ways it's civilized. I don't think I'll ever eat junk food again."

He thinks of Laura's nourishing dinner. The tacos are now sitting in his stomach with the mashed potatoes. That last quarter inch of beer was revolting.

"Yoko Ono was in Mendocino. Not in the canning factory. But around."

(". . . I think John should stay in the U.S.A., because he's a groovy musician. . . .")

"Yoko," he says.

"It's quitsville for John and Yoko, and believe me, with a woman like that I don't blame him. Women are yecch. It took me a long time to realize that."

Silence.

"But how are you? How are you, Charles?"

(". . . What have you got?" . . .)

"I'm fine," he says. "I've been running around a lot over the holidays and I'm pretty wiped out. . . ."

He hopes to avoid being asked either to go out or to have her come over.

"I was wondering if I could come over?"

"Sure," he says.

"Good. I can be there in about an hour."

"Good."

Good. He can take a shower. Brace himself. He hangs up, goes into the bathroom and runs the water. He takes his clothes off and looks at himself in the medicine cabinet mirror. Stubble. A double chin? No—he was looking down. His hair is dirty. Why bother to wash it for Pamela Smith? But it has to be washed before work tomorrow. Okay, okay. He drapes his clothes over the toilet seat and gets in the shower.

"I'm singin' in the tub, just singin' in the tub, a glorious feeling, I'm showering again . . ."

He learned that song from Sam. Sam does it complete with twirls and kicks. Charles is sure he's going to fall in the bathtub and break his legs. Charles holds on to the soap dish and gives a kick. Sam is crazy.

He gets out of the shower in time to answer the phone. It is cold in the kitchen. He jumps off the floor, jogs in place to stop his feet from freezing.

"Yeah?" he says. "Hello?"

"Hello, my boy. How are things with you tonight?"

"Hi, Pete. I'll call you back. Just got out of the shower."

"You do that, then," Pete says.

They did not talk long enough for Charles to be able to tell if Pete was drunk. Shivering, Charles goes into the bedroom and throws his towel over a floor lamp he never uses. He puts on a pair of gray socks, a pair of corduroy pants, and a blue button-down shirt. Over that he pulls a sweater with an antelope standing on top of a mountain. He bought the sweater because he thought it was funny: a very realistically knitted antelope on top of a pointed brown mound. Very stark, very ugly. "Hello, little fellow," the salesman writing up the sale said, stroking the antelope. Charles has not liked the sweater since then, rarely puts it on. He tried to give it to the dog, but she was only interested in sleeping on it once.

He looks around him. His room has looked just the same since the day he moved in. His mother used to have winter and summer bedspreads, winter and summer curtains. When he lived at home, his winter bedspread had been a yellow and brown plaid, a cheap, itchy bedspread that he didn't like to sit on. The summer bedspread was beige and green crinkle crepe with a large dust ruffle. He had said that he wasn't having a bedspread with any damn ruffle. She had said that it was a "dust ruffle," as though that excused it. He had threatened to cut it off. His father had been sent to his room. His father said that it was a bedspread in good taste, one that he wouldn't mind having on his own bed. "Then take the thing!" Charles had shouted. His father nodded. He removed the bedspread and carried it into the master bedroom, took the bedspread off their double bed and handed it to Charles. Charles was embarrassed; he felt as if he was holding a jar of tonsils, or the blown-off head of a friend. He held the big bedspread reverently. He watched his father put the single bedspread on the double bed. Of course it did not fit. It looked silly. "Do you want me to have this bedspread on my bed?" his father asked. Charles quickly gave him back his own bedspread, left in defeat and humiliation, trailing his green and beige bedspread with him. He put it back on his bed. "I didn't think you'd want my room to look like that," his father said, passing his room. His father never fought with him. He played dumb, as he did with the bedspread exchange, or explained patiently (which his mother was incapable of) why something had to be a certain way. Most logical men live a long time, but Charles's father dropped dead at thirty-nine. He would have been logical in his old age, but there was no old age.

Charles stands in the doorway of his room, thinking about how the room could be changed. Instead of being against the wall, the desk could be moved against the window. And the bed could be moved from the back wall to the side wall. There would be a little more space in the room that way. He no longer even questions that the room must be changed. He takes the things off the top of his bureau and puts them on the bed, shoves the bureau where his desk used to be, at the same time shoving the desk into the middle of the room. A lamp falls over, does not break. He stands it upright on the floor. He moves the dresser into place. He puts all the things back on top, shoved together: a picture of his mother and father on their first anniversary, a picture of him holding Susan when she was an infant (he can still remember his mother arranging the baby in his arms; he had thrust her forward, his arms straight out, so that she blocked his face in the lens, and his mother had rushed to him and crooked his arm and lowered her into it), a glass bowl with pennies, a hairbrush, a dirty ascot that got dirty not from wear but from dust settling on it over a two-year period, a dried-up philodendron, a fountain pen and bottle of ink, several magazines, and a flashlight. He pushes the desk across the rug. Maybe now that it faces the window he will enjoy sitting at it more. What will he ever use it for? He could figure out the bills there. He won't. He could do what his mother always did with useless pieces of furniture—put a tablecloth over it. He does not own a tablecloth. Maybe a sheet. No, that would look silly, to have a desk with a sheet over it. Everybody would know it was a desk. Sam would demand an explanation. Moving the bed is a bigger problem. He pushes hard, bunching the rug underneath the bed. He lifts the bottom of the bed and pushes the rug with his foot. He hopes that he does not get a hernia. There was a boy in the sixth grade who had a hernia that had to be operated on. The class sent him a card. Nobody knew what message to write, so almost everybody wrote: "I am sorry you have a hernia. See you soon." Some people asked how the food was. One girl refused to sign the card. She told the teacher that her mother would write a note saying she didn't have to. The teacher said that it wasn't necessary.

He gives the bed a final shove. The rug is a little bunched up, but so what? Sam can help him the next time he's over. He backs up, sweating, and looks over his work. He picks up the lamp and puts it back on the desk. The room looks much better. He should rearrange the whole house. Except that there is hardly any other furniture. He sold most of it to an antique dealer, a frail old man who went from room to room exclaiming "Staffordshire! Hepplewhite! A gateleg table!" Charles just wanted all the ugly, smelly stuff out of there. The antique dealer gave him a lot of money. At least at the time he thought it was a lot of money. He opened kitchen cabinets. "Peacock Feather!" the old man said, holding a bowl to his chest. He went away and returned with his "assistant," an enormously fat asthmatic woman who followed him from room to room repeating "Hepplewhite! A gateleg!" reverently. For a while Charles was afraid they'd just keep wandering like some poor damned souls in Dante, but after wheezing and exclaiming through the rooms they went away and came back with a blue truck and a terrier that ran yapping through the house. They did not allude to the dog. Charles could not figure out why it was there. When they did not summon the dog to leave, and it just appeared and ran out the door, Charles thought he might have been hallucinating. The fat woman lowered the antiques into piles of newspapers that she quickly wrapped around them, and the man removed drawers from dressers and tossed cushions onto the floor. "Any Sandwich?" the woman asked breathlessly, and Charles had thought that she was asking for food. She sang Billie Holiday songs as she worked; glass dishes were lowered into crates as she sang "God Bless the Child"; an oil lamp disappeared into a mound of paper as she crooned "Don't Worry 'Bout Me." Charles didn't know what room to stand in—whether he should appear not to notice what was happening or whether he should offer to help. Shouldn't they discuss money before the things were wrapped in newspaper? "You can help yourself, but don't take too much," the woman sang huskily, occasionally breaking off to get her breath. "Oh, Grandma!" she shouted with glee sometimes, when she saw a painted dish or a small colored photograph. The old man worked silently and very quickly. "I need your help, young fellow," he said, and Charles helped him carry the things out. "I want to tell you something," he said as they raised a love seat into the blue van. "That woman is my sister." Charles waited for what he was going to be told. The man nodded once, rubbed his hands together, and said, "Let's go." They carried more things out. Later, in the kitchen, the woman talked about her "husband," saying that the work was getting too rough for him. Their names were Bess and Bert, and their antique business was known as "Best Bird Antiques." There was a cluster of flying birds painted across the back door of the van with white paint. "Best Bird Antiques" was lettered above the clouds. In three hours they were gone, and Charles had one thousand four hundred dollars. The woman climbed into the back of the van and slammed the door behind her. She was singing "A Fine Romance." The old man gave him the money in cash. "She can't bear to see me actually part with money," the old man said. "I buy antiques on Mondays, if there's more you want to part with. Can't tell what you'll find that you want to part with. Things to part with in the attic, probably. We don't go into attics. But come to our store on Mondays, which is buying day. She makes that grocery day, because she can't bear to see me fork over money for antiques! Well, thanks mighty much, and here you go." He shoved a wad of money into Charles's outstretched hand. Charles's hand had been extended to shake the man's hand good-bye. In all the confusion, he had forgotten about getting paid. The little dog barked in the front seat. The man touched his fingers to his forehead in a salute as the van pulled away. Charles waved. He later took several hand-painted plates he found to the man's antique store. Sure enough, the fat woman wasn't there. "Don't look around the place, the inflated prices will make you sick," the man said. Charles took his advice, left with twenty dollars. There was a sign in an ornate frame over the cash register that said, "Best Bird Antiques Is Your Best Bet." "We used to have a racehorse named that," the man said, noticing that Charles was looking at the sign. "It broke its leg. I said, 'No more racehorses,' My sister was amenable."

Charles goes into the kitchen and dials Pete's number.

"What are you panting for?" Pete asks.

"I just moved some furniture around."

"Oh," Pete says. "Well, I've been straightening up around here the last couple of days, too. Furniture seems to creep forward in the room for some reason. I shoved it all back against the walls. Not right against them because of the paint, but about an inch away."

"How's Mom?" Charles asks.

"She's doing just fine. I know she'd want to talk to you, except that she's having a bath right now." Pete whispers, "Door's open."

"Christ, Pete, she's probably got a heating pad plugged in that she'll electrocute herself with."

"No she doesn't," Pete says, sounding hurt. "I told you the"—he lowers his voice—"the door's open."

He can picture it: she is sitting in hot water. She does not put any bubble bath in the water. She just sits there, sinks down in the tub until the hot water is collarbone level. She plays the radio. If she stays long enough (she takes many of these baths a day) she reads movie magazines, and if she stays for a very long time she starts to imagine pains and she cries. Someone has to haul her out. Charles and Pete have told the doctors about her dips. They think it's a good idea to "soak to relax." Even when they are told what really happens, they still say that there's nothing wrong with a hot bath. They think she is clever to have thought of that "to relax." She used to take Seconal and fall asleep with her chin on her collarbone, the magazines drowned in the tub, heating pads plugged into several sockets, radio blaring. If only one of them was home, they couldn't lift her. She was angry when they appeared in the bathroom and shook her awake. "I was relaxing! I have no privacy! I had a pain in my back—I was warming the heating pad for that!" The towels always smell bad and need to be washed. There is bath powder all over the bath rug. Movie magazines with moldy covers and curled edges are stacked on the back of the toilet. The bathtub and toilet are blue; the tile is brown and white—small brown and white tiles covered with a film of bath powder.

"What I called about," Pete says, "is that I thought it might be nice to have a little welcome home celebration for Mommy."

"Pete, you always put on that phony diction. When you're not thinking you call her by her name, or you say, 'your mother.' That sounds more dignified."

"How I wish I had a flesh-and-blood son I could kill for talking that way," Pete says. "But you're all I've got. I thought you and I were getting along better now after the—after the drink we had. The very nice time we just had."

"Yeah. That was nice. I only mention it, Pete, because I think we might get along better if you knew about the things that bothered me. Then I know you wouldn't do them and we'd get along even better."

"There's too wide a gap. I don't think we'd ever get

along very well. Maybe if you were my own flesh and blood you'd be indebted to me."

"I don't want you to take offense, Pete. I just want you to know that that's a little thing that annoys me."

"Well, I'll tell you something that annoyed me. You never even asked me to be a scoutmaster, and you knew I built birdhouses and did stuff like that. All the other kids asked their fathers, and you never even approached me."

"I never thought you'd be interested, Pete. We didn't talk much, so I didn't think you'd want to deal with a whole troop of boys my age."

"Maybe we would have talked more if we had had things to talk about. Birdhouses and things like that. I knew how to build stuff. I would have been a good leader for you boys."

"I'm sorry I never asked, Pete. I just assumed wrong."

"Well, it's too late now," Pete says.

"Don't worry about it, then. Just don't worry about it."

"That's right. What's that saying? 'Lord give me patience to change the things I can change and not worry about those I can't,' or something like that."

"Yeah."

"I find it very hard to talk to you on the phone, Charles. When I make a comment it doesn't seem to lead anywhere."

"I don't know what else to say, Pete. You remember the saying better than I do, so I don't have anything to add."

"You're a very impatient person, I think," Pete says. "But I want to get back to the reason for this call. You've got me so flustered I can't remember if I already said this, but I wanted to ask whether you couldn't come over on Saturday night for dinner to welcome Clara home." He punches the "Clara."

"Pete . . . you know she won't get a dinner together."

"I can get the dinner. I'm cooking. All you've got to do is grace us with your presence. If I can be blunt, I don't

even want you for dinner myself after this bad phone conversation, but your mother mentioned the idea. I'm going
to get a chicken. Anybody can cook chicken."

"Okay. I'll be there."

"Okay," Pete says. "Don't forget."

"It'll be on my mind all week, Pete."

"Talk nice to me! I'm sixty-three years old."

"I'll see you then, Pete."

"I hate to hang up this way. I feel like you've insulted
me, yet I'm on the defensive."

"Somebody's at my door, Pete."

"I know you're just saying that. You always get me in
some corner and make me stay there. What can I do but
hang up if somebody is knocking at your door? Yet nobody is."

The knocking continues.

"Somebody is, Pete. It's somebody I was expecting. I'll
see you for dinner."

"Aw, good-bye," Pete says, and hangs up.

Charles goes to the front door and opens it for Pamela
Smith.

"Charles!" she says. *"Plus ça change."*

"Hi," he says. "Come in."

"I *will* come in. I feel like I'm home now. You're the
only person I know who's still living in the same place.
People I left in poverty have got glass-topped Parsons
tables now. It's all *changed* so much."

"It's the same here, all right."

"How about family problems? Oh, well, I shouldn't
rush into that."

She hands him her coat. A black, long coat. She is
wearing a Wonder Woman T-shirt and black corduroy
jeans and work boots. A knee is torn out of her jeans.
The work boots have white paint on them. Why did he
wash his hair? He could have washed it when she left.

"Would you like a drink or some coffee or tea?"

"You don't have anything to *eat,* do you?"

"Cheese," he says. Does he have cheese?

"Oh, could I have some cheese?"

"Sure."

He leaves her standing in his living room and goes into the kitchen. She follows him out.

"I've become a vegetarian, and I feel so much better. When I ate meat a week ago, just to try it again, I actually stank afterwards. I could smell myself."

"There's Muenster and Swiss," he says. "Some of both?"

"That would be good," she says.

The phone rings. Charles picks it up.

"Hell," Pete says. "That was nuts of me to say there was nobody at your door. I'm sure there was, and I called back to say that it was just my nuttiness."

"That's okay, Pete. It was a friend of mine from a couple of years ago, just back from California. I was getting her something to eat."

"I'd really be a fool if I thought you were making that up," Pete says. "If I thought the knock *and* the food was imaginary, all to brush me off."

Charles hands the phone to Pamela Smith. "Please say hello to my stepfather," Charles says. Pamela Smith looks taken aback, holds the phone to her ear as if expecting an explosion, then says a tentative, "Hello."

"Why, hello," Pete says. "Charles says that you're here from California."

"Yes. I just got back."

Charles takes the phone away from her. She looks even more surprised.

"I'll see you on Saturday, Pete."

"Hell," Pete says. "Down with the phone and off with the pants."

"Oh my God," Charles says, and hangs up.

"It's a long story," Charles says to Pamela Smith. "To make a long story short, he gets his feelings hurt very easily, and he thought I was hanging up on him before when I said there was a knock on the door."

"Wow," Pamela Smith says. "That's sad."

"He's a sad case. I try to be nice to him, but it's just not in me."

"He might feel better in general if he cleaned out his system. Saunas and a fresh vegetable regime."

"He's stuck in his rut. He'll never get out of it. My mother is nuts, and he spends all his time coping with that and getting slowly crazier himself."

"Have they tried Gestalt?"

"No. She won't go out of the house."

"Wow," Pamela Smith says. "Even if she stayed in . . . she might try eating more fruits and vegetables and so forth."

Charles puts the cheese and some crackers on a plate, turns on the water to make coffee. He motions her to the kitchen table.

"So things are pretty much the same here," he says.

"All in all, things are pretty much the same with me, too. I feel a whole lot better, but things are otherwise the same. I've got to get a job. I don't know. Anything beats canning cauliflower in Mendocino. I mean, I just don't want to can at all any more."

"What else were you doing out there?" Charles asks.

"For a while I was living with this creep. He played the jew's-harp and had an imitation of Elton John doing 'Benny and the Jets.' It really got to me after a while. It was always raining in Mendocino, and I'd go home and he'd be on the bed, naked, twanging the jew's-harp, going 'Benny, Benny, Benny aaaaaand the Jets . . .' "

Charles laughs.

"I sort of had a thing with a woman out there, who turned me on to curried rice. She was older than me. Forty. Except around the eyes, she looked twenty. She had an amazing body. She fasted on Sunday and ate nothing but curried rice the next day. She was a silversmith."

Pamela Smith holds out her hand. There is a silver ring on her middle finger.

"That's very nice," Charles says.

"For a while I thought I'd be staying with her. She was going to teach me how to be a silversmith, get me out of that factory. She had a daughter. It was a weird scene."

Charles nods. He is sure it was. He does not want to hear.

"The daughter thought Dylan was coming for her. She had substantial proof from the last two records. She played them all the time. I was glad to get out to go to the factory some days."

"Is everybody crazy out there?"

"No. I think everybody's pretty relaxed. There are a lot of nice things about California. Her daughter, though, was always looking out the window, actually expecting Dylan. Her mother was shooting pictures of her in various stances by the window. She had been a student of Diane Arbus's. Things were really getting pretty tense when I split. And that's when I ended up with the guy who did the Elton John imitation. We both needed a place to stay. Marlan—that was her name—came over one night with her daughter, and she spent the whole night at the window. It was getting sort of weird."

"Do you want coffee?" Charles asks.

"I'd prefer tea, please."

He goes to the cabinet for cups. The cups are very cold from the cabinet. He rinses them in tepid, then warm water before putting the boiling water in.

"Actually, the daughter had a daughter too, but it was with its father. Its father was some hot shit San Francisco stockbroker."

"You mean that this girl was an adult?"

"She was twenty-one. She claimed she screwed Peter Fonda on the kitchen floor in an all-night health food restaurant, but I don't believe it."

"It probably happened," Charles says.

"Well, she says the same thing happened with Ahmet Ertegun, so I don't believe it."

Charles nods.

"But it's not all that crazy out there. Burbank is awfully ugly. I don't know . . . I think about going back, but I wouldn't want to go back to Mendocino."

"What did you come back East for?"

"Oh, I . . . started to feel I was expanding too quickly—that I'd end up like stretched taffy or something. I came back to compress."

Charles nods.

"But it's not all that crazy out there. And now it seems so unreal to me here. I think I may be going back there. Work some shit job for a little while and go back."

Charles nods.

"How's your job?" she asks.

He shrugs. "Money," he says.

"Do you wear a suit to work?" she says.

"No."

"That's Charles—a rebel at heart."

"Nobody wears them," he says.

"What kind of people work there?"

"Most of them are older than me. Family people. They're all sort of numb. They're what everybody says they are."

"I guess it could be worse. You should see the conditions in the canning factory in Mendocino."

"Yeah," he says. "I wouldn't want to work in a canning factory."

"I'm lucky to have my fingers," she says. "After a while it's hard to tell your own fingers from the cauliflower flowerets."

She takes a sip of tea.

"One day when Marlan's daughter was looking out the window Yoko Ono walked by."

Charles nods.

"I really don't have much *interesting* news. Tell me what's new with you."

"Nothing."

"Do you ever get away to go skiing?"

"I don't ski," Charles says.

"Oh. I must be thinking of George Nimkis."

Charles nods.

"Did you know Nimkis? Wanda's husband?"

"I don't think so."

"Totally forgettable. Cared about nothing but skiing. He taught Wanda to ski on their honeymoon, had skis hung on their living room wall. There was even an old pair of them in back of the toilet. She finally left him for a skiing instructor. God knows, she was expert enough at skiing, but the ski instructor didn't talk about skiing all the time. I don't know what happened to George. How could I have gotten you confused with George? He had ski masks in all colors, and he's pull them over the lamp shades. It looked like an evil jack o'lantern. I'm glad she got away from George. I wonder where she is now. . . ."

"You knew a lot of people around here, didn't you?"

"I went to school here for four years and worked here for a year after that. I was a silly little secretary. Well, you knew me then. You know."

"I should think that would beat the canning factory."

"It did, it did. I had to gouge out the centers of cauliflowers with a knife. It was a wicked thing, and it never got dull. I can't imagine what that knife was made of. I was terrified of it. I never worked fast enough."

"So you're going to go back to Mendocino, huh?"

"I don't know *what* to do with myself. I really think I could get interested in that woman if it weren't for her daughter. Besides being crazy, she's so piggish. She lies on the rug all day, and she eats anything that's put in front of her, and believe me, she expects regular meals down there. Sonny Bono wrote her a couple of letters. I don't know how she knew him."

"I heard that Dylan showed up at some party with Cher. I wonder what's gotten into Dylan?"

"I saw his kids at Malibu. They play with Ryan O'Neal's kid."

"What's he doing hanging out with Cher? 'Haff-breed.' Christ."

She puts her plate and cup in the sink. "I can't remember what you and I used to talk about," she says.

"Lesbians," he says.

"That's right," she says. "I was freelancing for that feminist newspaper. Well, I still feel very strongly that lesbianism is a good alternative. Like everything else, it has problems. Having a child, for one. And I *have* decided to have a child. If you have them after thirty they might be monsters. Not really monsters, but what do you call them when they have those oriental eyes?"

"Mongoloid."

"Of course. Mongoloid. I couldn't deal with that. For a while Marlan's daughter almost freaked me off the idea, but I think it's what my body wants. Ultimately."

He once lent Pamela Smith fifty dollars for an abortion. They got another ten from Sam, and ten from a friend of Sam's who came over with Sam and saw her crying. Her brother gave her some, and a neighbor in her apartment. And a friend of hers from college who lived twenty-five miles away gave her another fifty. The friend didn't have a car and Charles's wouldn't work, so they borrowed Pete's. When Pete found out about it a week later he gave Charles twenty dollars to give her. Charles explained that it was not his child. Pete took back a ten. "Give her the rest," Pete said. He and Pamela Smith ate at a cheap steak restaurant with the remaining ten. Pamela Smith dyed her hair after the abortion and lost a lot of weight, as if to make sure it was really gone. It was, although Pamela Smith was very upset all that summer, thinking that she saw infants' faces in the clouds.

"Would you do something very kind for me?" Pamela

Smith says. "Would you let me stay on your sofa tonight?"

"Sure. Just let me know when you're tired."

"Aren't you even going to question me?" she says.

"No. I don't mind if you sleep here tonight."

"I think I'd rather, because it's a very strange scene at the place I'm staying."

"You can stay here," he says.

"You've always been so *nice* to me."

"No I haven't. I used to beg you to shut up about lesbianism. I burned your Sappho book."

"We had a good talk once, didn't we, about Kate Millett?"

"You wrote me a letter about Kate Millett that I didn't answer."

"I met her. She's a brilliant woman."

"Maybe she is. I don't know."

"Aren't you interested to read *Sexual Politics?*"

"No."

"Of course there are better books. Would you be interested in reading any feminist writing?"

"Yeah. Send me something."

"How come you're interested in feminists, but not Kate Millett?"

"Hell, I was just being polite. I'll never read anything you send me."

"I really shouldn't sleep on your sofa. But it's an awfully weird scene."

"If you're mad at me you can go to bed and then we won't have to continue this conversation. I'm pretty tired, and I'm going to bed myself."

"What I like about you is that you're straightforward. Many men are not straightforward. I think that in business they have to compete, to at least appear very receptive and open, and when they're relaxing with women —that's what they think women are *for*—they assert their true self, which is generally not straightforward."

"Good night, Pamela," he says. "I'll bring you a sheet and a blanket."

"May I make more tea before I go to bed?"

"Sure. I'll put the stuff on the sofa. Good night."

"In your own way, you are really very nice."

He looks at her. Her Wonder Woman T-shirt ripples across her chest. She has gained weight since the abortion. Her hair has grown out. Medium-long, brown hair. Laura told him that medium could be medium-long or medium-short. She confused everything. He used to look at women and think they had medium-length hair. She did more than confuse him, she showed him that nothing was definite—even hair length. He thought that her head must reel with the complexities of everything. "When you say afternoon," she said, "do you mean early afternoon or late afternoon?" "What's two-thirty?" he asked. He accepted her answer for everything. "Mid-afternoon," she said. He felt that he really needed his apprenticeship. He felt that he really needed her. He didn't know all that stuff.

"Is there some woman you're in love with?" Pamela Smith asks.

"Yes," he says. "But she's married."

"Marriage is *dying*. We keep trying to cast the ashes of the dead institution away, but the wind blows them back in our faces. We *will* scatter that traditionalism to the winds."

"She'll never divorce her husband," Charles says.

"So you're lovers then."

"I never see her. Since she went back to her husband."

"Marriage is a retreat. It's wild animals in the rocks that curl together for protection. The wind will blow the ashes away."

"Will the ashes blow away tomorrow?" he says. "I'd like to see her tomorrow."

"If I could bring her to you, I would. I think you're a very nice person."

"Call her and tell her I've tried to commit suicide."

"I couldn't do that. She's my sister. There can't be sisterhood founded upon deceit."

"She's not your goddamned sister. She's a housewife in an A-frame across town."

"We're united."

"I want to be united with her. Give her a desperate call."

"I can't tell if you're serious or not."

"That'll make it easier not to take me seriously," he says. "I'll get the blankets."

Chapter 7

He calls in sick. It's true that he has a sore throat, but he's well enough to go to work. He just can't face it. Reports. Betty. Lunch alone. "What have you got?" The blind man there every day to remind him that, at the close of the day, he has nothing. It adds insult to injury to have to answer, "A peanut butter cup."

Pamela Smith left in the morning, deciding to borrow money from her brother and go back to California to become a silversmith. She told Charles this over breakfast, which he fixed for her. He went out and bought eggs, cheese, English muffins, raspberry jam, and sausage. She didn't eat the sausage, but he did and it tasted good. She told him not to go out, but he said that he wanted to. It was true; he did want to. He wanted her to exclaim again how nice he was. It would give him courage to call Laura. "You're a bully!" a girl in the sixth grade had once shouted to Charles as he ran by, nearly knocking her over, and he had been so delighted he almost stopped running and started strutting.

"You eat all that meat and you get sluggish, and when you're sluggish you're depressed. Try eating crisp celery in the morning and only fruits until night, when you can have soup or fish. I know you'll feel better."

She washed the Wonder Woman T-shirt before going to bed. She ate breakfast with a towel around her top, giving the shirt an extra few minutes to dry. He noticed a mole above her right breast, one that he didn't remember.

He tried to remember touching her. He couldn't. But he did remember what she looked like naked, and there was no mole. It must be a melanoma. Inoperable, of course. And if they operate, the cancer may have spread through the lymphatic system or through the blood. Persistent stuff. Laura probably thinks he is too persistent—he is a cancer. A cancer on the Presidency. An inoperable melanoma on the Presidency that occurred, strangely enough, through exposure to darkness. If only he could think of stylish political talk in her presence. Then maybe she would love him. Although she was never very concerned with politics. And he can never think of anything to say; he just talks about how much he loves her. Couldn't they have been like a Norman Rockwell family if they had met years ago, if they had been adults in the forties? There would have been a small black dog, an older son, younger daughter, a chubby baby on Grandpa's knee (his father—not Pete) and they would all be seated at the birthday party of his delighted son, Grandma carrying in a strawberry shortcake, the dog running to greet her, everybody slightly overweight and rosy. A white tablecloth, drapes to the floor, an unwrapped present, a bowl of vegetables on the table. Peanut-butter cups. The A-frame. Bob White's son throwing a brick through a window.

He walks the two miles to the park. It is a cold, sunny day. He has heard that hippies bury grass in this park, that if it ever burned, the firemen would be too stoned to fight it. Hardly anyone is in the park. He sees no hippies, suspicious or otherwise. The park has old wooden swings and a dented slide. The park Laura takes Rebecca to in the spring has orange plastic swings and large metal turtles to climb on. Rebecca will not eat turtle soup. She cries because she thinks that flesh—metal flesh, don't ask her to explain this—has been gouged out of this particular turtle to make turtle soup. He went to the park last spring, because he knew Laura was taking Rebecca there, and sat on a bench and watched them. He wanted to rush up to Rebecca and say warm, witty things to her that would charm her, but he had a very lazy floating feeling sitting on the bench and didn't want to change it by moving, so he only sat there, very still, watching them. Laura gave Rebecca a hand-up on the jungle gym (Sam, slapping his mother's hand . . .), sat on a bench to smoke a Chesterfield. When he first knew her—no, when he first became her lover—he got out of bed one night and rummaged through the ashtray to find out what kind of cigarettes she smoked, hoping they would be low in tar and nicotine. He shuddered when he lifted out the Chesterfield. He went back to bed and imagined that she was having trouble breathing—all that carbon in her lungs. In the morning, he begged her to have a chest X ray. When the Popsicle truck came, he wanted to buy one for Laura; the most expensive kind—vanilla ice cream in a sugar cone with chocolate and nuts and a cherry frozen on top. Then he would take her to the stone fountain for a drink of water. The next time he went to the park the stone fountain with the two steps had been taken out and there was a red plastic fountain shaped like a boomerang.

Charles is wearing a tweed coat that makes him feel like an old man. Other people his age wear ski jackets, navy-blue ski jackets that have no weight but that are stuffed with miraculously warm fabric, tied on the inside with secret drawstrings, buttoned and zipped on the outside. You can carry Kleenex on your bicep in those jackets. There is a three-inch zipper, just big enough to pull down and stuff a tissue in. He has examined the jackets, decided that his tweed coat from college is good enough. If he stays thin, he can become an old man in the coat, a powerful Yeatsian old man. She read Yeats to him. Swans, hills, valleys, islands. She read him Pound's parody of Yeats, and he wanted to kill Pound. Dead, she said. He disliked Pound so much that she told stories, trying to make him like Pound. It became important to her that he like Pound, but he could not stand the man. He couldn't laugh with her at Pound's rants about usury, and *ABC of Reading* seemed to him pompous. "But it's so funny," she said. When it all failed, she told him about Pound being shut in a cage. Now he pities Pound. Does not like him a bit, but pities him. She has made him feel so many ways. Now he feels a way about Ezra Pound and has no one to discuss it with. There is an old man in the park who looks like Pound. Can't be. The old man is wearing a tan coat and walks with slow steps in highly polished brown shoes. He is the only other stroller in the park. Charles suspects that when the old man's hand goes in his pocket it is for a peanut or a bit of bread. The old man blows his nose loudly, like a goose, honking. He stuffs the handkerchief in an inside pocket as he passes Charles.

Charles turns down a path that takes him to the main section of the park. There are graffiti on the benches. There are no drinking fountains. A dolphin that gurgles water in the summer has its mouth open to the cold wind. It looks, now, like a terrified caught fish. He never liked to fish. Susan did. She was too small to really fish, but she liked to watch, to jerk her arm as though it held a fishing pole. His father would take Susan fishing with him, and Charles would stay home with his mother. Some Saturdays she baked a cake (that dessert . . .) and let him frost it, awkwardly, moving around the cake instead of merely turning the plate until she laughed at him and showed him how easy it was to spin the plate. So he made cakes while Susan fished. Liberated children—Charles liberated out of revulsion at seeing fish twitch, Susan liberated because she loved to jerk her arm. She also did it in dancing. She'd stand on the floor, feet shuffling to a record, right arm flapping like a cowboy with a lasso. They said she would be a conductor. Conduct*ress*. Liberation. He hopes Pamela Smith does not waste her money on books.

It is too cold to think intelligently in the park (this is, after all, what he has taken the day off to do), and tea might soothe his throat, so he walks in the direction of the hill, below which lies a street with a coffee shop. It is next to a bakery he used to go to with Laura, one that stayed open very late. They would get there just as the fresh Danish were being taken out of the oven at two A.M. The old Italian woman who worked there (guarded by two German shepherds and one Madonna) would make motions—what looked like slapping—with her fingers, lightly touching the tops of the pastries. She would give one pastry to each dog and, if she was in a good mood, one to Laura and Charles before they even gave their order for half a dozen. His throat constricts, not so much from pain as from remembering. Old ladies always thought they were a sweet young couple. You could tell. He passes a bench that a young woman is sitting on, a little boy in her lap, face turned toward her to protect himself from the wind, a little girl pushing a noisy toy in front of her. It is a clear plastic cylinder with marbles inside. Charles stops to say hello. The young woman is very pleasant. They talk about the snow that is expected, and how hard it is to believe that this park is full of people in the summer. She has on a navy-blue ski parka, jeans and boots. Long (medium long) blond hair, a full mouth. Her name is Sandra. She does not give a last name, the way women in whorehouses, or waitresses, automatically state only their first name. He tells her his full name, as he would do with a new business acquaintance ("in business they have to appear very receptive and open . . ."). There is nothing left to say. He pretends to be amused by the little girl at play, asks her name. It is We-Chi, or something that sounds like that. The woman is obviously an American, the child too. "It means 'spirit rising from the great lagoon,'"—the woman says. She smiles. She has very white teeth. He says that the name is very pretty (Laura . . .), thinking she is crazy. "His name is

Mecca," the woman says, patting the blue bundle curved against her. Charles leans forward a little to see the smaller child's features. American. And sleeping. Charles nods, backs up a step to leave, and stumbles on We-Chi's rolling toy. He recovers himself, smiling foolishly, like the comedian deliberately flubbing an exit for laughs. If he had a hat, he could tip it, then trip again and fall on his face. "Good-bye," he says, and walks away. He has done a lot of walking and is getting tired. Good. If he gets tired, he won't have to think. Thinking this, he descends the hill. The sky is gray; it looks as though there will be no more sun before darkness. He sings a few words of "Mama You Been on My Mind" to himself as he walks down the hill and jumps over the stone border to the sidewalk. With his sore throat, he sounds very much like Rod Stewart. Tomorrow the sore throat may be worse, and he will have to take another day off from work. What a shame. Laura will call him at the office, a spur-of-the-moment desire to have lunch with him, and will be told that he is home sick. He will open his door and she will be there. She will simply be standing there, suffused in the aroma of chicken soup. Get this one down for posterity, Norman Rockwell. Sam's dog, who often visited my house, is dead; otherwise she could run yapping to another man's wife, who has come to bring me chicken soup. Maybe Edward Hopper? Or a cartoon?

He sits at the counter next to an old woman who smells of mint. Her hair rolls away from her face in even waves. A shopping bag is wedged between her feet. There is a dirty white towel over whatever is in the shopping bag. The woman is drinking black coffee, into which she empties three packs of "Sweet 'n Low." She is humming "Swing Low, Sweet Chariot." Charles orders tea with lemon. A priest comes in and greets the old woman enthusiastically. She moves from the counter to a booth with him, knocking Charles as she draws out her shopping bag. Something moves under the towel: a cat. A striped cat.

"Say 'I love you,' " the woman says, dangling the cat in front of the priest.

The priest laughs merrily. He'd do well in a Santa Claus audition, except that his eyes look mad—too many years squeezed in that collar. He orders a second cup of tea. The waitress says that he can use the same tea bag if he wants, but she will have to charge him twenty cents for water all the same. He says that's fine—and as he is sipping, the woman from the park comes in. She is carrying her son, who is still asleep. Or maybe he is dead. He always has fantasies of disaster. Squirrels crossing the street end up writhing and bloody in his mind, even if they make it safely across; sleeping people in public places are always dead; a knock on the door means machine-gun fire when he opens it to peek out.

"You look very upset," the woman says.

What did she say her name was? Betty . . . but last name what? Must remember to ask Betty her last name. This woman's name is something ordinary. Anne? Jane? Sandra! He says it out loud, victoriously.

"You had the right idea. It's cold today. It will snow."

"Is your little boy okay?" he says.

"Yes. He's had shots. For going abroad. They make him conk out. They don't bother you at all, do they, We-Chi?"

The little girl shakes her head. Her mother puts her on a stool beside Charles, unzips her jacket.

"Do you want hot chocolate?" she asks.

The little girl does.

"Where are you going?" Charles asks.

The Paris McDonald's . . .

"Turkey," the woman says. "My husband is working there."

"Do you remember Daddy?" the woman says to the little girl.

The little girl does not.

"She's just saying that. You get cranky in the afternoon, don't you, We-Chi?"

"Is your husband Turkish?" Charles asks. The children are so blond . . .

"Pittsburgh, Pennsylvania," the woman sighs. She orders one hot chocolate with whipped cream, one black coffee. There is a ring with a large sapphire on her left hand. Her hands look old, but the woman looks no older than thirty. The little girl spins around on the stool to look at the cat sitting on the table, licking its paws. The waitress looks as if she wouldn't say anything if someone brought an elephant in. Glassy-eyed, she shuffles over to the table to get the priest's order. "Sure the slaw is made with mayo," Charles hears her say.

"I want vegetable soup," the little girl says as the waitress lowers the cup in front of her.

"You're having that for supper," Sandra says. "Drink this now to make yourself warm."

The little girl turns away from the counter to look at the cat. The priest waves to her and she smiles shyly and swivels to face the counter again.

"Are you a student?" the woman asks.

"No. I'm playing hooky from my job."

"I played hooky all through college," the woman says. "I flunked out. Then I got married."

"What were you studying?" Charles asks.

"Math. After two years, when we get back from Turkey, I'm going back."

"Do you want to teach math?"

"No. I just like getting lost in calculations. I actually enjoy balancing my checkbook."

"I read somewhere that they were using calculators in elementary school instead of teaching arithmetic," Charles says.

"That's bright," the woman says. "My sister's got a kid in school down south and there are pictures in his textbook of black people in shanties, out on the front porch chewing watermelon. Educators are very bright."

Watermelon. Spring. In the park with Laura. "When you get done serving all the kids, take one of those ice cream cones to the woman on the bench and another one for her little girl," Charles had said, handing the ice cream man five dollars.

"The bright people are always in control," the woman says. "They're so bright that they sent my husband to Turkey, when he didn't know as much as the man already there that they sent back here to work in Wisconsin."

"How long has he been gone?"

"Five months. I have trouble remembering his face. I've got a friend whose husband died two years ago, and she says she has no idea at all what he looked like. He just looks like the picture on the piano. She says the picture was actually a consolation. It was taken when he graduated from college, so it was about ten years old. And she says now that's it—that's her husband."

Charles squirms.

"Here's my husband," the woman says, holding open the picture folder in her wallet. Her husband is a blond-haired, ordinary-looking man, tie knotted at his throat.

Charles nods.

"I'm bothering you," the woman says.

"No. You're not bothering me."

"I went to the park today because if I had stayed in that house another minute I was going to go nuts. My only friend is the woman I was telling you about, and she works all day. I don't know what to do with nobody to talk to."

"It's nice to talk to you," Charles says.

"I never thought I was *that* boring. I don't know why I don't have any friends. The only friends I had were his friends, and when he went to Turkey, good-bye friends. I've had to make arrangements to rent the house, take the kids to the doctors, I don't know. I'm always running around. There's always something to do. The days just get eaten up."

The woman finishes the last of her cold coffee, puts the spoon in the cup.

"We have to charge for second cups," the waitress says when she appears.

"That's all right. We-Chi, do you want another hot chocolate?"

We-Chi shakes her head. She watches the cat, curled on the table, swings her legs against the base of the stool.

"Does your wife work?" Sandra says.

"I'm not married."

"Man, there's days I'd like to be single. I might as well not be married, with my husband in Turkey."

We-Chi sneezes, rubs her nose on the back of her hand.

"Well," Charles says. "Soon you'll see your husband."

"It's a good thing. I've forgotten what he looks like."

Charles reaches in his pocket for change to leave a tip. The woman stirs her black coffee.

"I'll give you my phone number," the woman says. "You can come over some night for dinner. Would you do that?"

"Oh, that's very nice of you. Sure."

He wouldn't.

She writes her name and number on a napkin with a black felt-tip pen. Tiny lines wave off the letters. Her name is Sandra Ribert.

"Sandra Ribert," he says, folding the napkin.

"Ribert. Like the bread."

"Ribert," he repeats.

"I'd ask you for dinner tonight, but I just think that seems too bold, to be honest with you. So if you'd like to come, call. I'd like to have you."

"I was going somewhere tonight," he says. "But I will give you a call. Looks like your son is really sacked out," he says.

The woman nods. Leaving, he trips over a woman's umbrella. He pays at the cashier, sure that Sandra Ribert is staring at him. It makes him nervous, the way he always felt in high school, showering with everybody else. He always kept his eyes straight ahead, in case any of the boys thought he was looking at them. But they didn't, and that made it doubly hard to keep his eyes straight. Gym. Mr. Franklin was his gym teacher. He called everybody "you sons of bitches," even when he was addressing them individually. His wife taught girls' gym. She got pregnant twice and then quit. She called the girls "ladies." Every month the girls would compete against the boys at volleyball. Mr. Franklin would stand on the girls' side, blowing his whistle, and his wife would stand in back of the boys, blowing hers. Whistles blew and blew. It made it very exciting. Everybody thought the Franklins were pretty nice. After the second baby Mrs. Franklin didn't come back. Franklin was there, still shouting at the "sons of bitches." Once when Franklin was going around the track with them he grabbed his chest and fell in the gravel. Everybody rushed to him. Franklin smiled. "I just wanted to see if you sons of bitches really cared about me," he said. "I'll remember it at grading time." Nobody ever got less than a B from Franklin. Even the fat boys and the boy there was something wrong with got Bs. Franklin wrote a recommendation for Charles when he was applying to the state college. Charles had heard that a recommendation from a gym teacher would be a big help. He didn't know why. But he asked Franklin to write the recommendation and Franklin did it. He handed it to Charles the next gym period. Franklin had spelled the name of the month wrong, and he had commas where there shouldn't be any. Charles felt sorry for Franklin and had trouble looking at him after that.

Back on the street, Charles decides to climb over the stone wall and go through the park to get home. He was going to take the bus, but the buses are probably getting crowded by this hour, and since he's tired he might as well get exhausted. Nothing else to do. He crosses the street and pulls himself over the wall, walks up the slippery hill and back into the park. It is getting dark, and there is no one in the park. He jogs across the flat grass and doesn't slow down until he is ready to descend the hill at the opposite side of the park. He is panting. He doesn't even smoke. He swallows and realizes that his throat is much worse. He swallows again, to retest. It is much worse. He swallows again, fascinated with the soreness of his throat. He has to stick his chin out and swallow very hard to do it. Maybe he is getting the flu. He is sweating, too, but that might just be from jogging. He reaches in his pocket and takes out a tissue. Wait—that's not a tissue. It's Sandra Ribert's phone number. He puts the napkin against his forehead anyway, but stops before rubbing. Who knows. Maybe he will call her some day. She seemed okay. To be honest, she seemed better than Betty. He's not exactly sure what Betty lacks—other than not being Laura—but he's sure he deliberately forgot to get Betty's phone number. He even feels sorry for Betty. He feels sorry for himself, coming down with the flu. He thinks about something Susan said to him. She said, in effect, that everybody wasn't pitiful. Why did he feel sorry for all of them? Who's not pitiful? Sam, selling jackets? His mother, with her imaginary pains? Pete, stuck with her? Pamela Smith isn't pitiful. Sandra Ribert isn't pitiful. But Betty is. The blind man. Is the blind man pitiful? On general principles, sure. His boss? Nah—he's not pitiful. He has a summer cottage on Chesapeake Bay and a rich wife, and his son goes to an ivy league college. Sam's dead dog is pitiful. Only eight years old, and dead. It was such a good dog. Everything excited it: taking a ride in the car, going for a walk, dinner time, bedtime, playtime. Shit. He should have been nicer to the dog.

He walks all the way through the park without seeing anyone. Back on the sidewalk it's crowded, though. He starts jogging, wanting to be home sooner. He's too winded—can't do it. He resolves to jog more, to get in shape. He will have the flu, then get better and jog.

It gets dark too early in the winter. The streetlights are on when he gets to his house. He fishes in his pocket for his key. He has forgotten it. There is a spare in his car. He opens the car door and reaches around under the floor mat. Aha! The key and twenty-five cents. He lets himself in, walks across the living room and into the kitchen to start water boiling. There is a note from Sam: "Stopped by. Phone rang when I was here. Somebody named Pauline Reynolds. Will call you later myself.—S." Sam has gone away and left his own key to the house on the drainboard.

Charles puts up the thermostat before he takes off his coat. He rubs his throat, strokes downward, as though his throat might get soothed the same way a cat does. He is sipping his tea at the kitchen table, debating whether to go out to the grocery store for some food, when the phone rings.

"Hello?"

"Hello, Charles? This is Mrs. Reynolds."

"Yes," he says.

He forgot to call Susan. Elise is dead. Mrs. Reynolds is going to send hired killers after him.

"I have called to set your mind at rest. I knew you must be worried sick over my little Elise, although you were remarkably and reassuringly calm the other evening."

"Oh. She's okay. I knew she'd be okay, Mrs. Reynolds."

"Guess where she is?" Mrs. Reynolds says.

"There with you?"

"No. Guess again."

"At college."

He hates Elise. She bored him to death. This conversation bores him to death. It is better than being gunned to death by hired killers.

"No. Try again."

"I give up, Mrs. Reynolds."

"Guess! You have to guess!"

"New York?"

"No. Not New York."

Christ. Does he have to guess again?

"Guess again," Mrs. Reynolds says.

"Paris? I don't know. I have no way of knowing."

"I knew you'd never guess. Elise is in Vail, Colorado."

"That's good. I knew she'd be okay."

"I knew it too. Otherwise I wouldn't have let you placate me so easily on my last phone call to you. I was not drunk on that phone call, Charles, and it was not just flippancy, drunken flippancy, that made me terminate the conversation."

"I didn't think you were drunk, Mrs. Reynolds."

"I'm not drunk tonight either, but I will have to tell my husband I was because otherwise he sees no excuse for making long distance calls."

"I see," Charles says.

Charles thinks of a joke his father told him, the first joke he can remember: " 'I see' said the blind man. 'You do not,' said the deaf one." At the time, Charles had not understood. It was years before he could understand jokes. Jokes would be told to him tentatively, his father's face earnest and worried, knowing he would fail, much the way a doctor must set his face before telling his patient he has an inoperable melanoma, expecting, of course, that the man will never have heard the word "melanoma" before.

"What's she doing in Vail?" Charles says. Did Sam give her more than he said? Did he pay a lot for it and just not want to admit it? Maybe Sam has been down on his luck. . . .

"Skiing," Mrs. Reynolds says. "And here's another surprise. She's with *your* friend."

"My friend?" Charles says.

"Sam McGuire, the lawyer!" Mrs. Reynolds says.

Charles looks at Sam's note, at the key, at his cup of tea. Christ.

"You didn't know," Mrs. Reynolds says. "I've called with a surprise. They were going to send you a postcard, I'm sure, and I spoiled it."

"That's okay." Charles says. "I was wondering where Sam was."

"In Vail, Colorado. I'm so glad she's met a nice man. A lawyer. Is your friend very nice, Charles?"

A lawyer. Christ. Sam, who sells size thirty-eight regular jackets to men who wear forty-two extra long and gets commended for being made a monkey of. A lawyer. He didn't have the money to go to law school. He'll never have the money to go to law school, or to go skiing in Vail, Colorado.

"He's my best friend," Charles says.

"I'm sure he's a nice person if he took Elise skiing. That's where the President goes, isn't it?"

"Yes. I think so."

"Do you ski, Charles?"

She must be mistaking him for George Nimkis.

"No, I don't. It was very nice of you to call with this good news, Mrs. Reynolds, but I was just preparing my dinner."

"Wasn't your wife preparing dinner?"

"She usually does, but tonight I'm cooking."

"That's so nice of you. You and your wife must be such nice people. Was it your son who answered the phone earlier?"

"Yes. My son."

"It sounded like a grown-up."

"Oh, he's getting to be a big boy. Well, thanks again for calling."

He will call Susan and give her hell. He is getting pulled in deeper and deeper. If Sam the lawyer impregnates Elise, he will be held accountable. That's when she'd run home to her mother. The hired killers, after all.

"You're certainly welcome. And I appreciate you and your wife having Elise there. I think it's good for teenagers to be around young couples. My own husband is quite elderly. Elise always jokes that he's dead! Well, that isn't quite so. Elise said your wife was most gracious."

"She is. Good-bye, Mrs. Reynolds."

"Good-bye, Charles."

Charles picks up the phone again so soon after having hung up that there is no dial tone. He puts it down a few seconds, then picks it up again. He does not have her number. He hangs up and gets his name book, dials. Doctor Mark answers.

"Mark? Charles. How are you? Is Susan there?"

"Charles. How are you? I want to thank you for your hospitality of the other night. It was. Very nice of you to have me sleep over."

"I would have given you the bed, but I was in a bad mood. I'm still in a bad mood. May I speak to Susan?"

"She's at a sauna right now."

Christ. She's getting in the spirit of the bourgeoisie.

"Tell her to call me, please, when she gets back."

"Nothing wrong—not family trouble? If I may ask."

"Trouble with her bubbleheaded girlfriend. She's run off and told her parents Sam is with her. The guy who was sleeping at my place the night you were there."

"Ah. And it wasn't Sam, you mean. If I understand."

"That's right. And I don't want to get involved in this mess. So tell Susan to call me."

"So. How are things with you otherwise?"

"I think I'm getting the flu."

"That's been going around. Sorry I can't help you. That sounds. Like what a doctor would say. Ha-ha."

"Yeah. Well, tell Susan to call."

"Right," Mark says.

A sauna. Jesus Christ. Elise ought to be in the sauna. Trapped in it for good.

Charles dials Sam. Sam gets it on the second ring.

"Hello?"

"Hi. Guess where you are tonight."

"What do you mean guess where I am?"

"You think you're at home, don't you?"

"Are you drinking?"

"No. I'm on the rebound from a phone call with Mrs. Reynolds, who had turned up Elise. She's with you. You're both in Vail, Colorado."

Sam snorts.

"Guess what you are?" Charles says.

"You mean my profession?"

"Yeah."

"I don't know. What?"

"A lawyer."

"That bitch. I told her I wanted to go to law school."

"No sooner said than done."

"You sound funny still, Charles. You feeling okay?"

"Sore throat."

"I came by earlier. Did you see my note?"

"Yeah. You left the key here, too."

"Oh, yeah. I was wondering what happened to that."

"What did you come by for?"

"To see if you'd already eaten."

"Oh. Have you eaten?"

"Yeah," Sam says. "Three hot dogs and a can of beans."

"Ugh."

"I don't have any money."

"Then how were you going to go out to eat?"

"You were going to take me."

"Oh. Well, sorry I missed you."

"Where were you?"

"I took the day off from work and wandered around. Went to the park."

"Feed the birds and feel sorry for yourself?"

"No. Forgot to take anything for the birds and felt guilty."

The young in one another's arms, birds in the trees . . .

"They've been laying people off at work."

"They have? Are you worried?"

"Sure I'm worried. Where am I going to find another job." Sam doesn't ask it as a question.

"You could find another one."

"You said that with the same enthusiasm you give your mother pep talks with: 'You can find better things to do than sit in the tub. . . .' "

Charles laughs.

"I wish I could sit around in a tub. There's something comforting about that. Just sitting in all that warm water, nothing to do," Sam says.

"It's very Freudian."

"It's very comforting. The hell with Freud. I'm going to go sit in the tub."

"I'll be talking to you."

"Good-bye," Sam says.

Charles decides to take a hot shower. Have one more cup of tea—he drinks so much tea he can never sleep—and stand under the hot water. His legs are tired from so much walking. He's sweated a lot; he should wash his hair too. It would be so nice to lie on a raft, to float off the coast of Bermuda, sun shining, wind blowing, drifting. Rum drinks. White shells. Pink flowers. Bicycles. His parents used to take them to the beach in the summer. It was a crowded beach, Popsicle sticks everywhere, stores that sold dirty sweatshirts, fat women in straw hats, the men in matching straw hats, with miniature beer cans attached to the hatband. Auctioneers who kept shouting for everyone to move in, oriental rug shops, gift shops with naked plastic statues that could be filled with water so

they'd pee, drugstores that smelled of fish (they always
had tanks of goldfish in the back, and dyed birds), the
amusement park with puddles of beer and candy apples
half eaten. His father always had him by the hand in the
amusement park, guiding him around puddles. He went in
a house of mirrors with his father. It was a little too hot
in there. His father's laughter was forced. They bumped
their heads against the glass. They kept seeing the same
people inside over and over. Everybody groped forward
with their hands out, got knocked in the head anyway.
The kids ran around laughing, as though they knew where
they were going. And on the way out, when they finally
found their way out, there was a moving belt they had to
walk down, which made them teeter out the door. The
railing ended just before you came through the plastic
fringe curtain to the outside. His mother bought him a
bucket and shovel and several different molds at the grocery store to take to the beach. Two kids in the neighborhood had them and Charles had asked for one. The other
kids had a starfish mold, a fish mold, a circle, a square, a
triangle mold, and a mermaid mold. Charles's bucket and
shovel came with a bucketful of triangle molds in different
colors. "Maybe it's a different manufacturer?" his mother
said. "How should I know?" He took the label down to
his friend's house. Same manufacturer. He reported back
to his mother. "How the hell should I know?" she said.
"Can't you use that triangle thing? What's wrong with it?"
He thought she was very stupid for getting the worst one
in the store. She didn't even check. He told his father
that, behind his mother's back. "I'm sure she didn't check,"
his father said. "But she's awfully busy on grocery day,
you know." Charles hated grocery day. She was always
very busy, his sister in the grocery cart, his mother holding
his hand and pushing the cart with her other hand. Why
did he have to hold her hand? He wasn't like the other
kids: he didn't pull things off shelves or wander away. And
finally she said they were just too much for her and left

them with a neighbor when she went shopping. What had they ever done? It never failed—every time she'd get to the checkout counter she'd say to him, "Wait with your sister, I'll be right back," and run off for another item, and he'd stand there just knowing that his sister would start crying or that it would get time to unload the cart and pay for the food and he wouldn't have any money. When he had to start unloading and his mother wasn't back he was frantic. He dropped cans, couldn't get a grip on the things to lift them out. She always took so long. He used to think she'd run off and left them, that not only would he have no money to pay for the food, but he'd have to get Susan home, and he didn't even know for sure in which direction to walk. He used to watch the route his mother drove to the store very carefully. He memorized a couple of street names. Why couldn't she shop at a closer store? He had asked her that, and she had thrown a fit. "He even criticizes where I shop! Who does he think he is?" His father was always in the middle.

He picks up the phone. "Hello?"

"Hi. What's up?" Susan says.

"What's up? I'll tell you what's up. I'll tell you what I'd like to have up—my hand against Elise's bubble head. I'd like to slug her. What the hell would you bring a crazy girl like that home for? Why did I have to end up with her? Have you heard from her?"

"Don't get excited."

"Have you ever dealt with her mother? The woman is *nuts*. She called and nearly had me crazy because Elise never showed up after she left here. Tonight she called with the news that she was in Vail, Colorado, with my friend Sam the lawyer."

"Oh no," Susan says.

"Where she really is, I wouldn't know. But I want you to make it your business to find out and to tell her that she's not to implicate me in this, or the lawyer and I will beat her to a pulp."

"I'll call Denise. She tells Denise everything."

"She should have told *you* a little more about where she was going."

"Yeah. I'm sorry."

"That mother of hers is nuts, Susan. I've got a nut mother of my own to deal with. And I don't want to get dragged into this thing."

"She probably *is* in Colorado. She probably picked up somebody and went to Colorado with him."

"Find out. I want to know where she really is. And I want word to get to her that she should cool it about how nice my wife was to her and how swell Sam the lawyer is. Tell her to make up lies about somebody else."

"I will."

"And call me back and let me know where she is."

"Okay."

"Good-bye."

"Wait. Before you hang up, how's Mom?"

"I don't know. I'm going over there for dinner this weekend."

"She's cooking again?"

"Of course not. Pete is."

"That's nice of him."

"Yeah. We'll all have a great time. Especially if we don't have to haul her out of the tub at dinner time."

"I know. Well, I'm sorry about all the trouble Elise caused you, and I'll call back when I find out something."

"By the way, Susan. Is the funny way Mark talks an affectation?"

"I'll write you," she says.

"You can't tell me?"

"I'll write you."

"He's right there?"

"Yes. The sauna was great. I think you would enjoy it."

This is just the way Laura would talk to him if he had

called—a one-way conversation that made no sense. We have enough brushes. Thank you for calling.

Charles goes into the bathroom and begins undressing. He has lost weight. He has to remember to start grocery shopping again, lay in some food. Too bad Sam had already eaten. Not that he's hungry. He piles his clothes on the toilet and steps into the shower. It feels good. It would be nicer to be stretched out, though, on a raft in Bermuda, dangling his fingers in the cool water. Sharks would slice them off. He has always had problems with reality encroaching on his fantasies. One night when he was dreaming, a figure actually stepped into his dream and told him it was time to stop dreaming. Charles woke up and sure enough, the electricity had gone off and the alarm would not have rung. The only problem was that it was six A.M., and he could have slept until seven-thirty. Except that there was no way to set the alarm. So he sat there in bed, reading, for an hour and a half, thinking about the figure who walked into his dream. What to make of the fact that the man looked like Jesus?

The phone is ringing as he steps out of the shower. For a man with no friends, he thinks, the phone certainly rings a lot.

"Hello?"

"Charlie? Hello. Bill."

He did not need to identify himself. Only one person calls Charles "Charlie": his boss.

"Hi, Bill. What can I do for you?"

"What can I do for *you?* Hear you're not well."

"I'll probably be back tomorrow."

"What is it, the flu?"

"I thought so, but it's just a sick feeling. My throat's pretty sore."

"You ought to drink some whiskey with lemon. Put sugar in if it proves too much for you. Ha!"

"I might take that advice."

"My son goes to Dartmouth with a kid—his roommate,

actually—who had a sore throat for two months. Finally the doctor sent him to a shrink. The shrink told him his throat was sore because he was deliberately constricting it to stop himself from screaming."

"God. That's awful."

"Those shrinks are pretty clever fellows, huh?"

For some reason, his boss has been trying to find out for a year if he ever went to a shrink. He has not.

"I guess they are."

"But listen, what I called about was this: would you mind if I went through your desk if you're not there tomorrow? I *know* I left my silver pen in your office. You probably put it in the drawer."

"I don't remember seeing a silver pen."

"Must have left it there. I think I had my pen with me on Monday because I went over that report with you. Well, I wouldn't make anything of this, but my boy gave me the pen and he's going to be coming home and he wants to visit my office. My wife put him up to that, to make me feel good. Anyway, it was a present from him for my birthday, and I thought it should be on the desk."

"Sure, Bill. I don't care if you look."

"I thought it was only polite to call. It would look bad if you were out sick and I started rummaging through your things."

"You could have looked anyway, Bill."

"Thanks, Charlie. I was sure you'd be amenable, but wanted to check."

"How's your son doing at Dartmouth?"

"Very well. He wishes he could be at Harvard, though, and he's making his mother very unhappy. He writes her the silliest 'If only' letters. I don't know what to say to cheer him up. What can I say? Harvard wouldn't have him."

"Well, Dartmouth is a classy place."

Bill loves to hear that things are classy: his son's college, his shoes.

"Sure it's classy. Try to tell him that. He says it's cold, and he loves Harvard Square. I was at Harvard Square once. Cars and buses and cops. It was a mess."

"Well, maybe he can get into graduate school there."

"That's what my wife writes him. I tell her, don't write that. Drop the whole subject. But he's her son. You know."

"Yeah."

I have a son of my own, I should know. Just ask Mrs. Reynolds if I don't have a son. . . .

"So. We'll be seeing you later. I hope it's not the flu."

"So do I. See you later, Bill."

He goes into the bedroom, puts the towel over the lamp, and gets into bed. He is so tired he's almost dizzy. He gets up again and sets the alarm, then goes back to bed. The hell with the pajamas. He turns out the light.

He is almost asleep when the phone rings. It couldn't be Laura. But what if it is? He gets up and quickly walks to the phone. It is Pamela Smith, calling to thank him for his kindness and to say that he is really a very nice person. She is calling from a motel. She got a ride to California. She thanks him for helping her clear out her thoughts. She thanks him for the breakfast. "At one time I was in love with you," she says. He does not know what to answer. He realizes, standing there, that he should have slept with her. He tells her to have a good trip and to enjoy herself in California. She says that she will make him something out of silver. "I didn't get you out of bed, did I?" she says. He says she didn't. It's the truth; Laura did.

Chapter 8

He stops on the way to work to get gas. It is a self-service station. On the gas pump is a piece of cardboard: "See cashier for transaction settlement." Why not "Pay cashier"? He is in a bad mood. He was not going to go to work at all, except that he began to feel much sicker and thought that if he got out of the house he might not think about it. In the house, he had thought about weeping in bed, calling Sam at work to tell him to come right over. He had even thought of calling his mother. That's when he decided it would be best if he went to work.

When he walked into his office Bill was there, sitting in his chair, going through his desk.

"Thank God I called you!" Bill said, shooting up, as though he'd been caught doing something terrible anyway. "If I hadn't called, imagine what you would have thought if you'd come in and found me with my hand in the till!"

"Find your pen?"

"I *just* got here," Bill says.

"Try the drawer on the right," Charles says.

"How are you feeling, Charlie? Try my home remedy?"

"Didn't have any whiskey. I'll get some on the way home."

"You don't look good," Bill says.

"I feel awfully queasy."

"What are you doing here?"

"I just didn't feel like lying around the house."

"Yeah. It must be rough when you're sick, not having a wife to take care of you."

"Yeah. So I figured I'd come in."

"Well, take it easy."

"I will."

Charles sits in a chair against the wall, waiting for Bill to finish.

"Sometimes having a wife can present problems, too. Last night she got herself into a state about my boy not being accepted at Harvard. A very paranoid thing about how they would have taken him if he'd been black. I spent an hour calming her down. Her sister married a colored fellow ten years ago, and you should have heard her then. I told her—you don't have to see your sister. What does it matter to you? She hasn't seen her sister in ten years."

"There's too much emphasis put on what college you go to," Charles says.

"That's what I tell her. And Dartmouth isn't the small time. She cries because he's told her it's very cold there. She thinks he's suffering in the cold. She talks about him like he's a stray cat or something."

"That's too bad. I hope she starts feeling better about it."

Bill stands up. "I can't find it. Thanks for letting me look. If you see it around, let me know."

"A silver pen?"

"A narrow Cross number. My wife gave it to my son to give me for my birthday. You know."

Charles looks at the paperwork he has to do. He closes the door and takes out his cassette and earphones and puts on "John Wesley Harding." He works while he listens. When the tape has finished he clicks it off and stands up and stretches. His head is hot. He walks down the hallway to the library and stands looking at it. He goes in and asks for something he doesn't need—a financial report from 1970. The new librarian (he thinks, sadly, that she's not so new any more) writes the information down on a slip of paper and goes into the stacks to get it. He thinks about following her, whispering to her that he loves her, pinning her against the shelves. He shakes his head, smiling. Imagine Bill's reaction: "Why, I just left his office and he was fine. He'd been sick, you know. . . ." Imagine the librarian's reaction. Imagine even thinking of doing such a thing. When he gets the report he thanks the librarian and goes back to his office and gets four aspirin, goes to the drinking fountain and takes them, one at a time, tipping his head back to swallow each time. He reminds himself of a bobbing-bird toy he had when he was young. The birds would dip interminably over a glass of water. One night he felt sorry for them because they weren't getting any rest and poured the glass of water on the floor and attached the birds to the empty glass. He denied doing it. Not much was made of it. His mother showed his father the wet spot in the rug, his father shrugged and filled the glass again.

He leaves the office at quarter after eleven, kidding himself that he's going to meet Laura at school. He even drives to the school and circles the block, but of course Rebecca goes to school a full day now, and Laura won't be there for her until three. He could go back then. Except that he doesn't want to be pushy. Of course she would be polite. And beautiful. But she would think it was in bad taste. Maybe she'll call. Maybe he will drive over around three.

Three o'clock comes and goes, and he is still working. At three-thirty Betty comes in for the typing and asks how he's feeling. He is embarrassed, thinking, with his fever, that she knows he deliberately forgot to ask her number. Renounced. The villain.

"Okay," he says.

"Do you need aspirin or anything?"

"No thanks," he says.

If only she would leave him alone and not make him feel guiltier.

"Okay," she says, taking the reports out of the basket.

"I'll get these back to you in the morning. Is that soon enough?"

"Certainly," he says.

She leaves. He looks up only briefly, when she is almost out the door. The black boots are back. She has on a red miniskirt and a white sweater. She slumps. He should call her, put a little romance in her life, tell her he loves her, marry her. He still doesn't know her last name.

Leaving work early (four twenty-five), he sees Sid from his floor in the elevator.

"Sid, do you know Betty's last name? Betty in the typing pool?"

"I can't say that I do."

A curious look from Sid. Sid knows. Everything. Both sides of it. That Betty wants him to call, that he is going to call. Well, not without her name or number he isn't. He could call Laura and ask. That would be loutish; it would be something one of Sam's old girlfriends would do to him. And Sam wouldn't mind. Would Laura?

He remembers, finally, to go grocery shopping. There is nothing in the entire store he wants to eat. He buys two frozen pizzas, some soup, some salami and cheese, a roast beef, and a can of lima beans. He goes to the dairy counter and gets another kind of cheese and a half gallon of milk. A hippie is standing at the far end, a half gallon of milk opened and being poured into his mouth. What if he's caught? The hippie raises his milk carton in salute. Charles waves back. He leaves immediately, in case a store official thinks he knows the hippie.

Charles always has a moment of apprehension at the checkout counter, even though he has money. He checks his wallet several times while he's still in the store. Other shoppers probably feel sorry for him, having to economize, poor fellow, but that's all right. That's better than putting all his things on the checkout counter and not having the money. He leaves the store and drives home. Sam's car is out front. Sam is in the shower. He is doing his "singing in the tub" song, but he is quieter than usual. Usually he can hear Sam kicking (Sam has confessed to this), but the legs will not break tonight. Figuring that Sam hasn't eaten, he unwraps the roast and puts it in a pan in the oven. He opens the can of lima beans and dumps them in a pan. He takes a piece of salami out of the white paper it is wrapped in and rolls it into a little tube, bites into it. It's very strong. Too strong. He finishes it anyway, goes into the living room and turns the thermostat up, sits down with his coat still on. There is a postcard from Pamela Smith: "The Clocks: Walter Tandy Murch, American 1907–1967." The message: "Thank you again for being so nice to me. I've found a ride to L.A. Will try to call. P.S." It takes him a while to realize that there was never an additional message she left off; they are her initials. In fact, it takes that so long to register that he also goes into the bedroom and looks for the thermometer. He can't find it. He goes back to the living room and looks at the rest of the mail. Kittens are apparently no longer being thrown out in trash cans: there is nothing from the Humane Society. There is a notice that he should make a dentist appointment. There is also a note from Pete: "Mommy (crossed out) Clara suggested I send a note to remind you of your dinner invitation this Sat. We will be eating around seven, unless anything goes wrong with the chicken. I'm going to stuff it. I hope there are no hard feelings. Called the other night but the line was busy. Clara has been working a nice needlepoint footrest of a poddle that she thinks would be nice to put in front of my chair. Be sure to ask to see it. So far, the baths are at a minimum. I really enjoyed that drink you and Susan had with me. Maybe we can do it again sometime. I'll see you Sat. Clara suggested that I write. I'll show her the envelope now."

"Hi," Charles says to Sam.

"To dispense with formalities, I'm out of a job."

"What? When did you find out?"

"Five o'clock. I was going to work until eight tonight, when they came around and told me that it wouldn't be necessary."

"Oh, no. You said you were selling a lot of jackets."

"I don't know. They were very vague. They don't even do you the favor of saying one specific thing that can stick in your mind for you to brood over."

"What are you going to do?"

"Collect unemployment as long as I can."

"Couldn't they have switched you to another one of their stores?"

"I didn't ask. They actually sent two of them around, probably in case I decided to take one of them on. They were both big."

"Those bastards."

"I looked around me at the rows of jackets, and I just couldn't do anything but nod. I guess I'm glad to be out of there. At least for a while I can collect unemployment."

"How much will that give you?"

"I'm not sure yet."

"That's awful, Sam."

"Now that I'm out of work I won't have to pay back the college loan. Maybe I'll actually have it easier."

"It's a rotten way to have it easier."

"I don't know. What did I do with the money anyway? I just realized going home that I don't go out on dates any more. I don't do anything any more."

"You sound like Pete."

"Pete says he doesn't do stuff, but he does. He's always doing stuff for your mother. I used to do stuff for my dog. Now she's dead."

"Don't start feeling bad about the dog. Why don't you get yourself another dog? You'd have time to train it."

"Great. Get fired, and it gives you time to swat a dog's ass when it shits in the house."

"You get sarcastic every time I tell you to get another dog."

"I liked the dog I had."

"Go on, get another dog."

"Get another girl friend."

"Okay," Charles says. *"Touché."*

Sam slumps in the chair.

"I've got a roast beef in the oven. Maybe we ought to go out and get a bottle of wine and celebrate: your loss of a job, my loss of Laura."

"Maybe we should get a bottle of whiskey, too, and finish it off after the celebration."

"Come on," Charles says. "Want to go get some wine?"

"Yeah, I guess so. I haven't had a decent dinner for so long I can't remember."

"Your car or mine?" Charles asks.

"Mine's okay," Sam says. He gets up, shakes his head. "I don't think this is registering yet. I just realized that tomorrow I won't have anywhere to go."

They walk out the front door. The door on the passenger's side is frozen shut; Sam has to push it open from the inside. The upholstery on the front seats is ripped, and the rug has pulled away from the door and curled up on both sides. There is a crack across the windshield that begins in the middle and takes a ninety-degree turn across Charles's line of vision. A truck threw a rock into the window. Sam's insurance didn't cover it. Charles thinks about Pamela Smith talking about marriage as ashes—the wind will blow the ashes away. She should have been a poet. She did write poetry, in college, and then again for the feminist newspaper she wrote for. But that was ugly poetry, poetry about slippery tongues and pendulous breasts. He is glad he didn't sleep with her when she spent the night.

"Which one?" Sam says. "The new one on the avenue?"

"Sure. Whatever's closest."

"Do you have money, by the way? I guess it goes without saying that I'm broke."

"Yeah. I've got money." He knows he has thirty-some dollars. If he were going into the grocery store he would already have checked his wallet a couple of times, but this is just a liquor store. He has a twenty and a ten for sure.

"I actually think I might be doing better temporarily, not having to pay so much money back to that bank for the loan."

"Like I said—it's a great way to do better."

"Yeah, I know. Wait until my father hears about this."

"Don't tell him. What's he got to know for?"

"I don't intend to tell him."

Sam's father lives thirty miles away. He has an apartment. Sam's mother lives in their house, which is only fifteen minutes from where Sam lives. Although sometimes she moves into Sam's father's apartment. And sometimes, rarely, Sam's father shows up at the house. There are always suitcases all over. Sam's father retired, then went back to work; his mother took a job, then quit, and at last report was thinking about studying to be a beautician. There was a fight about that, and Sam's father moved out of the house, back to the apartment.

They should get rid of the house and live together in the apartment and send Sam to law school. Neither one likes him well enough to do it. Sam is their only child. Sam's mother had a hysterectomy after Sam was born. She tells people that she couldn't have another child because of a delicate heart. She tells them she has had heart surgery. She even buys a salt substitute for her bad heart.

"What do you hear from him lately, anyway?" Charles asks.

"He called to say that my mother was over at his apartment. I never call her—I don't know why he'd think I should know."

"How long have they been shuttling back and forth?"

"Eight years, I guess. Maybe a little longer."

"What was Christmas like?"

"Awful, as usual. His sister was invited to dinner, and she showed up at the apartment, and nobody was there. She called from the lobby and made a big thing of it—how they should tell her where they were living. She showed up late and everybody was crabby and hungry. It took her about twice as long to get there as it should have. She made a big thing saying that all the way over she kept thinking that she should just turn around and go back to her apartment and eat alone."

"That's all, though?"

"Well, every time my mother fixes dinner Eleanor makes her feel bad by saying, if there's no parsnips, how much she likes parsnips, or if there's no bread, how much she likes bread. And she pretends I'm still in college and asks how I'm doing there. I don't know why they invite her."

"Is she still working?"

"Yeah. It's her last year. She told her boss she was retiring next December and he said, 'I've been in hell so many years I've gotten used to it. What will I do without you?'"

"How long has she been there?"

"Forty years."

"Jesus. Imagine typing for forty years."

"I can't. My imagination is dead. I don't even dream any more. I was reading that Fritz Perls book over Christmas. Fritz suggests you sit down and ask your dreams why they are eluding you. You know: you set up two chairs and run back and forth."

"Tried it?"

"Are you kidding?"

Sam double parks in front of the liquor store.

"Since you've got the money . . ." Sam says.

Charles goes in and buys a bottle of bordeaux. The man behind the cash register has bushy white hair and eyebrows. He always says the same thing: "Should prove drinkable." Charles gives him the $5.80 and nods. Then the man asks if he wants a bag. He doesn't. He walks back to the car. Sam has turned on the radio and "Benny and the Jets" is playing. Charles wonders if that guy in Mendocino is still playing his jew's-harp and singing that song. He is glad he is not on the West Coast. He is too old for the West Coast. He found his Frisbee in the closet a few weeks ago and didn't even give it a toss.

"Pamela Smith was over at my house the other night."

"Is that right? I thought she was in California."

"She came back for some reason. She was working in a canning factory out there and it freaked her out, so she came back. Then she decided to go back out and not work in a canning factory."

"That girl was nuts. Interesting, though."

"She's got a friend out there who's going to teach her to be a silversmith."

Sam shrugs. "Beats selling jackets."

"You don't think there's any way you could go to law school, huh?"

"Nope."

"Well, maybe eventually."

"Sure. I'll marry a rich woman. Actually, even if I had the money, I think my brain has atrophied too much to understand what anybody's talking about."

"You exaggerate."

"I got a letter from my landlord last week saying that the rent was going up in March, and I had to read it twice to get it through my head what was being said to me."

"He probably wrote it that way on purpose."

Sam shrugs. "I don't know what I'm going to do if this car falls apart. Hear that? If it's the carburetor I'm okay, but if it's the engine, I'm sunk."

Sinking. Bermuda. The sharks. The fountain.

"It's probably the carburetor."

"It's probably the engine."

The car turns into Charles's block. The people in this

neighborhood go to bed very early. They are almost all asleep by ten, and some go to bed this early—before eight o'clock. Burglars are always breaking in on sleeping couples.

"Did you hear if Rod Stewart was dead?"

"No. Why do you think he's dead?"

"Some clerk in Housewares told me that this morning."

"Not as far as I know," Charles says.

Sam parks. This time Charles's door sticks from inside and Sam has to go around and pull on it. That doesn't open it. Charles slides across the seat, tearing it more, and gets out Sam's side.

"That's how it protests its existence. One morning I'll go out and both doors will be stuck."

They go into the house and Charles looks at the roast. It looks like it might be done. He sticks a fork in it. It might or might not be done. He leaves it in, uncorks the bottle of wine, and turns on the heat under the lima beans.

"This is going to be swell," Sam says.

"Yeah. We eat such rotten stuff usually that I'm surprised we're still alive."

"What the hell. You could know everything like Adelle Davis and still be dead."

"At least she got to take a lot of acid and trip for half a year until she died."

"Who'd want to trip for half a year?"

The hippie drinking milk in the food store?

"Susan says there aren't many drugs around any more."

"Yeah. Things must really be strange on campus now. Having fraternities and proms and swallowing goldfish again."

"What do you think they do to expand their minds now?" Charles says.

"Get engaged to doctors. I don't know."

"I wonder if she'll have a formal wedding. The whole bit."

"That girl I told you about before—the one in Housewares. She's keeping her wedding to five thousand bucks, she told me today. She's compromising and not having matches and napkins."

"That's sad."

"I don't know. Maybe there's something to it. It just seems silly to me."

"My sister seems silly to me."

Charles gets napkins and plates out of a cupboard. Sam gets forks and knives. "We don't need spoons, do we?"

Sam always asks that.

"No," Charles says.

"Shit. This is going to be great."

Charles lifts the roast out of the oven, puts it on a plate and carries it to the table. He goes back and gets the pan of lima beans, pours most of the water into the sink, and carries the pan to the table. He goes back and turns off the oven and the burner and gets the wine. He takes the wine to the table, where Sam is sitting, then goes to the kitchen for the glasses.

"I should have thought of glasses," Sam says.

He brings two thermal mugs (a gas-station giveaway of many years ago) and puts one in front of Sam.

"Thanks," Sam says.

"Sure," Charles says.

Sam picks up his steak knife and begins to cut the roast.

"Thick?" Sam says.

"Yeah. Please."

Sam begins to carve. "It won't cut thick," he says.

"Thin is okay."

Sam cuts several thin pieces and puts them on Charles's plate.

"Thanks," Charles says. "Lima beans?"

"Please."

Charles lifts the pan closer to Sam's plate, pushes the lima beans over the rim of the pan with his fork.

"Thanks," Sam says. "Wine?"

Charles nods.

"Say when," Sam says.

Charles says nothing, so Sam fills the thermal mug. He pours some into his thermal mug.

"Great wine," Charles says.

"It looks good," Sam says. He lifts his mug and sips. "It is good."

Charles spins the bottle to face him so he can read the label.

"What kind of wine is that?" Sam says.

"Bordeaux."

"French wines are expensive now, aren't they?"

"Yeah," Charles says. "But they've never been cheap."

"Well," Sam says. "This is a fine celebration."

"I'm glad you like it."

"Beats Christmas dinner all to hell. She really *had* parsnips, to shut Eleanor up. Have you ever tasted a parsnip?"

"Not to my knowledge."

"They're foul. They smell like Vanish."

"What's that?"

"Stuff you put down your toilet."

"Shut up about the toilet when I'm eating."

"Sorry. I was just thinking about those rotten parsnips."

"Drop it. I don't want to think about the toilet when I'm eating."

"More lima beans?" Sam says.

"Thanks," Charles says.

"More than that?" Sam says.

"That's fine."

Sam dumps the rest on his plate trying, unsuccessfully, to hold back the water with his fork.

"Some frozen vegetables taste very good," Sam says.

"Oh yeah? Well, they're very good. There's plenty of vegetables I don't mind. Hell. I never eat vegetables any more."

"We're probably going to get scurvy or something. Did you know that when old people have varicose veins it's the start of scurvy? Malnutrition?"

"Shut up about disgusting diseases while I'm eating. You don't hear me talking about the toilet, do you?"

"Stop mentioning the goddamn toilet."

"This is really very good wine," Sam says.

"It ought to be."

"It was awfully nice of you to fix us this big dinner."

"Don't tell me that. I had to endure a whole night of Pamela Smith telling me what a nice guy I was. I was so bored I forgot to lay her."

"You used to lay her, didn't you?"

"Yeah. I used to."

"That's what I thought," Sam says. "More roast?"

"Yeah. I could use some more. It's a big roast, isn't it? I never notice weight when I buy them. I just pick them up."

"What would Betty Furness say about that?"

"She's not the one any more. It's somebody else."

"Who is it?"

"I don't know."

"Well, you knew Betty Furness was out."

"I'm just smart. Like that girl who said Rod Stewart was dead."

"I'm pretty sure he's not dead. We could put on the news tonight, though."

"Yeah. We ought to check. He *is* a junkie, isn't he?"

"Not that I know of."

"Well, he could have died anyway."

"Sure," Charles says.

"She just sort of worked that information in when she was talking about her wedding. She talks about it all the

time to make me feel bad, I think. She always wanted me
to ask her out. Somebody told me that."

"Why didn't you ask her out?"

"Who's got the money to go on dates? Anyway, I'm
too old to go on dates."

"You're twenty-seven."

"Dates are a waste of time. I'd just as soon scrub the
toilet."

"Jesus! Shut up about the toilet."

"I'm sorry. I wasn't thinking."

"Do you want the rest of this wine?"

"No. You finish it," Sam says.

"Okay, I will."

"This was just great. I'm not even depressed now."

"It'll hit you in the morning," Charles says.

"Thanks for reminding me."

"Sorry."

Charles drains his mug. "You know, if you want to,
you can move in here. I don't mind having you around."

Sam looks up. His fork is raised above his roast.
"That's very nice of you. But I couldn't do that."

"Why not?"

"I don't know. It's your place."

"Hell, if your landlord's going to raise your rent, what
are you going to do?"

"I haven't thought about it. Maybe I could pay the rent
okay, not having to pay back the loan."

"How much is it being raised?"

"Twenty-five bucks."

"And how much unemployment will you be collect-
ing?"

"I told you before. I don't have any idea."

"Call tomorrow and find out."

"Stop talking about tomorrow."

"Would you like some coffee?"

"Please."

Charles gets up, taking his plate and Sam's, and goes to

the kitchen. He did not turn off the burner after all. He turns it off. Then he puts it on again—silly to turn it off—and puts the coffeepot on it.

"If you think there's milk, there isn't," Charles says.

The hippie raising the milk carton, smiling . . .

"I don't drink milk in my coffee."

"Oh yeah? That's good."

"You've been watching me drink black coffee for years."

"Yeah, but I've only seen you drinking coffee when you're sobering up. I thought you drank it black to sober up."

"No. I drink it black anyway."

Charles drums on the table with his fork. He puts his fork on the plate with what's left of the roast.

"Thanks for offering, though," Sam says. "I appreciate it."

"I think you're nuts not to take me up on it. It's a big house. I would have asked you years ago, but all those women trailing in and out would have depressed me."

"You've given up on me too, huh?"

"What do you mean?"

"On me finding a woman."

"I don't care if you find a woman or not. I just don't want a lot of them trailing in here."

"Women don't like me anyway."

Charles shrugs. "Women are getting strange."

"I read *The Dialectic of Sex*. You ever read that?"

"What are you reading all this junk for?" Charles says.

"That one's not junk. She's exactly right. Men are incapable of loving."

"You're out of your mind. Why did you start reading all that crap?"

"I don't know. I read a lot of stuff over Christmas."

"You ought to be in law school. Then you wouldn't have time to poison your mind with that crap."

"No. If you read this one you wouldn't think it was crap."

"I thought I was spared when Pamela Smith was here. She leaves with no feminist lecture at all, and you start in."

"I didn't start in. I mentioned that I read a good book."

"I'm getting the coffee."

"But anyway, it was nice of you to ask me over here."

Charles goes into the kitchen, lifts the boiling water from the burner, and pours it into two cups. He forgot the coffee. He gets a spoon and puts coffee in the boiling water, stirs, and walks back to the dining room.

"I was thinking about my dog," Sam says.

"Don't think about your dog. You'll get depressed."

"I already am depressed. I was thinking about my dog the whole time you were gone. You know what I was thinking? That I should have let the vet do an autopsy. She might have been poisoned. Somebody might have poisoned her."

"Nobody poisoned your dog."

"I'm not paranoid. I don't think it was deliberate. I just think that there might have been poison somewhere and she might have eaten it."

"Her heart gave out."

"Yeah. Unless she was poisoned."

"Stop depressing yourself."

"Shit. She was a great dog. I wouldn't want to think that anybody poisoned her."

"So. You don't have an autopsy, you don't have to think that."

"I guess so," Sam says. "But I feel like I ought to know for sure."

"If she was poisoned you'd go around mad all the time. She's dead, whatever she died of."

"Okay. I don't want to talk about my dog any more."

The dog, head thrown back, silly toy in her mouth . . .

"I should have bought something for dessert," Charles says.

"Couldn't hold it," Sam says.

"Ice cream," Charles says.

Sam looks into his coffee cup.

"What's the matter? Now you're feeling rotten because you think somebody poisoned your dog."

"Not just that. I don't have a job, and I'm in debt, and women don't like me any more. I've been reading those books to try to find out how women think."

"That's pathetic."

"It's not pathetic. You ought to read some of that stuff. You'd never believe what's going through their heads."

Sam, slapping his mother's hand . . .

"I don't want to know. I've got enough crap knocking around my own head."

"But you're right. Women have changed. You've got to try to understand them now."

"What for?"

"So you can get one."

"I don't want one. I mean, the only one I want is taken."

"You still thinking about her?"

"She was so great. How can I not think about her?"

"I don't know. I was just asking."

"Yeah. I'm still thinking about her. I used to dream about her, but now I've stopped. I wish I could still dream about her."

"Old Everly Brothers philosophy, huh?"

"Yeah. The Everly Brothers."

The dancing instructor, hands clapping together: get closer, get closer. . . .

"What are you grinning about? We're old fuckers. We remember the Everly Brothers."

"I wonder what happened to them?"

"They're still around, aren't they?"

"I don't know. You never hear about the Everly Brothers."

"I could check in with that girl at work and see if they're still alive. Except that I won't be going to work any more."

"Don't think about that. You'll depress yourself."

"Okay. Say something funny."

"One time somebody sent Cary Grant a telegram: 'How old Cary Grant?' Cary Grant wired back, 'Old Cary Grant fine, how you?' "

Charles's father had told him that one. He had had to explain it twice before Charles got it. The second time his father wrote it out, showed him what the telegrams actually looked like. "Think about it," his father had said, his face earnest. "See how Cary Grant kids around in the telegram he sends back? He pretends not to understand." His father has been dead for sixteen years.

Sam snickers.

"It doesn't take much to amuse you," Charles says.

"Not when I'm this loaded it doesn't."

Charles realizes, for the first time, that he is also a little drunk.

"How'd we get loaded on a bottle of wine?"

"I never drink any more. I never do anything any more."

"You do too."

"What do I do?"

"How should I know? You do stuff."

"I don't do anything," Sam says sadly.

"Let's go out to a bar," Charles says. "I don't want to just sit around here all night."

"Let's catch the news. See what we can find out about Rod Stewart."

"It's not time for the news."

"Okay. Let's go to a bar."

"Your car or mine?" Charles asks.

"Mine is okay."

They put their coats on and leave the house, dishes still on the table. Charles ducks back in to check the burners. They are off. He goes back out the front door. It is very cold, and almost every light on the block is off. Riding along, Charles stares at the dark houses with wonder. How can they go to bed so early? It must be habit, years of training. Got to get up for work, got to go to bed. And they *do* it. He once asked Laura what time she went to bed, so he could think of her. She wouldn't tell him. "It would end up depressing you," she said. She was right; it would depress him to know. But at least he would know—he wouldn't think of her asleep at ten, eleven, twelve, one. . . . He gives the finger to the house he thinks the cripple lives in.

They end up at the same bar he went to with Pete. The college kids are back, though, and it's crowded and noisy. The bar smells of sweat. There is a clock over the jukebox that shows a beer mug perpetually bubbling. Charles decides to drink a beer. He has more than twenty dollars. He can get good and drunk. In a few minutes a couple gets up to leave, and they sit at a table. The same waiter who took Pete's order comes to the table. Tonight he is wearing dark green slacks. They look like velvet. There is a big grease stain across the thigh. Janis Joplin says, loudly, "This is a song called 'Get It While You Can.' Cause it ain't gonna be there when you get up." Do the kids in the bar even know who Janis Joplin is, or do they accept anything that comes to them by way of the ceiling speakers? What a depressing song. Janis Joplin is dead. Maybe Rod Stewart.

"I don't think Rod Stewart is dead," Charles says.

Sam doesn't say anything. He is staring at a girl across the room. Charles orders a pitcher of beer for them.

"Hey, hey, get it while you can," Sam says.

"Looks like reading those trash books didn't do you any good," Charles says.

"It did. You don't see me getting up, do you?"

"Maybe you should go over. Don't listen to me. I'm just being witty," Charles says.

"To tell you the truth, I'd rather have my dog back than that girl," Sam says.

"Forget the dog. Stop talking about her."

The dog, sitting down, rolling over, shaking hands for a beef bone . . .

" 'Atta way, Maria!" a drunk shouts at the speakers. It is the same man.

"That clown was here when I came for a drink with Pete."

"He's always here."

"He looks like he's in bad shape."

"I heard that he was a sociology professor."

"You're kidding."

"That's what I heard."

Sam turns around and stares at the checked tablecloth. The pitcher of beer is put down in the middle of the table.

"Good centerpiece," Sam says.

"Amy Vanderbilt would think so."

"She doesn't think shit any more," Sam says.

"Oh, yeah. I forgot."

"That Elise was really a dummy."

"She wasn't even very good-looking," Charles says.

"She wasn't," Sam agrees. "I should have kept my fifteen. Then I could contribute to the beer fund."

"I've got plenty of money."

"That was a subtle hint, in case you'd forgotten I was broke."

"I didn't forget."

"Did you forget that you asked me to come live at your place?"

"Of course not. How drunk do you think I am?"

"I don't know. I just wanted to check."

"You ought to do it, Sam. I don't think we'd get on each other's nerves."

"I couldn't do that. It's nice of you, though."

"Think about it," Charles says.

"I'll think about it," Sam says.

"Oooooh, Mama," the drunk shouts. "Maria!"

"He's no sociology professor," Charles says.

"I'll ask him," Sam says. Sam gets up. Charles stares straight ahead, in case there is a fight. He doesn't want to get involved. If only Sam hadn't gotten up so quickly, he could have dissuaded him.

"He is," Sam says, sitting down again.

"You really asked him? What did he say?"

"He said, 'Yeah.' "

"Jesus," Charles says.

Charles pours another glass of beer.

"Then what did you say? You didn't just ask and then walk away, did you?"

"I said, 'You're not giving a graduate course this semester, are you?' And he said he wasn't."

"What if he had been?"

"I don't know," Sam says. "I would have thought of something."

Clever Sam, the drinking fountain handle twisted off . . .

Sam pours another glass of beer. "I wish I was back in college," he says.

"Yeah," Charles says.

"But I don't think I'd want to go to college now," Sam says. "With these people, I mean. They look just like they'd go to a prom."

Charles fills his half-empty beer glass.

"You want to hear something sad?" Charles says.

"Do I?"

"It's not that sad. It's just something I read. You know Jacques Cousteau?"

"Sure. You think just because I'm not in law school I'm an ignoramus?"

"I think you're very intelligent. That's why I wish you could be a lawyer."

"I don't have any goddamn money. Or motivation."

"Jacques Cousteau had this dolphin he was working with . . ."

"If the goddamn dolphin died, I don't want to hear about it."

"It didn't die. The dolphin liked Cousteau and all the attention he gave her so much that she always had her head out of the water, and she got sunburned."

Sam laughs. "That's not depressing," he says.

"I think it is."

"It's not as depressing as some things I could think of."

"Such as my unrequited love for Laura?"

"I was thinking more selfishly."

"I'm paying for the beer. Think charitably."

"Well, I wish she liked you."

"She does like me. She might even love me. She just won't leave her husband."

"We've been through this before."

"Be charitable, goddamn it. I love her."

"Yeah. She was nice."

"I know she was nice. Why did her husband have to meet her before I did?"

"I don't know," Sam says.

"I don't know, either. She says she doesn't know."

"Maybe you can shame her into leaving him or something."

"I doubt it."

"I don't know. I never have anything intelligent to say on the subject."

"I just like to talk about her. I'm a masochist. Susan says I am. Do you think I am?"

"I don't want to insult you. You're my best friend."

"You do think so, then?"

"I guess you are."

"Maybe I am. I don't know. I don't know anything."

"Mama Maria, ooh la la," the man hollers.

The waiter brings another pitcher of beer.

"You know what you could do for me?" Charles says.

"What?" Sam says, picking up the pitcher.

"You could just drive me past her house."

"What good would that do?"

"I want to see if the lights are off."

"You'll make yourself miserable."

"Come on, Sam."

"I don't think it's a good idea."

"Then we'll go over to your apartment and get as much of your stuff as we can haul and bring the stuff to my place."

"No, no. I can't move in with you. But thanks."

"What's the real reason you won't move in?"

"I just wouldn't feel right about it. It's your house."

"You can pay half the bills. That would still be a hell of a lot less than the rent you pay."

"Jesus, I can't do that. You mean just move out of my apartment?"

"Yeah. Then if you find another cheaper place to move, go ahead and move. Meanwhile, you'd be out of there."

"I don't know," Sam says.

"Anyway, there's a gas leak in your apartment."

"Everybody who's got a gas stove has a smell like that."

"That's because they leak."

"I don't want to fight with you."

"You're not able to fight with me."

"I wouldn't want to anyway."

"Come on, finish this beer with me and we'll get moving."

"What if you're just drunk and you wake up in the morning and I've moved into your house?"

"I asked you at dinner. I wasn't drunk at dinner, Sam."

Sam bends his fingers, cracks his knuckles.

"Well?"

"I don't know," Sam says.

"You could save some money. You could look around

and find some better place to live. You're not going to give them twenty-five bucks more a month for that place that's poisoning you, are you?"

"Let me finish this beer," Sam says.

"Will you at least drive me past Laura's?"

"Yeah. It seems maudlin to me, but if that's what you want."

"Maria Muldaur!" the man hollers.

Charles smiles. If Sam had said no, he was going to have Sam drop him off and drive his own car. He doesn't want Laura to look out her window and see his car, though. He doesn't want her to think he's harassing her. She doesn't know Sam's car. Not that she'll be awake.

"Maybe I could move in temporarily," Sam says. "Until I get another job."

Charles nods.

"That'll surprise the landlord," Sam says.

"Yeah. Just move out on him."

"It'll be strange not going home and riding in the elevator," Sam says.

"Apartments are for shit."

"Yeah," Sam says.

Charles pours the last of the beer into his glass. It's flat. He pours a little salt in. It will make him thirsty during the night, but so what. He stares at the head rising on his beer.

"There she goes," Sam says.

The girl that Sam had been staring at earlier is walking out of the bar. She looks about twenty, a tall, blond girl in a navy blue coat. This close, she's not as pretty. She's with another girl, a dumpy brunette. The brunette smiles at Charles. He smiles back, reflexively. The smile is too wide; he's pretty drunk. They walk out the front door. Charles stares at his fingers. Both his hands are on top of the table, as if playing with the Ouija board. He hangs his hands at his side. He feels the blood go into them. He puts them back on the table.

"Are we going?" Sam says.

Charles reaches in his pocket for his wallet, counts out the bills, and leaves them on the table. He folds the check and puts it in his pocket without thinking, shakes his head and takes it out. On the back is written: "Your Waiter" and under that "J.D.—Thank you!" in handwriting very small and pale.

They shiver walking to the car, but Charles doesn't feel the cold air sobering him up much. He reaches up and smoothes his hand across his forehead. "Don't drink so much," Laura used to say. His forehead is numb.

Sam fumbles putting the key in the ignition.

"If you make me drive over there and then get depressed, I'm going to be mad," Sam says.

"I'm not going to get depressed. I just want to drive by the place."

"You ever go in her house?" Sam asks.

"No."

"I just wondered what an A-frame was like. What's the point of them?"

"I never thought about it."

He has never been in her house, but he knows what it's like inside. The bathroom has white tile on the floor. Plain white. The tub and sink and toilet are all white. The sink in there is always getting stopped up. You'd think the tub would, since that's where they wash their hair, but it's the sink. The white sink, against the left wall. There is white tile halfway up the wall, and gray and yellow flowered paper the rest of the way. Tiny flowers. Rebecca's room is also done in this wallpaper. He has no idea what paper is in her bedroom, because she won't discuss it with him. The living room and kitchen are off-white. There is a gray and red rug in the living room. There isn't very much furniture. There are two comfortable chairs, and there is one uncomfortable chair. The sofa seat isn't wide enough—it hit everyone just wrong. She has a blender. There is no umbrella stand. There is an Impressionist painting on Rebecca's wall: Seurat's "Une Baignade Asnières." "La Grève du Bas Butin à Honfleur" hangs in the living room. No, there is no art in the bathroom. That's a little tacky, isn't it? He has bought a print of "Une Baignade Asnières," but can't find the other. It's a little depressing, to be honest. It's so empty, so washed-out. She bakes the gingerbread cookies in a white oven. There is a pale green refrigerator—not her choice, but it was on sale, that color only. There is a wood table in the kitchen, and chairs they got at an auction for fifty cents each. He imagines Jim bidding on them. He would never have the nerve to go to an auction. He would always look like he was bidding when he wasn't. He would be forced to pay for and take home everything in the place. Then he'd be stuck with it. He brightens; no he wouldn't. He could call Best Bird Antiques. He is a little drunk.

Charles has been silently pointing directions to Sam. "Turn," he says, pointing right. Sam turns just in time. He seems to be a little drunk also. Charles starts looking for policemen. What if Sam got stopped? This isn't such a hot idea. They should go home. But he wants to see her house. . . .

Sam makes another right turn. Not much traffic, even on this street. Charles looks at his watch. It is one in the morning. Work. Impossible. Work. No.

"That street," Charles says.

"This is where it is?"

"No. This takes you right into her street."

"It's like the country out here. It's nice."

"I was sort of hoping she'd despise it."

"It's a nice part of town. I was never out this way."

Charles closes his eyes for a minute. In the back of his head he hears the beginning of "Gimme Shelter." Was that playing in the bar? He opens his eyes and sees that Sam has put the radio on. "Gimme Shelter" is indeed playing. Charles imagines a dolphin leaping, that music in the background, a water ballet in cartoon style. He would really like to get out of the cold for a while, to stretch out on a beach in the sun. Inoperable melanoma notwithstanding. He points left, and Sam turns. The Rolling Stones are wailing as Sam coasts by Laura's house. There is a light in the kitchen. A light in the kitchen! Charles reaches over and grabs Sam's arm. Sam slows down.

"Christ, I knew this was a mistake," Sam says.

"Oh shit," Charles says. "She's baking gingerbread cookies. She's awake."

"Baking cookies? Are you out of your mind? It must be one in the morning."

"I know that's what she's doing."

Sam turns in a driveway, coasts past Laura's house again.

"How do you know that light's in the kitchen if you've never been in there?"

"She drew me a floor plan once."

"That's the sickest thing I've ever heard."

"I asked her to do it."

"I figured."

"Oh, Sam, she's baking cookies."

"Christ," Sam says.

"She's a room mother."

"What's that?"

"They give parties for the elementary school kids on holidays. That kind of stuff."

"We didn't have one of those."

"I know it."

"I didn't know anything improved in school," Sam says. "What do you know."

Charles closes his eyes. Gingerbread men dance with dolphins.

"Why don't you give her a call tomorrow? Why don't you just give it one last chance and find out one way or the other?"

Charles shakes his head.

"Don't tell me it's pride at this point," Sam says. "After you sent her four dozen roses you're acting coy?"

"I sent them years ago. I've gotten coy, as you put it."

"Why do you want to drag this out? Get an answer. You'll feel better."

"I don't want to get no for an answer."

Sam sighs. They are back on the main road, and Sam is headed for Charles's.

"Man, are you going to be suffering tomorrow," Sam says.

Charles puts his feet on the front seat and tips his head forward until it rests on his knees. He closes his eyes. The dolphins jump. Gingerbread men are riding on them. It's a ridiculous vision. Charles opens his eyes. What does the blind man do when he has a bad dream?

"Did you mean what you said before about moving in?"

"How many times have I got to tell you?" Charles says.

"Okay. I'm going to do it. But not tonight. I'm wiped out. I'll load some stuff over tomorrow."

"I'll see you then."

Charles prepares to leave, realizes that he is still riding in the car, miles from home.

He rides the rest of the way home with his head on his knees, no more disturbing visions.

"You want to know something?" Sam says.

"What?"

"When I first came here, you remember in the fifth grade? You remember how there was that valentine box?"

"Yeah, I remember. The girls decorated the thing."

"This is really awful. I shouldn't tell you this."

"Go on."

"Well, my mother bought me a box of valentines. I was addressing them at the kitchen table. My father came in and started picking them up. I was sending them to everybody, you know? He just about had a breakdown. He sorted out every envelope addressed to a boy and ripped it up under my nose. He said, 'A valentine is romantic.

What the hell are you sending valentines to the boys for?'
It really made me feel like hell."

Charles frowns. "That's awful," he says. "I didn't know
he ever pulled that kind of stuff on you."

"He was always having tantrums. I guess that was just
one more excuse."

They ride in silence to Charles's house.

"See you tomorrow," Sam says.

"Okay. See you," Charles says. The door opens, and he
runs to his front door, reaching in his pocket for his key.
He takes it out and opens the door. Sam drives off. Inside
the house, he leans against the front door as if he's es-
caped something terrible. He reminds himself of the
frightened heroine, hiding in the closet from the villain.
He laughs. He puts the light on and goes into the dining
room. The roast is there, in a puddle of blood. He puts on
the bathroom light and urinates. He sits in a chair and
looks into space. Work. Tomorrow.

As he is getting ready for bed, the phone rings.

"How's my boy? I hate to disturb you at this hour, but
I know you just got in because I've been calling."

"Hi, Pete."

"I've got to talk low. Can you hear me?"

"Oh, God. What's the matter now?"

"Nothing. Something good."

"What is it?"

"I'll bet I know where you've been," Pete whispers.

"Where?" Charles asks.

"With your California sweetie," Pete says.

"No. I was out drinking."

"Oh," Pete says. "Well, I've got very good news, but
when you come over Saturday you've got to promise to
act surprised."

"What is it, Pete?"

"I got it," Pete whispers.

"Got what?"

"The Honda Civic," Pete whispers. "White one."

Chapter 9

Coming home from work, Charles sees Sam's car parked outside. The car looks as though it has a flat tire on one side; it tilts noticeably to the right. Charles gets out of his car and looks it over. There is no flat tire. The car does tilt noticeably to the right. While he is there, Charles tries to open the door on the passenger's side. It doesn't open. He tries the driver's side. It doesn't open. Charles walks up his front lawn to take this good news to Sam. Sam is in the tub, doing his "singing in the tub" number. He is grunting, so he must be kicking. The radio is turned to a classical music station. There is a can of V-8 on the table.

Charles sits down and begins opening the mail. There is a letter from Susan. Not a letter, it turns out, but a brief note. "I couldn't tell you over the phone that Mark swallows to avoid stuttering. Isn't it amazing how well that works? Found out Elise is in Vail. But by the time you get this she'll probably be back at school. I'm sorry she caused you so many problems. I hope Mother isn't. Love, Susan."

"Hiya," Sam says. "I brought over a few boxes. I've decided to sell my furniture. I gave away the two black chairs today to people in the building. I might get some money for that crummy sofa." His mother gave him the sofa when his father got the apartment. His father went out and bought one just like it for his apartment, but still complains that the original sofa isn't still at the house.

"How did it go at work?" Sam asks.

"I got up the nerve to find out Betty's phone number."

"Who's Betty?"

"A secretary there. She used to pal around with Laura."

"You don't mean you're going to get at Laura somehow through her?"

"No. In fact, I'm so unimpressed with Betty that I left the piece of paper with her number on it out in my car. Which reminds me: you were right. Both doors *are* stuck."

"You're kidding me."

"No. I tried them. And there's something funny about the way that car is balanced. Your shocks must be gone or something."

"What do you mean?"

"It tilts."

"I'll just prop it up with cinder blocks."

"How are you going to drive it?"

"I'll put roller skates on the cinder blocks."

"You're in a jovial mood."

"My hangover finally went away. I've slept on every piece of furniture in your house today. Kept falling asleep. I finally feel okay again."

"That's good. Want to go out for dinner?"

"Yeah. Where should we go?"

"Some place close. The seafood place. Feel like that?"

"Those old men are depressing."

"We don't have to sit at the bar. We can get a table."

"I don't think they're too clean."

"Where do you want to go, Sam?"

"Delicatessen?"

"Okay. Sure. I want to wash my face first."

"You're not pissed off that I'm moving in?"

"No. I'm glad you took me up on it. You can save some money this way."

"Thanks a lot," Sam says.

"I'm really a very nice person," Charles says.

"You do a good imitation of her," Sam says.

"Thank you."

"I'm going to go out and see if I can get one of my doors open," Sam says.

Charles takes a swig of the V-8, goes into the bathroom, and runs the water. Sam's toothbrush is in the toothbrush holder: a red toothbrush. Even Sam's toothbrush is falling apart; the bristles splay outward. Charles fills the sink and leans over, closing his eyes and putting his face in the water. He puckers his lips and blows a thin stream of bubbles underwater. It would be wonderful to be submerged in water, to wade out, off the coast of Bermuda, until the water slowly covered his head, and then to blow a thin stream of bubbles before bobbing up for air. To arch his back and glide in the water until his body was horizontal, eyes on the blue, blue sky. The idea is so appealing that he runs the water in the bathtub. At least he can get all of his chest underwater before his knees come up. He sits on the toilet watching the water flow into the bathtub. He thinks of his mother, of the time she called him to get her out because she was having terrible stomach cramps, and how he had to go into the bathroom and lift her from under her arms. She was dead weight, and was complaining so much she wouldn't follow orders. He started laughing, because he suddenly thought of her as a big shark, a big, slippery fish that he could just let go of, and it would return to the depths of the ocean. He was laughing so hard, and she was complaining so loudly, that neither of them heard Pete come in. Charles didn't know he was there until Pete spoke from behind him, and then he was so genuinely surprised that he almost did let go. Pete held a towel in front of her as Charles hauled her out. After it happened about ten more times, though, Pete not only didn't even wrestle her into her bathrobe once she was on the bed. Saturday. He has to go over there for dinner Saturday. . . .

"Frozen," Sam calls, walking through the house. "Pipes in the kitchen, too. The water running in there?"

"Yeah," Charles says.

"Mind if I come in and fill a pan with hot water so I can pour it on the car lock?"

"Just a minute," Charles says. He gets up and sits in the bathtub. He ran the water too hot, and whistles as he sits down.

"Okay," Charles says.

Sam's cheeks are very pink, and his hair covers his forehead.

"Man, is it ever cold out there. I'll bet this is the coldest night of the year. If I'd only thought, I could have bought some groceries so we wouldn't have to go out."

"Delicatessen's not far. We'll make it."

"Why don't we eat at the seafood place? That was where you wanted to go, wasn't it?"

Sam turns off the water, leans against the sink facing Charles in his bath. His mother used to do that. "If you can wash yourself so good, let's see you wash," she'd say.

"Delicatessen's all right with me," Charles says.

"I'd just as soon have some oysters," Sam says. "Why don't we go ahead and eat at the seafood place?"

"I thought you said the old men depressed you."

"So we can eat at a table."

"I said that to you before."

"Okay. That's what we'll do then," Sam says, leaving the bathroom.

Charles sighs. He was all set for hot pastrami and potato salad. He leans back to relax, knocking over a shampoo bottle on the edge of the tub. He retrieves it, leans back again. He thinks about how nice it would be to be a fish, a trout, maybe, fanning his gills in the dark, cold water. A trout is a phallic symbol. He shakes the thought out of his head. "I know too much," he says out loud. He picks up the soap and makes a lather, drops it back into the soap dish. It slips out. He reaches into the water for it, then realizes that it is *his* bar of soap, and if he wants to be wasteful, he can be. His mother used to nag him about putting the soap back in the dish. "If you're so smart you can put the soap back in the dish so the next person who bathes can have more than a chip." Saturday. Maybe something will happen and he can get out of it.

"It's started to snow," Sam hollers.

"Did you hear me?" Sam hollers again. "It's snowing."

"Yeah," Charles says. "I heard it was supposed to snow."

"I really blew it," Sam says. "I should have gone out for food."

Charles runs a little hot water into the tub, swirls it around with his foot. He thinks back on his day; his boss's son came in to meet him, and he disliked him. He had on an argyle vest and black loafers, and mumbled like Marlon Brando. He had Brando's gestures, too—a wave of the hand to dismiss something (usually his own statement), a turn of the head to look first away, then down. He said very little, and what he did say was so softly spoken that Charles couldn't pick up on anything except the wave of the hand and the ironic laugh that followed. He is glad not to have children. He remembers sitting on a stool in his father's workroom. "You've heard of screwing, right?" He is glad he doesn't have a child he would have to explain sex to. Betty. Does Betty want to get married and have children? She seems to want only reports that she can type. He asked her today for her phone number. He said that he intended to call her to invite her to a small party he was giving soon. What small party? He doesn't know anybody. At the last minute he chickened out, couldn't say the word "date." Betty looked very hopeful all the same. She wrote the number, very efficiently, on his memo pad, coming around to his side of the desk to do it. Laura would know what her perfume was. A very heavy scent, obviously fake. Everything about Betty is obvious: the clothes she wears betray her bulges, the perfume is meant to draw attention. Today she had on one of the new longer skirts (he saw this in last week's Sunday *Times:* "the new longer skirts," they were called) and a pale blue blouse that wasn't bad. Except that she had on some ugly piece of jewelry that hung down the front of it. And the black boots. Maybe he could ask her to go puddle jumping.

The phone rings. Charles sits up, trying to hear Sam's end of the conversation. It sounds as though Sam is mumbling. Maybe Sam has left and has been replaced by his boss's kid.

"It was Pete," Sam hollers. "I told him you were in the tub. He said you don't have to call back, but he wanted to remind you to act surprised about the Honda Civic."

"Oh, Christ," Charles says.

"You didn't tell me he bought a new car."

"It's not the first thing I'd think to tell you about."

"He sounds happy as hell," Sam says.

"She'll ruin it for him. Just give her time," Charles says. He lifts the stopper and puts it in the soap dish. He lets most of the water drain out before he reaches in for the soap.

"I don't want to rush you, but if we're taking my car, we'd better get out there before the lock refreezes," Sam says. He is drinking V-8 and listening to the stereo through the headphones. He screams the statement. Charles nods, goes into his bedroom and throws the towel over the lamp. He puts on underwear, goes through his drawer looking for a clean pair of jeans. His clothes are all dirty. He has to go to the laundromat. Maybe on the way to his mother's. Saturday. He lies on the bed, suddenly tired. He flips the bedspread over him. He looks like a mummy. He closes his eyes. A party he's giving. My God. Call Audrey and the cripple, ask Pete to stop by? Have Sam carry around trays of little crackers with bits and pieces of things on top?

His mother and father used to give birthday parties for

him. His father would blow up balloons on the bicycle pump and hang them on crepe paper that was strung from tree to tree in the backyard. When the pin oak died there was nowhere left to string them to, so the crepe paper tapered down to his mother's clothesline—one of those metal things that look like an umbrella blown inside out. That was his last party. After that his father was dead. First the pin oak, then his father. Once he had a chocolate cake shaped like a football. Another time three kids gave him the same present, and he and his father rode down to the hospital to donate the other two to a playroom there. His father was pronounced D.O.A. at that hospital not long after that. He and his mother went to the hospital in the police car. Inside, Charles wanted very much to think of an excuse to go back to that playroom to see if the toys were still there. His attention kept wandering. His mother kept crying. The toy was called "Mr. Jumping Bunny"—a metal bunny that could be wound with a key to jump. He got a lot of nice presents at his birthday parties. One of his all-time favorites was a pair of wooden stilts that he wore to school to march in the Halloween parade, and that he later walked around the cellar with, pretending to be his dead father. Once he and his father had a "fencing" duel with the stilts, and his mother had run out into the backyard to stop them. "Those huge pieces of wood! What if one of you had an accident?" When Pete first married his mother he used to try to initiate games with Charles, but he never wanted to play because Pete didn't know how to improvise. He played everything straight, and it was a big bore: with badminton rackets he played badminton (his father had made a game of picking dandelions from the lawn and hitting them as though they were baseballs and the badminton rackets bats), with the Monopoly board he played Monopoly, there were no unexpected twists to the card games they played (his father had asked, "Ever play 52 pickup? Want to?").

Charles turns on his side, facing the wall. He closes his eyes and tries to remember his father. He can't. He gets an image of a black-haired man with a handlebar mustache and blue eyes, the man who was painted on the mug Charles gave him one Father's Day. He closes his eyes again and tries to picture Pete. He sees him perfectly, opens his eyes immediately.

He gets up and puts on a pair of dirty pants, a blue shirt, and an old sweater.

"Ready to go?" he asks. Sam looks at him blankly, takes the headphones off.

"Ready to go?" Charles says.

"Oh. Sure. Let me get my coat."

They put on their coats (he will have to take all that stuff out of the closet so Sam will have some place better than the upright ironing board to hang his things on).

"If you want to bring any of your furniture over here, even if you just want to stick it in the attic to store, feel free. We could use some tables and things like that."

"Oh. That's very nice of you," Sam says, starting the car. "If you'd like me to, I can bring the coffee table over and the round table."

"Sure. Bring it. I don't care what the place looks like."

Sam looks hurt. He has said the wrong thing.

"It's nice-looking stuff, anyway."

Sam looks less hurt. "I'll get it tomorrow," he says. "It's going to be here when you come home."

Big thrill. Tables will await him. He could, of course, have that little party, and there would be tables to put the hors d'oeuvres on. He and Sam would make the hors d'oeuvres he had at his boss's house three years ago: crackers with a slice of hard-boiled egg on them, topped with caviar. What a swell time they could all have. They could invite the man who comes around to inspect the meter in the cellar—a very nice man named Ray Roy. When Charles isn't home, he leaves a little piece of paper saying, "Be by end of week. Ray Roy."

Pete takes pride in the fact that no one has been admitted to read the meter since he came to the house. "Why let them down in my cellar? What for?" It would give Pete and Ray Roy something to talk about, as they nibbled hors d'oeuvres.

"What are you smoldering about?" Sam asks.

"I'm just in a lousy mood. I'm tired."

"Do a lot of work today?"

"No. I haven't had a lot of work to do for months, for some reason. I asked Betty for her telephone number today, though."

"Going to take her out?"

"I told her I was going to have her over to a party."

"When are you having a party?"

"When I make some friends."

"Oh," Sam says. "I don't get it."

"I didn't want to ask her for a date on the spot, but I'd asked her for her number, and I had to say something."

"Yeah. I was always giving my dog orders or calling her when I didn't need her. I was always retracting my statements to the dog. She got to know what 'never mind' meant."

"Why don't you get yourself another dog? Bring it to my place. I wouldn't mind having a dog around."

"It depresses me that I have time to train it, that I could actually just sit around all day teaching it stuff."

"Why should that depress you? Get the dog and teach it stuff."

"Nah. There's too much stuff to teach them. It's too much effort."

"Get one already trained."

"I like puppies."

"Sure is snowing like hell," Charles says. "Maybe this will get me out of dinner tomorrow."

"It's tomorrow, huh?"

"You're lucky your parents only expect you to show up on Christmas."

"I go over there more than that."

"Yeah, but they only expect you on Christmas."

"That's true."

"And at least you don't have to fish them out of the tub and watch them medicate themselves the whole time you're there."

"On Christmas I got to sit at a card table my father had put up in the living room that he was working a puzzle on top of. I had to pretend to be interested in fitting a pizza puzzle together."

"That's not as bad as having to fish somebody out of the bathtub."

"Why won't she stand up?"

"She sits there perspiring until she collapses. I think she soaks the strength out of her. Really. And then we have to pull her out. That causes bruises, and that gives her something else to complain about."

"She's really nuts," Sam says.

"Yeah."

"Maybe I *will* think about getting a dog," Sam says. "You have any preference?"

"No. Just some mutt from the pound."

"What if I find another job, though? Then I'd have to leave it, and it wouldn't be trained."

"I told you. Get a dog that's been trained."

"I'd miss not having a puppy."

"Then get a puppy and just figure on not looking for a job."

"I feel bad, just sitting around."

"You can go get the groceries."

"I feel like a goddamn wife."

"If you feel like a wife, forget the groceries. I can't see how you'd mind working with a dog, though."

"I'm just being silly. I'm going to get groceries tomorrow."

"I never had anything you cooked."

"Sure you did. I used to make banana bread."

"Is that what you plan on making for dinner?"

"I might make that and something to go with it."

"Go ahead. I can eat anything."

Another mistake. Sam doesn't look enthusiastic any more. He pulls into the parking lot next to the restaurant.

They walk into the restaurant and get a booth in the room next to the raw bar. One of the old men who works behind the raw bar has the underside of his thumb missing, a deep, perfectly shaped oval, from opening clams when he was drunk. Charles thinks about the thumb, even though he doesn't have to see it. Sam and Charles sit down in a booth. The person at the table next to the booth nods to Charles, and Charles nods back. Who is it? He'd ask Sam if he looks familiar, but Sam already has the menu in front of his face. Sam always orders the same thing: crab imperial. He also always looks at the menu. Charles picks up his menu. There is what appears to be a dancing cookie on the plastic cover: a circle with dancing feet and arms akimbo, pulling a fish out of the water. The water is represented by a wavy line. There are no other fish in the water; only the one the dancing cookie pulls out. The fish who has been pulled out is smiling. Inside, all the prices have been crossed out or inked over—fives changed into eights with strangely shaped tops—and there is a little piece of paper stapled to the top left, saying that there is a ten percent increase on all marked prices. Still, it's a good place for the money. The crab imperial is only four-fifty, and the shrimp are four dollars even. Beer is still fifty cents a bottle. The waitress comes to the table. She looks very much like the only other waitress in the restaurant, except that the other one has bright red hair. This one has bright blond hair, a black uniform, and hands ragged with varicose veins.

"I'll have the crab imperial and a Miller's," Sam says.

"The crabcakes," Charles says.

"What to drink?" she says.

"A Bass Ale," Charles says.

She walks away, leaving the menus. Charles studies the cover. At the bottom is written "art by Al M., 1973." He puts the menu on top of Sam's, looks around the restaurant. The hippie at the next table catches his eye again, and smiles.

"The waiter from The Sinking Ship," the hippie says.

"Oh, sure. I knew your face was familiar."

The hippie's plate is empty, and there are several empty beer mugs on the table.

"Good food here," the hippie says.

"Yeah. We come here quite often," Charles says. "This is my friend, Sam. My name is Charles, by the way."

"Oh, hi," the hippie says, lifting his hand to Sam. "I think I've seen you around." He spins an empty beer mug.

"Just don't eat the food there," the hippie says to Charles.

"Why?" Charles asks.

"I was making a club sandwich one night and cut my finger, and I was so fed up with the whole thing that I just turned the piece of bread over and served the thing anyway." He takes a long drink from his half-empty mug.

"My name's J.D. I don't guess you'd have any reason to remember that," he says. "They make us sign the checks. They tell us to use an exclamation point, too, after the 'Thank You.'"

"Been there long?" Sam says.

"I was there for a year part-time at night when I was in school. But after I dropped out I started working ten hours a day, six days a week. It's a drag. Today's my day off."

"That's rough," Charles says.

"It's rough, and I don't have anything to show for it. Last night somebody slashed my tires. I get out after eleven hours—my replacement didn't show—and there were the cut tires."

"Neighborhood's getting bad," Sam says.

"It is," J.D. says.

The waitress comes to their booth with the beer, puts it down on Miller's coasters.

"How about joining us?" Charles says.

J.D. nods, moves his almost entirely empty mug to their table, sits next to Charles.

"Who's that clown who's always shouting for Maria Muldaur?" Charles asks.

"He's a sociology professor. I kid you not. He takes a new one home every night. The way he operates, he'll get Maria Muldaur home eventually."

"Shit," Sam says. "I wish I was still a goon back in college."

"Fine goon you were. Phi Beta Kappa," Charles says.

"Yeah, but I acted goony. I hollered in bars."

"You should have been there last night," J.D. says. "Some drunk kept flicking matches at the ceiling speakers, and damn if he didn't launch one high enough to set it on fire."

"You'd think it would burn out before it got up there," Charles says.

"I can't understand it either, and I was in physics," J.D. says.

"If I had the money, I'd sit around in bars again," Sam says. "I used to have a good time sitting around bars."

"What do you do?" J.D. asks.

"Unemployed jacket salesman."

J.D. shakes his head, drains his beer.

"Hey, you guys do me a favor? Loan me fifty cents so I can get another one of these things. I'll give it to you next time you're in the bar."

"Sure," Charles says. "Just go ahead and order."

"I was supposed to have a date tonight," J.D. says, "but when I called she said—you're not going to believe this—she said, 'I'm not going to be ready at seven.' I said, 'What time should I come by?' She said, 'I'm not going to be ready ever.' Then she hung up."

"Why'd she do that?" Sam says.

"Beats me. She asked me if I'd take her to the movies. Called me and asked me if I'd take her. Hell, I'm better off not being with her, I guess, if I've got to sit through Paul Newman."

"Hey," Sam says. "Did you hear anything about Rod Stewart being dead?"

J.D. shakes his head.

"He's not dead," Sam says. "That girl was putting me on."

"Somebody told you he was dead?"

"Yeah. Girl I used to work with."

"Nuts. Women are all nuts. Another time this same girl, the one who called me to ask if I'd take her to a Paul Newman movie, had me take her to the zoo. She had me buy her an ice cream cone and a balloon, then she said she wanted to go home. 'Don't you want to do anything else while we're here?' I said, and she said, 'Yeah. Buy postcards.' That was it. We went home."

"She sounds like a million laughs," Charles says.

"I don't know. I don't have any luck finding nice chicks," J.D. says.

"I don't either," Sam says.

The waitress puts down their dinners.

"One more beer," J.D. says.

She nods and goes away.

"She's married to the guy behind the raw bar," J.D. says. "I saw them having a fight out in the parking lot one night."

"She's a beauty," Sam says. "There's just not many good-looking women around any more."

"They all wear brassieres now too," J.D. says.

"Yeah. What the hell's happening?" Sam says, spooning out some crab imperial.

"It's the fucking end of the world is what's happening," J.D. says.

The waitress comes back to the table with J.D.'s beer.

"When women put their brassieres back on and want you to take them to Paul Newman movies. I used to live with a woman in New Mexico. I wish I'd never left New Mexico. Small stuff pissed me off. I got tired of looking at roosters. *She* hasn't put any goddamn brassiere on."

"I don't care if they wear brassieres or not," Sam says, "as long as they've got tits. They sure don't act like they've got tits any more."

"Everything's going to hell," J.D. says. He swirls the beer in his mug. "I sure am glad I ran into you guys."

"I don't think we'll prove too uplifting," Charles says.

"You're making this beer possible. That's uplifting."

Somebody starts the jukebox. Tammy Wynette sings "Stand by Your Man."

"That's all that's left that thinks right," J.D. says. "Redneck women."

"You see that movie?" Charles asks. "That was a great movie."

"*Five Easy Pieces.* Yeah. I was so goddamn happy when Jack Nicholson gave that waitress a hard time, even if it was just a movie."

"I should think you'd sympathize with the waitress, being a waiter and all."

"No. She deserved it." J.D. points to Charles's piece of lemon. "Are you planning to use that?"

"No. Go ahead."

J.D. squirts lemon juice in his mouth, swallows beer. "I'm pretending it's tequila," he smiles.

"Have a tequila," Charles says. "You can pay me back next time I see you."

"That's mighty nice of you. It was a real break running into you guys."

"A tequila, please," Charles says to the waitress.

She gives no sign that she heard. In a few minutes she returns with a shot of tequila.

"To sticking together," J.D. says, downing the tequila.

"Whether we stick together or not, I've got the feeling

we're screwed," Sam says. "Take my friend here: his last lady visitor was a lesbian."

J.D. makes the sour face he didn't make when swallowing the tequila.

"But she's not my true love," Charles says. "My true love lies across the city, in the arms of her true love, a builder of A-frames."

"What's that?" J.D. says.

"You mean what's an A-frame?"

"Yeah."

"A house. A pointed house."

"Oh. She's in love with an architect?"

"So much in love that she's married the chap," Sam says.

"You wouldn't like her," Charles says. "She wears brassieres."

Charles orders three more beers.

Sam and J.D. have a long discussion of women's legs. They can not decide between short and lean and long and lean. "Just so the legs go over my shoulders," J.D. says. Sam laughs. Charles smiles. The next naked woman he will see will be his mother, screaming in the tub on Saturday. He starts to feel very tired again. J.D. sings a song about a black woman, to the tune of "On Top of Old Smokey." It gradually becomes apparent that J.D. is drunk and in no shape to get himself out—not that he's making any motion to leave. Charles tries to make a sign to Sam that he should stop encouraging J.D., but Sam's eyes are squeezed shut with laughter. Charles looks at the smiling fish. The fish is a goner, but smiling. That is the way artist Al M. conceptualizes it. Artists are all crazy. Everybody is crazy. Charles wants to go home and go to bed.

"J.D., how far away do you live?" he asks.

"Why?" J.D. says. "I don't have a thing to drink at my place. Cranberry juice. For my bad kidneys. That's absolutely all. You can't even drink the water."

"I was just thinking that we'd give you a lift on our way. You don't want to drive."

"Last person who gave me a lift was a queer. He said, 'I'd like to bury my head in that.' "

Charles winces. "We just want to get you home," he says.

"I didn't mean anything personal," J.D. says.

"What do you think, Sam? Can't we give him a ride home easy enough?"

"Sure," Sam says. "You come back for your car tomorrow. We'll take you home."

"I don't have my car. I took a bus. My car is still sitting there with slit tires."

"You left it there on the street?"

"What else was I going to do? I had just worked eleven hours. I was dead tired. What the hell did I care? Junk. Detroit junk. They could make tires that were indestructible if they wanted to."

"I'm going to take care of the bill, and you help J.D. into his jacket, Sam."

"I didn't mean anything personal about what I said before. I was just remarking," J.D. says.

"I know," Charles says. "Excuse me, while I pay the bill."

J.D. staggers to his feet. Tammy Wynette is singing "Stand by Your Man" again. J.D. collapses in the booth when Charles leaves.

Charles goes to the front counter and pays the red-headed woman. He buys a chocolate mint and stands looking out the front door, eating it. Then he goes back to the table, where J.D. has his coat on.

"Swear that you didn't take it personal," J.D. says.

"He doesn't take it personal. He knows you were just making a remark," Sam says.

"I like you guys."

The snow is falling heavily when they go out, and everything is blanketed in white. If it only weren't cold,

Charles would love to go to sleep in it, in the deep white on the sidewalk. He takes J.D.'s arm, expecting another outburst, gets none, and leads him slowly to the car.

"Where do you live, J.D.?"

"I'll give directions. Not so far."

J.D. gives directions. He will not name streets, or give the address of his building, but he keeps swearing that it isn't far. They are riding in back of a sanding truck. The road turns brown and ugly in front of them.

"Hell, I could live in New Mexico. Then what would you guys do?"

"Dump you," Sam says.

"Don't say that. You guys seem so nice."

"How would we get you to New Mexico?" Sam asks.

"I don't know," J.D. says. He looks crestfallen.

"Am I going right? You're watching where we are, aren't you?"

"Turn left." J.D. says. "That's it. That building."

There is a row of buildings.

"Which one?" Charles says.

"The ugliest."

Sam pulls up in front of a brown glass building.

"Two down," J.D. says. "I'm glad you don't think mine is the ugliest."

Sam coasts down another two buildings. It is uglier. He couldn't see it well from where they were.

"I want you to come in for cranberry juice," J.D. says.

"We've got to get home. It's bad driving, J.D."

"Aw, shit. I want you guys to come visit. You're sure nice guys."

"We'll give you a call tomorrow, if you'll let us have your number," Sam says.

"Just come up for a minute."

Charles feels very sorry for J.D. "Sure," he says. "We'll come up."

"That's great," J.D. says. He rolls down his window.

"Thanks," Sam says, looking out J.D.'s window to back

into a parking space. But that's not why the window was down. J.D. leans out and vomits.

"Don't hold it against me," J.D. says.

"We don't hold it against you," Sam says.

"You guys are really goddamned nice. Anybody else, I wouldn't have made the effort not to puke in their car."

"I'm glad you spared me," Sam says.

"Sure. I like you guys."

The lobby is carpeted in bright blue, and there are fake plants in the corners by the elevator. Muzak plays in the elevator. They ride to the second floor.

"This way, please," J.D. says. Charles is holding him up by the arm. J.D. reaches in his coat pocket and takes out a key ring.

"One of these," J.D. says.

Sam starts trying them. Finally the door opens.

"Please come in," J.D. says, as they lead him in.

There is nothing in the living room but a mattress and a black telephone. In the kitchen, four rubber plants are growing in holes in the stove where the burners used to be. There is a black wall phone.

"Look around, look around," J.D. says. To placate him, they go into the bedroom. There is nothing in the bedroom except a brown and white rabbit standing on a pile of magazines. There is no shower curtain in the bathroom.

"You just move in or something?" Charles asks.

"Lived here one year, four months," J.D. says, sitting on the mattress.

Charles nods.

"Well, now that you're here safely, I think we'd better get home before the storm gets any worse. Can you let us have your phone number?"

J.D. gestures toward the black telephone. Sam copies down the number.

"We'll be in touch," Sam says. "You okay now?"

"You guys are so goddamn nice. I'm not drunk now. I

realize that you wouldn't want any of that cranberry juice, and I'm not going to push it. When you guys can, come on over and I'll fix you a chili dinner."

"Right," Charles says. "Good night, now."

"You're not going to go out again, are you?" Sam says.

"I've ruined your evening," J.D. says.

"No, you haven't. We liked talking to you. You had a little to drink, that's all."

"I didn't puke in your car," J.D. says, lying down.

"No," Sam says.

"Well, good night," J.D. says.

They walk out of the apartment. J.D. waves.

Back in Sam's car, Sam lets out a long sigh.

"Everybody's so pathetic," Sam says. "What is it? Is it just the end of the sixties?"

"J.D. says it's the end of the world."

"It's not," Sam says. "But everything's such a mess."

"I told Susan I felt sorry for everybody, and she said there was something wrong with me."

"She's in love with that doctor. How can you expect her to be cynical?"

Charles shrugs. They ride home slowly, watching the snow mount up. Charles is glad Sam is driving, because Sam drives much better than he does in the snow. It has been such a cold, long winter. He used to like winter when he was a kid. He had a Fleetwood Flyer sled, and they'd close off the steep hill at one end of his parents' block, and there would be nighttime sledding parties, with a bonfire and hot dogs. Even his mother rode the sled down the hill once. He was so proud of her. Now she just sits around and goes crazy, but then she'd try things—go sledding, make new cakes—she even got a set of records and tried to learn Spanish. She failed. On the sled, she scared herself and said she couldn't get her breath and went home without eating a hot dog with them. The cakes were just mixes. Okay—so she never did anything right. At least she was pretty. Or prettier. She always had crooked teeth in the bottom of her mouth, and her hair never puffed out the way other women's hair did. Her hair always looked defeated. She had a pot belly as long as he could remember. But she used to wear high-heeled shoes. Now she wears white sneakers. She used to wear high-heeled shoes.

Sam tries to get his car in the driveway, but he can't do any more than get the nose a few feet up. The plow has been by, and it's impossible to park on the street. The cars that are parked there have been plowed in.

"We've got to shovel," Charles says. "You'll be hit for sure."

They get out of the car and go in the house for the shovel.

"There's just one shovel. I'll do it," Charles says.

"Let me. I knew it was going to snow. I'm the one who didn't get groceries."

"We'll take turns," Charles says. "When you've been out for five minutes, come get me."

Charles pulls a chair up to the kitchen window and watches. It is going to be a bad storm. He can hardly see Sam, even with the streetlights shining. He rubs the palm of one hand against the fingers of another, to warm himself. He goes into the living room and dials the thermostat up two degrees, then goes back out to relieve Sam, but Sam insists that he wants to shovel. Charles goes back to the house, takes his clothes off, and gets into bed. The bed is freezing. He lies there shaking, then falls asleep. He wakes up and hears Sam moving around the house, looks at the clock and sees that it is only midnight. He puts the pillow over his head and goes back to sleep, dreaming an intricate dream of sunflowers springing up in the snow, poisonous sunflowers that he is trying to rake under, that reappear elsewhere in deeper drifts. Confused, he wakes up again. Sam is sitting on the bed. He pulls himself up, asking, "What are you doing here?" Is Sam really there? Yes. Sam is talking to him.

"Sorry to wake you up. Pamela Smith is on the phone. She says that she's run into trouble and she was on her way back when she got stranded at the Clara Barton Service Area. She doesn't have any money. She doesn't sound very good. I said I'd try to get out to get her, but she said she wanted to talk to you."

"What?" Charles says.

"How much did you miss?"

"What do you mean the Clara Barton Service Area? On the New Jersey Turnpike, you mean?"

"Yeah. She came back East. She said there was trouble."

Charles gets out of bed, taking the quilt off and wrapping it around himself. He walks across the cold tile to the kitchen phone.

"Pamela?" he says.

There is no answer.

"Pamela? Hello?"

"Isn't she there?" Sam says. He takes the phone. "Pamela?" he says.

There is only silence on the other end.

"Hang up. She'll call back," Sam says.

Charles hangs up. They sit in the living room. The phone does not ring.

"Well, I don't know what the hell to do," Charles says. "It's a real storm out there. Did she say what kind of trouble?"

"It was garbled. I don't know well enough to tell you. The highway will be clear, if we can get off the block. What do you think?"

"I don't know. She always overreacts. Let's sit here a minute."

Charles looks over his shoulder at the falling snow.

"I was having some odd dream," he says. "I can't remember."

"Ask Fritz," Sam says.

"What garbage," Charles says.

Sam shrugs. "I don't know. Somebody's got to know something."

Charles gets up, staggers toward the bedroom. "I'm going to get my goddamn clothes on. We can take my car. It's got studded tires. If you even intend to come, that is."

"Yeah. I'll come."

"Are you awake enough to drive?" Charles asks.

"Yeah. But you will be too, man, when you hit that cold air out there."

"Pamela Smith," Charles says. "Pamela Smith doesn't mean shit to me."

"Why don't you wait for another call then? If it's important there'll be another call."

"She'd better goddamn well be there," Charles says. "You're sure that's the service area she said?"

"How could I forget that?"

There is no answer from the bedroom. Charles is putting his dirty slacks back on.

It is a long ride to the Clara Barton Service Area, and it is late Saturday morning before they are close to being home. Pamela Smith will not talk about what went wrong. When they persisted, she cried. "Everything I said to you, everything I talked about was just bullshit. I don't know what to do, I don't know what I think." She sat in the front seat wedged between them, and when Charles got in the back seat to try to sleep she moved over next to Sam. After half an hour of being bumped on his side, Charles sat up and sat cross-legged in the back seat, looking out the back window at the highway. He was so tired that he was giddy; he thought about waving to oncoming cars, seeing if they'd mistake him for a kid or think he was retarded and wave back. But he was too tired to play games. The morning sun was very bright, and it was tiring to squint so long fighting it. If only the sun warmed something. The radio was on, but it was turned down low, and Charles could only pick out a word or a phrase. Watching the bright highway, with all the cars, Charles felt even more fatigued: all of them going where? And what for? Pamela Smith turned around once and said, "I don't have any money." "It's okay," he said to her. Or he thinks he verbalized it. Pamela Smith looks very ill, with black circles swollen under her eyes. At the service area they bought her a glass of orange juice—all she would take—and she spilled some on her Wonder Woman T-shirt. She ran to Charles when he came in. He felt like a great savior, like he was really accomplishing something. The good feeling wore away as his body began to give out. Now he sits in the back seat, squinting. Occasionally there is a flurry of snow, and the sky clouds up, but for now it is mostly clear and harsh. The heater never makes the car warm enough.

"We're getting there," Sam says, to no one in particular.

Charles nods. Unless Sam was looking in the rearview mirror, he didn't see him.

"Wonder if J.D. made it through the night," Charles says. He thinks about the rabbit: a fat, bright-eyed rabbit in an empty room.

Sam did not hear Charles. He was mumbling.

"I figure maybe another half hour," Sam says. "We're lucky the snow stopped."

"How can you think of any of this in terms of luck?" Charles says.

Pamela Smith turns around. "I'm sorry," she says. "You're really my only friend."

"What about your brother?" Charles asks. Nasty, but he's curious.

"He just gave me the money on the condition he wouldn't have to see me again."

"That's brotherly," Charles says.

Pamela Smith shrugs. "He didn't want me to be born. My mother says he never looked at me in my crib. They'd have to call him over when they were giving me my bottle. He didn't look at me until I started walking."

"You didn't get raped, did you?" Charles says.

"No," she says.

"Are you ever going to tell us?"

"I'll tell you later. It wasn't any one thing."

"A combination of things," Charles says. That's why Laura went back to Jim. Not just because he was now making enough money building A-frames to support her, but because of a lot of little things. A combination of things.

He looks out the side window at a big blue truck rolling by. If he were Jack Nicholson in *Five Easy Pieces* he could hop a truck, start a new life. What new life would he like? The same life, but married to Laura. Or even living with Laura. Or even dating Laura. Or even getting to hear her holler out her car window again. She had looked so fragile, shouting out the window that she was sick. Once at her apartment she had been sick, and he had rocked her. There was no rocking chair, so he sat on the edge of a chair and rocked her by bending forward and back. His stomach muscles were constricted for a week after that. She liked to be rocked; she liked to pretend to be a child again. He bought her a mobile of little matchstick ships that he hung from the bathroom light. It was a small apartment, and they were always running into each other. He loved that. He'd quicken his pace when he turned a corner, hoping she'd be there so he could smack into her. He tries to imagine bumping into Betty, turning a corner and running into Betty. He could never take Betty in his arms and apologize for hitting her. There is no way he could even date Betty. He could, but he'd be miserable. What would they do? Go to a movie, or go out to dinner? What for? He stares at the passing cars, slumps lower in the seat.

"Don't you want me to take over for a while?" he says to Sam.

"Nah. This way I'll stay awake. If I fall asleep in a car I get sick."

"I could drive," Pamela Smith says. Neither of them acknowledges it.

Sam turnes up the volume on the radio. He quickly turns it down. "False alarm," he says. "I thought it was from the new Dylan album."

"I didn't think that was out yet," Pamela says.

"Supposed to come out sometime soon, isn't it?" Sam says.

They turn off the beltway and start down the exit ramp. Sam hums softly.

"I'll tell you what happened," she says. "I got robbed. That was the last straw. I had twenty-five bucks, and a woman with a little kid made me fork it over. She said we were stopping for a Coke, made her kid stay in the car, and walking into the service area she said she was going to stab me in the back if I didn't give her my money. I couldn't believe it. She looked so goddamned maternal, in a blue coat and loafers. 'What are you waiting for, to see the knife?' she said. 'It cuts. That's the first you get to see it.' I gave her the money, and she left me there."

Charles can see Sam's eyes in the rearview mirror. His eyes are wide.

"Why didn't you tell somebody inside? They could have called the cops."

"I didn't want to. I just didn't want to."

"You should have," Charles says.

"I should have, but I didn't want to. I thought: you might as well start doing what you want to do right now; this is as good a time as any other. So I called you."

Sam turns the volume up again. "Nope," he says.

Charles checks his watch. It is a little after noon, which will give him almost five hours of sleep before he has to go to dinner. His Saturday is shot. Sunday is always a bleak day, with nothing to do. Monday he goes back to work. His boss will come in and want to know what he thought of his son. He will lie. His boss always checks on his reaction: "Did you like those hors d'oeuvres my wife made for the party? I told her it looked pretentious. What did you think?" He has a new orange pencil sharpener he requisitioned, and the Steel City paper clips will be piled up on his desk, awaiting him. Also reports. He will eat alone. Maybe he will go to the Greek restaurant and have a good lunch, have Greek coffee and pudding for dessert. The food there is always very good, but it takes a long time to get served. What the hell. They're not going to fire him. He'll tell his boss that his son is a suave son of a bitch and take a long lunch hour. Pasticcio. He is hungry.

"Why don't we stop off on the avenue and get something to eat?" he says.

"Okay with me," Sam says.

"I'm starving," Pamela Smith says.

"If you were starving, why didn't you say anything?" Charles says.

"You're angry at me," she says.

"No I'm not. I'm not mad." He is a little mad. He is too tired to be really mad.

"I misjudge you all the time," she says. "When I came over the other night I thought you'd be very defensive and aloof, and you were very nice."

"Don't start that again."

"Can't a person tell you you're nice?"

"No. Absolutely not."

"Where do you want to stop?" Sam says. "Kentucky Fried Chicken or some place like that?"

"What do you want?" Charles asks Pamela Smith.

"Anything."

"Then stop at Kentucky Fried."

The Saturday traffic is heavy. Charles combs his hair and tries to open his eyes wider. He winces.

"I guess we'd feel worse if we were J.D.," Charles says.

"That's for sure," Sam agrees.

"Is that a friend of yours?" Pamela Smith asks.

"Guy we met last night . . . last night? Yeah. In a restaurant."

"He was pretty drunk," Charles says.

"What do you think he does with his money?" Sam says. "There's nothing in that apartment."

"Maybe the rent is high."

"How high can rent be for a place like that?"

"I don't know. How much can he make being a waiter?"

"I don't know," Sam says.

"Money is worthless anyway," Pamela Smith says. "I really felt like she might as well take it. What was twenty-five bucks going to do for me?"

Sam pulls into the Kentucky Fried Chicken parking lot. He gets out and lets Charles out of the back seat. Charles goes inside. There is a line. One man has a child sitting on his shoulders. The child is picking a scab off its arm.

"A family pack," Charles says when he gets to the counter. "And a large order of french fries."

"That's all?" the girl says. She rings it up on the cash register. He pays, and sits on the edge of a booth to wait for it. He looks around at all the families eating fried chicken. America is getting so gauche. If there's a McDonald's in Paris, is the Colonel there, too? Kentucky Fried bones thrown around the Eiffel Tower? He picks up his box, spots of grease dotting the outside, and walks out of Kentucky Fried Chicken. Sam gets out of the car again and Charles sits up front, the box on his lap. Pamela Smith begins to eat a leg. Sam takes a breast. So that he doesn't get both of them, Charles takes the other.

"Any more breasts?" Sam says after a few minutes. There are not.

Pamela Smith eats a wing. Charles eats a leg.

"I'm going to get something to drink," Sam says. "What do you all want?"

"Coke," Pamela Smith says.

"Milk," Charles says.

Sam opens the car door and goes into Kentucky Fried Chicken.

"What am I going to do?" Pamela Smith says. "I don't have any money. I can't just eat off of you."

"Don't worry about it," Charles says.

She licks her fingers. "You won't even let me say how nice you are."

"That's right," Charles says, dropping a bone into the bag.

Sam comes back to the car with a root beer, an orange, and a milk.

"Your choice," Sam says. "They were out of Coke."

"The orange," she says.

"Okay," Sam says, handing it to her.

They drop the tabs in the ashtray. Sam turns on the radio to hear what's playing. It is not Dylan. He turns it off.

"A watched Dylan never plays," Charles says.

They finish the rest of the chicken in silence. Pamela Smith reaches into the french fries box and puts several in her mouth.

"Give me some of those," Sam says. He puts several in his mouth.

"Delicious," Pamela Smith says.

"Now that I've eaten I'm sleepy," Sam says. "Got to get you kiddies home before old Sammy falls asleep."

"Why don't you let me drive?" Pamela Smith says.

Sam starts the car. He turns the radio on again, and he turns it off.

Charles wonders what they will do with Pamela Smith. Just have her sleep on the sofa, feed her? Suddenly there are two other people in his house. What would his dead grandmother think of a lesbian sleeping on the sofa and an unemployed jacket salesman sleeping in the spare bedroom, all her furniture sold to Best Bird Antiques? Sometimes he wants to move out of the house, move out of town . . . to Bermuda. He is obsessed with going to Bermuda. He would buy an underwater camera and take pictures of fish. Laura would be with him. Laura in a bathing suit. They would eat papaya or whatever they eat in Bermuda and drink rum. Their drinking rum is always part of his fantasy, so he no longer questions the reality of it. Maybe they don't drink rum. Whatever they drink. He would run around corners in Bermuda and collide with her. They would fish, pull starfish out of the water. Or whatever fish they have besides sharks in Bermuda. Laura would fix him fresh fish dinners. He would dance as happily as the restaurant menu cookie. They would walk the beach and look at the stars. They would fly to Paris and eat at the McDonald's because it was *très amusant* (this would be the reason they would give all their friends), and for a while they would be as happy and nutty as Scott and Zelda. Zelda died in the bin, and Scott drank himself to death. Didn't he drink himself to death? He fell over in Sheila Graham's living room. Whatever he died of. Once Scott and Zelda put ladies' purses in vats of spaghetti sauce because it was *très amusant*. They were assholes. The fun ended with a bang. He would be eaten by a shark; Laura would get an inoperable melanoma. Bermuda. It probably rains all the time in Bermuda. There are probably slums all around the beaches, to remind you of the real world. He would never have the nerve to spend a lot of money on an underwater camera. Maybe he should get himself a sunlamp and an aquarium and forget about it. He and Laura would probably be blown up in the plane flying them there. They would never get to Bermuda. The rum would be 151 proof and knock them out—they'd never want to screw. ("You've heard of screwing, right?") Charles sighs.

"I've screwed so many people this past year I don't even want to remember it," Pamela Smith says.

Charles starts. "That's just what I was thinking," he says.

"How do you know how many people I've screwed?"

"I wasn't thinking about you. I was thinking about my first sex lesson—a talk I had with my father."

"I was thinking about a pimply dyke I screwed who climbed out a toilet window and abandoned me."

"We must all go to church tomorrow," Sam says. He takes a bite of chicken leg.

"Did you ever go to church?" Pamela Smith asks.

"Me? Sure. I crayoned pictures of Our Lord in Sunday school that still grace my mother's bedroom wall," Sam says.

"What religion were you?"

"A Methodist."

"What were you?" she asks Charles.

"I was a Lutheran."

"I was an Episcopalian," she says. "I was going to switch to Catholicism. A long time back."

"Remember to pray for guidance on Sunday," Sam says.

"When was the last time you were in church?" she says.

"I think . . . twelve years ago. At Christmas."

"I was in church a couple of months ago. A Catholic church," she says. "With Marlan. Did I ever tell you that was her name?"

"What kind of name is that?"

"It was her mother's maiden name." Pamela Smith winces. "Listen to me; maiden name. As if there are maidens any more."

"Maybe there are," Charles says. "Maybe there are maidens in the jungle."

"What does 'maiden' mean, exactly?" Sam says.

"A broad," Charles says.

"It's funny that women got to be called 'broads,'" Pamela Smith says. "Does it mean they have broad asses?"

"I guess that's what it means. Yeah."

Sam pulls into the driveway. "Phew," he says. "Seems like a week ago I shoveled this out. Those cars on the street really got plowed in good."

"It does seem like a week ago," Charles says. "It'll be good to get some sleep."

"Thank you very much for bringing us here," Pamela Smith says to Sam.

"Oh," Sam says. "I live here now."

"Oh," she says.

"Yeah. I just moved in."

"He lost his prestigious, high-paying job," Charles says.

"I just realized," Sam says. "I should have showed up to get the dope after work. Now we don't have any grass."

"What would we do with it anyway?" Charles says. "Jesus. Imagine getting stoned on top of all this."

"If this were the sixties, we couldn't wait to get stoned," Sam says.

"Don't talk about getting stoned. Marlan's daughter was puffing away all the time, listening to Dylan records and saying, 'Yes, yes,' to herself."

"Get the chicken," Sam says. Charles leans over and gets the box from the floor. They get out of the car and go to the front door.

"Look at me," Sam says, and turns a cartwheel.

"I didn't know you could do that," Charles says.

"I don't think I ever had occasion to show you. You remember from grade school though, don't you?"

"No," Charles says. "And what's the occasion now?"

"That we get to go to bed," Sam says.

Charles puts the key in the front door. "If you hear my alarm and you don't hear me moving around, shake me," Charles says. "I've got to go over to my mother's for dinner tonight."

"That should top things off nicely," Sam says.

Pamela Smith flops on the sofa. She turns over, pulls the pillow under her head.

"I'll bring you a blanket," Charles says. "In a minute."

"Never mind. I'm already asleep," she says.

"I'll get you a blanket. Hang on," Charles says. He

hangs up his coat and pulls a blanket off the linen closet shelf. A pale blue blanket. His mother gave it to him. She usually gives him sweaters (the wrong size) and blankets. He has two other blankets in the linen closet: another blue one, and a yellow one. She also brings him light bulbs when she visits. When she used to go out of the house to visit. He puts the blanket over Pamela Smith.

"Take your shoes off," Charles says. "You're gonna wake up and be miserable."

He walks into the bathroom. Sam is in there, running water over his wrists.

"I froze my goddamn wrists," Sam says.

"Try to wake me up if you hear the alarm," Charles says.

"I will. Good night."

"Good night," Charles says.

He walks into his bedroom, undresses, leaves the clothes in a pile on the floor, and climbs into bed. He has forgotten to pull the drapes; it is light outside. He pulls the pillow over his head. It is still bright. He gets up and closes the drapes. He has forgotten to set the alarm. He gets up and sets the alarm, pulls the button. He will be getting up in four hours. Impossible. In five hours he will be in his mother's living room. He laughs. She will serve Hawaiian Punch with rum; Pete will have prepared . . . chicken. It won't be as tasty as the Kentucky Fried. They will have nothing to say to each other. That is, assuming he doesn't have to pull her out of the tub or hold her hand while she twists and turns in bed, during which time they can discuss her illness. She will have on sneakers, and Pete will be all dressed up in a sports jacket and tie. He will have on the damned wing-tip cordovans again. They will sit in the living room, saying nothing, sipping the Hawaiian Punch and rum. A real travesty of the Bermuda dream.

Thinking of Bermuda, he falls asleep and has a dream of a jolly fat man, water-skiing. He must be the fat man, because the fat man is wearing his clothes, except that they are bigger than the clothes he wears, all stretched out of shape. He is water-skiing down a narrow, wavy line—not the real ocean at all, but a line that has been drawn. There are boundaries to Bermuda—to the left and right there are concrete walls, and if the fat man isn't careful he will smash into one of them. There is nothing on the other side of the walls. The fat man is so jolly that he pays no attention, comes within a fraction of an inch of crashing into the walls. He laughs, soaring through the water in a full suit of clothes. Charles wakes up leaning on one elbow, smirking. "Jesus Christ," he says out loud, and falls asleep again. In his next dream he and Laura are underwater—without air tanks, though, with no cameras—and they are flopping easily, like fish, her hair billowing behind her. She is very white and beautiful, and the water is blue-green. He can feel the water against his eyeballs. They are turning somersaults, and then Laura doesn't come out of her somersault, but keeps sinking, bent in half, sinking deeper than he can go. He tries to make his body heavier, to sink with her, but he is light, buoyant, he can't follow. He wakes up at the bottom of the bed, his feet pressing against the bedboard. He pulls himself up to the top of the bed, taking hold of the sheet to pull himself. He feels dizzy. The sun is so bright. What was he dreaming? He reaches for the pillow, sees that it is on the floor. Leave it there. Sun shining through the drapes, he falls asleep again, and this time the jolly fat man is following Laura down, laughing, cackling. There are bubbles as the fat man sinks. He can no longer see Laura, only the fat man's head, grown immense, and the gush of bubbles. He wakes up with a headache. He sits on the side of the bed, after retrieving the pillow, but he's afraid to shut his eyes. He leaves them open, pressed into the pillow. His throat is aching. He has a sore throat. He puts one hand across the front of his throat and somehow falls asleep again, sitting on the side of the bed, falls backward. He is sprawled lengthwise across the bed, naked, when he feels a hand on his arm. He is trying to catch the fat man's arm, to hold him back, but he is sinking fast, and Charles is buoying upward, frightened, realizing that he has no air tank, that he will drown. He has to get to the top fast.

"Charles . . ."

But Laura. And the fat man. What does the fat man want with Laura? Why isn't he floating? Everybody knows fat people float easily, but Charles is floating upward, neck craning for the top, for air. . . .

"Charles. . . ."

He snaps his head forward and sees Sam sitting on the side of the bed.

"Charles . . . the phone. I called you, but you didn't answer."

"What? The phone?"

"Yeah. It's Pete. I said I'd have you call back, but he insisted."

"What time is it? I was dreaming something horrible."

"I figured you were. I couldn't get you to wake up."

"I was in Bermuda. Pete. Pete's on the phone now?"

"Yeah. He says he's got to talk to you."

"What time is it?"

"Four o'clock," Sam says, looking at the clock. The alarm is still pulled. The hand is going around and around. The clock. Dinner. Pete. He walks into the kitchen naked, forgetting Pamela Smith. But she's fast asleep, arms thrown open, feet hanging off the sofa.

"Pete?" Charles says. "What?"

"I'm sorry to be bothering you, Charles. Sam said you two had a rough night. I had to talk to you, though, because I know you were expecting to come to dinner. At least I don't imagine you forgot about dinner."

"No. What is it, Pete?"

"Well, I was washing the chicken. I had planned on a chicken dinner. Stuffed. I was rinsing it, and Mommy—

Clara—got a little upset, saying that she was going to prepare the meal. I thought that was great. I went out for a bottle of wine and left her there, and when I got back she seemed pretty confused. She was sitting on the kitchen stool holding the chicken. She said she wasn't feeling well. She wanted to make the dinner, but she wasn't feeling well. I told her I'd do it, to go lie down. She wouldn't get off the stool. She was sitting there holding this damned chicken. She refused to let me fix it. I finally got her to put it back in the refrigerator, but if she doesn't let me fix it, there isn't going to be any dinner, because she's not going to fix it."

"Oh, Christ, what's she pulling now?"

"She said she was your mother and she wanted to fix the dinner. I was just doing it to do her a favor. But now there's not going to be any dinner. She says so herself. I thought I'd call and let you know. Damn. And I wanted to show you my Honda Civic."

"Oh, Christ. I don't know what to say."

"She's in bed now. Everything's under control."

"Okay. I guess there's nothing I can do. I feel sorry for you, for what that's worth."

"I always thought you did. You and your sister are real nice kids. Sometimes I think about what you said—that my own wouldn't do any better by me—and it's a consolation. Well, I'd bought olives for you and everything. You remember you wanted them for that New Year's Day supper we had? Things don't go in one ear and out the other with me. I got olives and a chablis wine. Taylor chablis. If she had let me make it, it would have been a damn fine meal."

"I'm sure it would have been. If things get worse, call me."

"I'm getting hungry," Pete says, "but I don't dare cook the chicken, even just for the two of us. That chicken is better left forgotten. I'll go out and get us a pizza."

"I'll drive by on my way to work Monday and take a look at your car. I leave earlier than you do."

"No. Don't do that. I want to show you myself."

"Okay. You show it to me. I'll see you later, Pete."

"Promise you won't drive by and look at it."

"I won't. I'll see you, Pete."

"Good-bye," Pete says.

Charles goes back to bed. He sees that Sam is already in bed in his room. He pulls the covers up over himself and falls asleep. He wakes up at five o'clock when the alarm goes off. He gets up, pushes in the button, and goes back to bed. He doesn't wake up again until midnight, when he gets up to take some aspirin for his throat. The door to Sam's room is still open. Charles looks in and does a double take. Silently, Sam is screwing Pamela Smith. Charles closes the door. He goes to the bathroom and gets two Excedrin. He sits on the sofa, in the dark, swallowing the water slowly. He does not feel so much like medicating himself as like drowning. The water seems too cold going down; he finds it hard to breathe. He lies back on the sofa, listening to the whispers and creaking mattress in the other room, and falls into a deep sleep.

Chapter 10

Driving home from work on Monday night, Charles notices that it is staying light longer. When he gets home from work he will have nothing to do: Pamela Smith cooks, and Sam does the dishes. They keep the house clean. Pamela Smith has dyed her hair again. Sam has gained a little weight. Charles is sure that they screw all day, although they show no affection for one another in his presence. And he hasn't seen her in Sam's bed again. They have to screw all day. What else could they do?

Today when Betty came in to get the typing he was embarrassed not to have called her and asked again for her number, saying that he'd lost it. Worse than that, he was specific about the lie: it blew out the car window. It sounded awful. To cover for that, he blathered on: he was going to call and invite her to a small party he was giving. Then he inquired about her sister: had she found work? No—she married a man and is packing to move to Detroit. "Does the man work in the car industry?" Charles asked. "No, he's an accountant," Betty said. He has no idea how to make conversation with Betty. He went back to talking about the party: maybe she could come over a little early to help him get things organized. How is he ever going to get out of this?

Somebody answered his phone when he was at lunch and took a message that Pete called. Is his mother back in the hospital? Surely Pete will call him at home and he'll find out.

Maneuvering through traffic, he is very tempted to turn around and head for Laura's. This could be it: a scene with her husband, a fight which he would lose, but maybe Ox would hurt him so badly that he'd go into a coma and never come out of it. He thinks about cutting his wheel sharply to the left, plowing into the car coming toward him. The car passes. It was a middle-aged woman. Good he didn't kill her. Maybe the next car? It passes. Another middle-aged woman, wearing a hat. A white car, woman inside with a green (green?) hat. He begins to make a game of counting the cars with middle-aged women inside. He counts eight before he tires of the game. When he first started counting there were four cars in a row containing middle-aged women, and he thought, nervously, that the country might have been taken over by middle-aged women while he was working. But the next car was a teen-ager. The next was an old man, the next was a teen-age girl, and there was a car full of nuns. What a silly game.

2001 is playing at the movies. Pete told him a horrible story about how he took Clara to see it, and she screamed when the fetus came on the screen. Pete says that for a long time before seeing the movie she had been worried that she'd go to hell because Susan's twin died. The reason she thinks this, according to Pete in a whispered late-night phone call, is that she wore a red dress to the funeral. She just wasn't thinking. She had a gray raincoat over it, but still. He told her it was perfectly all right, and she got out Amy Vanderbilt's book of etiquette. Amy Vanderbilt. How could anyone fall out a window? Of course she jumped. Why don't they admit she jumped, that knowing you don't wear red dresses to funerals didn't make her everlastingly happy? Because they don't admit anything. Amazing they ever admitted the *Pueblo* was a spy ship. Now Bucher is growing avocados. Tortured by the North Koreans, he returns to the U.S.A. to grow avocados.

Charles stops for gas, sees cashier for transaction settlement, parks in the parking lot next to the gas station, and goes into the store. He has been craving devil's food cookies. Infantile. He checks his wallet and sees that he has ten dollars. He will have to go to the bank. The lunch at the Greek restaurant set him back seven dollars, and ten will never be enough to get through the week. He walks down the aisle, looking for cookies. He sees the dog food and misses Sam's dog. There are a lot of toys in plastic, too. He wishes that he'd bought more toys for the dog. The dog only had three or four, and she loved them. If anybody poisoned that dog, they ought to burn in hell. They could burn in hell with the North Koreans and former President Nixon. And Mrs. DeLillo, if she really killed all those animals. And the people who do all the things the Humane Society keeps him posted on. He hopes that he does not burn in hell for adultery. He wishes he could be committing adultery now, instead of looking for the cookies in the supermarket. But the devil's food cookies will be some consolation when he finds them. He intends to rip them open and eat them on the way home. It is nice to know that there will be a good dinner to follow the cookies. He is very glad that Pamela Smith forgot and ate the chicken—he heard about that for hours—and no longer considers herself a vegetarian. ("Oh no!" she said. "Do you know what I did without thinking?" And he was overcome with horror, expecting her to announce that she had stabbed somebody on the New Jersey turnpike and rolled him into a ditch. She's just crazy enough to forget something like that.) Last night she fixed a platter of vegetables and chicken with spaghetti. She keeps out of the way and doesn't bother him. She certainly isn't bothering Sam. He gets the devil's food (two packages) and a box of vanilla wafers and laments the fact that Hydrox are no longer the same. He gets some Pepperidge Farm Lidos. He puts them all back on the shelf and rechecks his wallet. Yes, that bill he saw was a ten. Is ten dollars enough to buy four packages of cookies? Of course it is. He adds them up in his head, finds that it is plenty. He re-adds. He forces himself to pick up all the cookies again and move away from the cookie counter, where he is lost in calculations.

The rush-hour traffic is subsiding. He puts a devil's food cookie in his mouth and chews. His mother always told him to bite twice on cookies. Therefore, he always puts the whole cookie in his mouth, no matter what the size. With very large cookies from the bakery, he breaks them in several pieces—which is not the same as biting them. Still, although the bakery cookies are very good, he prefers the ones he can shove in his mouth all at once.

He turns right and drives down the street that will take him to his block. He should go out at night—go to the movies—do something. Maybe he will suggest that they all go to the movies. He rolls into his driveway, Bob Dylan singing "Like a Rolling Stone." It feels like every other day. He thinks about Bob Dylan's children running around on the beach at Malibu. Imagine having Dylan for a father. Imagine if his own father were alive. That would be nice. His father made cookies once a year, at Christmas. Then he and Charles went out looking for cookie tins. They bought some, and covered Crisco cans with wrapping paper for others. He made German cookies with chocolate sprinkles on top that were wonderful—ruined only slightly by the fact that his mother told him to bite twice.

He opens the front door and walks in. There is a copy of *The Second Sex* on the kitchen counter. He puts the bag of cookies down on top of it and goes into the living room and looks at the thermostat. He takes off his coat and is hanging it up when Sam comes out of his room.

"She's over at her brother's," Sam says. "She said not to wait for her for dinner."

"Is there anything to eat, then?" Charles says.

"I don't know. I haven't looked. I was taking a nap."

"It was a gray day," Charles says. "Maybe more snow. It's getting colder."

He goes out to the kitchen. There is a box of dried litchi nuts next to a bottle of wine. There's isn't much in the cabinets.

"We ought to go out for dinner," Charles says.

"I don't have any money," Sam says.

"I've got money. Wait a minute—I don't. I mean, I've got six bucks."

"We can get a pizza," Sam says.

"That's right. Okay. Do you want to go now?"

"I want to talk to you."

"What?" Charles says.

"You remember when you closed the bedroom door?"

"Yeah. You want me to leave it open in the future?"

"There won't be any 'in the future.' That's what I want to talk to you about."

"Your cock fell off?"

When Charles was a child he read an article about leprosy. He thought that his limbs were going to fall off, go clunk on the sidewalk. He was very young when he read it, and didn't understand that it was a gradual thing. For a long time he went around expecting to hear a clunk. What a twisted childhood.

"She came into my bedroom that night and wanted to know if I thought it was okay to wake you up and lay you. I said I thought it was a good idea to let you sleep. So she jumped me."

Charles laughed. "Whisper women's liberation propaganda in your ear?"

"Seriously."

"Oh, I believe you."

"And I wanted to tell you, because I didn't want you thinking, I mean, I want to apologize if I did you out of anything you wanted."

"I don't find her attractive," Charles says.

"I don't either. She and I don't talk about it."

"Hell, there goes a treasured illusion: that you and Pamela Smith were shaking ass all over my house while I worked."

"Nah," Sam says.

"Did you go to get signed up for your money?" Charles asks.

"Yeah, I went down this morning. They suggested jobs I could look for and I said, 'uh-huh.' I hinted around that I wanted to work in something related to religion—as a janitor in a church or something like that."

"What did you do that for?"

"Just off the top of my head."

"So what did they say?"

"That I can't get a check for two weeks."

"That's nice of them. Do they let you starve for two weeks, or what?"

"I guess they figure I've got a lot salted away, making all that money selling jackets."

Sam holds open the door and they go out to Charles's car.

"Good you headed for that one," Sam says. "Mine gave out. Died."

"When you were driving?"

"Fortunately, no. Battery's dead. It just wouldn't turn over. I took the bus down to unemployment. That was really something. Everyone on the bus looked like a fat person in a sideshow. Except for the ones who were so old they looked like dried leaves."

"I almost took a bus the other day and decided to walk instead," Charles says.

"I'd say to avoid them if you can," Sam says.

"I'm going to the bank tomorrow during lunch, so I'll remember to bring you some cash. You can pay me back when they come through."

"Thanks," Sam says. "No wonder she says you're so nice. You are nice."

"You're my only friend," Charles says.

"You're *my* only friend," Sam says.

"That's pathetic," Charles says. "How did this happen?"

"I don't know. I just stopped seeing people or they moved or something."

"You used to have women falling all over you."

"I did, for a while. I don't think women like me any more."

"They don't like me, either. I think Betty might, but she's giving up on me. I can tell."

"They never give up once they're interested."

"Yeah, but you haven't met Betty. She's very, well, she's a zombie. I don't think she thinks about anything much."

"Sounds like you'd do well to get her, then."

"What do I want some dumb woman for?"

"To screw."

"She's fat."

"Get her to lose weight. Once you get her you can start talking that up."

"I wouldn't know how to tell a woman to lose weight."

"Find some way and tell her. Tell her now and wait a few weeks before you ask her out."

"I don't want to ask her out. I just have no motivation to do it."

"I think Susan might have something. That the two of us are depressed all the time. Too bad she didn't tell us what to do about it."

"She's nineteen. You're going to listen to advice from a nineteen-year-old?"

"I don't know," Sam says. "Maybe we shouldn't have cut her off."

"Sam, she reads those paperbacks about people who relive their childhood by screaming and things like that and she thinks we should try it."

"Screaming?"

"I mean, just as an example. She thinks we should do

something that a book tells us to do, something that's supposedly made everybody else happy."

"Well, what book would you read?" Sam says.

"I wouldn't read any book, and you wouldn't either if you were in your right mind."

"We don't encourage each other. You should urge me to try something," Sam says.

"It's *1975*, Sam. I urge you to try pizza with green pepper, the way I like it."

"Hell, you're paying," Sam says.

"You really are sounding defeated. I thought you couldn't stand anything but cheese."

"I'm not complaining. You're paying."

"Shit," Charles says. "Im going to order it half plain, half with peppers."

They drive in silence to the restaurant: a small brick pizza house with the Parthenon jutting out over the front door. It's a good, cheap place. A large pizza is $3.80. If this were a food store, Charles would be in a panic with only six dollars.

"Maybe I should try green pepper," Sam says. "I should try again and see if I like something like that."

"Why would you try it? You don't like it. You can have it plain."

"I want to try green pepper."

"Jesus. What am I arguing for? What do I care how you eat your pizza?"

"You're mad at me," Sam says.

"Well, what am I supposed to think when you suggest we let Susan straighten us out? She's my kid sister. She's so straight it's pathetic. She doesn't even drink."

"She screws," Sam says.

"That's straight," Charles says. "Screwing a doctor is straight."

"Keep your voice down."

The waitress stands at their booth.

"A large pizza, half green pepper, the other half mozzarella only, and a Coke for me. What do you want?"

"A draft," Sam says.

"One Coke and one draft," the waitress says. "Thank you."

"You missed my point before," Sam says. "I meant that she seems normal and happy. She must know something."

"She's nineteen. She doesn't know shit. You could be happy too, Sam, if you were nineteen in 1975 and you hadn't had your eyes opened in the sixties."

"She was alive then."

"In 1968 she was twelve years old."

"Oh," Sam says, "1968 was the best year. That's the time I was the happiest."

"In 1965 when 'Satisfaction' came out she was nine."

"Okay, okay," Sam says.

"The goddamn sixties," Charles says. "How'd we ever end up like this?"

The waitress brings a Coke and a draft.

"Who gets the Coke again?" she says.

"The clergyman," Sam says, pointing.

"He stutters," Charles says. "She wrote me a note explaining that he speaks so haltingly sometimes because he's swallowing the stutter."

"C-c-c-clever," Sam says.

Charles laughs. Even when Sam is down, he is still funny. Sam even used to make his mother laugh. His mother used to laugh at jokes. "It's not dirty, is it?" she used to ask Sam. "Filthy," he'd say, and start in. It was never dirty. His mother used to like Sam. Now she never asks about him. Now she doesn't know what's going on. She's her own joke.

"I've got a load of books at my apartment that I've got to get out of there," Sam says.

"Drive me to work and you can have the car."

"Okay. Sure."

"You don't think the battery on yours can be charged?" Charles asks.

"It's dead."

"I swear this is the last time I'll bring this up, but do you ever think about getting another dog?" Charles says.

"Yeah. I think about it."

"Why don't you go to the pound tomorrow and get a dog?"

"I don't know."

"You'd have a lot of fun with it."

"It would crap all over your place."

"Put down newspapers. Keep it in the bedroom with them for a while."

"I've got to sleep in there."

"How many times a day can it shit?"

"I'll think about it."

The waitress puts the pizza down.

"Let me just have a slice with green pepper," Sam says.

"Take it."

Sam cuts a piece with his knife. He bites off the end.

"Well?"

"I don't like it. Here."

Charles takes the piece of pizza and begins eating.

"She's a good cook, isn't she? Pamela Smith, I mean."

"Yeah, pretty good."

"I mean, she's not *Laura*," Sam says, "but . . ."

"Shut up about Laura."

"That's what you were thinking when I mentioned Pamela Smith's cooking. You got that Laura look on your face."

"I don't want to hear about Laura."

"You brought up my dog again."

Charles sighs.

"The new Dylan isn't on the jukebox, is it? It might be there even if it isn't in the stores."

"I doubt it," Charles says, flipping through. "You want to hear 'Lay Lady Lay'? That's on here."

"I don't want to think about screwing."

"I was just offering," Charles says, breaking off another piece of pizza.

"I really don't have any luck with women any more," Sam says.

"Maybe when you get older you don't have luck with them."

"You really think that's it? My age?"

"No."

"What do you think it is?"

"I don't know. You're not going to meet any, in the first place, sitting around the house."

"In 1968 I could pick up the prettiest girl in the park just by walking through."

"I met a woman in the park the other day. I can't remember her name."

"Wouldn't have done me any good anyway."

"Yeah," Charles says. "She was okay."

"You mean just okay?"

"Yeah," Charles says. "And she was married."

"Who cares if they're married or not?" Sam says.

The waitress frowns down at him. "Do you want another draft?" she says.

"Oh. Please."

She takes the glass away.

"Nice one," Charles says, shaking his head. "Glad she didn't hear the clergyman saying that."

"Did I tell you Pete called?" Sam says.

"Say what he wanted?"

"No. But he sounded okay. Sounded cheerful."

"Maybe she sank in the tub."

"Do you think he'd be happy if she died?"

"According to him, what would make him happy would be to have his own kid."

"I don't guess he'll be getting one of those now," Sam says.

"That's what he says," Charles says.

"Well, that's sad, I guess. If you want a kid and you don't have it."

"If we don't get married and have kids we're going to be up shit creek. What's going to happen when we're old?" Charles says.

"Are you serious?"

"Yeah. I'm serious."

"If we had kids they'd probably have to be taken care of in their old age by us."

"If we had a lot we might get one good kid."

"Great. You pull off shitted diapers for years, hoping for one good kid."

"It's just an idea," Charles says.

"Talk about your sister being straight," Sam says. "That's what straight people do—pump 'em out, change the diapers, and sit back waiting for the payoff."

Sam takes a drink from his new mug of beer. "This is a miserable topic of conversation," he says.

"How did we get onto it?" Charles says.

"I said that Pete called."

"That's right. I wonder what he wanted."

"Maybe he got the chicken cooked."

"He said he was going to forget about it. He didn't want her to see it and start again."

"That must be hell on earth, living with your mother."

"I feel pretty sorry for him lately."

Charles takes his money out of his wallet and puts it all on top of the bill. The waitress takes it away.

"Listen. Would you mind riding over to Laura's?"

"That's pathetic!" Sam says. "What do you want to do something that pathetic for? What's the point of it?"

"I'll drop you at home."

"Oh, shit, Charles. It's not that I won't ride over. I just think it's pointless."

"She might be outside."

"Just walking around at the end of the drive, soaking up the cold air?"

"The light might be on."

"Of course the light will be on. She wouldn't be in bed this early."

"Then I want to see the light."

"What's this, *The Great Gatsby* or something?"

"Shut up. I said I'd take you to the house."

"I'll come, I'll come for Christ's sake."

They get up and walk out of the restaurant. The waitress doesn't look at them. She is standing in front of the cashier, talking.

"Take me home," Sam says. "I can't bear to watch you make a fool of yourself."

"It'll take ten minutes longer than driving straight home."

"This is ridiculous," Sam says.

"I just want to see what's going on over there."

"All you can see is a house! A lit-up house."

Charles heads for Laura's. He hopes that she will be outside the house. Maybe she went out because . . . she heard a noise. She wouldn't, though. She'd mention it to her husband and he'd go outside. Ox. To drive all the way over there to see Ox.

Eric Clapton on the radio. Layla. Laura. Ox. Ox had better not be in sight. Sam slides down in the seat, sighing and shaking his head.

"You're nuts, this is completely nuts," Sam says.

Once he and Laura made a fruitcake. It took them all afternoon. They were going to give it to a friend of Laura's who was sick, but they wanted it when it was done and ate it themselves. It cost a fortune to buy all the things that went into it. They bought a bag of walnuts and he cracked them. They joked—how did that joke start?—about sending the shells to the Smithsonian, writing a letter claiming to be archaeologists, saying that they found these peculiar things on a dig in the Blue Ridge, and did they think it might be petrified caveman shit? He showed her the trick with the Land O' Lakes butter box—how you could make it look as if the squaw had big tits. They ate the fruitcake and drank the brandy they had bought to use in the fruitcake. It was so rich and delicious that they were almost sick, but they couldn't stop eating. He put candied cherries in their brandy. In the morning she went out and got a get-well card for the friend. They ate the fruitcake for lunch and after dinner. Weekends were so nice with Laura. The time seemed to go so fast. She had a calendar hung in the kitchen that he insisted she get rid of. He didn't even want to look at it. "But where will I write down appointments and things?" she said, and he gave her an engagement calendar. "I'm half flattered and I half think you're crazy," she said. He wonders if she has a calendar in the A-frame. If she and Ox ever do things like making fruitcake. He would like to soak Ox in brandy and beat him well and shove him in the oven. Ox wears size extra-large undershirts. Charles wears medium. Ox would pick him up by the collar and put *him* in the oven. Does Ox know about him? And if he knows, does he know about the fruitcake they made, about all the giggling they did in Laura's kitchen? It would take her years to fill him in on all that. He couldn't know it all. He might even get bored hearing all of it: we baked fruitcake, he showed me a trick with a butter box, we went to the movies, we did the laundry, we ate at a Japanese restaurant and didn't like the soup, we cleaned his kitchen, we . . . Maybe Laura left because she was bored. Maybe that was one of the many things. She wouldn't have been bored in Bermuda. He should have taken off from work, made her go to Bermuda with him. He should have cleaned the kitchen himself. He could go tap on her kitchen window: "Another chance, Laura." Ox would be in the kitchen. He would walk outside and kill him.

"I mean it," Sam says. "This is pathetic. It's not like you call her and write her and make yourself obnoxious. All you do is slink over there to look at the lights on in her house. If she killed somebody you'd take the rap for her, wouldn't you? The whole Gatsby trip."

"She wouldn't ever kill anybody."

"Yeah, but what if she was driving your roadster along and a woman ran out in front of it?"

"Okay, okay. Enough."

"What can I say that will talk you out of this dreary driving by her house?"

"Nothing."

"There's no point to it. What does driving by her house prove?"

"Nothing."

"You just intend to do it anyway."

"I just intend to do it anyway."

"Goddamn it," Sam says. "You remember how we used to double-date in college, and how we even had girlfriends in elementary school?"

"I never had a girlfriend in elementary school. You had Bess Dwyer."

"Are you still denying that you had a crush on Jill Peterson?"

"I never liked Jill Peterson. That was always just something in your mind."

"You're still denying it. I can't believe it."

"I can't believe that you're still going on about it. I never liked her."

"Then you're just not admitting it to yourself."

"You've brought her up for years. I'm not even clear on which one Jill Peterson was. Was she the scrawny blond kid?"

"Exactly! You remember just which one she was."

"What made you think I liked her?"

"You bought her a special valentine, don't you remember that?"

"She transferred into our school just before Valentine's Day. I remember that. My box of valentines had all been addressed, and then she showed up, and I thought I'd better . . ."

"I'll be damned! You're still rationalizing!" Sam breaks in.

"I'm not rationalizing. I'm trying to set you straight. It doesn't matter to me if you want to think I liked her, but I never did."

"Everybody knew you did."

"Even if I did—which I didn't—she wasn't a girl-friend."

"You've always liked thin blondes. Laura is just like Jill Peterson! Didn't you ever think that?"

"Laura is twenty-nine. Jill Peterson was a kid I knew in the fifth or sixth grade."

"You know it was the sixth."

"Okay, I knew it was the sixth. I don't know why I said that."

"Because you always try to pretend to be vague about her. Actually, every woman you've liked has been thin like Jill Peterson."

"They were all different. All the girls were different. You're talking nonsense."

"Okay, even if they were. Laura is just what Jill Peterson would look like grown-up."

"You sound like my sister. This is incredible."

"She might be right. You really might not understand yourself."

"Leave me alone."

"I'm trying to help you."

But they are already on Laura's block.

"There are a million girls with blond hair. Skinny blond girls. Is that all you see by way of similarity?" Charles says.

Sam is slumped in the seat, disgusted. He won't speak. Charles sighs.

"If it were true, why wouldn't I think about Jill Peterson?"

At five miles an hour, the car rolls by Laura's driveway. The light is on in the kitchen again, but the kitchen window is too far from the road to see through. She could be standing right in the window and he wouldn't know it. If only the house were closer to the road. If only she didn't live in that house at all. She could live in his house. Did he ever make that clear enough to her? Yes. A hundred times. She even agreed that his house was more spacious. She is in there, somewhere in that house, in one of those lighted rooms. He turns in a driveway and rolls by again, this time even slower. The trees are blowing in the wind. He is nothing like Jay Gatsby. Gatsby waited all his life, and then Daisy slipped away. Charles has only been waiting for two years, and he'll get her back. He has to get her back. He will get her back and take her to Bermuda. "Bermuda?" she will say. She always thought the things he said were strange. Maybe he was a weird conversationalist. And he can't blame her for thinking him peculiar when he said the calendar had to go. In general, though, she didn't think him peculiar. She loved him, in general. If she still loves him, he will get her back. She has to still love him. She just has to. She laughed wildly when he showed her the butter box trick.

"Jesus Christ." Sam swears under his breath as they turn back onto the main road.

"I've got to get her back. Wasn't she great, Sam?"

"Here we go. I knew. I just knew it." Sam sighs dramatically. "Yeah, she was a swell woman."

"I'm going to get her back."

"I hope so," Sam says. He shakes his head.

"If she didn't like me, why would she have driven to school that day she said she'd meet me?"

Driving home, Charles realizes that it's too late to suggest going to a movie. Just as well, because he spent all his money at dinner.

"I sure am waiting for that Dylan album," Sam says. "I

really want to know what Bob Dylan's got to say in 1975."

Charles thinks of the cookies at home and drives faster. Devil's food cookies. In fifteen minutes they are there. Charles heads for the cookie bag as he goes through the door. He is suddenly starving.

"Have some," he says to Sam, then sees the note next to the bag: "My brother is driving me to California. It's a long story. I had intended to stay with you, but I realized talking to my brother that I really had to head west. I can never thank you enough for coming out that night to get me. I'm leaving some books here that you and Sam might like, and when I get to California, I'll call with a longer explanation. My brother is waiting. Long explanation later. Love, Pamela."

"Oh no," Sam says, reading over his shoulder.

Charles shoves another cookie in his mouth. "I'm actually disappointed," Charles says through the cookie.

"Why?" Sam says.

"After all we went through to get her, it seems like she should have stuck around for a while."

"I know what you mean," Sam says.

"She left her sweater," Charles says, looking at the kitchen chair. "She left in a hurry."

"You think that's true? About her brother?"

"Maybe he figured he'd transport her himself, be sure to get rid of her."

"Yeah. That could be it."

"Wow. It really seems strange that she's gone," Charles says.

Sam takes another cookie. "Well, back to cooking for ourselves," he says.

"Yeah."

"We still might hear from her before she hits the West Coast, knock on wood," Sam says, rapping his knuckles on the kitchen cabinet.

"Women," Charles says.

"She's a very odd one," Sam says. "Do you remember when women didn't use to be odd? I'd pick up some girl in the park and she'd be a nice, normal chick."

"I've got to get Laura back," Charles says, putting another cookie in his mouth.

The phone rings.

"Don't tell me," Sam says. "Should I answer it?"

"Go ahead."

"Hello?" Sam says. "Yes. Just a minute." He covers the mouthpiece. "Pete," he says.

"Hello?" Charles says.

"How's my boy? Did I disturb you?"

"No. We just got in."

"Get into those pants, ha, ha, ha?"

"She's gone back to California."

"That's the breaks," Pete says.

Silence.

"I don't have anything major to report," Pete says. "I think sometimes that you must dread a call from me, because it might bring word of your mother being in trouble. It's too bad I can't just call you and we can't chat without that hanging over us."

"Yeah," Charles says. "What's new?"

"Well, the reason I called, I've been by two hardware stores today, and damned if I can find Turtle Wax. You know, that's the stuff you want to take to your car. Get it waxed up while it's new, you'll never have a problem. But I can't find the stuff anywhere. Now, it's not what the manufacturer recommends, but I know my car wax, and I want to go over it with Turtle Wax. If in your travels you come across it, why, buy the stuff and I'll reimburse you."

"Sure," Charles says. "I'll look."

"Cooked the chicken and it went fine," Pete whispers.

"Good," Charles says. "Things are looking up."

Silence.

"I'll hang up now and let you get on with it," Pete

says. "Good to talk to you, and thanks for keeping an eye out."

"Sure," Charles says. "Good-bye."

It is nine-fifteen. He puts on a record that has always been one of his favorites: The New Lost City Ramblers with Cousin Emmy. Cousin Emmy has her red-painted mouth open wide. She looks like his mother being hauled out of the tub. He gets up and moves the needle to "Chilly Scenes of Winter." Sing it, Emmy. He eats a cookie and tries to think what to do to get Laura. Sam is right; he can't keep driving by her house. He will call her. Tomorrow. He'll call her and ask to see her again, ask whether he can meet her at the school for just five minutes. Or maybe that doesn't seem self-assured enough. He'll ask if he can see her and put no time limit on it. He'll be a little casual. He won't say it's important the way he did the other time. He will just say that he'd like to see her. He won't tell her he loves her on the phone—nothing to scare her away, nothing to give her an excuse to say no. And then he'll see her. What will he say? What will he say to persuade her never to drive home again? He gets up and walks around the house. Pamela Smith's things are everywhere. He will have to box them and send them. He hates wrapping things for mailing. Maybe there's a way to get Sam to do it. Sam has more time than he does. Get Sam to do it. He opens the Lido cookies. They are wonderful. He gets a glass of water and paces the kitchen. What can he say to her? What can he say to Laura?

He takes a shower and watches the eleven o'clock news. He gets in bed with a magazine. At midnight he calls good night to Sam and turns off the light. He thinks back over the day. One thing keeps coming back to him: when he was leaving work he stopped at the blind man's stand for a Hershey bar. "What have you got?" the blind man said and Charles was suddenly tempted to break into song with, "I've got a never-ending love for you. . .

He laughed out loud when he thought of singing that to the blind man. "Hershey bar," he said, and laughed again. The blind man reached out and felt the Hershey bar before he took the money from Charles. He felt all along it, and had his head cocked to one side when Charles left. The blind man is beginning to distrust him.

Chapter 11

Standing on the eleventh floor waiting for the elevator, Charles sees Betty out of the corner of his eye. She had her coat on and must have been leaving, but she ducked back in the doorway when she saw him. She has given up on him, doesn't even want to talk to him. She picked up his reports today without even saying hello. He couldn't think of anything to say to her, so he didn't look up. Now she won't even wait for the elevator with him. He feels sorry that he has been cruel to Betty, but he just can't get interested. He has been in a bad mood all day because Laura's phone rang and rang. She never did answer. He stayed at work later than usual, hoping to catch her before Ox got home. He finally stopped dialing, sure that Ox would pick it up. He could have hung up on Ox, but he doesn't want him suspicious. He doesn't want Laura blaming him for anything. He has to be very nice and very careful and get her back.

Betty and another woman walk through the corridor to the elevator. The doors open just as they get there. Charles puts his hand over the edge of the door to make sure it stays open for them. The elevator is packed. He gets on along with ten people from the eleventh floor. Bob White is pressed in the back. He nods hello. Betty is standing next to Charles.

"How are you?" Charles says.

"Tired," Betty says. She turns and talks to the woman next to her about dinner.

"If you're not doing anything for dinner, why don't you two come over to my place," Charles hears himself say as he walks off the elevator in back of them.

They stop, looking confused. He has never seen the other woman. She is much prettier than Betty. Sam wouldn't mind.

"I was just saying that I couldn't go at all," the woman says. "I have no baby-sitter."

"Oh, that's too bad," Charles says.

"Maybe some other time," Betty says.

"Oh," Charles says. "If you can't make it."

"I'm awfully tired to go out," Betty says. "But thank you."

"Let me walk to your car with you," he says. Why is he saying this?

She shrugs. She says good-bye to the other woman at the door.

"Change your mind," Charles says to Betty.

"Actually, I have no car. It's in the shop for a valve job. I was walking to the bus stop."

"Let me drive you home, then."

"All right," she says. "Thank you."

They walk silently to his car. He thinks of his dancing teacher: "Closer, closer." He is walking six feet away from Betty. He moves over about a foot. She doesn't seem to notice. Her coat collar is turned up. She looks like a turtle. She has a sharp nose like a turtle. On all fours she might look very much like a turtle.

"Are you sure you wouldn't like to stop by for dinner? I have to go to the grocery store anyway. A friend is staying with me and his battery's dead, so he couldn't go out to get groceries."

"If you'd like me to," Betty says. "Thank you for inviting me."

"What would you like for dinner?" he asks.

"Whatever you'd planned to have is fine."

He never plans dinner. He would have gone home and had water and cookies.

"I'll stop and get us some steaks." He opens the car door for her. Her legs are fat. He averts his eyes—shower room etiquette—as she climbs in. He walks around the car and opens his door. She did not pull the lock up for him. She doesn't like him. He doesn't want her, and she doesn't want to come.

"How long have you worked there?" he asks.

"Four years," she says. "I started when I was twenty."

This woman is only twenty-four? How could anyone be so . . . solid at twenty-four? He turns on the radio and catches the end of a plea for money. Just like going home and opening the mail. The Indians want him. The starving orphans in Ghana. The mistreated kittens. He realizes, suddenly, that this was the day Sam was going to drive him to work so Sam could clean out his apartment. They are both so disorganized that nothing gets done. He is amazed by people who can shop for a whole week's groceries on one day—that they know what to get, and how much of it, and that they will want to eat those things for sure during the next week. He looks in his wallet at the first red light. There is plenty of money. He has forty, and there is a twenty tucked in the back to lend Sam. He could even use that in the grocery store if necessary. Betty looks at him looking in his wallet out of the corner of her eye.

"I'm fascinated by men who can cook," Betty says. "My father wouldn't even open a carton of milk for himself. My mother or my sister or I had to do it. It seems lately that quite a few men cook."

"It's that or go out," Charles shrugs.

Betty says nothing. He has botched it. He cut her off, and she was making polite conversation.

"Your father really wouldn't open a milk carton?" he asks.

"No. He wouldn't. When my mother bought the things

she'd always open and close the milk again, and she'd take the caps off the soda bottles and put on those rubber ones to seal them. He'd pop one of those off. He'd carry on if he had to use a can opener or rip open the milk, though. That's part of the reason I moved out. That and my mother telling me to use my salary for plastic surgery."

"What for?" he says.

"My nose."

"You don't have a bad nose."

Her nose is her worst feature. That and her weight.

"Thank you. I'm very self-conscious about it."

He should say something else: flatter her more. He changes the station on the radio.

"What did you do before you started working?"

"I worked at Western Union for a while, and as a checker in a supermarket. I trained to work in a bank, but I quit after the training. The people were so nasty, and the money looked so ugly."

"That's quite an assortment of jobs."

"I kept kidding myself that I was going to college. How can you save money working at Western Union? When I had a little extra money at the supermarket I spent it joining a health club. The exercises made me sore, and I got a kidney infection around that time and had to give up on it. So then I went to the bank and started learning the ropes. And then I took the exam to get into the government. I always knew how to type."

"When did you get your apartment?"

"Over a year ago. A girl was living with me, but she quit and went back to Georgia."

"She didn't like the job?"

"She didn't like the city. She had me so upset that after she left I was afraid to go out at night, and I had a bolt put on the front door. When you live with somebody who's always telling you what danger you're in you start believing it."

Betty lights a cigarette. "Do you mind if I smoke?"

"Go ahead," he says. Cigarette smoke makes him sick. They are almost at the supermarket, though. He concentrates on not coughing. He always coughed in Laura's car. Laura, smoking Chesterfields. She will die young. He had better get her in a hurry.

He pulls into the parking lot. As he walks in, he takes his wallet out of his pocket and checks. The forty is still there. He puts it back. He takes it out again, going through the electric door, and searches for the twenty. Because if it took more than forty, he would need that money. He knows he is being silly. He knows that steaks for three people don't cost forty dollars.

"Do you have enough money?" Betty says.

"Oh, yes. Checking my wallet is a nervous habit."

Betty nods. He is sure she doesn't believe him.

He goes to the meat counter and gets three T-bone steaks. "What else do you like?" he asks.

"Potatoes," she says.

"Potatoes. Where would they be?"

He follows her. He picks up a bag of potatoes. He gets a package of spinach and a large bottle of Coke. They stand in line. He wonders if anyone in the grocery store mistakes her for his wife. People used to mistake Laura for his wife. "Your wife left this," the woman at the bank said, when Laura left her hat on the table. People used to smile at him when he was with Laura. They don't smile now.

"Working makes me so tired," Betty says.

"You could do some isometrics," he says. What is he talking about?

"Do you know the exercises?" she says.

"I have a book you can borrow." Pamela Smith left the book. What is she going to think if all those women's lib books are still lying around? She'll think it's peculiar he reads Germaine Greer and Kate Millett and Simone de Beauvoir. And if she asks for an opinion on any of them he's sunk. Maybe Sam cleaned. He is sure that Sam did not.

"I'll probably be having that party this weekend," he says. What did he bring that up for?

She nods. She does not believe him. She has no reason to believe him. There is no possible way he could have a party over the weekend. He could call J.D. J.D. might come to the party if he didn't have to work. That would make him, J.D., Sam, and Betty. Pete would come for sure. Pete would be so flattered. What a travesty that would be. What would Betty say to Pete?

"I'd be glad to come over and help you get organized," she says.

"Thanks," he says.

He pays for the food and is very relieved when he sees that he has enough money. How would a psychiatrist work him through this trauma? Tell him to go to a store and get more food than he has money for and see that it's not the end of the world? Probably. Shrinks. The indirect approach. "Don't you think . . ."

They get back in his car and start toward the house. Sam is going to be very surprised. Charles himself is very surprised. It would be nice to take all this food home and have dinner with Sam. He pulls into traffic.

"Where do you live?" she asks.

"Colony Street."

"I don't know where that is."

"It's not far from here."

"Is your friend visiting from out of town?"

"He's actually staying there. He just lost his job."

"Things are awful," Betty says. "What was he doing?"

"He had a shit job selling men's jackets, and last week they fired him."

"That's too bad. Do you think he'll find another job?"

"Eventually."

"So many people are out of work. My sisters' fiancé

says you wouldn't believe the lines in Detroit for welfare checks."

Come on, Charles. Keep the conversation going. He stares straight ahead at the line of cars he is in. When the light changes, the line begins to move. He turns right and is on an almost empty stretch of road that goes to his house.

"It's nice out here."

"Yeah. My grandmother bought the house I live in not too long before she died, and she left it to me in her will."

"Wow. You never hear of things like that happening."

"The other house was nicer. Handmade by my grandfather, but she sold that and got this newer one. Still, you're right. It's a nice house."

"Are your neighbors nice?"

"I don't know my neighbors."

"That's what Ginny—the girl who lived with me—complained about. That everything was so impersonal. In Georgia everybody knew everybody else, I guess."

He turns into his driveway. She opens her own door and gets out. He carries the grocery bag, walking in front of her. Sam opens the door.

"Prepare yourself," Sam says. "Oh—hello," he says to Betty.

"What's wrong? What's the matter?"

"Nothing bad."

"Betty, this is Sam."

"How do you do?" Sam says. He has on a pair of ripped pants and his snowmobile socks and a black sweater with a hole over the left nipple.

"Hello," Betty says.

Sam turns and pushes open the door. A black dog is sitting in the kitchen. It wags its tail and walks up to Charles. It is one of the ugliest dogs he has ever seen.

"Oh, a dog," Betty says.

"I can explain why I got him. It was next in line, if you know what I mean. It cost me five dollars."

"Look at it," Charles says. "It's a male?"

"Wait until you hear what they told me it was a mixture of. Can you guess?"

"Dachshund?"

"Right. And what else?"

"God. I have no idea."

"Cocker spaniel. It's seven months old."

The dog does, on close inspection, have some cocker spaniel features. It has long curly ears and the sharp nose of a dachshund. Its fur is curly and a little long, but its body is all chest and no rear, like a dachshund. It is definitely one of the oddest dogs Charles has ever seen. It looks like a very old dog. There is white on its coat.

"Are you sure this is a puppy?"

"Yeah. They told me."

"It's . . ."

"I know. I just got it because it was so ugly I knew it would never be saved before nine A.M. tomorrow. I know," Sam says, shaking his head.

"I think it's a nice puppy," Betty says.

"It is nice. It follows me around, and it's not at all wild."

Charles shakes his head. He picks it up and examines it in his arms. Its narrow rat-tail looks doubly awkward coming out of the soft, curly hair. He cannot believe that there is such a dog.

"Well. You got a dog."

"You'll get to like it. You really will. I like it already, and I've carried out the newspapers twice."

Charles puts it back on the floor. "Got a name for it?"

"No. Can you think of anything?"

Charles shakes his head. "Well, come in," he says to Betty. He leads the way into the living room and takes her coat. He hangs it over Sam's coat on the ironing board.

"Have a seat," he says. She sits in the chair. On the footstool in front of it is *The Female Eunuch*.

"I'll get the steaks ready to broil," he says. "Excuse me."

Sam is in the kitchen, stroking the dog. The dog is a terrible genetic mistake. And he urged Sam to get a dog.

Charles gestures with his thumb. "Go in there," he mouths. Sam gets up and carries the dog into the living room.

"So. You work with Charles?" he says.

"Yes," he hears Betty say.

He rummages around for the broiling pan. He unwraps the steaks and puts them in the pan. He takes the spinach out of the package and dumps it in a pot. He runs water over it, pours the water out, runs more water over it, pours that out, fills the pot with water and puts it on the stove. He rinses three potatoes and puts them in another pot and turns the fire on under them. He takes them out and slices them in half so they will cook more quickly. He drops them in. He goes back to the counter to get the cellophane to throw away and picks up a lottery ticket. Sam has bought a lottery ticket. He looks at the lottery ticket and feels very sad. He is embarrassed to have seen it. It reminds him of another thing he saw by accident: a bloody Kotex of his mother's that tumbled out when he dumped the trash. He didn't know what to do. He couldn't touch it. He pushed it back of the trash cans with a stick.

"No," he hears Sam say. "I was born here."

He gets three plates down and stacks them on the counter. He pushes the lottery ticket away with his elbow.

"Yeah," Sam says. "Jackets."

Charles goes into the dining room and begins to clear the table. He takes *The Second Sex* into Sam's room and throws it on the bed. The dog runs into the dining room and looks at Charles.

"Hi," Charles says.

The dog wags its tail. It goes into Sam's room, in pursuit of *The Second Sex*. Charles hears it skidding on the newspaper. Charles takes several record albums off the table, and his pajamas. He puts them on a chair they won't be using. Sam seems to be conversing very easily with Betty. They are talking about Marvin Mandel. How did they get on that? He would never have the ingenuity to talk to Betty about Marvin Mandel. Maybe Sam is regaining his old touch with women. The dog stands at Charles's feet, looking up.

"Hey, did you feed this dog?"

"They had fed it. They said to try again tonight. When they're scared they like to eat."

"The dog doesn't seem scared."

"I didn't think so either. That's good, huh?"

"Yeah," Charles says. He pats the dog. He has nothing else to do, so he goes into the living room.

"Betty was saying that she worked in a bank with a woman who grew up with Mandel's new wife."

"She let everybody know she was her friend, too," Betty says. "She brought it up all the time and said she didn't think it was scandalous."

"That's liberal of her," Sam says.

"That's just the way she put it: 'I don't think Jeanne's romance with the Governor is at all scandalous,' she said. She quit after training just like I did."

"What's it like looking at all that money?" Sam says.

"After a while you forget it means anything. It was depressing because I'd look at my paycheck I'd worked for and think that *it* meant nothing."

"Must be strange," Charles says.

"I thought I'd like the hours, but you always end up staying late."

"You know what?" Sam says, looking at Charles. "I forgot to drive you to work so I could have the car."

"Tomorrow," Charles says.

"Or maybe I could just take it later tonight. Do it tonight. I haven't done anything all day."

"That's a good idea. After we drop Betty off I can come help you."

"You were living in an apartment?" Betty says.

"Yeah. A real dump."

"It's nice you can stay here," Betty says.

"It is. There's not a bug in the whole place. How come you don't have bugs?"

"I don't know. It's not too dirty."

"I guess bugs are mostly in apartments. I swear to God, if you left a glass of water out overnight, you'd find something floating in it in the morning."

Betty makes a face. "My apartment is pretty clean," she says.

"I'd rather have bugs than rats, though," Sam says.

"Don't talk about it before dinner," Charles says.

Betty laughs.

They eat in the dining room with four white candles burning in a wooden candle holder Susan gave him for his birthday. The dinner is good. They concentrate on eating because they have run out of things to say to each other. Ry Cooder's "Paradise and Lunch" plays. It is not exactly dinner music, but Amy has gone out the window, so what the hell. Ry Cooder is doing a splendid job of "Mexican Divorce."

"Have you ever been to Mexico?" Betty asks.

"I've never been anywhere," Sam says.

"No," Charles shakes his head.

"I went there when I was ten. I bought a stuffed armadillo. At customs they opened it underneath with a jackknife. They sewed it back up, but they did a sloppy job. That was traumatic, to have my toy taken away and sliced open."

"Drugs, huh?" Charles says.

"I guess."

"What's it like in Mexico?" Sam asks.

"I don't remember too well because I was so young. I

just remember things like what the children looked like, and all the fruit stands."

"It would be great to have money to take a vacation," Sam says.

Bermuda. . . .

He has forgotten to buy dessert. They go back to the living room, where the dog is sleeping. There is a small puddle on the floor by the lamp. Sam gets a sponge and wipes it up.

"You're a nice puppy," Betty says, patting it.

"Think of a name for him," Sam says.

"I can't think of anything," Betty says. She looks proud of herself for not being able to think, the way Marilyn Monroe always smiled in the movies when she was apologetic.

"Did you two meet in college?" Betty asks.

"Grade school. A long time ago."

"That's amazing. You've known each other that long and you still like each other?"

"Yeah," Charles shrugs.

"I was friends with a girl since we were sixteen, but lately we're so different that we don't get along. She married a stockbroker."

Sam gets on the floor and plays with the dog.

"That was a very good dinner," Betty says. "Thank you."

After another half hour of awkward conversation (damn—he should have bought two of those big bottles of Coke) Betty says that she should go home.

"You don't mind if I ride along?" Sam says.

"Of course not," Betty says.

On the ride to her apartment Sam sits in the back. Betty wanted to sit back there, and both kept insisting until finally Sam pushed her aside and climbed in. Charles felt sorry for her, trying to act like one of the guys, to act indifferent. He thinks she is starting to like him again. He looks quickly at her legs. They are so fat. She is so plain.

They have nothing to talk about. He knew it would be this way.

"What do you hear from Laura?" he asks, going around the circle. It is the same circle the old man shook his stick in, the circle he rode around with Laura.

"Oh, that's right. You know Laura. I was over at her apartment a couple of nights ago for spaghetti."

"What? What do you mean?"

"She asked me over for dinner. What's wrong?"

"Didn't you say her apartment?"

Betty nods.

"But she lives in a house."

"Oh. I told you she was living with her husband, didn't I? She's moved out, into an apartment. She seems pretty unhappy about it because of the little girl. Did you ever meet her? She brought her to work one day."

He has pulled over. He is shaking his head back and forth.

"What's wrong?" Betty says.

"She can't have moved. Where did she move to?"

"A place not far from where I'm living. I forget the name of the street."

"You're kidding me. You have to be kidding me."

"I didn't know you knew her so well."

"Yeah. I do know her well."

Sam sighs loudly in the back seat.

"Sam," Charles says. "Laura left him. And she didn't call."

"She'll call," Sam says mechanically.

Betty turns around and looks at Sam. She looks at Charles.

"Did I say something wrong?" she says.

"No, you . . . I had no idea she wasn't still with him. What happened?"

"We didn't talk much about it. I didn't want to press her. She was just there in this apartment, and she said she'd left him."

"Was she all right?"

"Sure. She was all right." Betty gives him a funny look. His foot has gone dead, and he doesn't think he can drive. He tries the gas pedal. The car starts off.

"Is there a phone? Do you have her number?"

"It's unlisted," Betty says. "I've got it somewhere."

"Can you get it? Can you give it to me right now?"

Of course she can't give it to him right then. They are driving down a street. Very fast, as a matter of fact. He checks in the rearview mirror for cops, sees Sam shaking his head.

"Oh my God. She's left him and I didn't even know. She didn't even tell me."

Betty looks very uncomfortable. She looks out the window.

"That next street is mine. No—past the stop sign."

He turns.

"Which building?" he says.

"The last one on the right."

"Betty, don't forget to find that number."

"I'll look for it," she says.

"You can find it, can't you?"

"I'll give it to you tomorrow," she says.

He wants it that second.

"Thank you," he says. "Please find it."

"I will," she says. "Good night."

Betty doesn't look at him. She gets out and runs toward her apartment, and he sits there, in a daze, knowing he should have escorted her, but his legs are feeling too funny to walk on them. What's the matter with Betty?

"Sam? What's the matter with her?"

"What do you think?" Sam says.

"I wasn't rude, was I? Did I say something rude?"

"You made it plain who you liked, let's say that."

Oh no. Poor Betty.

"What am I going to do? I can't just let her run off like that."

He wants to let her run off. He wants never to see her again. Or anybody but Laura. Anybody else is a waste of time.

"I think it's pretty obvious what you can do," he says.

"Okay. I'm going to get out of the car for a minute."

He walks slowly toward the building. His car idling sounds very loud. He doesn't feel well. He pulls the door handle. The doors are locked. He pulls harder. They are locked. There is a list of names outside underneath glass, but they're only last names. What is Betty's last name? He never did know her last name. He has to get Betty so . . . so what? So he can apologize. It wouldn't do any good to apologize. She would be polite. If she isn't up there crying. Why did she run? How did she get away so fast? Did she even say what floor she lived on? He leans against the building, looks through the darkness back to the street where his car is. Sam is getting pretty tired of all this. He is likely to lose his only friend. He will have to get himself together and go over to Sam's and help him pack books and move clothes. He straightens up and begins to walk. The trees to either side of him might as well be a firing squad.

Chapter 12

Laura's number is waiting for him when he gets back from lunch. He went to work over an hour early, thinking that for some reason Betty might get there early, too, and he would have Laura's phone number sooner. Betty did not show up early, or at all. When he saw the memo (it did not have his name on it, and there was no explanation—only the number and Betty's name) he was relieved that Betty was feeling well enough to come to work, and in a burst of sympathy before he called Laura (and to give himself a little more time to think) he walked down to the typing pool. Three women were there, but Betty was still not at her desk. He asked one of the women. She said that Betty had called in sick, but there had been a message for him. She asked the woman typing at the next desk if she hadn't taken the message. Yes, and left it on his desk. "Thank you," he said. He was bothering them. "Do any of you know Betty's number?" The same woman who took the message knew Betty's number. She opened her bottom desk drawer and took out a huge purse, a lavender purse, and found a little book inside with Betty's number. "Thank you," he said again, and went back to his office. He dialed Betty. There was no answer. He hung up and tried again. Still nothing. He put on the earphones and listened to a song. He went out for a drink. He came back to the desk and ran his hand over the pile of reports. It is just not the right moment to call Laura. He is worried about Betty, and he is sore from lifting cartons of

books, and his lunch was horrible, and he's sure that
when she picks up the phone he will blurt that he loves
her and plead with her to let him run over immediately.
He has already told Sam he won't be home for dinner. He
opens a box of Steel City paper clips and examines one
("Doctor Dan wants to know who shot that paper clip.
Come on . . . which one of you?"). How could she have
moved without telling him? He picks up the phone again,
then puts it down. No sense in calling and sounding annoyed. Best to treat it casually: "I hear you moved." Shit.
Why didn't she call him; what's that supposed to mean?
He picks up one of the reports and begins making nota-
tions. He finishes the report and leans back in the chair.
It is an orange chair with upholstery that looks and feels
like burlap. He is reluctant to say that it is burlap, however, because he doesn't want to think that he is sitting on
burlap. That's what they bag potatoes in. He puts his
head back and stares at the sun, mid-point in the window.
He is tired; last night after cleaning out Sam's apartment
he tried to sleep, but he kept thinking that the next day
he'd get Laura's number and he couldn't sleep. Then the
dog started walking around, jingling its collar. Sam finally
got up to take the collar off, and the dog thought that it
was a game and ducked its head (Charles eventually got
up to help) and sprinted from the room. Then he was
wide awake, and worrying about the way he had treated
Betty and wondering if it was true that Pamela Smith left
with her brother. What if some maniac had a knife on her
and made her write it? He should have looked to see if
there was a hidden message. How could she just leave like
that? How could Laura? Why isn't he calling?

What is your favorite meal? he asks himself.

Lasagna.

What is your favorite day?

Friday.

What is your favorite sport?

Skiing. (He chuckles.)

He begins again, trying to be honest, no tricks, just honesty. It is a game Susan taught him years ago that she said would help him fall asleep. She did not use the word "game," but that's what it is.

What is your favorite meal?

Lasagna, chili.

Just one.

Lasagna.

Who is your best friend?

Sam. . .

What is your favorite country?

America.

Who was your favorite President?

Kennedy.

Whom do you idolize?

Nobody.

What was the best year of your life?

The year I met Laura.

What was the happiest month of your life?

Same.

Hour?

Same.

Then why aren't you calling?

Fear.

Why are you fearful?

Don't know.

You do know.

Too many reasons to go into.

Go into one of them.

Afraid I'll be overcome and will sound too desperate, blow the whole thing.

What if you blow the whole thing?

Don't know.

You do know.

The end.

Sam would ask the same questions, prodding him. He would give the same answers. The game is not relaxing him at all; it's not divorced from life, it is life. He closes his eyes and tries to count sheep. What do sheep look like? ("And now she says the picture on the piano *is* her husband. . . .") Sheep have curly hair and little ears. In a pasture. Green grass. They bleat. He can't see them, though.

What do you see?

A fruit stand.

That makes no sense.

I know. . .

What kind of fruit?

Apples, pears, bananas, peaches, grapes, and lettuce. No, not lettuce. Melon.

Do you want to eat the fruit?

No.

Want to buy it?

No.

Explain.

Can't.

Can.

Can't.

He is feeling very uncertain. If he doesn't call now, he will be in a worse state of mind when he does call. The phone rings. It is his boss. He has found his pen. It was on the windowsill, behind the venetian blind. Charles tells him that it is wonderful that the pen has been found. "I'll be having a small get-together soon, and will let you and your wife know." His boss says that that is splendid. Why did he say that to his boss? Because he is making nervous conversation, hoping his boss does not sense that he's goofing off. He congratulates his boss again. His voice is so insincere that it cracks. His boss chuckles. Spirits are high.

This is just not the right phone to call from. There is nothing pleasant about the phone or the surroundings. He puts on his coat and walks down the corridor to the elevator. He rides to the ground floor, walks past the blind man's stand, out the doors. He runs across the highway to the shopping center. He goes into the Safeway and gets a brown bag and fills it with fruit. He checks his wallet. Fruit could not possibly cost more than thirty-eight dollars. He throws in another pear, a bunch of grapes.

"Weigh this, please," he says to the teen-age boy standing at the produce scales. The boy's face falls. He spills it all out, separates the different kinds and puts them on the table the scale sits on. One falls. He picks it up, face red. He writes 89 on the bag and drops the apples in. He weighs the bunch of bananas; 72 appears under the 89. He weighs the single grapefruit. "Wait, these are ten for ninety-nine," he says. He writes 10 on the bag. The oranges cost 49 and the single pear 16. He adds it up, circles it in red. Charles almost runs to the checkout counter, where he has a long wait. A woman in front of him, her cart full of boxes of disposable diapers, stands reading *Family Circle*. She has a pug nose and bangs. Her clothes are all different colors. Charles rechecks and finds that he has only thirty-five dollars. Still—the fruit costs so little. Thirty-five. He recounts and sees that he's right. Finally he gets to the cashier. She has on a pink smock. She is pregnant. She rings up the amount on the cash register. He gives her a ten dollar bill and starts to leave without his change.

"Sir," she calls.

He doesn't want the change; he wants to get on with it. But wouldn't they go after him if he ran? Sweating, he turns back. She counts it out loudly. A woman in line stares at him.

He goes back to the office and walks through the lobby. The blind man is asleep (looks it, at least) in a chair in the corner. Charles takes out one piece of fruit—the pear—and puts it on the blind man's counter. He walks quietly away. The blind man does not move. Someone will pick up the pear on their way home and the blind man will say, "What have you got?" and they will answer, "A pear," and the blind man will be completely mystified. He sells no fruit. He will have no idea where it came from. Charles chuckles. He goes to his office and sits in the chair. Reports. He has reports to do. The bag tips over on his desk, the bananas stick out. An apple hits the floor. He retrieves it, sits down and dials Betty's number. No answer. But at least he knows her last name now. It is Betty Dowell. He will know what buzzer to ring.

But Laura, Laura . . . he really went out to find a suitable place to call Laura. He has taken care of Betty now—he will drive to her apartment after work and give her the fruit and apologize—and he should just pick up the phone and dial Laura, not make a big thing of it. He does. The phone rings exactly fifteen times.

Charles does as much work as he can between then and five-thirty, then leaves the building and goes to his car in the parking lot. He gets in and puts the key in the ignition. He leans back and closes his eyes. Laura. He sits forward and turns on the ignition. He begins to drive, through the heavy rush-hour traffic, to Betty Dowell's apartment. It's oldies time on the radio. "The Name Game" plays. "Laura, Laura, bo bora banana fana fo fora, fee fi mo mora, Laura," he sings. He takes a banana out—he has a bit of trouble tearing it off the stalk with one hand—and peels it. He bites into it. He went to the store and he forgot to buy food for dinner. Damn! Why don't housewives all go mad, go completely crazy, run naked down the streets, stampeding, screaming? How could he be right in the grocery store and forget? Wait. How could he be going to call Laura, how could he be going to go over to Laura's and still eat at home? Oh, shit. He is terribly confused. He finishes the banana and throws the skin out the window. He double parks in front of Betty's apartment. A driver rolls down his window and curses him. "Think you own this lane, you bastard?" A couple is walking into the apartment building. The woman holds the door open for him. Just like that! He won't have to stand on the street shouting that he is there. He will surprise her; she will have to let him in, have to accept the fruit. Maybe he should have sent a fruit basket with a big bow. Maybe this looks tacky. But wouldn't the other have seemed too presumptuous? Muzak plays in the elevator. A note above the controls: "I found a brown glove. Also have cat to give away. Apt. 416." He has forgotten to look and see what floor Betty lives on. When the elevator stops at three for the couple, he pushes "lobby." He goes out the door, holding it open with his foot, and peers at the list of tenants in the corner. Dowell, Dowell . . . 512. He goes back to the elevator and rides to five. He stands in front of apartment 512. He knocks. There is no noise inside. He knocks again. He reaches in his coat pocket for a pen, writes "For Betty from Charles" on the bag of fruit and leaves it leaning against her door. He goes back to the elevator and rides to the lobby, walks across the blue patterned carpet to the door, walks out the door to his car. He drives home. Everything is fine now. She will get the fruit, she will forgive him; he will call Laura, *she* will forgive him. But what has he done to Laura? What did he ever do that she wouldn't call him? He has got to find out. He drives faster.

Sam holds the door open for him.

"I thought you weren't coming home."

"I wasn't. I couldn't reach her. Thought I'd call from here."

"Well, you're not going to believe this, but I was baking a tuna casserole. You can have some."

"Yeah? That's good."

"I'm the perfect little housewife'"

"You ought to go to law school."

"We went through this before, Charles."

"I kept after you about the dog and you got a dog."

There is silence. The wrong example. And speak of the little devil, there he is sauntering into the kitchen, a little late to appear enthusiastic about his homecoming.

"You had a fine time making monkeys of us last night, didn't you?" he says to the dog.

"Sorry," Sam says.

"It wasn't your fault."

"I know," Sam says. He opens the oven door and looks in.

"You got a postcard from Pamela Smith. In case you were still worried that she was abducted, or whatever you were thinking. A Special Delivery. Just came this afternoon. I read it. I don't get it."

Sam goes into the living room, hands him the postcard. On the front is a statue of the Winged Victory. On the back is written:

                    L
          ARICA
                    B
                    E
                    R
                    A
                    T
                    I
          OF MIND AND SPIRIT
                    N

It is signed, "Pamela Smith."

"Wow," Charles says.

"What does it mean?" Sam says.

"Arica's some sort of therapy, something like that."

"Oh. You want to eat pretty soon?"

"Yeah. Call me."

Charles goes into the bathroom and shaves and showers. He pinches the roll of fat around his waist. So what?—Ox is repulsive. He saw a picture of Ox in a bathing suit once that made him almost physically sick. So what if he has an inch of fat? He brushes his teeth. He urinates. He used to urinate in the tub, but he didn't want Sam doing it, and he thought that if he stopped, somehow Sam would sense that he was not to urinate in the tub. At the time, it made sense. He flushes the toilet. He examines his teeth in the mirror. They are fine teeth. He looks at his hair. He should have washed it.

"Dinner," Sam says.

Charles goes into the bedroom and squirts on deodorant, drops the towel over the lamp. He puts on fresh underwear and goes out to the table.

"That looks very good," he says to Sam.

"I took the bus to the store. We didn't have shit."

"Good idea," Charles says. He burns his tongue. Damn! It won't be any fun kissing her with a burned tongue. He glowers at the casserole.

After dinner he ceremoniously pulls a chair up to the phone on the kitchen wall and calls her. He has memorized the number. Or at least he thought he had until a strange woman's voice answered.

"Hello?"

"Hello. Is Laura there?"

"Not right now."

"Is she expected back?"

"Yes, but I'm not sure when. Who is calling?"

"Charles."

"I'll tell her you called."

"Are you a friend of Laura's?"

"I live here."

"Oh."

"Good-bye," the woman says.

"Good-bye," Charles says.

He walks over to the sink, where Sam is doing the dishes.

"She's living with some woman," he says.

"Huh," Sam says.

"I wonder what's going on," Charles says. "She said Laura would call back."

Sam shrugs; Sam thinks that his affection for Laura is disproportionate.

At eleven o'clock the phone has still not rung. He calls again. The same voice answers.

"May I speak to Laura?"

"Just a minute."

A long time passes, and then Laura says hello. Her voice is very faint. He wants to shout at her to get her mouth closer to the phone. She always does this; she's impossible to talk to on the phone.

"Laura. What's going on?"

"That's a good question, isn't it?"

She answered him! He didn't blow it by shouting that he loved her!

"Talk to me. What's happening?" Charles says.

"Well, as you've somehow found out, I've left Jim. I'm . . . living here."

"You're living with some woman," he prompts her.

"Yes. She's also leaving the man she lived with. She just started graduate school."

"What about you? What . . . what are you doing?"

"I was getting ready to go out for a drink with a friend."

"But have you left him? You've left for good?"

"Yes. Look, this isn't a very good time for me to talk to you. I have to think about some things. I can call you . . ."

"When?" he says.

"Well, another time. When I'm feeling more like talking."

"Who are you having the drink with? You'll be talking then."

She laughs. No answer.

"Laura, I couldn't believe it when I found out you'd moved. I didn't believe it had happened. Are you okay? Can you just tell me what's going on?"

"Nothing very mysterious. I wish there was something I could say. . . ."

"Say anything!"

"How did you get this number?"

"From Betty."

"Oh."

Silence.

"You're okay?" she says.

"Okay? I don't know how to feel. I've got to see you. You've got to tell me exactly what's going on."

"Charles, I *don't*. I don't mean to sound nasty, but I'm not in the best mood now, and I don't feel like sorting everything out in a second just so you can *know*."

"When would you . . . when are you going to call me?"

"Soon."

"You mean not tomorrow?"

"A second was just a convenient way to put it. I'll call you when I can call you."

"Laura, shit! I'm sorry if I made you mad, but I've got to see you. I stayed away when you went back to him, but now I'm coming over there."

"If you come over tonight I won't be here," she says.

"Then tomorrow. All right?"

"If it means that much to you."

"It does."

"I don't think you're thinking of me. I think you're thinking about what's best for *you*."

"I love you!"

Silence.

"I know," she says. "I'll see you tomorrow."

"Where do you live?" he says.

"On Wicker Street—140 Wicker. A small building."

"Okay. I'll see you then."

She hangs up. What went wrong. What's happening? Where is Wicker Street?

That night he dreams that he is launched in a spaceship

to the stars. His mother is there. She is taking a bath on a star. He gets back in the rocket. Mechanical failure! That strange jingling! He sits up in bed, eyes wide open. The dog is walking again, his collar jingling. By now it is clear; the dog has insomnia.

Chapter 13

J.D. and Sam are sitting in the living room, listening to "It's Only Rock and Roll" and drinking Bass Ale. Charles had one beer with them when he came home, but wants to be perfectly sober when he sees Laura. He slept only four or five hours the night before, thinking about her, wondering what had made her move, what had stopped her from calling, why he seemed so incapable of impressing upon her, why he had always—almost always—been incapable of impressing upon her that he loved her and had to have her, and when the dog jumped on his bed in the early morning he was actually glad to see it. By now, the dog responds to the name "Dog." There is something wrong with his mind if he can't think of a name for the dog. He should get referred to a psychiatrist. "I can't name my dog, Doc." So many situations he finds himself in remind him of the beginning of a good joke. "And the doctor said . . ." He should forget about a conventional shrink and let the people in Arica work on him, become a different person. Of course he won't. It's going to be all he can do to get up the courage to tell Laura that they must set out for Bermuda. Fly, or take a boat? Die in the air, or sink in the ocean?

J.D. says, "She must have been some chick." Charles had just told him the outline of his relationship with Laura.

"She's messed up," Sam says. "I hope she doesn't fuck you over tonight."

"She was okay on the phone," Charles says.

She was mad at him on the phone. He went too far. Somehow.

For a while, when things were going very well, he'd be talking to Laura and he'd forget she hadn't been with him all his life. He'd mention kids from grade school and assume she knew them, too, talk to her about how he lied his way out of the Army and forget that he'd never before mentioned the Army to her. She never told him much about her past. Her mother died when she was in high school. He has no idea what happened to her father, whether he is dead or alive. And he can't remember where she went to high school. In Virginia, but what part of Virginia? She worked as a waitress in high school. A man on the street in New York, where they went for their class trip, gave her his card and told her he wanted to sign her for his modeling agency. She was scared to call him, and is glad that she was. She jumped on the trampoline in high school, wanted to be an acrobat. She was a waitress. Did she ever tell him what waitressing was like, though? Or even a funny story? Doesn't seem like it. She has a brother who runs a hunting lodge. She has not seen him for years and years. One Christmas he sent her a deer head. She wrote asking for a bearskin rug for Rebecca and got no answer. She met Ox when he was in the Marines, dated him a few times. He remembers, in fact, that they went dancing, and then she forgot about him. By chance, she saw him again a year later. He was married, then, and unhappy. He called her a year after that and said that his wife was in the bin. Then his wife got out of the bin. She lost contact with him. Then he called again, and she went to the house for dinner and never left. Rebecca loved her. That was that. Then how could she mind his calling and putting her on the spot a little?

And what else, what else about Laura? That she jumped on the trampoline because somebody told her that she would drive her shinbones into her feet and she wouldn't grow any taller. She worried that she was too tall. She took photography lessons, but was never very good at it, and there never seemed to be a convenient photo lab to develop the film, so. . . . And she took dancing lessons, and paid a French woman ten dollars a week to let her stand around her kitchen on the weekends and watch her cook. The French woman was always pregnant, and always out of some spice. Laura tried to have a baby and never did. No, no tests. That was that. She went to college for a while. Some day she might go back, to study botany. She could model to make money, but she'd really have to go to New York to do that, and anyway—she was old now, too old to model. The French woman made things with fish heads. None of her professors tried to pick her up, none of them even knew her by name. She said once that she would like to meet Ox's wife. They became friends. His wife married him because he was captain of the football team. He married her because she was crazy and funny. Laura went to see her, taking food and perfume. Ox drank, had another woman once—at least once—and stopped building houses, lost a lot of business, drank some more, she left. She left for a lot of reasons.

"I left New Mexico for a lot of reasons," J.D. says. "Shit on me."

Her hair always crackles with electricity. She puts hair spray on the brush, hoping this will cure it. George Harrison is her favorite Beatle. She never had to wear braces. She likes expensive, delicately scented soaps. Her hair is long and wavy. She was so thrilled when she got her own car, even if it was an old car. She got Bs in college. The first drink she ever tasted was at eighteen, a rum collins. Now she drinks scotch. She feels sorry for giraffes. She doesn't care what's on her pizza, as long as it isn't anchovies. She loves Caesar salad, however, and was surprised to find out that crushed anchovies were in it. She likes *Jules and Jim*. She thought about being a filmmaker. She

saw Otto Preminger on the street. Of course she was sure.
She stirred tiny slivers of meat, almonds, and vegetables
in her wok, grew violets the same colors as her round,
pastel bars of soap, showered in water too hot for him.
She asked, once, why May Day was celebrated. She does
not remember names or dates well and is not apologetic
about it. She has big feet. Big, narrow feet. Butchers are
kind to her, men in gas stations clean her windshield.

"What time are you going over there?" Sam asks.

"Around eight. Another half hour or so."

Actually, Laura set no time. He could go right this
minute, but he doesn't want her to think he's too eager.
He is very eager. At work, he thought about going out
and buying her a diamond ring, proposing to her on the
spot, pushing the ring on as he talked. He had no idea
what size ring she wears. Or if she liked diamonds. Ox
had given her only a silver band.

"Anybody call me?" Charles asks.

"No," Sam says. "Unless it was when I was out."

"How long were you out?"

"To get my check. I don't know how long. I remember
looking at my watch when I got there, and it had
stopped."

"If you want to go out tonight, I've got my car," J.D.
says.

"Nah," Sam says. "I'm happy to sit here and drink."

"I guess I didn't tell you," J.D. says to Charles. "I finally got tires to put on the car, had the guy come around
and jack it up and put them on. The next morning when I
came out of my apartment there was a kid with a crowbar, getting ready to take it to my trunk. I chased him for
two blocks, then didn't know what I'd do if I caught him.
He had the crowbar."

Charles shakes his head. "Place you live didn't look
like a very bad area."

"There he was, just getting ready to pry it open."

"Maybe it was a narc," Sam says.

"My God. I never thought that. Do you really think that?"

"Got a lof of stuff around?" Sam asks.

"Hey—you guys could be narcs for all I know."

"Sure," Sam says. He puts his empty beer bottle in line with the others.

"Clever thinking," Charles says. "You're under arrest."

"I've got a gun! Don't make a move!" Sam hollers.

"Okay . . . I was just thinking," J.D. says.

"Get your head together, J.D.," Sam says.

"I wasn't thinking it seriously," J.D. says.

"We fooled you, then," Charles says. "Stick 'em up."

"Forget it," J.D. says.

"Narcs," Sam says. "Jeez."

"I didn't really think that," J.D. says.

"My long-suffering ass," Sam says. "Narcs!"

"I wonder who becomes a narc nowadays?" Charles says.

"Abbie Hoffman," J.D. says.

"Your mother," Sam says to Charles.

"My mother. That would be funny. She'd find the stuff and sit there staring at it, and when they got back she'd be in the bathtub with it."

"What's this?" J.D. says.

"His mother is nuts," Sam says.

"Oh," J.D. says. "My aunt was." He opens another beer. "She was a waitress, and she went out into the kitchen and cooked up a whole box of eggs and went out and dumped them on a customer who reminded her of her first husband."

"How many husbands did she have?" Charles asks.

"Two. The second one was a cop. He'd practice his fast draw on her. She'd be walking through the house, and the gun would be pointing at her."

"Need we ask what happened to her?" Sam asks.

"She's milking cows in Vermont." J.D. takes a long

swig of beer. "At Christmas she sent me a picture of her milking a cow, and two dollars. Jesus."

"Well, we've got enough information to run him in," Charles says.

"Cut it out," J.D. says. "I never really thought that."

Charles goes into the bathroom. The toothbrush. He keeps meaning to get Sam a new toothbrush. He takes his own toothbrush down and brushes his teeth. He wants to take the toothbrush with him, to take his toothbrush to Laura's and put it next to hers and never leave. The other woman's toothbrush is next to hers. Who is she? He combs his hair. It is quite a bit longer now. He can't tell if it looks good or not. Why is he standing around the bathroom? Why isn't he at Laura's? He leaves the bathroom and asks Sam and J.D. if either of them knows where Wicker Street is. J.D. thinks he does and gives directions. Charles has trouble concentrating. There is a ringing in his head. He feels like he might black out. He sits on the floor, hearing J.D.'s voice faintly in the background.

"What's the matter with you?" Sam says.

"Nothing," Charles says.

"You look awful. She's getting to you already, and you haven't even seen her."

"I'm okay," Charles says. He wishes he were okay.

"Got it?" J.D. says.

"No. You'd better write it down."

Sam goes out to the kitchen to get paper for J.D.

"Drink a beer before you go. You don't want to be too sober," Sam says.

"Why do you say that?"

"How much has sobriety ever helped you?"

Charles shrugs, accepts the beer. J.D. mumbles street names as he writes.

"Thanks," Charles says, taking the piece of paper from him. "You two going to be here?"

"Yeah," Sam says.

"If Betty calls, don't tell her where I am. Say that I'll call back."

"She'd never call you after what you did."

"Yes she will. Just say I'll return the call."

"I'd be plenty surprised," Sam says.

Charles leaves most of the beer in the bottle, puts it on the hearth. "See you," he says.

"Yeah," J.D. says.

Sam says nothing. He shakes his head.

It is very cold outside. The bushes bordering the driveway look very stark; black twigs shoot in all directions. They are almond bushes. His grandmother made a list of all the bushes and trees and flowers in the yard that he discovered in a drawer when he moved in. There were instructions on how to prune them, feed, and propagate each. He has never done anything for the bushes, and they are all doing fine, but he still feels guilty when he thinks about that piece of paper. He never takes up the tulip bulbs, and every year they bloom. The lilies of the valley have crept out into the sunshine, and they, too, multiply.

He would like to marry Laura and move to another house, a big house in the country with no other houses around, and gardens that Laura would dig and plant in. Does she have any interest in gardening? Of course she must, if she once considered majoring in botany. That will be something he can tell her tonight—that they can sell his house and move to a big house in the country. What will happen to Sam? Sam can come, too. He can stay with them. They will get Rebecca, too, somehow, to make Laura happy. And then they should probably get a dog. It sounds too Norman Rockwellish to be true. Who would somebody assume Sam was, if they saw him seated at a table with a happy family in a Norman Rockwell picture? They might think he was an uncle. They would never think he was there because he was unemployed and didn't have enough money to live. He imagines a conversation between a mother and her child:

MOTHER: Who's this?

CHILD: The daddy.

MOTHER: That's right. And is this the mommy?

CHILD: Yes. And that's the doggie.

MOTHER: And who's this?

CHILD: I don't know.

MOTHER: An unemployed jacket salesman.

Charles laughs. But not for long, because he has made the wrong turn. He puts the light on and looks again at J.D.'s directions. He should have turned right back there. He makes a U-turn and takes the correct turn, and then he's on the road that will lead him to Wicker Street. He hopes that she will be glad to see him, that she's not acting funny the way she was on the phone. Even if she does act funny, he can talk her out of it. Remember the mobile I bought you, Laura? The night I rocked you? Remember that dessert you used to make—the one with oranges? He wants to rush in, hand her a diamond ring, sit down in a chair in the kitchen and watch her make that dessert. He wants to eat the dessert, then jump into bed with her. What should he really do? What should he say when she opens the door? Wicker Street cuts across the road to the left and the right. He turns right and sees the numbers going down. Naturally, he made the wrong decision. He turns around and goes the other way on Wicker Street. He should have brought something. The ingredients for that dessert . . . no, he should have brought flowers. But that would be corny. He'll just park the car and casually go into the building and . . . and . . . what should he say? There are no parking places. He has to park the next street over and walk through the cold to her apartment. His nose will run. He reaches up, to check. That would be awful. The building is drab and brown, no locked doors, no list of tenants under glass. There is a brown bag crumpled on one of the chairs in the lobby. He goes up the four steps, past the mailboxes to the elevator. There is no Muzak in the elevator. He gets off at her floor. Incredible. He can't believe this is happening. She has left Ox, she is living here, he is going to knock on her door, and she is going to open it. He stands in front of the door. Music is playing inside. He knocks and Laura opens the door. Incredible! There is Laura, in a pair of jeans and a wraparound sweater. She gives him a half-smile. "Hi."

"Hi. How are you?"

"Fine. Come in."

There is a bowl of crocuses blooming on the little table next to the closet she hangs his coat in.

"The last time I saw you you were sick," he says.

She gives the half-smile again. "Yeah. And I thought I felt bad that day."

"What's the matter . . . now?"

"Come in," she says. They walk down the short hallway to the living room. There is a mattress on the floor, covered with a yellow Indian bedspread. There are no curtains. There is a sofa, and a small rug in front of it. There are plants in the windows. There is a stereo playing.

"I'm sorry not to act nicer," she says. "I'm glad to see you."

He doesn't know what to say. He stares. She looks the same, but she's plucked her eyebrows. They're thin arches now. Her eyes look much larger. He stares into them.

"I don't know where to begin," he says.

She smiles.

"Coming in, I started remembering that dessert you used to make with the chocolate and the oranges, and I thought about begging you to make it immediately."

"Oh. I know the one you mean. You can come over sometime and I'll make it for you."

Sometime? What is she talking about?

"Tomorrow?" he says.

"Tomorrow? I guess so. If you want to," she says.

The conversation has started all wrong. She is sitting on the mattress, her back against the wall. He sits down at the end of the mattress, looking up at her.

"You've got a roommate?" he says.

"Yes. She's at the library. She's in graduate school."

"Oh. Well, what are . . . what are you doing?"

"Looking frantically for work."

"Why don't you come back to the library?"

"I don't want to," she says.

"Are you looking for another job like that?"

"I wouldn't care. I've just got to get a job."

"Sam's out of work. You remember Sam?"

"Of course I do."

Of course she would.

"That's too bad," she says. "Does he get unemployment, or. . . ."

"Yeah. He gets that. He's over at my place now."

"That's nice," she says.

"Are you okay?" he says.

She can't be. The half-smile has become frozen on her face now.

"No, I'm not very happy, if that's what you mean. I didn't want to leave Rebecca."

"Why did you?" he says.

"I didn't, really. Jim told me, well, I don't remember the exact way he told me, but he wanted to live alone. I thought it would be better for me to go than to have Rebecca living in a new place, maybe having to leave her school."

"Why did he want to live alone?"

"How should I know? We didn't talk."

"You didn't?"

"You're so curious," she says. She gives him a half-smile.

"I love you. I want to know what's going on."

"I can't tell you. I don't know myself. He told me that

one night, and the next morning I explained as best I could to Rebecca, and I left. Frances let me stay with her, until I can find work."

"You can stay with me."

"No. I just want to think things out for a while."

"What do you mean?"

"That I don't know what I'm doing. I don't even know if I'll stay around here. I only would for Rebecca, but now I hear that he's going to move."

"Couldn't you stay with me until you found out?"

"No," she says.

"Why not?"

"Because I want to be by myself."

"Frances lives here, though."

"That's the same as being by myself. She doesn't make any demands on me."

"I never made demands on you, did I?"

"People always make demands on other people."

"What did I do wrong?"

"I wasn't saying you did anything wrong. You were very nice to me. I didn't start this conversation."

"Laura, you're talking funny. I can't understand you."

"You don't want to understand me."

"I don't want to, but I think I do. You're saying that you don't intend to come back to me."

"Not right now, no."

The dizzy feeling comes back. He is very glad that he didn't finish the second beer.

"But you will come back? You just want time to think? Time to think about what?"

"Charles, what are you talking about? I just said that I had to have time to think about where I would work and live."

"With me."

"I don't want to live with you."

"Why not?"

"Because I want to be on my own. I don't want anyone

dependent upon me, and I don't want to have to depend on anybody else. I just want to . . ."

"Laura, you've got to come back. We don't have to live in my house. I was going to tell you we'd sell it and that you can pick out some place you'd like to live."

"You really are crazy about me, aren't you?"

"Of course I am."

"That makes me feel awful. It's not that I don't like you . . ."

Like!

"But I don't want to get into anything like that right now."

"Laura, you love me! If you hadn't loved me, you wouldn't have gotten out of bed when you had the flu to tell me you couldn't meet me. Don't you even know that you love me? Remember the mobile I gave you?"

"The mobile?"

"Don't you remember?"

"Yes. I remember it. But I don't know why you brought it up."

"I don't either. I was just thinking about the other apartment."

"Would you like some tea or coffee? Or scotch?"

"No! I want you! I want you to be sensible. I love you."

"I know that. There's nothing I can do about it. I didn't call you, you got my number and called me."

"You mean you never would have called?"

"I don't know."

"What do you think?"

"I just don't know. I do think about you."

Think about!

"You love me! This is the craziest thing imaginable. You love me and don't even know it. Don't you remember in the other apartment, how we ate dinner together and went to the movies and . . ."

"I remember it perfectly. It was very nice. It was peaceful."

"Then move in with me. Or we'll both find some place to move into. What's happened between then and now?"

Laura shrugs.

"Somebody else?"

"Nobody I'm serious about."

"Who, Laura?"

"I went out with somebody a couple of times. I don't even know why I mentioned it, since it's not what happened between then and now."

"Who?"

"A taxi driver," she says. "I went out with him for a couple of drinks."

"Two times?"

"Yes. Two."

"That's all?"

"Yes. That's all."

"Where did you meet a taxi driver, Laura?"

"In his taxi."

"You're kidding! He picked you up?"

"I don't want to get into an argument. I'm feeling very low. I did not call you because I knew I could not cope with you. I am very fond of you. I remember the mobile, and I will cook you that soufflé tomorrow night. I want you to go home."

"No! I can't leave you like that. Shit, Laura. I never bothered you when you went back. I called *once*. I didn't even call again after you said you'd call and you didn't. I just drove around your goddamn house at night, looking at the lights. I can't concentrate at work. I can't stand the thought of dating other women. I hate other women. The only woman I can even stand the sight of is my sister. Cut this out! Come back with me. What is there for you here?"

"Peace. Look at the way you're acting."

"You mean if I'd been calm and subtle you would have come?"

"No."

"Then I'm going to act this way. I'm going to talk truthfully."

"Stop thinking about yourself and think about me. I need peace. I don't need to be told what to do. I've lost Rebecca and my marriage has fallen apart and I can't find a job, and you're telling me it can be like it was before."

"It can!"

"It can't. I'm miserable. Before I was just unhappy."

"A taxi driver! How the hell am I supposed to feel about that? You got in a goddamn taxi, and you let the driver pick you up."

"So what?"

"That's awful. It's incredible. Taxi drivers don't just pick up great women like you. Look at yourself. God, Laura."

"I never saw as much as you did," she says.

He gets up, legs shaky, and walks to the sofa. She is so unreasonable. He looks up at the picture on the wall: two parallel black lines are pushing a rainbow off the canvas. He looks at the rug: a circle of brown inside an oval of green, bordered with black. He wants to see something familiar—something from the old apartment.

"Isn't there anything of yours here?" he says.

"It's all back at the house," she says. "I thought about going back to get some things, but I can't face Rebecca."

"She knows it's not your fault, doesn't she?"

"I don't think seven-year-olds make intellectual distinctions."

"Is there any chance of getting her?"

"Seemingly not. I've spoken to a lawyer. She *is* his daughter."

"Maybe he'd let you take care of her because it would be better for her."

"I don't even know that it would. He's nice to her. He's her father."

"But did you ask?"

"Yes."

"He said no?"

She doesn't answer. He stares at the little rainbow, at his feet on the rug. There is a magazine on the floor and a small mirror. There are old wood floorboards, wide boards that have been painted brown. One of the panes in the window is cracked. The paint on the ceiling is chipped. The ceiling is painted light gray; it is white where the paint has peeled away. There are silver radiators. It could be a nice apartment, but it would need work. Strip the floors, paint the ceiling . . . he is already trying to imagine the place theirs, even though he has to leave it, even though she will probably leave it, too. She'd better leave it.

"If I come back tomorrow you might not be here."

"I'll be here after six. I have to go out looking for a job. And I'd better go to the store. After seven would be better."

"You say that, but I might show up and you might be gone."

"You mean deliberately? No, Charles."

"Some goddamn taxi driver might pick you up."

"I do not get picked up by just *any* taxi driver. Anyway, I don't have the money for taxis."

"So he was special to you. That's what you're saying?"

"I'm losing patience. I've been as nice to you as I can. Tomorrow I'll even try to be in a better mood to put up with your telling me what to do with my life. Please go home and come back tomorrow."

He simply cannot do it. ("Closer, closer . . .") He looks at his feet. They won't move. He's sure of it. He smiles at Laura. Isn't she going to cut this out? Isn't she going to come over and sit beside him? She stretches out on the mattress.

"I'm tired," she says. "I was out all day."

"Did you eat? I could take you out to eat."

"No thanks. I think I'll just get ready to go to bed."

"But you do like me?" he says.

"Yes," she says.

"And you'll be here for sure."

"Yes."

He looks at the broken windowpane. He should offer to fix it. He doesn't know how to glaze windows. He should find out and fix it tomorrow night. He should demonstrate to Laura that he is very useful; there's something to what she says—that he makes demands on her. He will make no demands at all, and will fix the window and offer to strip the floors. If he were only bigger, he could volunteer to go to her house with her and carry out furniture and paintings, but of course Ox would kill him or, even more degrading, just pick him up by the back of the neck like some trespassing cat, and drop him in the yard.

"Remember taking me to the zoo, and how upset I got when I asked what giraffes did for fun and you said, 'How could they do anything?'"

"I should have thought of a nicer answer," he says. "Like the cab driver Holden Caulfield asks about the ducks in winter."

"That's an awful scene," she says.

He gave her *Catcher in the Rye,* and when she liked that he gave her *Nine Stories,* but after she read "A Perfect Day for Bananafish," she couldn't read any more. She even made him take the book back, and she knew that he already had a copy. She just wanted it out of her sight.

"I guess I'll see you tomorrow, then," he says.

He has to go. He shouldn't press his luck. He rubs his shoes back and forth on the rug. He looks at the broken windowpane.

"Where's the bathroom?" he says.

She points. He gets up, legs still shaky as hell, and walks around the corner to the bathroom. It is painted an awful shade of blue. There is a white shower curtain patterned with whiter flowers. Breck shampoo (not Laura's—unless she's changed) on the back of the toilet. He closes the door. He sits on the side of the bathtub, the curtain wadded beneath him. He just can't go. If he stays in here for hours she might come to the door and ask if he is all right. He wants her to show concern. He wants her to act interested in him. When he was a kid, his mother used to ask if he was all right when he stayed in the bathroom too long. That annoyed the hell out of him. Mary Tyler Moore's water-spattered face smiles up from the cover of *People* magazine, at his feet. Her roommate is messy. He looks behind him to see if Laura's shampoo is in the tub. No. Where is Laura's shampoo? He wants to smell it. He gets up and runs the cold water, puts his hand under it and raises the wet hand to his eyes. His eyes burn when he holds his hand against them. He sits on the small stool against the wall, looking at the toilet and sink. The music goes off in the living room. He hears Laura walk across the floor—the floor creaks—and then the music begins again. It is classical music, but he doesn't know who. Mournful music. Albinoni, perhaps. It would be nice to bring her some records. She wouldn't like flowers (he tried that in the past, and it turned out that she felt sorry for them because they had been cut off the plant and would soon die. She has a way of feeling sorry for things, even inanimate things), but she would probably like some records. He could bring wine and records. He could bring a diamond ring if he had the nerve. He could leave the bathroom if he had the nerve, if he could go out there and say good-bye. He cannot. He gets up and stands at the sink, running the cold water again. He holds his hand under it, turns the water off and rubs his hand down his face. After all this time he is seeing Laura again, and he is locked in her bathroom. He shakes his head—not to deny it, but because it's so ridiculous. As ridiculous as driving to her house and looking at the lights, imagining what room she might be in when she'd already moved. Ox is in the house now, and his daughter, Rebecca. He still has Rebecca's bird in his glove compartment. He would give it to Laura, but it might make her sad. She'd feel sorry for the bird. To say nothing of the fact that it would remind her of Rebecca. Laura buys plants that are dying in supermarkets—ones that have four or five leaves, marked down to nineteen cents, because she feels sorry for them. Couldn't she feel sorry for him? Sorry enough to go back to his house tonight? He will never find out standing in the bathroom. But it smells good in the bathroom, and as long as he's in the bathroom he doesn't have to leave. He will never tell Sam about this. He probably will tell Sam, hoping for sympathy, since Laura probably isn't going to give any. The metal fixtures are very bright, the floor is dirty. There is a small red rug, with hairs all over it. He opens the door, goes back and turns off the light, and walks slowly to the living room.

Laura is lying on the mattress. She sits up when he comes back.

"I thought you might be sick," she says.

"Why did you think that?"

"Were you? You look pale."

"No," he says.

"That's what I thought. Rebecca was sick so much that the slightest thing makes me think somebody's sick."

"I was just standing around in there."

"What?"

"I mean, I was washing my face."

She frowns. "But you're okay?"

"Yeah."

She turns on her side, propped on one elbow. Why did she pluck her eyebrows? She looks constantly quizzical.

"What record is that?" he says.

"I don't know. One that Frances had on. You can look, if you want."

"No," he says. He sits on the side of the mattress.

"Would he let you take your things?" Charles says.

"Jim, you mean?"

He nods.

"I guess so. I don't think there are bad feelings." She sighs. "But I don't really have anything. The furniture isn't nice. He bought it."

"It's half yours."

"I can't haul it around like a pack rat," she says. "Might as well leave it. I'm not attached to furniture, anyway. Sometime I'll get around to going back for my clothes."

"You could store anything you wanted at my house."

"That's nice of you. I might."

He thinks about having boxes of her clothes near him. He could raise the lid and—better than a genie—Laura's clothes. They would all smell like Vol de Nuit.

"Cookbooks," she says. "I guess I should get them. Most of them are out of print. And the ones the French woman gave me."

"It must be strange to walk out and leave all that stuff. It's sort of the reverse of me walking into my grandmother's house and being faced with all of it."

The half-smile.

"Can I go to the store for you tomorrow?"

"I'll have time," she says. "And at the moment I can't think of the ingredients. It'll come to me in the store."

"Would you like me to take you out to dinner first?"

"Let's just eat here. I don't feel like going out right now."

"Whatever you want," he says.

"I'm going to go to sleep. Come back tomorrow at seven," she says.

"Okay," he says. He does not move. He wants to say: Could I watch you sleep, Laura? He would just sit there and not make a sound all night. He has better sense than to ask—but not enough to leave.

"Don't worry about the cab driver," she says. "I wasn't interested."

"Good," he says.

He gets up and looks at the record. It is Albinoni. The crack in the windowpane. At least the apartment is well heated. He remarks on this.

"You're as trying as Rebecca. *Good night,*" she says.

"Good night," he says. He even walks to the closet and gets his coat out. She gets up, then, and stands by the door. Without high heels on, she is shorter than he is. He puts his hands on her shoulders. She puts her arms out. He hugs her. He will never be able to let go. But what to do. It's a gamble, but it's all or nothing. He picks her up a few inches off the floor (she giggles) and waltzes her into the living room, spinning and dipping, dancing fast around the floor, the old boards creaking like mad. He hums to the music. He has Laura, and they are dancing a beautiful waltz, completely out of time with Albinoni. She is telling him to stop, and he is swirling, remembering, suddenly, Pete asking him what dances he knows. Pete, in the elevator: "Young people dance nowadays, don't they?" "La, la," Charles sings, and with a final dip deposits her on the floor. He stands back and looks at her, but he doesn't see her clearly. He had his eyes squeezed shut for the dip, and the light is blinding. Is she happy or angry? She smiles the half-smile.

"Go," she says.

"I'll see you tomorrow," he says, and goes to the door. He listens. No floorboards move behind him. If he turns and looks at her, he will never go. She says she wants him to go. He opens the door and walks out into the hallway. He leaves the door open behind him, but he walks all the way to the elevator without hearing it close. It is too silent in the elevator. He worries that it will crash. And where did he park, exactly? The cold air outside makes his face burn and he runs for the car, hoping that the tires aren't slit. They are not. Neither has he forgotten the key. He gets in the car and starts it, his hand shaking. Someone on the radio is droning the news. He listens and gets more and more depressed until he realizes that he can turn it off. He does not have to hear Henry Kissinger's well-modulated voice, speaking the words Henry Kissinger always speaks. With the radio off, he feels a little better, but it's still too silent. Few cars are out this late, and the lights are flashing yellow. That means it's after midnight. How did that much time go by? He says Laura's name out loud a few times, to interrupt the silence. He puts on the heater, and by the time he is halfway home his legs have stopped jerking. He watches the speedometer and the rearview mirror; this is the time of night cops like best, watching for drunks speeding home. He would not want to be given a sobriety test. He knows he could not walk a straight line. He would lurch and weave and stand shaking in front of the policeman. He drives five miles below the speed limit, and has to stop at every light that isn't just flashing. Well, it wasn't a bad visit. He can't tell if anything he did was very right or very wrong. He stayed too long. She kept telling him that. But other than that, he didn't do too badly. Tomorrow he will do better. And she said the taxi driver didn't mean anything to her. A taxi driver. Jesus.

J.D.'s car is still at his house, parked on the street. Charles pulls into the driveway—it seems steeper than usual, or perhaps he's just a little sick to his stomach—and turns the ignition off and gets out. He walks to the front door and opens it. J.D. is passed out on the sofa, a blanket over him. The dog barks a greeting, and J.D. groans and rolls over to face the back of the sofa, the blanket falling on the rug. Charles picks up the dog, strokes it, and walks through the living room to his bedroom. The light is on in Sam's room, and Sam gestures for him to come in.

"What did she do to you?" Sam says.

"Nothing. It went fine."

"I'm surprised. But that's good."

"You look like you don't believe me."

"You look half dead. You don't look good."

Charles shrugs. "Neigher does J.D."

"J.D. got good and drunk. We walked the dog for a mile, and he still didn't sober up, so there he lies."

"Does he have to go to work or anything?"

"He's just working part-time now."

"Oh. Well, see you in the morning. You want the dog?"

Charles puts the dog on the bed. The dog walks up to the other pillow and curls up.

"Get me up when you get up," Sam says. "You can drop the dog and me at the animal hospital in the morning. It's got worms."

Charles makes a face. "Worms?"

"Yeah. All dogs get worms. Drop me at the animal hospital and I'll only have to pay for a bus home."

"Okay. See you."

"Hey, Charles?"

"Yeah?"

"Those worms don't crawl out or anything, do they?"

"Of course not."

"Good." Sam says. "You should have seen the things."

That night, as usual, the dog paces (Sam removes the collar at night, but you can hear the dog's toenails on the floor if you listen carefully) and J.D. groans and goes to the bathroom many times. Charles is glad he isn't either of them. He is glad to be himself, now that he's going to get Laura. And he *is*. He reassures himself of this, and eventually falls asleep. He awakens several times, though (flushing toilet, the dog pacing), from nightmares that he is losing her. In one nightmare he meets Frances, and instead of being a woman, Frances is a tall, handsome man, and Laura is obviously in love with him. They tell him to go away, and he jumps out the window (these nightmares are faithful, down to the last detail: he sees the shattered pane of glass as he crashes through the window), and he awakes spread-eagled on the bed, his face in the pillow. J.D. flushes the toilet. He is now only half glad he's not J.D. J.D. will vomit a few more times, and eventually it will be over with.

He calls Laura when he gets to work. If she hasn't left the apartment, he can at least tell her that he loves her and to have a good day. The phone rings and rings.

His boss asks him if he will have lunch with him. Charles is sure he is going to be fired. He works diligently until noon, when Bill said he would come for him. Bill does not appear until twelve-fifteen.

"Kid was on the phone. Sorry to be late."

Bill is losing his hair. He is wearing a blue blazer and navy blue shoes—that's something Charles has never seen before—and he has new glasses.

"Kid's going nuts in the cold, wants an electric blanket. Jesus. My kid doesn't even try to be self-sufficient. I said, 'I sent you money galore. Can't you go out and buy a blanket?' and he says, 'Do you want me to get into Harvard or not? Getting into Harvard requires that I do a lot of studying.' So I said—I've always wanted to say this—I said, 'I think you place too much importance on getting into Harvard. I don't care if you get into Harvard or not, personally!' *That* shook him up."

"I'd be afraid to sleep under an electric blanket," Charles says. He thinks of his mother: God—what if that occurs to her? What if she plugs herself in and roasts?

"Nothing's going to happen to you," Bill says. "I've been sleeping under number three for years. My wife's nuts for the thing. She wants to be under number four. As I'm dropping off I hear her click it up a number."

Charles smiles, waiting to be fired. The elevator doors open and they walk out of the building.

"That blind man gives me the creeps," Bill says, when they are outside the building. "I'm all for hiring the handicapped, but that blind man's something else."

"What is it about him?" Charles says.

"I don't know. I just can't account for it."

"Maybe he's the devil," Bill says. "Other morning I came in and bought a paper from him and he said, 'Up late last night, huh?' As it happens, I was out damned late. Playing cards. You don't play cards, do you?"

"No," Charles says.

"That's too bad. I mean—it can be overdone. But an occasional game of cards." Bill slaps Charles on the back. "That's what I tell my wife. She doesn't like me out playing cards. What the hell. An occasional game of cards. Not that it's always cards exactly."

Bill's face lights up, and what started as a conspiratorial smile ends up a sneer.

"You play *those* cards, don't you, Charlie?" Bill says. "Ha!" Bill says.

They are crossing the highway. That means either the drugstore or the delicatessen.

"How about some hot pastrami?" Bill says.

"Fine," Charles says.

"You're a very quiet guy," Bill says. "Notice that?"

"I guess so," Charles says.

"So's my kid. And then I get a phone call about an electric blanket. I worry that he's not getting any action up there at Dartmouth. I was going to say something about that to him, but he's a great one for confiding in his mother. If he wants an electric blanket, though, that means there's nothing else to keep him warm, huh?"

"I guess," Charles says.

"That's a shame," Bill says. "Nice-looking kid like that. Always work work work."

"Yeah. He's a nice kid," Charles says.

"He works so hard he doesn't remember his mother or his father's birthday. Top that. You don't have kids, but when you do you'll see that things like that matter. I still go out and get his mother a gift and sign his name, and she does the same thing. Sometimes I feel like shoving that pen up his ass."

Bill holds open the door. The delicatessen is mobbed. Bill stands in the longest line, the one for "twos."

"Reason I asked you to have lunch with me, I thought that you were closer to my son's age than I am . . . I've got a few years on you, huh? And maybe you'd have some idea what I might say to him to slow him down."

"I don't think there's anything you can say if he doesn't intend to slow down."

"Aw, Charlie, there's got to be some way to tell him to limber up. Are there any poets or singers or people like that I could introduce him to who would, you know, urge him to limber up?"

"I don't know. I'm not as up on things as you probably think. Uh—you could get him a Janis Joplin record, one she sings 'Get It While You Can' on."

"Tell me more."

"Janis Joplin? You never heard of her?"

"I think I've heard of her."

"She killed herself. She was a singer, at Woodstock? She was very free, you know, hippies identified with her. That one song . . ."

"Isn't my kid going to know she killed herself? Won't that make him think she's nobody to listen to?"

"I don't know. If he thinks that way."

"I don't know what he thinks, Charlie."

"Well, try that one. Get him *Pearl*."

"What are you talking about?"

"The name of the record."

"I *knew* you'd come up with something," Bill says, slapping his back and moving him up in line.

In a few minutes the hostess seats them. She brings menus and a bowl of bright green pickles. Bill's hand shoots into the bowl.

"That record's going to surprise him," Bill says. "I'm not going to send it with a note or anything. I'm just go-

ing to let him figure the thing out. That song's plain
enough that he'd figure it out?"

"Couldn't miss it," Charles says.

They eat their sandwiches in silence. Bill looks very
pleased with himself. Charles is let down; he expected to
be fired. All that adrenalin surging around for nothing.
For that asshole kid. He would like to break the record
over the kid's head. Harvard. Just as bad, Dartmouth.

"Would you send an electric blanket to your kid?" Bill
asks.

"No."

"Why not?" Bill says.

"That's just a lot of crap. Anybody can pile some stuff
on and keep warm in bed."

"They're good things," his boss says.

Oh yeah. His boss has one.

"Maybe you ought to send it, then," he says.

"I never know when I'm talking to you exactly what
you're thinking. Tell me honestly, now: should I send an
electric blanket?"

"No. They're useless crap manufactured to make
money."

Bill nods.

"But that record will go over okay?" he says.

"I imagine," Charles says.

"No poets that you can think of, though?"

"I don't know any poets who deal specifically with the
problem of not agonizing if you don't get into Harvard."

"Yeah," Bill says. "My impression is that they never
speak specifically to any point. You ever sense that?"

"Yeah," Charles says. It is the easiest thing to say.

Bill insists on paying for lunch. "Not only will I pay,
but I'll teach you poker if you want to learn."

"Thanks. Sometime I might."

"Tell me the truth, Charlie. Forget that I'm your boss.
You were very honest about the electric blanket. Would
you ever take me up on my offer to teach you poker?"

"No," Charles says. "Cards bore me."

"Ha!" his boss says, and slaps him on the back, pushing him against the door to the outside.

They walk down the arcade, to the record shop. Charles finds *Pearl* and hands it to Bill.

"Look at that," Bill says. "That looks like an old lady."

"She's only around twenty-five," Charles says.

"I thought you said she was dead."

"I mean in that picture."

"That looks like my mother. Except for the way she's dressed."

"Yeah. She burned herself out good," Charles says.

Bill takes the record to the cashier. It is put in a bright orange bag for him. He swings it back and forth as they walk back to work.

"What do you think of these fancy shoes?" Bill asks.

"I was noticing them."

"Yeah? My wife put me up to getting them. She said she'd seen enough of black and brown. I don't know. Everybody looks liks a clown nowadays."

Back in their office building, Bill turns left and Charles turns right.

"Thanks for the advice," Bill says. "I'll keep you posted."

"Sure," Charles says.

Charles stops at the typing pool on the way to his office. Betty is still not there. Back in his office he tries to reach Betty, but there's no answer. He tries Laura again; nothing there. He reaches in his coat pocket for the piece of paper he discovered early in the morning, when he was rummaging to see if he had his house key. He unfolds the piece of paper and stares at Sandra's number. He dials that. A woman's voice says, "Hello?" He has no way of knowing whether it is Sandra or not, because he doesn't speak, and he can't remember what her voice sounded like that day in the park. Why has he even dialed her number? He hangs up and throws the piece of paper away. He begins work on a report, then reaches in the waste paper basket and retrieves the number, smooths it out and puts it in his top drawer. Sandra somebody-or-other. It seems like months and months ago that he ran through the park. Why wasn't he at work that day? Sore throat. But why . . . ? Can't remember.

He stops at a florist on the way home and buys yellow tulips for Laura. They are in a pot, so they won't make her sad. It is a silly blue pot, with a ceramic windmill at one end. At least the tulips are pretty. Coming out of the florist's he sees a hardware store across the street. What the hell. He puts the tulips carefully on the seat and locks the car. He runs through the heavy traffic to the hardware store and asks where they keep the car wax. A salesman points him to the back of the store. "Aisle two," he says.

Charles picks up three containers of Turtle Wax and checks out. He runs back to the car. A day of good deeds: advice to his boss, a present for Laura, and Turtle Wax for Pete. He drives to his mother's house. The Honda Civic is parked outside. He will lie to Pete and say that he didn't notice it, swear that he didn't notice it. It is so silly-looking—a toy.

Pete's face is white when he answers the door.

"Charles! How's my boy?"

"Fine, Pete. I stopped by with something for you."

"Is that so? Well, I'm mighty glad to see you. What a surprise."

"How's everything?" Charles says. He never comes here uninvited.

"Today things couldn't be better. Come upstairs and see."

"She's in bed?" Charles whispers.

"Mommy had, Clara had a bit of a setback, but she's as bright as a firecracker now. Come on up." Pete gestures nervously from the steps.

"Honey," Pete calls, "you've got a visitor."

"No!" she shrieks.

"What's the matter with her?" Charles says.

"It's just Charles," Pete calls.

They reach the top. Charles whispers to Pete: "What is it?" Pete shakes his head, keeps walking.

"What a nice surprise, isn't it?" Pete says loudly. They stand in front of his mother's door.

"My firstborn," she says.

"Isn't this some surprise, Mommy?" Pete says.

"How are you doing?" Charles says. The room smells very perfumy.

"She's as fresh as a daisy in the field today, aren't you, honey?" Pete says.

Clara stares at them.

"Were you . . . sick?" Charles asks.

"I was in the hospital," she says.

"What?" Charles says, turning to look at Pete.

"Well, now, you were in the hospital a while ago, but you haven't been back now, have you?" Pete says.

"You mean when Susan and I came before?" Charles says.

"I know you did," Clara says.

"We all know that," Pete says, slapping Charles on the back. "How about taking a seat?" he says to Charles. Charles sits in the pink tufted chair. Pete strolls around like a master of ceremonies.

"I was quite sick," she says.

"You're looking fine now," Charles says.

"Oh, Pete says that I have to be freshened up. He throws me in the tub, Charles, and squirts perfume all over me and I'm too weak to get away."

Charles looks at Pete in confusion. Pete reddens.

"We have to freshen up," Pete says. "We can't lie in bed without a bath for a week, can we?"

"I hate to be freshened," she says.

"Look at Mommy's—Clara's—nice pink bed jacket. Her thoughtful husband got that for her. If Mommy—Clara—takes to bed, she might as well look cheerful."

"What's new?" she says to Charles. She looks like she expects to hear the worst.

"Not much. Back to work and all that."

"I can't seem to do my household work," she says.

"That's all right," Pete says automatically. "If you're going to get all confused when you get out of bed, I'd just as soon have you in bed."

"I get confused," she says to Charles.

"Yeah?" he says.

"Don't I?" she says to Pete.

"We don't want to dwell on this," Pete says. "Aren't you mighty glad to see Charles?"

"I know it's Charles," she says. "I'm not confused when I'm in bed."

"Can I fix coffee for anyone?" Pete says.

"No thanks," Charles says.

"Susan wrote me a nice letter," Clara says.

"Mommy *mislaid* it," Pete says.

"Oh. That's nice," Charles says. "How is she?"

"I want you children to keep contact. You do keep contact, don't you?"

"Sure we do. I was just talking to her on the phone."

"I talked to her on the phone," Clara says. "It was in the day, and Pete doesn't believe me."

Pete turns red.

"What did she have to say?" Charles says.

"Mice and rice and everything nice," Clara says.

Charles looks at the floor.

"Say," Pete says. "What about a look at a little something I've got?"

"What's that?" Charles says, playing dumb.

"Come on, come on, don't tell me you've forgotten."

"A death car," Clara says.

"A Honda Civic," Pete says, louder than Clara. "Come take a look."

Charles walks in back of Pete, out of the room and down the stairs.

"Here," Charles says. "This is to celebrate the new ar."

"What's this?" Pete says. "Hey! Turtle Wax!"

Charles nods.

"I knew you didn't really forget. Say, thanks a lot. Vhat do I owe you?"

"Nothing," Charles says.

"Come on. . . ."

"Really, it's a present."

"Hell," Pete says. "My own son couldn't have given me unything I wanted more."

Pete puts the bag on the hall table, puts on his coat und walks outside.

"She's much worse," Charles says.

"She's out of her goddamn mind, to be honest with you. She gets up and flips around like a fish when I'm not there. Not that water ever touches her. I have to do that once a week. Throw her in. What else can I do?"

"Christ. Have you spoken to a doctor?"

"No. I don't want to."

"Why not?"

"What are they going to do but take her to the hospital? Then what happens? I'm there all the time, the house is like a tomb. . . ."

"What if she does something to herself?"

"She'd forget what she was doing if the knife was poised at her heart. Really. You can't imagine what bad shape she's in."

"I think I get the idea."

"I'm not calling any doctor," Pete says. "I'm not going to run back and forth to the hospital. They don't do anything for her there, anyway. Put her in a room with a murderer."

"How do you know that?"

"That foreign broad told me she was a murderer. Showed me all these photographs of kittens and puppies, one hand showing the picture, the other clutching her throat."

Charles sighs. They are standing in front of Pete's Honda Civic.

"You know what my consolation is?" Pete says. "You want to know what my one consolation is?"

"What?"

"That car," Pete says.

"Well. It's very nice."

"That car must get a thousand miles to the gallon. I get in that in the morning and just leave the past behind."

Charles smiles.

"I do. You don't believe me?"

"Sure."

"Sure is right. That thing gets a thousand miles a gallon."

Charles stares at the little white car.

"Looks like a whale, doesn't it?" Pete says. "Friendly like a whale?"

Charles resumes his smile.

"Wait till I take that wax to her. Some shine."

Pete unlocks the car. "Take a sit," he says.

Charles sits in the car. His legs are cramped.

"What a beaut," Pete says.

Charles gets out.

"So what brought you by?" Pete says.

"Just wanted to give you the Turtle Wax."

"Jesus, that's very nice of you. When I saw you standing there I thought: he's come to tell us he's getting married."

"What? Why would you think that?"

"I thought for sure. I don't know."

"I'm not getting married," Charles says.

"If you were my own boy I'd pry," Pete says. "Ask what happened to that California honey."

"She went back. She's a lesbian, anyway."

"What?"

"Yeah."

"You're kidding me. How'd you meet one of those?"

"Long time ago. When she wasn't."

"No kidding," Pete says. "Must make you feel bad."

Charles shrugs.

"Whew," Pete says. "Glad I don't know her." He shakes his head sideways.

"I guess I'll be getting home," Charles says.

"Don't bother to go back in," Pete says. "She'll have all her clothes off."

"What do you mean?"

"Every time you have—I don't mean *you,* I mean anybody—anybody has a conversation with her and they turn their back, she's as naked as a jay."

"Pete, you're going to have to do something."

"I'm sitting tight. I know eventually I will."

"Well. Call if you need me."

Pete nods. Charles shakes his hand.

"See you," Charles says.

Pete stands on the sidewalk waving as he pulls off. He waves back, and lets out a long sigh when he turns off their block. His father is dead, his mother is crazy, Pete is all alone. He puts on the radio for the appropriate song. It is "Rocket Man" by Elton John. He listens to the radio and worries all the way to Wicker Street. Once again there is no parking space on Wicker Street. He parks on the same street he parked on the night before and cuts through an alley to Wicker Street, holding the tulips, in their white bag, inside his coat for extra warmth.

Laura opens the door wearing a black sweater and a long gray skirt. He is so surprised by how beautiful she is that he forgets to hold out the bag of tulips.

"Hi," she says.

"You're beautiful," he says. "These are for you."

"Oh, thank you."

He walks into the apartment. Incense. He watches her put the bag on the floor and pull it apart at the top.

"Tulips! They're beautiful!"

"They're in a thing. A container. So they won't die or anything."

"Thank you, Charles. It's so gray out. These will be beautiful." She looks around for a place to put them, settles on the coffee table.

"Your roommate studying again?"

"Yes."

"Do you really have a roommate?"

"You don't believe I have a roommate?"

"I don't know."

"I do. She's at the library. She studies there until midnight. Sometimes later."

"Did I make you mad?"

"No," she says. "It was just a foolish question."

"What's that on the stereo?"

Damn! He was going to bring her records. He was right in the store and he forgot.

"Keith Jarrett."

"Beautiful," he says.

He sits on the sofa. The two black lines have not yet done in the rainbow.

"Would you like a drink?"

"Yes," he says.

She goes into the kitchen and takes a bottle off the counter and pours scotch into a glass. She drops in an ice cube.

"Just scotch, or water with it?" she says.

"Just scotch."

"I might have a job," she says, handing him the glass. There is writing on the glass: Hot Dog Goes To School. A dog, knees crossed, is beaming. He holds a piece of paper that says 100.

"A job?"

"A job selling cosmetics."

"Oh. Would you like that?"

The perfume in his mother's room . . . Pete throwing his mother in the bath. . . .

"It's a job."

"When will you hear?"

"Tomorrow."

"Then you have to wait home for the phone call?"

"Yes," she says. "You're not very subtle about playing detective."

"If you're here I can call and say good morning. I like to hear your voice."

She sighs. He looks at the window—the cracked glass. A nightmare: he had some nightmare about that glass. He takes her hand.

"If I'm not all smiles it's because I just visited my mother."

"How is your mother?"

"Loony."

"But, I mean . . ."

"She's loony and well cared-for. She's stopped bathing, and I think she's stopped getting out of bed."

"What is your stepfather going to do?"

"That's a funny way to think of Pete. I always think of him as Pete."

"What's he going to do?"

"Nothing, he says. Unless she gets unmanageable."

"That's so awful," Laura says.

"I shouldn't tell you my problems. You've got enough of your own."

"I've got a job, probably. What problems do I have?"

"You're feeling good now?" he says, his mood lifting.

"No. Heavily ironic."

"Oh," he says.

"Would you like another?"

He gives her the empty glass. The ice cube hardly melted at all. It is the last scotch he will drink.

He looks at her standing in front of the kitchen counter, pouring. He stares at her ass.

"I'll tell you something funny. My boss asked my advice today about his son, who wants—in this order—to get into Harvard and an electric blanket."

She laughs. "What advice did he want?"

"He seemed to want to know if there were some poets who advised young men not to worry about getting into Harvard."

"Were you able to help him?" She is coming back with the drink. The drink is yellow. Her sweater is black, her skirt gray, her boots black, her hair brownish blond. It is Laura.

"You must have been," she says, "with that grin."

"Actually, I was. I recommended 'Get It While You Can' by the late, great Miss Janis Joplin."

Laura nods. "A fine selection. Sure to change his thinking entirely. Then all he'll yearn for is the electric blanket."

Laura has fixed herself a drink. "You don't mind eating a little late, do you?"

He shakes his head no. She is really quite beautiful in profile.

"You're smiling too much," she says. "You've had enough scotch."

"No," he says. "I'm just smiling."

The radiator hisses. He looks at the plant hanging in the window above the radiator and at the yellow tulips. There is loud applause as the record ends.

"Jesus," he says, stroking her shoulder with his free hand, "I'm going to get that dessert."

"I didn't realize you liked it that much."

"I was wild for it. I crave it constantly. A riddle: how is orange and chocolate scoufflé like Laura?"

She sighs again. "You're so subtle," she says.

"You're so lovely. Imagine a taxi driver getting lucky enough to pick you up."

"Enough! I don't want to hear any more about the taxi driver."

"Imagine *me* being that lucky. When I was that lucky."

"I've never understood why you like me so much," she says.

"I know it. And you always talk about my 'liking' you. You won't even say out loud that I love you."

"I don't understand why you love me."

"The orange soufflé."

"Sometimes I think it really is something as crazy as that. You love me because of a dessert I make. The recipe is in a cookbook."

"I looked through all the ones at my house. I couldn't find it."

She laughs. "That's the one book I took, I think."

"You do have the recipe here, don't you?"

"If I don't, I can remember it."

"Tell me. Tell me how you make the orange soufflé."

"You're kidding me."

"No. I want you to tell me."

He closes his eyes.

"You peel four oranges and . . . I can't tell you. I'm embarrassed."

He opens his eyes, drinks more scotch.

"You peel oranges . . . go on."

"I can't. I feel too silly."

She laughs. She has big front teeth. He loves her.

"Then I'm going to watch you."

"You can watch if you don't talk. I don't want you to embarrass me. Then I wouldn't be able to make it."

"No! You can't threaten me about the orange soufflé. You promised you'd make it!"

"You're crazy," she says.

"I am completely normal. So normal that others come to me for advice. My own boss, for example. I know more than my boss."

"You don't know how to make dessert. I'm the only one who knows that," she says.

"No kidding around. I want that dessert."

"Would you like me to make the dessert and forget about dinner?"

"Yes."

"Seriously?"

"Yes."

"Okay," she shrugs.

"And I'm watching," he says.

"You're drunk, I think."

"I'm not. If I were drunk I'd be on a talking jag. When you go into that kitchen I am going to stand there and be utterly silent."

"You'll have to say something. Otherwise I'll get nervous."

She gets up and goes into the kitchen. He follows (far enough behind to stare at her ass). He sits in a chair. He gets up, pours a glassful of scotch, sits in the chair again. Laura takes a white pot out of the cabinet, opens cream and pours it in, puts it on the stove.

"Say something," she says.

"I was thinking about that snow fort we discovered in the park that winter when we had a bad storm. How strange it was that no kids were in it, just a big white enclosure."

She jiggles the handle of the pot on the stove, stares into it.

"Which further made me think about not being able to get to work because of the snow, and how bright the glare was that day in the apartment."

She opens the refrigerator, takes out a carton of eggs.

"In support of the fact that I really am crazy, I never called you—except that once—when you went back."

"I don't know why I did," she says. She is separating eggs. The yolks slide from the shells into the bowl.

"And that, in turn, made me think about you running out in the kitchen naked for something to eat, and me finding you jumping around in misery in front of the refrigerator. You couldn't decide what you wanted, but your feet were cold."

She laughs. She begins to whip the egg yolks. He takes a long drink of scotch, thinking how good the orange soufflé will taste.

"And how I told you I had a bath toy for you, and it turned out to be me."

He takes another drink of scotch. "It would be nice to have a huge bathtub, one big enough to go under and come up, like seals. To really float in."

"The dream tub bath," Laura says. The cream bubbles to the top of the pan and she lifts it off the burner, adds it to the eggs, pours in cognac, leans over to smell.

"That was a swell apartment," he says. "I miss it."

She turns around. "Why are you so nice to me?" she says.

"What do you mean?"

"Why don't you hate me for walking out like that? For making you so unhappy?"

"What would I gain by not being nice to you?"

"You mean you're just acting nice to get me back?"

"Sure."

"What do you really want to say? Go ahead and say it."

"You just want to hear bad things. I don't know any bad things I want to talk about. It'll give you an excuse to stop fixing this soufflé."

She shakes her head (brownish-blond hair). She begins to whip egg whites.

"And you love me because I make this dessert," she says.

"Because of all of the above."

Her head is still shaking. "I guess I should follow through and let you down again," she says. She puts the whisk aside and walks over to his chair, sits in his lap. She smells like oranges. He puts his nose in her hair. He kisses her hair.

"I got my way," he says.

"You did," she says.

"A story with a happy ending," he says.

He rocks her in the chair. The kitchen is a mess. If he rocks her for three and a half more hours—which is possible—her roommate (who exists) will come home to find the kitchen a mess. He looks out the window, sees through the steamy panes that it has begun to snow.

"Look at that," he says. She raises her head a little.

"Just before I left," she says, "there was a snow. We went to see his wife. We stopped on the way for all the usual disgusting food, and we got her magazines—because the magazines there are all ripped apart—and soap, and things like that. When we came in she had her chair sideways, by the window, looking out at the snow, and she said, without even looking up to know that it was us, that the doctors had said that sitting and staring at the snow was a waste of time; she should get involved in something. She laughed and told us it wasn't a waste of time. It would be a waste of time just to stare at snowflakes, but she was counting, and even that might be a waste of time, but she was only counting the ones that were just alike."